MALACHI MOON

Journey of a Bluesman

By

Robert Crudup

*Our mission is to efficiently provide the world's finest, most comprehensive
book publishing service, enabling every author to experience success.
To find out how to publish your book, your way, and have it available
worldwide, visit us online at www.trafford.com*

Trafford rev. 4/22/2010

 www.trafford.com

North America & international
toll-free: 1 888 232 4444 (USA & Canada)
phone: 250 383 6864 ♦ fax: 812 355 4082

CHAPTER ONE
Hard Times

The intensity of the sun's heat made Malachi's light skin feel as though it was burning into the depth of his soul. He moaned with a strenuous effort as he continued to plow the harden ground that always refused to give in to his brutal strength. Malachi stopped. He licked his parched full lips while he removed the yellow, dingy, straw hat. He wiped his forehead with the back of his dirty hand. The sweat burned his eyes as he squinted up at the hot intense sun as it released its brutal heat down on him. He grunted as he shook his head and replaced his hat. His right hand grabbed the handle of the plow while he pulled out a small pebble from his left pocket. He threw the pebble at the mule in front of him who was harnessed to the other end of the plow.

"Let's keep it moving, Stella! If Pa were to see you

1

fooling around, he'd be whipping us both," Malachi said. He watched the pebble bounced off the mule's head. "Let's go girl."

Stella, a mule who'd seen better days, heehawed. She was stubborn. She whined a course of dislike when the pebble hit her. She put her head between her shoulders, and began to pull the plow as she lazily walked forward.

"I don't know, Stella. I get tired of working this field every morning. I don't see any progress at the end of the week. Maybe it's the sun burning out my brains that make me think the way I'm thinking, but life has got to be easier somewhere else besides Mullebur, South Carolina. What do you think, Stella?"

Stella stopped. She turned her head around to look at Malachi. She took a hoof and kicked up some dirt in front of her, and then she made a loud whine.

"I know how you feel, girl. Come on. Pa will want us to have this side done by the time he returned from town. Let's go, Stella!" Malachi snapped.

Stella nodded her massive head as she turned back around. She kicked her hoof into the dirt, and then she flopped down on her hindquarters all in one swift motion.

"Oh, damn it, Stella! Don't go acting hardheaded on me!" Malachi shouted. "You can take some hard licks to that thick backside of yours, but my skin ain't as thick as yours when it comes to the switch. Get up, girl!"

Stella's hindquarters quivered as she sat her full weight onto the ground to get more comfortable while wiggling her large hindquarters into the ground.

"Stella! Sweet shit! Stella, don't act this way. I'll

give you an apple if you get off the ground," Malachi pleaded.

Stella turned toward him. She pulled back her lips to display her large teeth, and then bayed.

"Well, I'm not going to give it to you if you're sitting on the ground. I'll give it to you when we get to the other side of the trench," Malachi said, as he hiked up his worn, faded gray overalls as he gave Stella a defiant stare.

Stella continued to look at Malachi.

"I promise, Stella. I got a few apples in the barn. Now come on, get up," he pleaded.

Stella didn't move.

"Sweet shit! Girl, come on!" Malachi shouted as he yanked on the reins.

Stella bayed, but didn't move.

Malachi let go of the plow and the reins, and turned around. When he turned back around seconds later, he was holding a red, small apple that he'd taken out of his overalls.

"This is yours if you get moving, Stella," Malachi said. He held the apple out in Stella's direction.

Stella didn't budge.

"Go ahead. Eat it," Malachi said. He pushed the apple closer to Stella's face as he neared her.

"All right," Malachi said. "Go ahead. I trust you, and I hope you trust me."

Stella looked at the apple, and then Malachi as she watched Malachi's hand draw closer to her mouth with the red shiny apple.

"Eat it," Malachi gingerly urged.

Stella slowly moved her head toward the apple. She was hesitating. She sniffed at the apple. She looked at

Malachi, and then she sniffed at it again. She opened her wide mouth, and was about to bite into the apple when Malachi pulled it back.

"Are you going to act right?" Malachi asked, as he held the apple behind his back. "No more tricks if I give it to you."

Stella tilted her head sideways while making her eyes become cross-eyed as she displayed a bemused quizzical stare.

Malachi held up his index finger. "If you eat it, you work for me," he said.

Stella continued her nonchalant stare as she lifted her right ear while letting out an intimidating baying sound.

"Okay. Here's your apple."

Malachi slowly moved his hand toward Stella's mouth. He snatched his hand back the moment Stella bit into the apple while yanking it out of Malachi's hand.

"Damn, you're fast. Chew it quick and let's get back to work," Malachi said.

Malachi watched Stella chew on the apple slowly. He thought she was chewing on it a little too slow as he walked back to the plow and picked up the reins.

"Are you finished?" Malachi asked.

Stella bayed.

"We had a deal, Stella. Come on, girl. We have work to do!" Malachi whined.

Stella snorted and bayed. She shook her head, and pressed her hindquarters deeper into the ground.

"Sweet shit, Stella!" Malachi shouted. "You good for nothing, stubborn ass mule! You eat my apple, and then you get even lazier." He started kicking dirt on Stella with the side of his worn, brown shoe. "This wasn't part of our deal!"

"Do you know you're talking to a mule?"

Malachi turned around.

"An ass has no feelings after it has eaten Malachi, and no desire to work either."

Malachi looked at the small, dark skinned girl as if she'd come up behind him and kicked him in his butt. He shook his head. There were times when his twelve year old sister had a knack to drive him crazy with her snide remarks.

"Thank you, Rose Ann for your good words of encouragement in this situation." Malachi's words were so southern that Rose Ann, at times, had to strain her ears to understand what he said. "But I can handle it without you," Malachi said.

Rose Ann, her long, gray flowered dress dragging on the ground, smiled. Malachi watched her raise her dress displaying her bare feet, as she walked toward him.

"What are you going to do that I couldn't?" Malachi asked.

"The difference between you and me is that Stella knows what she's doing when it comes to me pulling the plow and when it comes to you," Rose Ann said as she bent down and picked up a palm size rock. She went behind Stella. "The difference being that we're both girls."

Malachi watched Rose Ann raise the rock above her head, and throw it at Stella's hindquarters with all her strength. When the rock hit Stella, she leaped up as she bayed with pain.

"Get your lazy ass plowing, Stella!" Rose Ann shouted.

Stella began moving the plow.

"You better get behind her, Malachi," Rose Ann said.

Malachi looked at his sister. He grabbed the plow while wrapping the reins around his hands.

"I have to finish milking the cows," Rose Ann said as she began walking away.

"Yeah, you do that, so a real man can do his job," Malachi said.

Rose Ann looked at Malachi. "What real man? You couldn't even make an ass move," she said. 'Think about it. It's an ass leading an ass."

By late afternoon every muscle in Malachi's body was hurting. He was sitting at the kitchen table watching his sister make biscuits. He looked down at his hands. They were red, swollen, and blistered.

"You better go put that ointment Pa uses on your hands," Rose Ann said. She'd been watching Malachi as he winced in pain while examining his hands.

Malachi looked up. His sister's back was toward him.

"And wash that stink off you. You smell like Stella!" Rose Ann snapped.

"You'd smell like Stella, too, if you'd been walking behind her for most of the day while she shit, burp, farted, and whined most of the day!" Malachi snapped, as he stood up.

"Malachi, you smell like that even when you don't plow," Rose Ann said. She laughed.

"I do not," Malachi said defensively. His forehead

wrinkle as a quizzical look appeared on his dirty, handsome face.

"Go by the well and wash that dirt off you if you want to eat lunch," Rose Ann said. "And you might think of changing those dirty, wretched smelling clothing. Throw them in the washtub so I can wash them."

"For someone who is only twelve, you're very bossy, Rose," Malachi said as he glanced down at his worn, ragged overalls and smelly body. He could remember when they were slightly new after his father had given them to him. "They're not that bad."

Rose Ann turned around. She crossed her thin arms across her large bosom chest. "I'm bossy because I know that if I don't stay on top of you, you're going to slack off, and Pa will come in here and start acting like a fool," she said.

"Hmmf. Pa acts like a fool regardless of what I do," Malachi said.

Rose Ann turned back around. "Maybe that's because you two are the same," she said.

Malachi walked to the door. He opened it. "Could be," he said.

As he stepped outside, Malachi stood on the boarded porch and looked around at the scene he'd been looking at since he could remember. The greenish mountain to the right of him always looked as if the grass never changed no matter what season was in effect. His mind raced with memories of the past. He thought about the time he first raced out of the door and into the full, dark grass thirty paces away in the middle of spring when he was eight years old. When he turned his attention to the large oak tree to the right of him, he smiled. He remembered falling out of the tree four or five times while growing up. He lifted his left arm and looked at the scar running along his forearm. He could barely see it now. He had been five years old when he first fell out of the tree. He began to walk around toward the back of the house. As he did, he began removing the shoulder straps on his overalls. He let them fall to his waist.

He glanced down at his callous hands. They were dirty and they were big. He rubbed them together gingerly because of the pain. He continued looking down at his body, and was amazed at the sight of his hard abdominals. They looked like little rocks in rows of three. He could feel the tightness in his biceps and chest as he flexed his muscles repeatedly. He realized that the past winter had him working long hours, and hard days. At fifteen, he was bigger than most kids his age.

He saw the large, wooden barrel in front of him. He stripped off his overalls. He didn't wear underwear, so his nakedness from the waist down was apparent. He removed the dirty tee-shirt and dropped it beside his overalls. He stood there naked as he looked around for the lye soap that always made him itch for a day or two after using it. Locating it on the windowsill that was behind the barrel, he stepped on the small stool that was beside the barrel, and climbed into the very cold, murky water.

"Ahh!" Malachi shouted as he settled down into the cold water. "Sweet shit, this is cold!"

"Lordy, Lordy, my heart is filled with pain. Lordy, Lordy, ain't nothing like some sweet rain on a hot day to take away this Devil's heat. Rain down on me... Rain down on me. I want to drown in my Lord's tears and cleanse my body with that sweet water from Heaven. Cause my head is on fire and

my soul's beginning to sweat. But that Devil ain't gonna get my soul just yet," Malachi began to sing with a melodic voice.

Rose Ann could hear her brother singing. A smile formed. Enhancing her cute dimples. Her brother could sing the draws off a virgin if he wanted to. Every time he sang, she felt goose bumps.

By the time the sun went down four hours later, and the night had cooled, Rose Ann and Malachi were finishing up the last of their dinner, which, consisted of dumplings stew with chucks of beef. Malachi was putting the last portion of his food into his mouth when the front door exploded opened. His father walked in as big as life with his chest sticking out.

"Hi, Pa! How was the market?" Malachi asked, as he watched his father drag in his tired two hundred and ten pound frame through the door. "We have supper ready for you."

"We?" Buford Moon said to his eldest son gruffly. "You cook today, boy?"

Malachi watched his father hang his hat on the hat rack beside the door. Malachi didn't know why he still wore the ragged hat. Most of the brim was missing in the front and back of the hat. It looked more like a cap than a hat.

Buford had the half hindquarters of a buck slung over his shoulder. He walked over toward a leather canvas lying on the floor and dropped it next to the small cast iron cooking stove. Without missing a step, he walked to the kitchen table and sat down. He ignored the blood stains that were on his shoulder from the dead buck and the fact that his fingernails were caked with dried blood.

"You children take care of your chores today?" Buford asked. His eyes fell on Malachi, and then Rose Ann. They lingered on her for a full minute as he looked at her face, and then let his eyes rest for three seconds on her ample chest before looking away. "You two know I don't like no slacking when it comes to your work around here."

"Yep," Malachi said, as he licked the greasy remains from his dinner off his fingers. "Everything is done, Pa."

Buford stared at Malachi. The gray hairs on his short-cropped head were reflecting off the dim light emanating from the cabin lamps. He placed his large hands on his tired eyes and rubbed them.

Rose Ann, sitting at the table, quickly stood up and hurried to the cast iron pot. She filled her plate with food and brought it to her father.

Buford reached for a spoon as he watched his daughter push the food toward him.

"It's good, Pa," Rose Ann said. She lowered her eyes when her father gave her a long stare.

"Thank you, honey," Buford said as he began eating fastidiously. "Your brother's been taking care of you and the place?"

"Of course, Pa. I—"

"Boy, don't go into the long of the situation damn it. If your sister wasn't keeping you right, I know you wouldn't be doing what I asked you to do. Ain't that right, Rose Ann?"

Rose Ann looked up at her father. "Uh…No, Pa. Sometimes Malachi reminds me of the chores you told him we had to do," she said. "I don't always have to tell him."

Buford stared at his daughter. "You putting on some

weight, girl. You are filling out just fine. Soon, I'm gonna have to find you a husband to keep you right."

"Oh, Pa," Rose Ann said. She lowered her eyes bashfully. "I'm too young for that kind of talk."

"You're twelve years old, girl. Back in my day, girls your age were getting hitched at thirteen. Regardless if they knew how to cook," Buford said. He put some more food in his mouth. "Hell, my problem is when you do go, who am I going to have around here to look after your brother to make sure he's doing his chores?"

"Aw, Pa," Malachi said.

"Aw, Pa, hell. Boy!" Buford snapped, as he scratched his rough beard. "You can get lazy if I don't keep my foot in your ass."

"Pa, Malachi ain't lazy. You should see how he worked that field today," Rose Ann said. She always defended her big brother. "His hands were cut holding the reins with Stella, but he didn't complain."

"Um-hmm. "How many times did you tell him to keep at it?" Buford asked Rose Ann.

Malachi shook his head as he stared at his father. "Pa, I do what you ask me to do. Sure, I protest a little, but that's because I don't see the logic in us working this field to make money a bank that gets half of our profit." Malachi ran his fingers through his curly black hair as he stared at his father. "When the bank is finished with us, then Mr. Miller at the local store gets another third from the credit he leads you to get us through the rough times during the winter. With his interest rates, what are we left with? A simple third of our sweat and blood that we put into this land of dirt. That's all! We've been working this land for ten years now. I remember Ma complaining that we're working our skin to the bone to pay other peoples bills except our own. I might get a little fed up, but you know you can depend on me to do my chores."

Buford stared at Malachi. He put his spoon in the unfinished dumpling stew. He stared at his son with the one good eye he had. The black patch covering his right eye always gave him a menacing appearance. "You raising your voice in my house like you're paying the mortgage. You know I don't cotton to that kind of talk under my roof. You are not big enough for me to take a switch to your backside. Anyway, you know you don't mention that woman's name in my house. How many times have I you that, boy?" he said.

Malachi looked down as his father's intensified gaze bore into him. He was gingerly wringing his hands under the table to keep from becoming even more disrespectful. There were times when his father acted as if he was dimwitted or something. He hated when that happened.

"This land has promise. If you don't own something in life, you work until you can own something. We work this land because in a few more years we'd be able to call it our own. Before you know it, your children will own it and their children after that. Nothing in life comes free. You remember that, boy. Everybody has to earn their own way to get better things in this life. If you're lazy and shiftless, then nothing good is going to come your way," Buford said.

Malachi nodded. He still hadn't lifted his head out of respect.

Buford pushed his chair from the table. "Rose

Ann, you get this kitchen cleaned up. Where's my corn liquor?"

Malachi and Rose Ann watched their father stand up and stretch. He glanced at them, and then walked away as he headed toward the other side of the room. He reached into the small chest that was underneath the window and removed the dark brown bottle of corn liquor.

When he'd gone into his room, Malachi began gathering the plates as he stood up. "I don't care what he says. I don't see any logic in farming someone else's land!" he said. He was angry. "We do the hard work, and others live high off the hog while we bust our butts to get this land right. And for what? So we can say it's ours? If I ever own anything, it's going to be mine from the start!"

Rose Ann took the plates Malachi had given her, and walked over to fireplace where a large, black pot was hung on an iron ring. She put the plates inside the hot water that was in the pot.

"Why we can't we be bankers and store clerks?" Malachi asked.

"Maybe because we don't have the proper education, Malachi."

"Hell, we don't need education to steal from people who don't know any better than what they're told. When Pa got this land ten years ago, Ma told him he was a fool for signing on the dotted line and taking on the responsibility of this place. She said that the land wasn't fertile enough to bring in a profit. But your Pa—the man who knows everything—didn't listen. What do we have out in that field? Some potatoes. A few rows of corn that's never sweet. Some tomatoes, and that's about it."

Rose Ann shrugged. "He's your father, too."

"We have two cows that are as thin as shoestrings. Stella," Malachi threw his arms up while shaking his head in frustration. "A mule so damn stubborn that if I had my way, I'll shoot her in the ass to put her ass out of her misery," Malachi said. He made Rose Ann laugh. "Don't laugh, Rose Ann. That damn mule is enough to drive a man crazy. One day she wants to work. The next day she doesn't. The following day she won't even come out of the barn." Malachi shook his head. "I'm going out to check on the thin cows and the stubborn mule."

Rose Ann laughed harder.

"Rose Ann! Rose Ann! Girl come and help your Pa take these damn boots off!"

Malachi glanced at his sister. "The poor king is calling you," he said, and rolled his eyes.

Rose Ann shook her head and smiled as she walked toward the back room of the cabin.

Buford was sitting in his old rocking chair in the far right corner of the room. He raised the large brown corn liquor bottle to his mouth, and gulped down its contents. He brought the bottle back down, and placed it on the floor. He watched his daughter walk into the room.

"Malachi is a good boy, Pa. He's trying to do the best he can," Rose Ann said.

She walked over to her father. She turned her back to him as she sat half way on his right knee while he lifted his right, big booted foot for her.

"Girl, you take up for that boy too much. The boy is lazy! Come back some so you can grip the boot, child!" Buford said. He grabbed Rose Ann's hips and pulled her further up on his thigh toward him. "You know I have trouble with these boots when it's time to take them off."

Rose Ann moved back a little further toward her father. She knew what was next as she gripped his boot by the heel and tried to pull it off.

"Girl, you really starting to fill out in all the right places. You going to make a man mighty happy one of these days when you come of age," Buford said, as he reached for the bottom edge of Rose Ann's dress.

Rose Ann tensed as she felt her father's hand on her left calf.

"A good man when you find him, girl, is going to treat you right," Buford said. He let his hand slowly travel a little farther up her calf.

She tensed her stomach. She felt a sense of nausea flood over her body, as she clenched her teeth tightly. She shivered as she felt her father's hand slowly travel further up her leg. Closing her eyes, she concentrated in expanding her lungs. Seconds later, she let out a bellowing fart while at the same time tugging hard on Buford's boot.

The sound of the fart and the immediate horrendous smell that followed made Buford remove his hand.

"Damn it, girl! Don't you know it's not ladylike to be passing gas like that?" Buford asked. He wrinkled up his nose as the wretched smell of dead fish filled the room. He started fanning his hand in front of his face. "I'll take off the other boot myself. You go see if you messed on yourself. Whew! Child, I hope nothing crawl up in you and died. You stink!"

"You sure you don't want me to get the other one,

Pa?" Rose Ann asked as she turned around while hurrying away from her father.

Buford continued fanning his hand in front of his face. "No. Go on and finished straightening up in the kitchen," he said, as he stared at Rose Ann while reaching for his corn liquor.

Rose Ann smiled as she left the room.

That night, Malachi lay in his bed looking at the ceiling. He had his forearm across his head. He was naked underneath the gray wool horse blanket. His thoughts were far away.

"Malachi?"

He looked to the left of him at the worn blanket hanging up beside him. The blanket separated his sister and himself. Giving each some privacy. Since they'd both shared the same room. It made them both feel as if they had their own rooms. They'd been in the same room since Malachi had been seven and Rose Ann was three.

"Yeah, Rose Ann," Malachi said.

"Are you decent?"

Malachi looked down at himself. He pulled his blanket up to his waist. "Yeah," he said.

Rose Ann pulled back the blanket. "Can't sleep?"

"No. Thinking. Why?" Malachi asked.

"I can't sleep either," she said.

"We should try. Before long the rooster will be crowing and we'd be doing the chores again," Malachi said.

Rose Ann looked at her brother. "You don't like farming, do you?" she asked.

Malachi continued to stare at the ceiling. "I don't know. I don't see any purpose in it, Rose. I mean, I feel there's something better in the world out there then shoveling cow shit, chasing chickens around to get some eggs, and plowing a ground with a stubborn mule that don't give you nothing but headaches. Pa likes this way of life. His Pa and his Pa before him liked farming. Maybe I'm different in some way. I might be more like Ma. She said what was on her mind, and did what made her happy. You don't remember Ma much. You were little when she…Well, Pa and her used to argue a lot about the farm, and where life was taking them. Ma had a mouth on her that made me cover my ears sometimes as she'd curse Pa."

Rose Ann looked at her brother. "Was Ma pretty?"

"Pretty? I don't know. Maybe. She always smelled like honeysuckle whenever she hugged me. She always had a fresh smell. It could be the hottest or coldest day outside, and she always smelled…lemony," Malachi said.

"I don't look like her, do I?" Rose Ann asked.

Malachi turned toward his sister. "You have her eyes. Those dark brown eyes that makes a person look at you more than once," he said.

"Do you think I'm pretty, Malachi?"

Malachi rolled his eyes. "Nope. You're as ugly as the butt of a squirrel," he said.

"Malachi!"

"I don't know, Rose Ann. What do you mean by pretty? Are you prettier than Stella? I don't have anyone to compare you to. You're my sister. I guess you look okay."

"Pa is always talking about how pretty I am, and how I'm going to make some man a good wife someday," Rose Ann said. She pushed out her bottom lip in a childish gesture. "What if I don't want to get married, huh? I don't need a man groping me, and trying to make me do things I don't want to do. Worse, I don't need a man in my life that's going to tell me what I can't do and can do! A man can't do anything for me that I can't do for myself!"

Malachi stared at his sister. "What are you talking about?" he asked.

Rose Ann looked at him. "Huh?" She lowered her brown eyes. "Oh…nothing. I just thought you might think I'm pretty," she said.

"I don't know. Well, you're getting bigger. This time last year, you looked like a stringy boy. Now…."

Malachi quickly glanced at Rose Ann's large breasts, and then back up.

"Oh. These," Rose Ann said, as she followed Malachi's quick glance. "They're more a burden than anything else. I can't swing the ax like I used to because they're in the way. Then when I run, I have to hold them down because they're bouncing all over the place. If you had them, you'd know what I mean."

"I don't want them," Malachi said. He turned his attention back to the ceiling. "I like my flat chest just the way it is."

Rose Ann pulled back the blanket separating them and curled up with her hands shielding her breasts while pulling her blanket up to her neck. The night had become cool and she felt a small chill run through her body. Maybe the chill had to do with the way she was feeling whenever her father touched her. She was young, but she knew there was something nasty in the way her father touched her and the way he looked at her. She was not comfortable with it.

"Sing me a song, Malachi," Rose Ann said.

"Why? You're only going to laugh at me."

Rose Ann smiled. "Go ahead. I won't laugh at your wolf howling sound," she said.

"Wolf howling?" Malachi asked.

"Go ahead, Malachi. Please."

Malachi smiled. He closed his eyes for a moment, and let the words form. When he opened his eyes, he was grinning.

"I was walking down a dirt road looking for a chicken-chick. I'd been walking three days, and four nights while licking my juicy lips. I didn't see noth ...ing...noth... ing but darkness on the sweeeetttt...cold...cold... road. I heard the croak of a toad, and my eyes got as wide as a spring tide. My hands shivered, and I missed a step. I swallowed hard while stretching my longgg, longgg neck. I know that old chicken-chick is out there hiding in a hole. I am going to find me that chicken-chick and pluck its feathers. Skin it good and fry it lonnnnggg. That ole chicken-chick is going to keep me strrroonngg and keep my stomach full. Cause, I'm as hungry as a fool on a rainy, rainy daaayyy with nothing to look forward toooooo."

Malachi stopped singing. He listened to the heavy breathing of Rose Ann. She had fallen to sleep. He smiled. Closing his eyes, he tried to sleep. He knew his day tomorrow would be a tiring one. A day full of chores and hard work on a hard ground that yielded nothing but blood and sweat.

CHAPTER TWO

Loss of

Innocence

Malachi's day was going to be one of pain and suffering when he went to the barn to get Stella. It was still dark out. He yawned as he opened the barn doors and saw Stella staring at him. The mule bayed and turned her ass to him as she turned around as if she'd seen something she detestable. Malachi took that as an insult as he closed the barn doors. Also, he knew it was Stella's way of saying she wasn't going to do any farming today.

Malachi went to Stella's stable. He opened the stable door and walked in. He leaned on the doorframe and stared at the stubborn mule. "Look, Stella, I ain't gonna take you acting like you running this damn farm. I've been patient with you. I understand you're being dumb

20

and all, but it's too early in the morning for you to be acting this way," he said.

Stella turned her massive head slightly around to look at Malachi. She arched her eyebrows and shook her head as she returned her attention to the back of the barn wall.

"I don't need you looking at me as if I've lost my mind for asking you to come on out and do your chores, Stella," Malachi said.

Stella whined but didn't turn back to face Malachi. Her tail lightly swung out, and, purposely brushed it against Malachi's face.

Malachi shook his head as he ran a hand across his face. "If I go get me one of those damn switches out yonder from the tree, and come back in here and take it to your hide I bet you'd listen to me then!" Malachi snapped.

Stella he-hawed as she continued to swing her tail.

"So now you think I'm a fool, huh? Stella, I'm telling you to come on out of there. Right now, doggone it!" Malachi shouted.

Malachi took a step further into the stable. When he did, Stella raised her hind legs, and kicked out. Her hoofs lightly hit Malachi in the stomach. It wasn't as hard as it could've been, but the force of it did lift Malachi off his feet and out of the stable as the door of the stable slammed shut. He landed on a pitchfork that was partially hidden in straw. He let out a horrible scream as the pitchfork pierced his butt.

At that moment, Rose Ann came running into the barn. She'd been in the chicken coop gathering eggs near the barn. There was a basket in her hands. She was wearing the same dress from yesterday. The only difference was she was wearing a white handkerchief tied around her head. She looked from Malachi to Stella. She quickly assessed the situation. She started to laugh.

Malachi leaped up. His handsome face was twisted in anger as he rubbed his sore backside. "That's it! I've had it with that damn jackass!" Malachi snapped. He turned around and snatched up the pitchfork. "I'm going to show you what it is like to feel pain."

"Malachi!" Rose Ann shouted.

As Malachi took his first step toward the stable, Stella slowly turned around to face him. The mule walked the feet to the stable door. She used her head and pushed open the stable door. Malachi stopped. He watched Stella walk out. She headed to the barn door. Stella didn't rush. She simply sass-shay out of the barn with grace. In her hurry to see what was going on, Rose Ann had left one of the barn doors open. Malachi stood there and watched Stella exit. The pitchfork was gripped tightly in his sweaty right hands.

Rose Ann watched the mule and her brother. She had to admit. If she hadn't seen it with her own eyes, she wouldn't have believed it. She started laughing.

Malachi dropped the pitchfork and stormed pass his laughing sister.

"Malachi, you get angry too quickly. Stella knows that and that's why she does what she does," Rose Ann said as she followed her brother out of the barn.

"If that stubborn mule wasn't the only one on this farm, her ass would be wolf meat by now," Malachi said. He continued walking.

Stella ears pricked up at the sound of Malachi's harsh words. She stopped.

"Malachi," Rose Ann said.

Malachi continued to walk toward Stella, but he slowed down his quicken pace as he neared the mule. He took three more steps before stopping a few feet from Stella.

"Well, I didn't really mean it like that..." Malachi said.

"Malachi," Rose Ann said as she came and stood beside her brother. "I think you made her mad."

"She's a damn mule, Rose Ann! Why is she getting upset? We feed her lazy ass after she works, and if she won't work, we still have to feed her," Malachi said.

Stella head abruptly turned toward Malachi. Her nose flared. She grunted and dropped her big rump on the ground defiantly all in one swift motion.

"Now you've done it, Malachi. Offer her some sugar."

"I didn't do a damn thing, Rose Ann! We treat this mule like it is human. The only sweets I'm going to give her will be a sweet kick in her stubborn ass if she don't get up and start working!" Malachi snapped.

Malachi walked around and stood in front of Stella. Stella followed his every step with her large brown eyes.

"If you don't get your lazy ass off the ground, you're going to be in some real trouble, Stella," Malachi said. His neck was bulging with veins as his anger grew.

Stella gave him a look of disdain. She didn't move.

"Malachi!" Rose Ann shouted.

"I know what I'm doing, Rose Ann!" Malachi snapped. "Stella, I'm gonna tell you one more time."

Stella replied by letting her forelegs collapse. She was now lying completely on the ground.

Malachi crossed his arms over his chest. He leaned in close to Stella's nose. "I'm going to go get a switch," he said. He spun around and headed toward a large old tree several feet behind him.

Stella sat there and watched Malachi walk away. When Malachi was twenty feet away, Stella stood up. She gave a loud whine, and took off running toward Malachi at a full gallop.

"Malachi!" Rose Ann screamed. Her scream was ear-shattering as she dropped the basket of eggs.

Malachi was determined to let Stella know who the boss was. He glanced over his shoulder when he heard his sister scream. He did a double-take as he saw Stella running toward him. He shrieked and took off running.

"Run, Malachi, run!" Rose Ann shouted as she lifted her long dress that went down to her feet, and ran after them.

Malachi's heart was racing. He'd never seen Stella move as fast as she was moving now.

"Keep running, Malachi!" Rose Ann shouted. "Keep running!"

Stella increased her speed as she tried to catch Malachi. The massive muscles in her powerful legs expanded each time they hit the ground.

Malachi was nearing the cabin. He'd been running in circles to throw Stella off, but the mule was slowly gaining on him. He was breathing hard. His chest was on fire. A few more feet and he would be on the porch.

Stella, seeing Malachi nearly on the porch, increased

her speed by lowering her head and expanding her lungs while stretching her legs.

Damn mule never ran this fast before. Malachi said to himself. If Stella had been running like this when they were working in the fields, he might've finished planting seeds for the next two weeks. No, he had to get her angry to get her going. The mule was crazy.

The front door of the cabin opened. Malachi leaped into the air and through it in one swift motion. Stella whined as she watched Malachi leap through the doorway. She slid a few feet forward before coming to a stop.

Buford looked at Stella, and then at his son who was lying on the floor of the cabin staring at the ceiling and breathing hard.

"Boy, what did I tell you about chucking your chores?" Buford said, as he stared down at his son. "That's your problem, son, you can't get the job done when I expect you to."

"Huh? I...was...wasn't... chucking...my chor... chores. Stella took...took after me... Pa," Malachi said, as he tried to catch his breath.

Buford shook his head. "Get your no-good-for-nothing ass off the floor and take care of your chores," Buford said. He walked over and kicked Malachi on the leg as he stood in the doorway. "And stop playing with that silly mule." He turned back around to see Rose Ann running toward him with her dress hiked up. "Girl, where's breakfast? I hope you ain't getting shiftless habits from your brother. Get in there and start cooking, damnit! What's wrong with you two this morning?"

Rose Ann, her bountiful chest heaving up and down, lowered her eyes; as she dropped her dress, and hurried pass her father. She noticed Buford looking down at her chest as she passed him. She shivered as she increased her pace to get by him.

"Yes, Pa," she said.

"Stella, get on over yonder in them fields and start working," Buford said, as he glanced at the mule. "Malachi, get off the floor and go do your damn chores or you won't be getting anything for breakfast."

Malachi, taking his time, rose from the floor. "It was Stella's fault, Pa," he said.

"You and Stella keep playing around, and I will be bringing my whip down on both your backsides," Buford said.

As Malachi walked pass his father and out the door, he felt his father's foot slams into his butt. The kick knocked Malachi off the porch. His face landed in the dirt. He found himself staring up at Stella. As he stared at Stella, Malachi would've sworn on a stack of bibles that the mule smiled at him.

When he finally stood up, he saw his father slamming the cabin door.

Malachi turned toward Stella. "You see what happens when you don't listen, Stella?" he said.

Stella looked at Malachi. She cocked her head to the left, and quickly turned her ass around, slightly brushing against Malachi's shoulder. Stella headed in the direction of the fields.

"You ornery mule, Stella," Malachi said as he began to follow Stella. "Some mules can listen. Some mules can work, but you, you can't do either. Sure they might act up a little, but you. You're a different story altogether."

Stella stopped.

Malachi stopped.

Stella turned her head in his direction.

Malachi swallowed hard as he watched her. He took a step back.

"Sorry, Stella," Malachi said.

Stella dropped her head between her shoulders.

"I tell you what. We won't work as hard as we did yesterday," Malachi said. He held up his arms as if he were warding off a bad spell.

Stella stared at him.

"Cross my heart, Stella," Malachi said. He ran his right hand across his chest.

Stella raised her head, and turned back around heading toward the fields.

"Damn mule," Malachi whispered.

Rose Ann was busy gathering some pots together to make breakfast when she turned around to find her father standing nearly on top of her.

"Girl, you're too big to be running around with your...things jumping up and down. Something is gonna fall off you or out of that there dress, child," Buford said. He looked down at Rose Ann's small five foot seven frame. "What if something popped out of that dress? You would've been embarrassed."

Rose Ann could see Buford sneering down at her mischievously. She shrugged as she tried to maneuver pass him, but he blocked her. Thrusting his groin forward, and grabbing her shoulders.

"Pa, I have to get breakfast going," Rose Ann protested by trying to squeeze by her father. She tried to gently break free by shaking her shoulders. "Pa, you're hurting me!" she said.

Buford grunted. His good eye squinted. "Girl, you act right with your Pa. I done raised you and I can do what I want with you. You're my child. Now go in my room and wait for me. I have to show you something."

Rose Ann shrugged a little more, and then she stopped. She looked up at her father. She saw his face had changed. His lips were pulled back revealing his blacken teeth. She shivered.

"Pa…You're hurting me," Rose Ann said in a frightening voice.

Buford reached out toward Rose Ann's ample left breast. He cupped it with an urgency that made spittle fall from the corner of his mouth. "Ain't no man going to be your first but your Pa, girl. I feed you, cloth you, and I raised you, so you're mine. Go in my room and wait for me like I said."

"Why, Pa?" Rose Ann protested.

Buford's callused left hand came crashing down hard on Rose Ann's soft innocent left cheek. She fell to the floor.

"Don't question me. Take you ass to my room!" Buford shouted.

Fright filled her entire body. She felt her stomach turn to jelly as the pain from the blow made the left side of her face go numb. With slow deliberation, Rose Ann pushed herself off the floor and stood up. She glanced at her father and walked toward his room. She was crying as she walked toward his room with her head down. Each step she made was one of hesitation.

By late afternoon, Malachi was exhausted as he headed back to the cabin to wash up and eat lunch. He knew breakfast had long been over.

"I'm telling you right now. If we had another mule, Stella would be mule meat for the wolves out there," Malachi said as he came through the door. "What did you make for lunch, Rose?"

Rose Ann sat at the table breaking green beans and placing them into a wooden bowl in front of her. "I made some beef stew with potatoes," she whispered.

"That sounds good," Malachi said. "But why we keep having stew? "I saw Pa heading into town. I guess he's going to go and try to get us some credit. This damn land ain't worth any man's sweat and sore muscles. A dead land trying to give some life to its rotten soil."

Malachi walked to the overhead cabinets and removed a small wooden bowl. He headed toward the large skillet in the fireplace. He reached for the metal spoon in the pot, and began scooping up the stew and placing it in his bowl. When he'd filled his bowl to the rim, he walked to the table and sat down.

"You know what I think Rose. I think Pa ought to sell this land back to the bank. Get whatever few dollars he can get, and we find us some land that's going to give back the effort we put into it," Malachi said. He lowered his head toward the bowl and began shoveling food into his mouth with his big spoon. "This is good Rose Ann."

Rose Ann leaped out of her chair and ran out of the kitchen.

Malachi looked up. He watched her. He arched his eyebrows in confusion and shrugged. Picking up his bowl, he went to the chair Rose Ann had been sitting in. He was about to sit down when he saw blood on the seat of the chair. His thick eyebrows creased in confusion.

Why was there blood in the chair? He didn't see

anyone bleeding. Maybe it had come from the buck his Pa had brought in the night before. Malachi shook his head, and went back and sat down in the chair he'd left.

Malachi stretched his tired, long body as he lay in bed that night trying to adjust to the heat around him. In the summer time, it was hotter in the cabin than outside on some nights and tonight was one of those nights. He could feel every ache in his body as he tossed and turned to get comfortable in the small bed.

"Rose Ann, I need a new body. If you were a boy, I would have some help in the field," Malachi said. "Hell, I need a few boys out there working with Stella. Lazy ass mule."

A small whimpering sound could be heard coming from Rose Ann's side of the blanket.

Malachi turned toward the blanket. "What are you doing? Trying to sing?" he asked.

The whimper turned into crying.

"Rose Ann? Are you crying, girl?" Malachi asked.

The crying grew louder.

"I'm going to open the curtain, Rose Ann," Malachi said as he propped himself on his elbows. He reached for the blanket and moved it enough to see only Rose Ann's face. "You are crying. What's wrong?"

Rose Ann, her face puffy around the eyes, stared at Malachi. "Nothing," she said. She wiped her nose with the edge of her sheet. "I'm all right."

"If you are, how come you're crying?" Malachi asked. "Is your face swollen? What happened? Did you fall or something?"

Rose Ann shook her head.

"You don't have to hide anything from me. What's wrong, Rose Ann?" Malachi pleaded. "It's all right."

"Pa…Well, Pa's been acting funny these past few days, Malachi."

"Funny? Pa's been telling you jokes? Hell, I didn't even think he knew any. Were they really funny?" Malachi asked as he stared at his sister.

"No, Malachi. Not funny like that, but funny like… crazy. I've been trying not to tell you, but today…."

"Today? What about today, Rose? Now that you mentioned it, you did act a little strange when I came in to eat lunch. What's wrong, girl?"

"Pa. He's been saying things to me," Rose Ann began. Her breathing had become labored. "I don't know. Things a Pa shouldn't be saying, and then this morning he…he just lost his mind, Malachi!"

Malachi stared at his sister. He didn't know what she was trying to say, but he did know that whatever it was, it was something that was very hard for her to say.

"Tell me what happened. I can't help you if I don't know, Rose."

Rose Ann looked at her brother. It felt funny trying to explain what she had to say to the opposite sex, but she knew Malachi loved her like any big brother who loved their little sister. And, hopefully, he would understand.

"Pa grabbed my…" She lowered her head down to her chest.

Malachi looked at her. He arched his eyebrows as confusion etched itself onto his face. "What? He touched your what?" Malachi asked.

"He grabbed my chest, Malachi."

"Your chest?" Malachi asked.

"These!" Rose Ann snapped, and pointed to her breasts.

Malachi looked at her breasts, and then quickly looked away.

"Pa grabbed them," Rose Ann said. Her nose was running heavily, and she wiped it with the back of her hand.

"What?" Malachi snapped.

"He told me to go to his room. When I didn't go, he slapped me. Oh God! He slapped me so hard, Malachi, that I saw blue lights in front of my eyes when I opened them. I was scared that he was going to hit me again so I went to his room. I thought he was going to get the switch for me, but he came in and locked the door behind him. He told me to lift my dress and drop my underpants. I told him no because he always beat me with my clothes on. He slapped me again. When I fell to the ground, he picked me up and threw me on his bed. I kicked at him, and that made him mad because I kicked him in his... you know. Between his legs where the soft spot is. He cursed me and punched me in the stomach. Next thing I know, I'm leaning over the footboard of the bed with my dress over my head and my underpants at my ankles. A few seconds later I feel something hot and hard hitting me on my legs and moving up toward my...secret place. I hear Pa behind me breathing hard and grunting. Next thing I know this pain hits me down there in my secret place. It was a horrible pain, Malachi. I ain't never felt pain like that before. And Pa's pushing himself in and out of me. I tried to get away from him, Malachi. It was hurting something awful. I fought as best I could but he had a tight grip on my waist. I couldn't break free!"

Malachi listened to his sister tell her story. In his mind he tried to picture the incident. To compare it to something that he could relate to. As the story unfolded, an image of a stallion and a mare formed. He remembered watching the horses one day on Mr. Bale's farm last year in the corral. The stallion, a big red one, had been sniffing behind the mare for days. The mare had always pushed the stallion away. But on this day, the stallion followed the mare to a corner of the corral, and mounted her from behind. Malachi remembered how the stallion's large member had grown to an unbelievable size as it took the mare from behind. The stallion's first thrust into the mare, knocked it to its knees, but the mare quickly got back on its legs and stood the onslaught of the stallion thrusting in and out of it for a full minute. That image of his father pounding into Rose Ann from behind like the stallion and the mare, infuriated Malachi. He balled his fists and snarled.

"He's our father!" Malachi whispered through clenched teeth.

Rose Ann, her eyes dry, stared at Malachi. "Malachi, when Pa was...doing that—

Malachi lifted his hand. "I know what you mean," he said.

"Pa said I'm not his daughter. He said that Ma came home with me one day wrapped in a sheet and said that she was going to raise me as her own. He said that you were too young to remember me being brought home. I think he said that to make me feel...Well, I don't think it's true. He hurt me something terrible, Malachi."

"What?" Malachi said.

"Your ma and pa are not my ma and pa, Malachi."

Malachi stared at Rose Ann. The veins in his temple were standing out as he continued to tightly clench and unclench his fist. He began to grind his teeth together. These were the signs as a child while growing up that he was becoming angry.

Buford lay in bed dreaming peacefully that night as Malachi and Rose Ann talked. He'd consumed so much corn liquor before going to bed that he was in a complete stupor. It was only when he felt a sense of warmth beside his left thigh that appeared to intensify with each passing second that he became conscious of something wrong with his left hand. He opened his red bloodshot eyes while lifting his left arm.

They had grabbed as much of their things as they could carry and placed them in sheets that they tied into knots. They each were carrying a bundle sheet with their belongings as they walked out into the airless, muggy night. They were a mile and a half away from the cabin when they heard the hair curling, soul-wrenching scream. They stopped.

Rose Ann glanced behind her, and then looked at Malachi. "You didn't have to cut his hand off Malachi!" she said. "He was our father!"

Malachi, with a piece of straw in his mouth, twisted his lips back and forth as he chewed on the straw. "He didn't have to do what he did to you with that hand either. He's your father, too. That story he told you was for his own satisfaction justify what he was doing to you in his own crazy mind. Now let me see him try to toll the fields with Stella and one hand," he said.

Malachi tossed something into the woods behind him.

When the object rolled out of the sack, the moonlight fell on it. It was Buford's hand.

CHAPTER THREE
The Pains of Change

Malachi and Rose Ann walked for five days on the road heading out of Mullebur. Their worn shoes had become even more worn as the days progressed. They'd stopped every four hours to rest their tired feet. Their journey became longer as each day passed into the next. When the late evening fell on them, Malachi knew they had to find some shelter and get off the dirt road. They'd been sleeping in the woods since their trek.

"Rose Ann, I see an old barn a couple of yards away. We can rest there a bit," Malachi said, as he pointed to a large dark figure to the right of them.

Rose Ann was too tired to protest. She nodded her head and followed Malachi.

When they'd reached the barn, neither one of said a word as they headed for the old, dirty straw that was piled up in the middle of the barn. They dropped their belongings, and each fell onto the straw in exhaustion. Rose Ann drew close to her brother for comfort and security as they placed straw around them.

"We'll be all right here. We only need a few hours sleep, and then we'd be on our way," Malachi said. He closed his eyes. He could feel sleep engulfing him as he let his body relax and succumb to the darkness while slowly closing his eyes.

Malachi felt something nudge him in his right side. In his deep sleep, he tried to get away from the source of the nudging by moving away from it. He heard himself moan. He protested by saying something that was unintelligible. He felt a sharp pain dig deeper into his right side. He opened his eyes.

There was a tall silhouette figure a few feet from him looking down at him as Malachi adjusted his eyes. He couldn't make the image out due to the darkness in the barn. The only light illuminating came from the corner to the left of him on the other side of the barn.

"Boy, you'd better have a good reason why you're trespassing on my property."

Malachi looked up toward the voice. He had to force his vision to focus on the man standing in front of him while using the back of his hands to get the cold out of his eyes. When he did get better vision, he saw the man pointing a double-barrel shotgun at his face. He was startled as he stared at the man wearing a pair of ragged overalls, and a blue checkered shirt that had seen one wash too many over the years.

Malachi glanced around to see where his sister was. He saw her standing a few feet to the left of him. She was frightened. He could tell by the way Rose Ann was tightly clutching the collar of her dress. Her eyes were bulging out of her head, and her legs were trembling.

"Mister, I don't mean you any harm. My sister and I got tired of walking. We saw this barn and thought we could rest here for a few hours. I swear to you, we were going to leave as soon as we were rested," Malachi began. He attempted to stand, but the man in the overalls pushed the double-barrel shotgun closer toward his face, it forced him to stay in the same spot. "We didn't do anything wrong, and we meant no harm to you or your property…sir."

"You're trespassing, boy, and that's wrong. It's also enough for me to pull on this trigger and watch your head explode."

"Mister, we ain't got much money, but we can give you a dollar for letting us use your barn," Rose Ann said. Her trembling voice made Malachi look at her. She gave Malachi a quick glance and a weak smile. She turned her attention back to the man with the gun. "We mean you no harm. Honest!"

"Uh-huh. Sure you don't, girl. I bet when you two awoke, you probably would've been hungry, and took one or two of my chickens on your way out, huh?" The man asked.

"What?" Malachi asked. His eyes grew wide. "No, sir. We weren't going to steal any of your chickens. We just needed some sleep. That's all!"

"You're a liar, boy!" The man in the overalls snapped. He pushed the double-barrel shotgun closer toward Malachi's face as he took a step forward. The double-barrel shotgun was two inches from Malachi's nose. "You were probably going to go to my house and rob me, and then rape my wife. Every time someone stops by here, they're lusting for my beautiful woman. I can see their intentions in their eyes. They want her. You want to take away my woman, don't you, boy?"

Malachi, his hands beginning to shake, looked at the man as if he'd lost his mind. Why would he rape a woman for? What did the word rape mean anyway? He asked himself. What did he get Rose Ann into? Maybe he should've waited to find somewhere else for them to sleep. The man in front of him was going to kill them. Malachi could feel it in his bones. He felt perspiration running down the small of his back as he glanced around. He had to make sure nothing happened to Rose Ann, even if it meant forfeiting his own life.

"Mister, I swear to God as my witness. My sister—"

"Sister! That girl over yonder is your sister? Boy, you must take me for a darn fool. She's probably your wife. Ain't a girl as pretty as her going to be related to an ugly thing like you! I ain't stupid! Are you calling me stupid, boy?" The man asked. "Go ahead and call me stupid one more time, and I'm going to let one of these barrels loose on ya."

"Huh? No, sir! Rose Ann is my sister. We were traveling to get—"

"To get to where, boy? Huh? Trying to get to my chickens? You and your wife wanted to fry some chicken and make some corn bread with the grease? Then after you two had your stomachs filled, you were going to go into my house while was sleeping, crack my head open with one of my cast iron skillets, then have your way with my beautiful wife. I raised those chickens. Don't nobody take my chickens!"

Malachi mouth became dry from fear at that moment. Right then and there. He had to pee. He felt a tinkle of pee run down his right leg. He willed himself to hold onto his bladder. The man was obviously crazy. He didn't want to embarrass himself by peeing in his pants when he got shot. If he was going to die, then he wanted to die with dry pants on.

Maybe he could grab the double-barrel shotgun, and get the advantage, and then he could talk to the man. No. The way he had the weapon so near to his face, Malachi knew if he reached for the double-barrel shotgun, he would be shot in the face immediately by the angle in which it was being pointed at him.

"I can see it in your eyes, boy. You were going to steal my chickens and rape my wife," he said. "I might've let you rape my wife, but nobody steals my chickens. I'm going to put a hole in you!" the man whispered menacingly. He moved the double-barrel shotgun up an inch closer to Malachi's nose. "This is the last thing you're going to see, boy."

"George Lewis! If you don't put that empty shotgun down and stop scaring those children, or I'm going to split your head open with a log!"

They all turn in the direction of the voice standing in the barn doorway. The woman's cherubim, caramel face, and two salt and pepper pigtails in her hair, were a blessing to Malachi. To him, she was his miraculous savior that rode in on a cloud.

"Aw shucks, Maybelle, I was just playing with the children," George Lewis said. He lowered the empty shotgun, and took two steps back. "Woman, you should've seen the fright on that boy's face. He darn near dropped a load of mess in his pants." George Lewis laughed. His wrinkled, dark face displayed a mouth full of crooked, dark teeth. "Another minute, the boy would've been begging me to let him live." George Lewis slapped his leg with mirth. "The boy was ready to beg me to spare his life, I tell you!"

"You're an evil, old cuss of a man, George Lewis," Maybelle said. Her long, flowered yellow dress bellowed with the early morning wind. "Bring those children in the house."

Malachi looked from Maybelle to George Lewis. His eyes were blinking fast as he tried to sort out what had happen. He watched George Lewis offer his hand to him. Malachi stared at it.

"Come on, son. It ain't all that bad. I ain't going to bite you…no more, anyway," George Lewis said with a smile.

Malachi reached up and took George Lewis' hand. George Lewis yanked Malachi up.

"Don't look so serious, boy. I don't get too many laughs out here. Maybelle is a strict woman. So, when I find something that can take the boredom out of my day, I reach for it," George Lewis said as he shrugged.

"I don't think that scaring people with a double-barrel shotgun is funny," Rose Ann said. She'd walked over to stand beside Malachi.

"When you've lived as long as I've lived, you try to get as many laughs as you can to keep on living. Anyway, you try to find anything that will keep you laughing to keep away the pain of arthritis and her," George Lewis said as he tossed a thumb over his finger in the direction Maybelle. "Let's go. Now I'm going to have to hear Maybelle's mouth for the rest of the day and night. But, it was worth it."

George Lewis took the lead. Malachi looked at Rose Ann. He shrugged, and then followed George Lewis out of the barn with Rose Ann behind him.

Maybelle was placing plates on the small kitchen table when they walked in.

"Son, in the back of the house is a washbasin with fresh water. You go clean up. Little girl, there's another one in my room. I just poured some fresh, warm water for you, too. You go on in there and clean yourself," she said. She never looked up from what she was doing. "George Lewis, you're an old coot. Put that shotgun back under our bed, and the next time you touch it, it better be to go coon hunting."

George Lewis looked at the woman he'd been married to for twenty-four years. He stuck out his tongue at the exact moment that Maybelle glance up at him.

"If you stick it out again, I'll cut it off," Maybelle said. She looked at the three of them. She clapped her hands loudly and repeatedly. "Let's get!"

The three of them were startled as they headed off in the directions Maybelle had told them to go.

Twenty minutes later, they were all sitting at the kitchen table eating breakfast.

"What are you children doing out so late in the early morning? Where do you live?" Maybelle asked. She looked from Malachi to Rose Ann.

"A couple of miles not far from here," Malachi said.

"A couple of miles? Where? Dandridge?" George Lewis asked.

Malachi stared at him.

"Waverly?" Maybelle asked.

"Clarksville?" George Lewis said. He slammed his hand down on the table, as if he'd found the answer.

Neither Malachi nor Rose Ann said a word.

Maybelle placed her large, dry elbows on the table. She stared at Malachi and Rose Ann. "Are you children running away from someone or something?" she asked.

Both Malachi and Rose Ann shook their heads in denial. Neither one of them looked at Maybelle.

"You want me to get the shotgun and put some shells in it and then we can ask them some real questions, Maybelle?" George Lewis asked. A grin expressed his mischievousness.

Malachi and Rose Ann quickly glanced up at Maybelle.

Maybelle looked at George Lewis. The right side of her lips turned up, and then her eyes rolled upward. "No, fool," she said. She turned her attention back to the children. "Are you two in any trouble?"

"No!" Malachi and Rose Ann said in unison as they both looked up from their plates of food.

"Hah! That's a doggone lie!" George Lewis shouted. "They said it too quickly. What ya'll steal. Who ya'll steal it from? And how much is it?"

"George, stop agitating the children. Are you two in some kind trouble? Don't worry I won't judge you," Maybelle said. "You can talk to us."

"Why not, Maybelle? You judge me," George Lewis said. He put his face in his plate, and began rapidly scooping up the pork and beans with his spoon and stuffing them into his mouth. "These damn beans are burnt, Maybelle!"

"George, hush! What are you children running from?"

"Well, yesterday our parents die—"

"Boy, tell the whole story," George Lewis said. "How did they die? And it better be the truth. We don't cotton to any lies around here."

Malachi looked at George Lewis. The man was beginning to get on his nerves. He sighed. "Our parents were killed in a car crash…yesterday at two-thirty in the morning. We didn't have any other family, so they were talking about placing us in an orphanage with the state. They said we might be separated, and I didn't want that. I don't think my parents would've wanted that, so we took what we could carry and we left," he said.

George Lewis, his head partially in his plate, looked from Maybelle to Malachi. His black eyes darting back and forth as he continued to place one spoonful of food after another into his mouth.

"You children are too old to be in an orphanage," Maybelle said. "Hmm. I don't know. Well, I tell you what. You two will stay on here for a couple of days. Just to rest. How about it?"

Malachi looked at Rose Ann sitting beside him. She was piercing her lips together. A telltale sign that she was thinking. She glanced at Malachi and nodded.

"Okay, ma'am we'd like that," Malachi said.

"All right," Maybelle said. She leaned back in her chair. "You two know our names. What are yours?"

"I'm Malachi Moon and this is my sister, Rose Ann."

"We have a small room in the back for Rose Ann. I guess you can sleep in the overhead area in the barn, Malachi," Maybelle said.

"Yes, ma'am," Malachi said.

Maybelle waved her chubby hand in the air. "Boy, you ain't got to be calling me no ma'am. I'm Maybelle and that's George Lewis. I'll get you some blankets for the barn when it's time," she said.

Maybelle stood up and walked out of the room.

"I think you two are on the run. That's what I think," George Lewis said. He didn't look at either of them. "Uh-huh, that's what I think. And if I think that way, I'm gonna find out who ya'll running from."

Malachi looked at Rose Ann. Rose Ann shrugged and began eating her food. Malachi glanced at George Lewis. His attention was on his food as well, as he picked up his spoon and surreptitiously glanced at him.

Maybelle and Malachi were walking to the barn twenty minutes later. George Lewis was a few paces behind them whistling.

"Malachi, you sure Rose Ann ain't your girlfriend who's pregnant and you two are running away from your parents?" Maybelle asked. "That child and you don't look nothing like kinfolk. It's all right. You ain't got to lie to me. If she's your girlfriend, it's okay."

"Maybelle, Rose Ann is my sister. I'm telling you the truth."

"Hah!" George Lewis shouted.

Malachi lowered his voice. "What's wrong with him?" he asked.

Maybelle being two feet shorter than Malachi, smiled. "He's a good man. Ain't never run from his duties as a husband, and he ain't never once put a hand on me. When you find a man like that, you keep him. If one day you find you a woman who will take care of you when you're sick, and feed you when you're hungry, then shows you love when you are in time of some emotional need, that's a good woman. Anyway, I love that crazy man," Maybelle said.

"I love you, too," George Lewis said.

"The man has ears like a hawk," Maybelle said as she leaned in toward Malachi and whispered. "Be careful what you say around him, though. He's a sensitive man."

Malachi nodded.

As Malachi headed toward the barn, he stopped at George Lewis' voice.

"We'll be doing chores in the morning, boy."

Malachi winced.

Every bone in Malachi's body was aching when George Lewis awoke him several hours later that morning. His chores weren't simple. He had to give feed the chickens. Feed the pigs their slop. Milk the three skinny cows that were in the stable in the barn. Toss the straw, and fix a broken fence. After he washed up, he sat on the ground and let his head fall to his chest. He was exhausted.

"Malachi! Boy, I know you're not tired!" George Lewis said, as he walked around the corner of the house and saw Malachi sitting on the ground. "Hell, boy, it's only eight o'clock in the morning. After breakfast, we have a few more things to do around here."

Malachi shook his head as he stared at George Lewis. The man's southern drawl was so thick, that he could barely understand what he was saying at times. The morning had been very hard for him. He felt like he was back home attending to his father's farm. The only difference being he didn't have to hear his father's irritating voice or the frustration that came with trying to get Stella to plow.

Two hours later Malachi was fixing the fence that held the pigs. When he'd finished that, George Lewis had told him to toss new straw in the barn. Malachi threw himself into his work. And why wouldn't he? He was used to working when it came to the farm.

When the year 1936 rolled, the morning sun was high. Malachi realized that he'd been working George Lewis and Maybelle's farm for over a year. He'd also noticed that his muscles had grown.

By the time his sister came out and told him to come eat lunch, Malachi was tossing the last of the pig's slop into the pen. He was famished to the point of starvation. He dropped the pail he was holding, and ran toward the house ten minutes later.

"I hope you boy's clean yourselves up before sitting at my table," Maybelle remarked, as she sat a bowl of collar greens on the kitchen table. "I don't like dirty, stinking men eating at my table."

Malachi glanced at George Lewis. George Lewis raised his arms to show his clean hands. Malachi did the same thing.

Rose Ann followed Maybelle carrying a plate full of fried chicken. She sat it on the table, and smiled at her brother.

The kitchen was a drab gray color with an assortment of small pictures on several walls. To the left of Malachi, he saw a picture of a white Jesus Christ staring upward. He never understood why most southern homes had a picture of Jesus Christ on their walls.

Maybelle brought over a plate of hot biscuits with a mason jar of strawberry jam. The white apron she was wearing looked new to Malachi. Maybelle and Rose Ann sat at the table after setting the table.

"Say our blessings, George Lewis," Maybelle said. She placed her elbows on the table and folded her hands in front of her. She closed her eyes, and lowered her head.

George Lewis glanced at the food on the table, and then his wife. He licked his lips. He cleared his throat, and then looked at his wife again.

"George," Maybelle said as she stared at him expectantly. "The blessing."

"Damnit, Maybelle! How come we're always saying a prayer to the food?" George Lewis asked as he stared at his wife. "It's already dead! Hell, I didn't bless it when I killed it!"

Maybelle continued to stare at George Lewis. She slightly cocked her head to the right side. Her hair was pulled back into a tight bun. The streaks of gray were apparent. "George, we're giving thanks to the Lord for giving us this food that's on the table," she said.

George Lewis, his eyes fixated on the food, licked his lips again. "I do all the chores around here and the Lord gets all the credit," he said. "When there are things to be done around here, I don't see any phantom spirit helping me take down a door, tending to that field out there or painting."

"George Lewis! How dare you talk like that about the Lord? Especially when we're in front of company. "You stopped going to church last year, and lately you been questioning the Lord's work. You keep on acting like this and you going to feel the wrath of the Lord," Maybelle said.

George Lewis turned up the left corner of his mouth. It was a devilish smirk. "Maybelle, the Lord moved on when it comes to us, woman. Now if I'm going to pray to the man, I'll pray when I think he's done something good for me," he said.

Maybelle shook her head. "You're a bad man, George Lewis. Do you think it was the Lord that made that mule kick you in the head a few years ago?"

George looked up at his wife. "That damn mule was just too ornery. If he hadn't kicked me, he would've kicked someone else. That mule kicked some sense into my head that day."

"That mule kicked the good sense out of your head, George Lewis!" Maybelle snapped. "Say a prayer before I take this food off this table."

George Lewis placed his cupped hands in front of his face, and closed his eyes. "Lord," he began, "We here today to give thanks to this food that I worked the fields everyday to make possible." He opened his right eye, and winked at Malachi, who'd been watching him with one eye. Malachi closed his eye and smiled. "And to give thanks to us for having these two children around here to help. Unless, of course, I get sick, and then we starve, because I know you only give those who can provide for themselves. Amen!"

"George Lewis!" Maybelle snapped. Her eyes were opened wide in shock. She glanced at Malachi and Rose Ann. "You children don't pay that old fool any mind.

Old people like him tend to do and say silly things when they start aging."

George Lewis reached in the bowl and removed a chicken breast. "Pass me those collard greens, boy," he said.

Malachi quickly looked at Maybelle for confirmation. She nodded. He reached over and picked up the bowl of collard greens and gave them to George Lewis.

"Thank you," George Lewis said.

Everyone watched George Lewis pile food on his plate.

George Lewis stopped. He looked up from his plate and stared at them. "Ain't ya'll gonna eat?" he asked.

Maybelle looked at Malachi and Rose Ann. She nodded, as she reached for a bowl of candy yams. Malachi looked at Rose Ann and shrugged his massive shoulders. He reached for a piece of chicken. Rose Ann smiled as she reached for the bowl of collar greens.

No one said a word for a full ten minutes. All that could be heard was the sound of smacking lips, and utensils falling to the side with the sounds of pleasurable grunts.

"Boy, you ever play a guitar?" George Lewis asked.

"Nope," Malachi said, as he bit into a chicken leg. He didn't look up.

"George Lewis used to sing in the vaudeville. That's how I met and married him," Maybelle said. She dapped the corner of her mouth with a napkin as she looked at Malachi.

"What kind of songs do you sing?" Rose Ann asked.

"You ever hear of the Blues?" George Lewis asked. His mouth was filled with food as he chewed. He looked from Malachi to Rose Ann. They shook their heads. "The Blues ain't about feeling sad or happy, girl. It's about feelings you can't let go of."

"How can you know if someone is singing the Blues?" Rose Ann asked.

George Lewis reached for the pitcher of lemonade on the table. He poured him a glass, and gulped it down fast. "The Blues are words you'll feel from the bottom of your feet to the top of your head. Every word is meant to make a person feel like they experienced what is being said. A good blues singer will have the audience eating out of their hands when the song is finished. Tossing silver dollars on the stage to show their appreciation of a good song," George Lewis said.

"Could you teach me how to play the guitar?" Malachi asked.

"Why do you want to learn to play the guitar, boy?" George Lewis asked. "It takes time to fiddle with them their strings. Anyway, you and your sister didn't say how long ya'll was staying on."

Malachi glanced at Rose Ann. "We ain't in a rush. So I figure since you're feeding us and we can't pay you. I can continue to help you around here, and Rose Ann can help Maybelle do women chores for a while. And, well, being that I'm here you can teach me to play the guitar," he said.

"How you know I need you around here, boy? I have been doing all right by myself all these years," George Lewis said, as he glanced at Maybelle. "Anyway, you complain too much when it comes to doing chores."

"You don't need me? I complain at anything," Malachi answered.

George Lewis looked at Malachi. "You sassing me, boy?" he asked.

"Huh?" Malachi asked. He changed his expression. His eyes became innocent and non-condescending. He displayed a smile that made Rose Ann and Maybelle laugh. "I'll never sass you, George Lewis."

George looked at him. "You better not. Anyway, it depends on how you work around here. Sure you been doing all right over the past year, but how I know you won't get shiftless on me when I need you?" he asked. He took a quick glance at Malachi. "We'll see, boy. If you continue to work right, maybe I'll teach you how to play."

"All right!" Malachi said. He looked at George Lewis. "I'll do right around here."

"You better," George Lewis said.

The passing of the days turned to weeks as Malachi and Rose Ann lived with Maybelle and George Lewis. Rose Ann learned how to bake cake and pies; to sew, as well as how to make big dinners for the times they had special evenings, and Malachi learned how to play the guitar.

One night Malachi and George Lewis were sitting on the porch. George Lewis had the guitar on his lap playing it while Malachi sat across from him watching.

"Look, Malachi, each string on the guitar has its own distinctive sound. You want to play those strings as if you were caressing a woman's…Well, you're too young for that now, but you want to play the strings as if they were your individual friend. One octave is different than the last. You, as the player have to find out which sound you want the people to hear. You can tell by the reaction on their face. Now watch my fingers as I play," he said.

Malachi, sitting attentively in his chair, placed his elbows on his knees as he cupped his face with his hands and leaned forward. He gave George Lewis his undivided attention.

"...*I have been working them fiiieeelllddds like a demon was on my taaaailll. The heat on my baaaaccckkkk, the thiiinnggss my mind. I don't care about no sleep, I got to get that field done, because the slower I wooorrkkrk, the more I gonna be in them there fields. My minds on fiiiirrreeee, and my feet burning something terrible. Whoooee! I got to get me some waaatttteeerrr. It's hot as hell in them there fields. Hellllll is hot! But them fields I working iiinnn, is hotter!*"

Malachi was amazed at George Lewis's voice. It sounded so smooth. And he had to admit the man could play the strings on the guitar with dexterity. He was impressed. The sound of clapping from the doorway made Malachi looked up and George Lewis stop playing the guitar.

"You still got it!" Maybelle said gleefully. "Husband, you wooed me when I first heard you sing, and you can still woo me. Can't he sing, Rose Ann?" she glanced at Rose Ann standing beside her. Rose Ann nodded.

"Shucks, woman. My voice had so many cracks in it; I thought I was going start croaking like a rooster. How long you two been standing there?" George Lewis asked.

"From beginning to end," Maybelle said. She was still clapping.

"That was nice, George Lewis, but Malachi can sing better than that," Rose Ann said. She smiled.

Malachi shook his head as if to stop Rose Ann from finishing her sentence, but she ignored his gesture.

"Can he now? Well, boy I'll play a tune and you come in when you feel its right," George Lewis said. He looked at Malachi and displayed an evil, wicked smirk.

Malachi swallowed. He had never sung in front of anyone before. He looked from Maybelle to Rose Ann. Rose Ann smile grew as she winked at Malachi. The pride beaming from Rose Ann's smile made Malachi blush. When he looked at George Lewis, the man was grinning like a banshee.

"I—"

"Go on and sing, boy," George Lewis pressed urgently. "Your sister said you can sing. Let's hear you sing."

"He will do it. He's a little nervous," Rose Ann said. She nodded. "Show them you can do it, Malachi."

Malachi cleared his throat. He took in three quick breaths, and then he glanced at his sister. She had put him in a corner.

"Sing them to sleep, Malachi," Rose Ann said with laughter.

"I been walking on a road filled with the sight of fools gold. Bright gold that makes my eyes blind from its brighhhhtttttht glittering sight. It don't make me a mind that I can't hold it in my haaaannnnddddnd, because I don't need gold to love that woman in reeeeddd. Her fine, short dress, and her candy apple red shoooeeeesss, is enough to make me want to beg for her looovvveeove. I'll skip, and I'll run. I'll bump my head on the ground...just so she could keep me around. I don't mind if you won't love me like I love you... All I need is for you to hold me...to scold me, but don't you loath me...Because I'm yours for life...I'm yours

*and one day you'll be my wife. I'm a heartbroken fool…I'm a
heartbroken fooooolllll. But you know something, woman…
I'm your heartbroken fool, and I ain't never, never, never
ever gonna let you go."*

George Lewis played the strings on the guitar with
the expertise of a man who'd been playing it for most of
his life. The C chord he'd chosen to play was done to see if
Malachi could sing at the octave he'd chosen, and, by the
end of his song, George Lewis had found that he could
sing. He strung the last note and stared at Malachi.

Malachi mouth had become dry. The nervousness
and the singing had made his mouth feel as if he hadn't
had any water in days. He looked from one face to the
other.

He smiled when he saw Rose Ann offering him a
glass of water. He grabbed for it as if he thought she was
going to pull it away. He brought the glass to his mouth,
and began drinking it very fast. His wide eyes looking
over the glass at George Lewis.

Maybelle began to shake her head.

George Lewis placed the guitar against the house. He
crossed his arms over his chest and stared at Malachi.

"Um…That's," Maybelle began. "Uh, real —"

"Sonofabitch!" George Lewis snapped, as he slapped
his hand down on his thigh.

"George Lewis, watch your mouth!" Maybelle
shouted. "There are children present."

George Lewis slapped both his hands down on his
thighs. He stood up and pointed a finger at Malachi. "I
ain't heard blues singing like that in all my life! Hell, boy,
I'd never thought you were a fifteen year old. You sound
like you've been through the wretched of the earth. Boy,

you made my toes curl, and that ain't easy to do with George Lewis. No, sir. It ain't at all. How long you been singing the blues, son?"

"The Blues?" Malachi asked.

"Yeah. That's what you were singing," George Lewis said.

"I've been singing Rose Ann to sleep like that since she was a baby," Malachi said.

George Lewis looked at Rose Ann. "How long?" he asked.

"I can remember him singing to me. That had to be about when I was five or six years old," Rose Ann said.

"Five or six, huh? So that would make Malachi about eight or nine years old," George Lewis said. He looked at Malachi. "Son, I know men that have been singing most of their adult lives. And their voices don't sound nothing like yours. You have the gift, Malachi."

"What gift?" Rose Ann asked. Her voice had cracked with fear that Malachi had gotten some kind of roots spell cast on him. "Is it something bad?"

George Lewis began walking back and forth. "We can go on the road like in the old days. Set us up a tent at the edge of town, and charge ten cent at the gate. No…No, twenty-five cents," George Lewis said. He words were like a rapid machine gun. "Never mind that now, son. I'll handle the gate purse. We'll get you some clothes. Something flashy to keep audience eyes on you."

"George?" Maybelle said.

"Son, at your age, and in the coming years, you'll get better with time. That voice of yours and life experiences will make you a man not to be reckoned with. I done been around a lot of blues singers in my younger days.

Men like Son House. Arthur Blake. Fulton Allen. I played with some great men in my time. Great men who could sing the underwear off some fine—"

"George Lewis!" Maybelle snapped. She looked at her husband with her head cocked to the side.

"This could happen, son," George Lewis continued. "This could make you an important man. I'll be there with you, Malachi. They won't beat you like they beat me. No, sir. I'll watch them like a hawk."

"Goddamn it, George Lewis, stop it!" Maybelle voice was so loud that everything around them stopped moving. "You're working yourself up for nothing. Now you stop it this instant," she said, stamping her foot.

George Lewis stopped. He looked around, as if he finally realized where he was at. He sat down in his seat dejected by the reality of what he'd experienced.

Malachi had been smiling. He'd seen something he hadn't seen in George Lewis before. He saw…joy. Now as he watched the man sit down, a dark cloud appeared to take hold of him.

"During George's vaudeville days, he was billed as a new star among Blues singers," Maybelle said. She walked over to George Lewis, and placed a hand on his shoulder. "It didn't last long though. Three years later, George was no different than any other Negro singing blues songs. When I met him, he was drinking heavily and near death. He'd been walking around sick with some kind of chest pain. If I hadn't made him go see a doctor, he might've died from a heart attack. I followed his career during those years. Wherever he went I followed him from town to town. He didn't know I was attending all of his shows. It would be some time before he realized that my face was always in the crowd urging him on. Always in the front row clapping the hardest. A real musician will play their hardest to please an audience, and George Lewis could do that. Over the years, though, it starts to wear you down. After seeing a doctor, I asked George to get away from it all. To let it go. We decided to buy this farm from the money my folks had left me when they died and the little money George had saved. I asked George Lewis to marry me, he did and we been living here ever since."

"The boy has something I never had," George Lewis said with pride. "He has the gift, Maybelle."

"Come on now. It's getting late and we need to be in bed," Maybelle said softly.

George Lewis stood up. He reached for the guitar. As he turned around to go into the house, he stopped. Turning back around to look at Malachi, he offered him the guitar.

"The two cords that I showed you will help you get comfortable with playing," he said. "Don't rush it. Let your fingers strum it like you caressing a woman's," George Lewis stopped. He smiled. "Just be gentle with the strings, and everything will be fine."

Rose Ann stepped out of the doorway as George Lewis and Maybelle neared. She walked over to her brother.

"He looked like he wanted to jump in the car and take you away, Malachi," Rose Ann said.

Malachi nodded. "He's a strange one, but it seems to me that he has a good heart," he commented.

"Well, I'm heading to bed," Rose Ann said. She leaned over and kissed Malachi on the right cheek. "You made me feel proud tonight, big brother."

Malachi watched her walked away. She was growing

up, he thought. "You made me feel like a fool," he said, and then chuckled.

Rose Ann laughed as she went into the house.

Malachi extended the guitar outward. He stared at its worn base and discolored neck. He could tell that George Lewis had been playing it for years by the fading of the lines that used to be on it. It was probably brown at one time, he surmised. Tossing the base of the guitar over his shoulder as he held it by the neck, he stepped off the porch whistling. Tomorrow, he knew, would be just another workday, and George Lewis would forget about tonight as he handed out his chores. He smiled at the thought.

CHAPTER FOUR

Growing Up

Soon, the days turned into weeks and the weeks into months. The months eventually turned into years. Before Malachi and Rose Ann knew it they'd been living with George Lewis and Maybelle for three years. Rose Ann learned all there was in regard to taking care of a house. She'd also learned the ways of a woman. The first year she'd received her menstrual. Rose Ann had awoken one morning to find her bed covered in blood. She'd leaped out of bed screaming that she'd been stabbed while sleeping. As she ran through the house with blood running down her legs and her nightdress drenched in blood, her screams grew louder. Maybelle, her eyes partially closed from sleep, exited her room at the moment Rose Ann ran pass her. She grabbed her, and slapped her a few times before pulling her into one of the rooms and explaining to her what she was going through while stripping her of the nightdress, and washing her. She had given Rose Ann some cloth to place in her to stop the bleeding. Maybelle had told her what to expect each month concerning her body and how to keep herself clean once the cycle was over.

One early morning, Malachi, sitting behind the steering wheel of a 1928 Dodge Victory Six Sedan with anxiety as he glanced at George Lewis was calmly sitting in the passenger seat.

"Listen, Malachi, driving ain't easy when you first learn. You have to have faith in your skills and be comfortable while sitting behind the wheel," George Lewis said.

Malachi nodded as he nervously gripped the steering wheel.

"Don't be trying to learn everything in one day, boy. Hell, it took me weeks to learn how to drive my father's old jalopy, and that piece of junk used to smoke as soon as you stuck the key in the ignition, "George Lewis said, as he glanced over at Malachi. "What're you sweating for, Malachi?"

"I'm a little…scared," Malachi said.

"Scared? What are you scared about? I'm the one sitting in the passenger seat. Hell, if anybody ought to be scared, it ought to be me. Put your left foot on the clutch while placing your right foot on the brake. Put the gear shift in the first gear by shifting the stick upward and to the left. You'll get the feel of the gear shift as you continue to learn," George Lewis said.

Malachi did what he'd been instructed to do.

"Can you feel the power under there, Malachi? Sure, this baby is old, but that eight-horsepower cylinder can still hold its own. Now, I want you to slowly ease up off the clutch while lightly pressing on the gas, and then placing that foot from the clutch onto the break. Don't rush it, boy. Take your time. Give the car a little bit of gas. When you do, the car will lurch forward a little," George Lewis said.

Malachi licked his parched lips as sweat began to form on his forehead.

Maybelle and Rose Ann were sitting on the porch watching George Lewis and Malachi. Maybelle was showing Rose Ann how to knit.

"Malachi ain't ever driven before, Maybelle," Rose Ann said, as she unwinds yard for Maybelle while displaying a look of despair and concern.

"No one has ever learned to drive when they first get behind a steering wheel, Rose Ann. You learn by practicing," Maybelle said. "George Lewis is a good driver. He will teach Malachi good habits when driving."

"All right, boy. Keep both hands on the steering wheel, and slowly ease off the break while giving it some gas, Malachi," George Lewis said.

"Okay," Malachi said.

Malachi took in two quick breathes as he slowly let off the break. He smiled as he felt the strength of the car under his control.

"You're doing good, Malachi," George Lewis said.

Malachi eased off the break some more. When he did, he glanced at George Lewis and unconsciously pressed harder on the gas. The car leaped forward and took off down the dirt road.

Maybelle looked up at the sound of the engine of the car reveling high. She watched as the car shot down the road at a speed of thirty miles an hour.

"Was that George Lewis screaming?" Maybelle asked Rose Ann.

"Uh-huh. It didn't sound like Malachi. I know his voice," Rose Ann said.

"Lord! Sweet Jesus! Malachi, stop this car!" George Lewis shouted as he held onto the dashboard.

"I got it!" Malachi said. "I just have to keep the steering wheel straight!"

"God! Look out where you're driving, Malachi!" George Lewis screamed.

Malachi saw them at the same time that George Lewis screamed. There were five chickens about to cross the road. Malachi swerved from left to right to avoid them. The movement made George Lewis scream louder.

"God, who art in Heaven, hollow be thy name—"

"I'm doing good," Malachi said, as he laughed hysterically. "I thought you didn't think anything good of prayer."

George Lewis looked at Malachi. His dark skin had become an ashen gray with fear. He quickly looked back onto the road at the precise moment that Malachi nearly went off the road and into the ditch.

"Lordy! Lordy! Save me!" George Lewis shouted.

Malachi twisted the steering wheel to the right, straightening it out and pressing harder on the gas while shifting into second gear while laughing hysterically.

"Slow it down, Malachi! Boy, you're gonna kill us!"

"This is fun!" Malachi shouted.

"Stop the car! Stop the car!" George Lewis hollered at the top of his lungs.

Malachi hit the accelerator. The car buckled for a fleeting moment, and then it shot forward with increased speed.

George Lewis closed his eyes. He tightly clasped his hands together. "As I walk through the Valley of Death," he began.

The car came to a screeching halt.

George Lewis opened his eyes.

"How did I do?" Malachi asked.

George Lewis looked around. He began touching his body to make sure nothing was broken. Sighing, he turned to Malachi. With a quick right hand, he slapped Malachi in the back of his head.

"What the hell were you doing, Malachi? I almost… Get from behind that steering wheel. I'm driving back."

"Aw, come on, George Lewis," Malachi said. "I can get us…" Malachi stopped. He tilted his head, as his nose flared opened. He began sniffing. "What is that smell?"

"Huh? Smell? I don't smell anything. Let's go. We're switching seats," George Lewis said as he climbed out of the car.

Malachi did the same. He and George Lewis pass one another as they switched positions.

"Now watch me," George Lewis said. He clutched and then hit the brake while shifting the gear. "You got to drive with caution, boy."

Malachi nodded. He sniffed the air. "What is that smell?" he asked, as he leaned closer to George Lewis. "It's you. You stink, George Lewis!"

"You'd stink, too, after that ride," George Lewis said, as he began driving back toward the house. "All right. I might've had a little accident."

"That ain't any accident. You done gone and do-do," Malachi said.

"Okay. My bowels got a little loose," George Lewis said with shame. "We can keep this to ourselves, Malachi."

Malachi placed a hand over his nose. "All right," he mumbled. "Whew! You stink."

"If it wasn't for your driving, I wouldn't be stinking," George Lewis said.

Malachi started laughing.

George Lewis joined him after a few seconds.

The cold winter blast greeted them harshly as they stood outside that morning. It was near the end of January and the Dodge Victory Six Sedan was idling nearby with an engine that didn't have many miles left on it.

They stood huddle together in their winter coats. Maybelle's arm was draped around Rose Ann's shoulder as she watched Malachi and George Lewis shake hands.

"Ya'll gonna be missed, son," George Lewis said.

"You both treated Rose Ann and me real good. You took us in and made us feel like family," Malachi said. "I thank you kindly."

"You are family," Maybelle said. She leaned over and kissed Rose Ann on the cheek. "Our house is always open to the both of you, ya'll hear."

Rose Ann turned and gave Maybelle a hard hug. "Thank you," she whispered. "I love you."

Maybelle pulled back and looked Rose Ann in her eyes. "Child, I love you, too," she said. "I love the both of you." She reached over and took Malachi into her arms.

"You two are good children. Ya'll watch yourselves, and respect those who respect you. Some things you can't worry about in life, so let the Lord guide you."

"All right, Maybelle. Let them go. They have to be going," George Lewis said.

Everyone began walking down the stairs to the car.

"Look, son, remember what I said. Keep the car oiled. Watch the road. Check your tires regularly…" George Lewis stopped. He turned toward Malachi, and gave him a strong, long hug. "Ain't any sense in me telling you things I already done said." He let go of Malachi. "Just remember them."

"I will," Malachi said.

"Ya'll go on now," George Lewis said. He prodded them to get into the car. "Drive carefully."

Malachi and Rose Ann entered the car. They tossed the two small suitcases into the back seat along with the guitar George Lewis had given Malachi. Malachi started the engine. The old, rusty, Dodge Victory Sedan sputtered and sputtered before the engine turned over and came to life. Dark smoke emerged from the exhaust pipe, and it backfired two times, but it stayed on.

"Rose Ann you keep what I gave you close to you at all times, baby," Maybelle said. She leaned in the car and gave them both a kiss. "Trust doesn't come easy. Remember that.

"You got everything you need, Malachi?" George Lewis asked.

"Yeah," Malachi said. His face, though etched with concern, wrinkled and smiled.

"Where ya'll headed, son?" George Lewis asked.

"We're going to head out a little bit toward the east," Malachi said.

"And then?" Maybelle asked.

"We'll let the wind at our backs lead us from there," Malachi replied.

"Don't let it push you too far," George Lewis said.

"No, we won't," Rose Ann said. "You two take care of yourselves. We love the both of you."

Everyone said their last goodbyes. Malachi eased off the accelerator, and the car jerked forward. Stopped. Then jerked forward again. Its speed slowly increasing as it moved forward.

"What did Maybelle give you?" Malachi asked. He kept his eyes on the road.

Rose Ann glanced at him. She lifted her overcoat at the leg, and then her dress. Her thick legwarmers had a leather case strapped to her leg near the ankle.

"She gave me a pearl-handle straight razor," Rose Ann said. "And she taught me how to use it."

Malachi nodded. He began unbuttoning his heavy overcoat. He pulled it open to reveal a wooden-handle hook knife in a leather case connected to his belt. "George Lewis made me take this," he said.

They both started laughing.

Two days into their long drive, they had to find a lodge that was open. Night had fallen quickly and the weather had turned for the worse. Snow had begun to fall. First it came down lightly and then very heavily as the darkness set. The lodge, Malachi noticed when he got out of the car, was in an area that was isolated from any other houses. He looked around and all he could see were thick trees and a road leading out to nowhere. He heard the passenger side of the car door close.

"This place looks…scary," Rose Ann said, as she came and stood beside Malachi, who was getting out of the car. Rose Ann tightened the wool scarf she had wrapped around her head to ward off the cold. "Is this the only place we can stay?"

Malachi nodded. "I don't think we should drive in this weather, Rose. We could stay in the car, but it'd get mighty cold in there," he said. "What do you want to do?"

"I don't know. It's cold out here."

"Stay in the car while I go and see what it's like," Malachi said.

Rose Ann got in the drivers side of the car. She watched Malachi walk up the three stairs that led to the entrance of the lodge.

Malachi walked into the lobby of the lodge. He wrinkled up his nose at the scent that had penetrated his senses. The smell inside had a wretched scent of defecation and urine with a mixture of disinfectant. He walked toward the front desk. The man sitting behind the desk never looked up as he approached.

"Howdy, do you have any rooms to rent?" Malachi asked.

The thin man sitting behind the desk looked up.

Malachi gasped when he saw the man's left hand cradled to his side. It looked like his hand was nothing more than a knob of crippled flesh. The man's piercing blue eyes were like the color of lapis.

"Rooms? How many with you?" The man with the

crippled arm asked, as he searched behind Malachi with urgency.

"My sister is outside. It's just the two of us," Malachi said.

"Sister?"

Malachi nodded. He had to listen very hard to understand what the man was saying. His words were thick with an accent he'd never heard before. An accent that wasn't southern.

"You're not from around these parts, huh?" The man asked. "My name is Bo. I'm the sometimes manager here. It'd be three dollars for the night. You got any bags or any valuables you'd like to keep in the safe until the morning?"

Malachi stared at the man as if he'd lost his mind. He was dressed in a brown suit that looked moth eaten, and his blond greasy hair looked like it hadn't been washed in days. "We can carry our own things," he said, as he reached into his pocket and took out six dollars. He hated to depart with the little money they had, but a warm bed was better than a cold car seat. He reluctantly offered the money to Bo.

Bo nodded as he turned around the sign-in book while extending his hand toward Malachi. "I have room 412 and 418. They're both on the same floor just a few doors down," he said.

"You don't have any rooms that are right next door to each other, do you?" Malachi asked.

Bo took the money and began counting it. He ran his hand across the wrinkled bills. "Nope. That's all we got," he said.

Malachi turned to go get his sister. While walking to

the door, he turned back around. "Bo, why do you talk like that?" he asked.

"Hmm. Oh. I'm from Austria, Germany."

Malachi turned around and walked out. He didn't know where Austria, Germany was located.

Rose Ann, her coat collar up around her ears, and her arms wrapped around her to keep warm, watched her brother approach. When he opened the car, she saw a perplex look on his face. "What's wrong? They don't have any rooms?" she asked.

"Yeah. I have two for us," Malachi answered as he reached in the back of the car and got their bags. When he was taking the bags out of the car, he turned to his sister. "You ever hear of a place called Austria, Germany?"

Rose Ann was getting out of the car. She closed the door, and turned around to face Malachi. "No. Is it in the South?" she asked.

Malachi shrugged. "I don't know where it is. Come on; let's go find some warm beds. I'm tired."

When they walked into the lodge, Bo watched them. "Hey," he said. "She doesn't look like your sister."

Malachi ignored him. "Which way to our rooms?" he asked.

"Take the stairs, and make a right turn when you get to the top. You can't miss them," Bo said.

Malachi and Rose Ann headed for the stairs that were to the left.

"I don't like this place, Malachi," Rose Ann said.

"It's only for tonight, Rose. We'll be okay," Malachi said.

They ascended the stairs.

When Malachi's head touched the small, sweat stain

pillow on his bed after he'd settled Rose Ann into her room, he immediately fell into a slow, deep sleep. He was so exhausted that he didn't even take off his clothing.

Malachi slept for three hours when he suddenly sat up. His eyes were bloodshot as he looked around the room. He licked his dry lips as he tried to focus his vision. What was that noise? He threw his tired legs out of bed, and stood up on wobbly legs. He walked to the door, and opened it. He stuck his head out the door at the exact moment he saw someone turn the corner that lead down the stairs. He watched the area for a moment, and then closed his door. His mouth felt like chalk. He needed a glass of water. He walked back to his bed. As he was about to sit down, he stopped midway. He was frozen in that position for a second, and then he strengthen up. He decided to go check on Rose Ann.

He didn't feel like putting on his shoes. He walked to the door and opened it with one swift motion. He stepped out into the hallway, and headed toward his sister's room to the right.

As he walked toward the door of his sister's room, he felt uncomfortable. The creaking of the floor made him shiver. He didn't know why, but it did. When he reached Rose Ann's room, he knocked on the door.

"Rose Ann?" Malachi whispered.

There was no response.

"Rose Ann. It's me, Malachi. Open the door."

Nothing.

Malachi leaned closer to the door. "Rose, are you awake?" he answered.

The creepiness of silence was the only answer that greeted him.

"Rose Ann?" Malachi said. He turned the doorknob.

The door swung inward as it opened.

"Rose Ann, why isn't your door locked?" Malachi asked, as he walked into the room.

He stopped when he saw that the room had been ransacked. All of Rose Ann clothing were thrown everywhere. Two chairs in the room were turned over. The mattress was on the floor, and a lamp lay on the floor. Malachi took it all in and realized that a fight had taken place. That thought and the fleeting image of someone hurrying down the stairs came back to him. He spun around and headed for the front desk.

"Bo! Bo! Something has happened to my sister," Malachi said as he jumped down the last three remaining stairs, and ran toward Bo.

Bo, who had his head on his arms as he lay sleeping, looked up at Malachi. "What?" he asked.

Malachi, out of breath, stared at the calm Bo. He didn't look like he'd been sleeping. His eyes didn't look tired or red. Malachi knew when a person is coming out of their sleep they usually blinked more than once or twice to get their eyes adjusted. But as he stared at Bo, the man looked like he was wide awake and alert.

"Relax. Now tell me what happen," Bo said.

Malachi lifted his bottom lip as he pierced his lips together. It was his way of thinking.

"I didn't see anybody come down this way," Bo said.

Malachi might've been a country bumpkin at times, but he was no ones everyday fool. Bo was in on whatever happened to Rose Ann. He could tell by the way the man acted. He knew he had to calm himself and think everything out carefully. Rose Ann's life was at stake.

"My sister's gone." Malachi said, as he willed himself to control his breath. Inside his body was boiling with rage. "I went to her room and she wasn't there," he said.

Bo shrugged. "Maybe she decided to go back home. She got homesick, you know," he commented.

Malachi shook his head. "No, she wouldn't leave without telling me first." Malachi stared into Bo's blue eyes. "You had to see her come down the stairs," he said.

"No. I was sleeping, but I sleep light. I would've heard her if she'd come down the stairs."

Malachi stared at Bo. He was lying. The bastard was hiding something, and he knew what happened to Rose Ann.

"Look, you better go on back upstairs before you catch a cold," Bo said. "If anything changes or I hear her, I'll come and get you."

Malachi glanced down at himself. He wasn't wearing any shoes.

"If she comes back, I'll tell her you were worried and send her to your room," Bo said. He smiled.

The smile infuriated Malachi. He wanted to reach over the counter and strangle Bo.

"Go on. She probably went out for some air, or smoking a cigarette." Bo said. "She'll be back."

Malachi bit his lower lip. He had to feel some pain to prevent himself from leaping over the counter and wrapping his large hands around Bo's thin neck while smashing in his lying face, but he knew if he did that, he might not get any information as to where his sister might be. He turned around and headed for the stairs.

"That's right. You head on back to your room. If anything should come up, I'll come get you," Bo said.

Malachi didn't look back. Bo's words were too sarcastic for him. He took his time walking up the stairs. When he reached the top, and out of Bo's vision, he took off running toward his room. He knew he was working with little time as he burst into his room and ran toward the bed. He quickly put his shoes on. He leaped from the bed and reached for his heavy wool shirt and overcoat that was on a chair in the corner of the room. As he hurried toward the window, he stopped. He turned back around and grabbed his hook knife that was under his pillow. He quickly opened the window, and climbed out on to the house wooden awning.

Bo had watched Malachi climb the stairs. When he'd disappeared he'd placed his head back down on his arms. He lay there for fifteen minutes with his eyes closed. Suddenly, his eyes popped opened as he searched the lobby. He sat up. Grabbing his small coat that was underneath the counter, he hurried from around the desk. He stopped as he tilted his head to the right. He listened for any sounds coming from the stairs. Hearing nothing, Bo went out the front door.

Bo stepped out onto the front steps of the lodge and was greeted by a heavy snowfall. Flipping up his collar, he walked down the stairs and hurriedly took off to the left.

Malachi had swung down from the roof and landed on the ground. He'd been standing around the corner of the lodge watching the front door for a good three minutes. He saw Bo come out and run down the road.

With the darkness to conceal him, Malachi stealthily took off behind Bo. He knew if he lost Bo, he would probably never see his sister again. He had to be very careful.

Bo was grinning as he walked down the street. He wanted to get to the Hole before everyone took their turn on the girl. The crackling of a twig several paces behind him made him stop. He turned around. Searching the darkness behind him, and, seeing nothing, he grunted and started walking again.

When he felt the twig break under his foot, Malachi threw himself into a wooded area in deep darkness to prevent from being detected at the same time that Bo had spun around. If he'd been a second late, Malachi knew, Bo would've seen him. Malachi didn't know where Bo was leading him, but he had to make sure he wasn't seen.

Bo walked for ten minutes. He got off the main road to the right and took an old worn trail into the woods. He didn't care about the lack of illumination from the moonlight; he knew where he was going by feel.

Malachi had begun to perspire. He was scared. He was following Bo, but didn't know if Bo was with the people who had taken his sister or not. If it turned out that he wasn't, then Malachi would really be in trouble. Then, he knew, there would be no way of locating his sister. He tried his hardest not to step on any more twigs as he continued to follow Bo.

Bo stopped. He was in an area thick with foliage. He walked to a large tree that was on his left. He placed his ear on it, and knocked. He nodded when he heard the hollowness of the tree greet him. Placing his right foot in front of his left, he began walking straight ahead of him.

Malachi watched Bo from behind a large boulder.

Bo dropped to one knee. He reached for the rung that was on a door. He pulled on it.

Malachi was surprised when light lit up the dark woods. It was a trapdoor. He watched Bo go down and slam the door behind him. Malachi, his heart racing, ran to the tree where Bo had been. He placed his right foot in front of the other and began counting to fifteen. The number of steps he'd counted as he watched Bo. When he reached the trapdoor, he bent down. He smiled when he felt the iron ring.

His smile faded quickly as the reality of what lay ahead. His head became light. His mouth was dry. With slow deliberation, Malachi began to lift the door with caution. As he did, he saw light emanating from below. He cautions himself in regard to lifting the door fully open. When it was partially opened, he slid through.

Malachi feet touched a ladder. He climbed down them with his eyes opened wide. It was partially dark. The little illumination coming from a lamp somewhere was his only guide as he continued to descend the ladder. He could feel perspiration running down his back and into his underwear. He was frightened, but he pushed aside his fear in hopes of finding his sister. When he reached the bottom of the ladder, he crouched down at the waist. Although there was no danger of him bumping his head on the ceiling, he kept low out of instinct. He walked for about twelve paces when he noticed the hanging bulbs from the ceiling. He looked from left to right. Not knowing which direction to take. Taking a deep breath, he decided to go to the left. Why? He thought he smelled a scent of Bo's dirty hair coming from that direction.

Each step Malachi took, he did it with trepidation.

There was a chill down below that made him shiver. Maybe it was the coldness drying his wet, perspiring body, or the intensity of fear building inside of him. He didn't know which one it might be, but he continued to walk down the long semi-dark tunnel ahead of him.

"Goddamn it, Luther! I told you to clean up that room before we left so it wouldn't look as if there'd been a fight in there."

Luther, his gray eyes blank of emotion, stared at Henry. He disliked doing things with Henry because he always complained when things weren't going the way he wanted them to. He looked Henry up and down. His expression was one of distaste. Henry unkempt appearance and smelly body odor made him keep his distance. His clothes always seemed to be barely hanging on his thin body. Worse, thought Luther, the man's brown hair looked like a mangy dog's coat.

"You know what happened last time, Luther. We had the sheriff on top of us in that other town," Henry said. He was pacing the floor. "We don't need any attention like that now. We got a good thing going on here."

Luther, a piece of wood in his hand, was chipping away at it with a large eight-inch knife. Luther stood up. Henry took a step back. The room they were in suddenly became too small for Henry as he watched Luther stand up.

"I'm tired of your whining, Henry," Luther said. "You make me want to snap your frail neck sometimes. Luther tossed his black hair back out of his eyes. You always want to lead."

Henry's hands began to tremble. He stared up at Luther's six foot two inch frame, and began to stammer.

"It's...it's not that...seri...serious, Luther. I mean...We can work this out," he said.

Luther pointed the knife at Henry. "We better. Where's Bo? He should've been here by now," he said.

"I'm here," Bo said, as he came out of the darkness to the left of them.

Luther and Henry turned around. Bo was hurrying toward them hunched over and wringing his hands.

"Well, what happened?" Luther asked.

"The boyfriend came—"

"Boyfriend? I thought you said they were sister and brother," Henry said, as he walked toward Bo.

"Do they look like kin?" Bo asked. He watched Henry tilt his head to the side, thinking of an answer. Bo rolled his eyes at Henry. "Anyway, the boyfriend came downstairs asking questions about her being gone. I told him I didn't hear or see anything. Where is she?"

"In the back room tied up. How much are we getting for her?" Luther asked.

"She's young. I figure...maybe...three hundred dollars," Bo said. "If we get the right buyer for her."

"Three hundred smackaroos! Hot damn! I can use that money," exclaimed Henry, as he began doing a small foot dance.

Luther and Bo looked at Henry.

"Uh. Do you think I can spend an hour with her before we ship her off to those people?" Henry asked.

"We don't want the nigger banged up and bleeding when we bring her to the people that are buying her, Henry," Bo said. "You try to keep that peckerwood zipped up."

"Or else I'll shorten it for you," Luther said. He cut the air back and forth with his knife. "Real short."

Malachi was outside the room. His back pressed hard against the stone wall as he listened and tried to control his breathing. He realized that Bo wasn't as stupid as he'd thought. What was he going to do? They were thinking so selling Rose Ann. There were three of them. How could he get Rose Ann out of there without them getting caught?

"What time are they supposed to be here?" Luther asked. He went and sat back down. "I ain't got all night and day."

Bo walked over to where Luther was sitting. He leaned down toward his ear. "They'll be here tonight. Before the sun comes up," he said. He straightens up.

"Well, they better. Every time they say they're coming, they don't make it until the next fucking day. I don't like it," Luther said.

"Me either," Henry said. He lifted his head in an arrogant stance. "They ought to be more aware of the time."

Luther looked up.

Henry smiled.

"I'm going to go check on the girl," Bo said.

Henry looked at him. "No funny business back there...Unless I join in," he said. He began snickering like a hyena.

"Shut up, Henry," Luther and Bo said in unison.

Closing his eyes, Malachi willed himself to take a look at what they were doing.

"Keep the blindfold on that darkie," Luther said.

"It's her word against us white folks, but ain't no sense of suspicion headed our way."

"Yeah, I know. You tell me the same thing every time we get us some fresh meat," Bo said.

Malachi looked around the doorway. The move was quick. He saw Bo walking toward a closed door and Luther and Henry sitting around.

"Hey, my little black bird," Bo said as he opened the door. He saw Rose Ann tied up to a chair that was placed in the middle of the room.

Rose Ann, her brown eyes staring at Bo, narrowed in a threatening matter as she watched Bo approach.

"I'm sorry we couldn't let you get dress. We were in a hurry," Bo said as his eyes took in the sight of Rose Ann's tied up ankles and followed upward. His eyes stopped on Rose Ann's breasts. "You're a pretty Negro."

Rose Ann continued to stare at Bo. His eyes were lingering on her breasts. She knew what to expect as he drew nearer. Her father had stared hard at her breasts before grabbing and squeezing them to the point of making tears come to her eyes.

"Whew! I didn't know you were as pretty as this. I ain't never seen a nigger as pretty as you. I should've sold you for a little bit more money. Three hundred dollars ain't enough when they get a sight of you," Bo said.

Rose Ann's eyes hardened.

"Um. Um. Um. "I ain't ever had any nigger juice on my wood before. Never liked ya'll that way. But I can make an exception with you," Bo remarked. He stood directly in front of Rose Ann. He licked his cracked lips. "I wonder if I can get to that bush between your legs without untying you."

Rose Ann eyes felt her body tense. She wished she had the razor Maybelle had given her.

Bo stood in front of Rose Ann. He placed his hand on his crotch, and began slowly rubbing himself. "I can pull this big thing out and you'll see something you ain't ever seen before," he said.

Rose Ann eyes widen as she stared at Bo.

"We white men know how to handle you black bunnies." Bo said. He smiled as he unzipped his pants. "If you beg me for it, I might let you lick it."

With the handkerchief tightly bound over her mouth. Rose Ann began to mumble. She started to struggle in hopes of breaking free. Her eyes became wild. If Bo touched her, she would kill him.

"Uh-huh. I know you want it," Bo commented. He began searching inside his pants.

Rose Ann watched him. He seemed to be searching far too long, she thought.

"Here it is," Bo said. He whipped out his penis.

Rose Ann tried not to look at it. She kept her eyes on Bo's face.

"Come on. This is what you want," Bo said. He began shaking his hips. "This is what you nigger women always want."

As much as she tried to avoid looking down at Bo's crotch area, curiosity got the best of her. She looked.

"I put this on you, ain't no man gonna be as good to you when I finish," Bo said.

Rose Ann, who was scared when they'd first grabbed her, had turned that terrible feeling of fright into anger. Now seeing Bo's penis, that anger turned into laughter.

Or what little laughter she could muster behind the handkerchief.

Malachi had made his way back a few yards. He'd paced back and forth with indecision as to what to do. His answer had been slow coming, but when it did, he knew what he had to do. He had to take his hook knife and go in there and get his sister. While taking in deep breaths. He calmed down. He was going to head back toward where his sister was being held when his eyes fell on a shovel standing up in the corner.

"You ain't never seen nothing this big before, have you?" Bo asked.

Bo couldn't see it, but Rose Ann was laughing. The thing in front of her was no bigger than her pinky finger, she told herself.

"If I take your handkerchief off, you better not scream," Bo said. He watched Rose Ann shake her head. "All right. I'm gonna take it off."

Bo put his penis back in his pants. He reached for Rose Ann's handkerchief. When he pulled it off. He was shocked to find Rose Ann laughing.

"Nigger what the hell is you laughing about?" Your black ass is in trouble and you're laughing!" Bo snapped.

"What is Bo doing in there?" Henry asked. His back was to Luther. He was rolling a cigarette. "He better not be doing what I think he might be doing, and then telling me I can't do it."

"Henry, you need to shut your trap," Luther said. He didn't look up as he continued to shave the wood in his hand. "You are as about as dumb as this piece of wood I'm carving."

Malachi had taken off his shoes. He needed surprise

to save his sister as he crept into the room with Luther
and Henry. He knew if either one of them turned toward
him, he was a dead man. He clutched the shovel in his
hands with so much force; his knuckles were beginning
to hurt. Each step closer into the room, made the dread
of being caught more appending. He prayed that Luther
didn't look up. Everything in the room became one for
him as he drew closer to Luther. He could smell his own
fear as it permeated through his skin.

"You know, Henry. You might be right. Bo's skinny
ass has been in that room with that girl a mighty long
time," Luther said. His knife continued carving the
wood. "I think I might go in there and see what the hell
he's doing."

"I'm going with you," Henry said. He began to turn
around to face Luther when he saw Malachi nearly on
top of Luther. "Luther!"

Normally Luther would ignore Henry whenever he
called him, but it was the tone of his voice that made
Luther look up.

Malachi, a mere foot from Luther, brought the heavy
shovel up and brought it down hard. It smashed into
Luther's face. He'd put all his strength into the swing
hoping it was enough to knock him out.

It was an eerie scene to Luther, for as he was looking
up; he caught the sight of the shovel coming toward him.
Mentally he wanted it to stop. To reach up and prevent
it from descending, but his body refused to respond to
his mind. Anyway, he realized, the effort would've been
useless, he admitted.

The blow from the shovel was so hard when it hit

Luther that it knocked him out of his chair and broke in half. Luther fell to the dirt ground unconscious.

"What the hell!" Henry shouted. He dropped his cigarette as he stared at Malachi.

Malachi put his index finger to his lips. "Shush! Call him out here," he said, as he approached Henry with the handle of the shove in a clubbing fashion.

Henry looked at Malachi, and then at the door where Bo and Rose Ann were behind.

"Call him!" Malachi whispered with venom. He grabbed Henry by the collar while raising the broken shovel handle. "Make it believable."

"Bo!" Henry shouted. "We need you out here."

Malachi raised the shovel handle.

"We need you now!" Henry shouted louder, as his eyes became as big as saucers at the sight of Malachi raising the wooden club.

Malachi didn't hesitate as he brought the wooden club down across Henry's head.

"What the hell do they want?" Bo asked through the door. He looked down at Rose Ann who was still laughing. He put the handkerchief back over her mouth. "When I come back, black bitch, I want to see you laugh when there's something warm and big in your mouth." He spun around and headed toward the door.

Bo pushed open the door and stepped out. "What the fuck is it? Did the people come?" he asked. He looked and saw Luther on the floor. He glanced and saw Henry unconscious as well. "What the hell—"

Malachi, who'd been standing behind the door, stepped out and brought the wooden club down hard on Bo's head. Bo grunted as he took two steps back and then collapsed. He twitched for a second, and then his body went still.

Rose Ann, who'd stopped laughing after having the handkerchief placed back over her mouth, felt her heart leaped with delight when she saw Malachi walked through the door. He hurried toward her.

"You all right, Rose?" Malachi asked. He began untying her legs while pulling the handkerchief from her mouth.

"Yeah. A little scared, but I'm okay," Rose Ann said.

Malachi ran behind the chair and untied her hands. "We have to go," he said. He helped Rose Ann from her chair. "I don't know how long they're going to be out. But we better hurry."

Rose Ann stood up. He legs felt weak and she shivered. She gathered her strength and headed to the door. She nearly tripped over Bo's unconscious body lying at the door.

Malachi urged her on with a little push on her lower back.

As they neared the first door, Malachi stopped.

"Wait Rose Ann."

"Huh? What? Let's go," Rose Ann urged. She looked around to see if anyone was moving. "Come on. They're going to wake up," she said.

Malachi ran over to Luther. He turned him on his back, and began quickly raffling through his pants pockets.

"What are you doing, Malachi?" Rose Ann asked, as her eyes darted back and forth from Luther to Henry, and back to Bo. "Leave him alone, and let's go!"

"These bastards were going to sell you for three

hundred dollars!" Malachi snapped, as he pulled out some dollars from Luther's front and back pants pockets. "Go check on that other one over there."

"I won't!" Rose Ann said. She stamped her barefoot.

Malachi put the money in his pocket. He hurried over to Bo. He ran his hands in both of his front and back pockets. He removed what little money was in them. He glanced up at Rose Ann. She gave him her disapproving look, which, he shrugged off. He hurried to Henry and began going through his pockets.

"Okay, let's go," Malachi said, as he stood up after stuffing his pockets with the dollars he'd found.

"Have you finished robbing them?" Rose Ann asked.

Malachi took his sister by her elbow and guided her out of the room in a hurried fashion.

It took the both of them ten minutes to gather their things from their rooms and put everything in the car. The guitar he placed on the floor in the back seat. When everything had been secured in the car, Malachi, sitting behind the steering wheel looked at his sister.

"I know you want to get away from this evil place because of what they'd put you through, and if it makes you feel any better, Rose, I left something for them," Malachi said. He started the engine. "Something they'll always remember us by."

"What?" Rose Ann asked. She tightened her collar around her neck.

Malachi smiled.

They were nearly half a mile away from the lodge when Rose Ann began sniffing. "Do you smell something burning?" she asked.

Malachi laughed.

Rose Ann turned around in her seat and looked out the back window.

"Malachi, I think the lodge is on fire," Rose Ann said.

Malachi glances at the rearview mirror. "I know the lodge is on fire," he said. "They will never kidnap anyone else and sell them. Stinking bastards!"

Rose Ann turned to her brother. "You set the place on fire?" she asked. Her expression was one of horror.

"Yep!" Malachi said with glee.

"Malachi!"

"Malachi nothing. Who knows what they'd done to you if I hadn't followed Bo."

Rose Ann was about to protest when the image of Bo pulling out his penis filled her mind. She sat up straight and watched the road. Silence being her wall of protection.

Malachi glanced at her, and then gave his attention back to the road. "You don't have anything else to say?" he asked.

Rose Ann shook her head.

"No?" Malachi was surprised. "You sure?" he asked. He scratched his head. He glanced at Rose Ann again. She was looking straight ahead. "Okay."

"Where are we going?" Rose Ann asked after fifteen minutes of silence.

"I've been thinking about us heading to New Orleans. I heard George Lewis telling Maybelle one night that it was a city that you could live a good life once it got some good people in it."

"New Orleans?" Where is it?"

"Take that map from under your seat that George Lewis gave us," Malachi said.

Rose Ann reached under her seat and removed the road map. She began unfurling it on her lap. "Where are we?"

"We were on I-232 going south. Do you see it?" Malachi asked.

"See it? I can't even read it. It's a bunch of colored lines crisscrossing everywhere."

"All right. I'm going to pull over," Malachi said.

Malachi drove ten more feet, and then pulled over to the right shoulder of the road. He turned off the engine, and put on the brake. He turned toward his sister and reached for the map.

"How do you know how to read a map?" Rose Ann asked.

Malachi, his head down, began running his index finger over the map. "George Lewis taught me. Okay. We're here, and we want to get to Interstate 43. That will take us to Highway 14, and we can take it to Interstate 9 which will take us to New Orleans," he said.

Rose Ann looked at her brother with newfound respect. "You gathered all that from reading this colorful paper?" she asked.

Malachi began folding the map up. He gave it to Rose Ann. She took it and put it back under the seat. "The way I figure it," he began. He looked up in the sky. "The sun will be coming up in another hour. We can be on Interstate 43 in about…two hours. You should sleep."

"If we're going to be driving a lot, I think you ought to teach me how to drive," Rose Ann said. She leaned back in her seat and tried to get comfortable by placing her knees under her. "This way when you get tired, I can drive."

Malachi started the engine. "Humph. I don't know about that," he said. He pulled back onto the road. "Driving is not easy. You have to learn how to clutch, brake, steer the wheel, and always be alert when driving."

"You make it sound like it's hard. You learned."

"George Lewis was patient with me, Rose, and there were many times when he had let go."

"Let go of what?" Rose Ann asked.

"You don't want to know, and I don't want to do the things he did when I was learning how to drive. You don't want to smell it," Malachi said, and smiled.

"Huh? You can teach me," Rose Ann said.

"No."

Rose Ann looked at Malachi. She put her chin on her chest. "How far is it to New Orleans anyway?" she asked, as she felt sleep slowly coming on.

"Whew. About five days," Malachi replied.

Rose Ann closed her eyes. She smiled.

CHAPTER FIVE

The Queen

Malachi was beginning to feel the effects of driving on the road after three days. He'd had diarrhea for most of the morning and every two hours he was jumping out of the car and running to the woods to relieve himself. An hour later he watched the car jerked forward, then stop, move about three feet, and then jerked forward again. Malachi looked at Rose Ann sitting behind the steering wheel. She returned a toothly grin that displayed her deep, pretty dimples.

"Rose Ann, you have to let loose of the clutch the moment you press on the gas," Malachi said, as he sat in the passenger seat holding his stomach. "Everything has to be done with ease, sis."

Rose Ann sat behind the steering wheel clutching it tightly. Anxiety filled her face. "I am," she said. She leaned over closer to the steering wheel. "It's just that it won't do it the way I'm trying to do it."

"You're doing it wrong, girl, that's why we can't get anywhere! Take your time. Clutch. Change gear. Brake. Slowly press the gas," Malachi said.

"It's easy for you to say. You know how to drive," Rose Ann said.

Malachi shook his head as he watched his sister go through the jerking of the brake, and the horrible screeching sound of the transmission not being in gear every time she shifted.

"Rose Ann!" Malachi shouted.

"What! What? You're scaring me, Malachi!" she snapped.

"You're scaring me by the way you're trying to drive. You're scaring me to death each time you jerk the car. Look, let me drive, and watch what I do. This way you can learn," Malachi said.

Rose Ann stopped the car. She put it in neutral and watched Malachi get out and come around to the driver side. He opened the door for her, Rose Ann crossed over to the passenger side by climbing over the stick shift while hiking up her dress and coat.

Sitting behind the steering wheel, Malachi looked at Rose Ann. "Everything is easy once you get to know how to do it. Everything that I told you will move the car."

Rose Ann watched as Malachi went through the motions of preparing to drive the car. She said nothing as Malachi drove forward a few yards, and then stopped.

"You see," Malachi said. He raised his hands in a victorious gesture. "It's easy. Now you try it again."

Malachi got out of the car and was walking to the passenger side when he stopped.

Rose Ann had already gotten behind the steering wheel the same way she'd changed seats previously as she watched her brother walk around to get into the car. She smiled when she saw Malachi grab his butt and run off into the woods.

"Lucky we're on this dirt road or a whole lot of people would be stepping in your mess," Rose Ann shouted out of the window. She laughed at seeing Malachi running and holding the back of his pants. "I hope you got some leaves near you because if you don't, you're gonna have some funky draws."

Malachi returned five minutes later and climbed into the passenger side of the car. He looked at Rose Ann. "Take your time," he said.

Rose Ann nodded. She reached for the stick shift after clutching and slowly began releasing the brake while pressing on the gas. The car jerked forward so hard that Malachi bumped his head on the dashboard.

"Oh, sorry," Rose Ann said.

Malachi shook his head. "Let's try it again," he said. He rubbed his forehead and felt a knot growing.

By the time they reached New Orleans, Rose Ann, Malachi had to admit, had become a better driver. They drove into a small town called Gatesville. Malachi noticed from the sign at the entry of the town, that the population was no more than eight thousand people living in the town.

As Malachi drove down the muddy street, he took in the sights.

"This place looks…deserted," Rose Ann said.

"Yeah."

"How long are we gonna be here, Malachi?"

Malachi saw a man in a bright red hat and wearing all black come exploding out of a doorway to the right of him. Seconds later, a man wearing a dirty gray uniform came running out behind him. The man in the bright red hat was distancing himself when a gunshot rang out. Malachi saw the man in the gray uniform crouching with a gun extended toward the man in the red hat. The man in the bright red hat arched his back, and then fell face first into the muddy, dirt road.

"Oh, God! Malachi, did you see that? He shot that man," Rose Ann shrieked.

Malachi was pulling the car to the side of the street to park when a crowd came running out of the building the two men had emerged from and headed toward the man who'd fired the gun. Malachi saw the man in the dirty gray uniform turn around and aim at the crowd, but realizing there were too many of them, he decided to run while dropping his gun.

"That was stupid," Malachi said.

"What? The fact that he shot the man?" Rose Ann asked.

"Nope. That fool dropping his gun and trying to run from that crowd. If he'd kept the gun, he could've at least had an edge. How is he gonna outrun anybody in all this mud?"

Malachi and Rose Ann watched the man in the gray uniform run. But there was someone in the crowd who was much quicker than the rest. He caught up to the man in the gray uniform within five quick strides and dived on his back. Knocking him down. The crowd fell onto the both of them with in a rabid frenzy.

"What'd I tell you," Malachi said.

"This place doesn't look very friendly," Rose Ann said. She crossed her arms over her chest. "It looks downright frightening."

"At our age, a lot of places will look scary, Rose. We're gonna have to find a place to sleep, and some jobs," Malachi said.

"Jobs? Like what?" Rose Ann asked.

"Anything that will keep money in our pocket. You can wait on tables, and I'll probably get any job I can find. The little money we have ain't much, and if we keep spending it without putting some of it back, we're gonna be broke in a week or two."

"Okay," Rose Ann said.

Malachi and Rose Ann exited the car. Malachi grabbed their suitcases. Suitcases they'd bought the day before from the money they'd taken from Bo and his friends. Rose Ann had picked up Malachi's guitar. They stood by the car searching the street for a hotel.

"There's one down there," Rose Ann said, as she pointed straight ahead.

Malachi followed her direction. The hotel's sign was hanging down, and the building hadn't seen a paint job in years. "Let's go see if we can get us a room," he said.

When they reached the hotel, they walked in with several eyes on them from white patrons standing around. Malachi walked up to the clerk behind the desk.

"We're looking for some rooms," Malachi said, as he neared the desk.

The clerk, his rim glasses hanging on the bridge of his

nose, and his blond hair plastered to the side of his head with pomade, looked at Malachi. He was reading a book, and his attention went back to it after dismissing Malachi with a distasteful stare.

Malachi leaned down a little in front of the man. "Hello, we're looking for a room," he said.

The clerk lifted his left hand, and slowly rotated it to the left of him while pointing in the air.

Malachi followed his hand. On the wall was a wooden sign painted with white letters:

No Niggers Allowed!

Rose Ann saw the sign. She gasped. "Malachi, let's go," she said. She reached for Malachi's arm. "Come on."

Malachi, his fist balled tightly, looked at the clerk who was still reading his book and ignoring them. He wanted to grab the man by the collar and spit in his face, but that thought disappeared when he looked around and saw other white people staring at him.

"Thank you, sir," Malachi said. His tone was cold and distant. "Come on, Rose Ann."

Malachi and Rose Ann were headed to the door when the clerk stopped them.

"Boy, there's a shanty town about two miles out of town that cotton to your kind. I suggest you and your girlfriend head that way. Take the next right turn by the old mill, and ride it straight out. You can't miss it," the clerk said.

Malachi never turned around to acknowledge the man. He continued walking.

On the street Malachi and Rose Ann looked around. It was then that they realized that they were in the middle of a white town with no real law because at every turn, there was some sort of fight going on or some other lawless act.

"I think we better take the white man on his word and go see that town," Malachi said. He headed toward the car.

They rode in silence. Rose Ann staring out the window, and Malachi trying to keep his anger in check by concentrating on the road. If he didn't, he might find himself turning the car around and going back there and put some lumps on the white clerk's head.

What he thought was a two mile drive turned into ten miles. Malachi and Rose Ann didn't see anything but dirt road and big trees.

"Do you think that man lied to us?' Rose Ann asked.

"I know he did! Damn cracker!" Malachi snapped. "George Lewis always said that white folks are evil incarnate. We didn't bother him. We weren't disrespectful. Only thing we were looking for was a room."

Rose Ann nodded as she looked ahead. She leaned forward a little at the sight of illumination further down the road.

"Us Negroes don't mean anyone harm unless it's coming to them for trying to bother us. White folks think they own the damn world because they're white," Malachi said.

Rose Ann was still leaning forward. "You're not that far off. A few more shades lighter and you can pass for white. Your straight black hair, green eyes, and thin lips don't make you pass off as a Negro too often. If your nose wasn't big...."

Malachi glanced at his sister. "That ain't funny, sis," he said.

"What's that light up ahead?" Rose Ann asked.

Malachi looked. "I don't know, but we're going there," he said, as he pressed down on the accelerator.

When they finally reached the illumination, they saw why. They saw lanterns on the top of tall poles that lit up the street. Malachi slowed down as he continued to approach the entrance. In the streets, there were large planks of wood for crossing over the muddy water. The streets were busy with people going on about their business.

"What does that sign say?" Rose Ann asked as she squinted to decipher it.

"Where?" Malachi asked, as he looked around.

"To the left of you," Rose Ann answered.

"The one leaning up against the wall with the faded paint?" Malachi asked. He began to read: "This town is for you. Treat it like you would your own home. Welcome to Blackenfield."

"Blackenfield?" Rose Ann repeated.

"Population: Nine hundred," Malachi said.

"That's a whole lot of Negroes in one place," Rose Ann said.

"Yeah, and you know what they say about Negroes," Malachi said as he looked for somewhere to park. "Too many Negroes in one place draw heat. And in this case, we need it. I'm cold."

Malachi directed the car to the back of an alley. The bright lanterns hanging from the pole gave off good lighting so he didn't have to worry about the car being broken into. He hoped. They'd seen a hotel a half a block away. With their suitcases in their hands, they headed for it.

As they walked down the street, Rose Ann was amazed at how some of the women were dressed in beautiful dresses and wide, sweeping hats with flowery shawls. Whenever she passed a man, their eyes would make contact, and the man would wink at her, making Rose Ann turn away quickly with embarrassment.

When they walked into the hotel, there was a big, black man whose skin looked like leather sitting down behind the counter. They headed toward him.

The large black man watched them approach. Malachi saw him move his right hand toward his waist. It was a subtle move, but he saw it anyway.

"Hi. We're looking for a room…two rooms really," Malachi said.

"Two rooms?" The man repeated as he stared at Malachi. "Why two rooms? You and your little honey done had fallout or something?"

Malachi could see that the man was used to intimidating people. He raised his chin. "She's my sister," he said. "Do you have the rooms?"

The clerk stared at Malachi. "You two are not from around these here parts, are you?" he asked.

Malachi reached for the sign-in book. He turned it around so that he could write in their names.

The clerk slammed down a six-inch barrel .38 five-shot revolver on top of the sign-in book. Malachi jumped back as if a snake had bitten him.

"My name is Bear. I own this hotel, and when I ask you something, I expect to get an answer," he said.

Malachi looked at Bear. He gave him a really good look. He could see that Bear's left eye didn't move like his right eye. Malachi could also feel Rose Ann clinging tightly to his arm. He knew she was frightened. He had to stay calm for her sake.

"No, we're not from around this area," Malachi said.

Bear looked at them. "Uh-hmm. I can tell. You didn't come in here with your eyes shifting. As you can see," Bear began, as he reached for his left eye. "My eye is on everyone and everything."

Rose Ann screeched and put her face into Malachi's shoulder when she saw Bear remove his glass eye and lay it on the counter.

"I used to have a good eye until my best friend plucked it out several years ago," Bear said. "Now I let my other five eyes watch over my good eye." He patted the gun very gingerly. "And those eyes don't miss much when I take aim."

Malachi stared at the black hole in Bear's face. He'd never seen anything like it before.

Bear reached for his eye. He pushed it back into his eye socket with ease. "You got money for two rooms? If you do, for how long? Blackkenfeild is a town that takes money and pisses it away. When your money is gone, then what?" he asked.

"We'll be working before that happens," Malachi said.

"You will, huh?" Bear placed the gun back in his waist. "Doing what? I see you got you a guitar. Can you do anything with it besides carry it? What about your girlfriend? Can she sing? Can she dance, or is she your money ticket?"

"She's my sister!" Malachi snapped as he took a step forward. He stopped when he saw Bear's hand reaching for his waist. "We'll find whatever work we can to pay our way," he said.

"You're young boy. You don't wait until the rabbit decides to jump into the trap. The rabbit won't take the bait unless it smells something worth the effort. You have to make sure you got enough lettuce to lure it out of its hole," Bear said.

"What does that have to do with jobs?" Malachi asked. He was becoming angry.

"You can work here for your room and board, and save your money," Bear said.

"Work here? For you?"

"Why not? You're new in town, and you don't bring any other baggage that could be considered trouble, so I can trust you," Bear said.

"You don't even know us," Rose Ann said.

Bear reached up and began scratching his mangy beard. "Nope, I don't, but I think I can trust you two. I have a nose for these things, and until my nose gets cut off, I'll go with it. So, what do you say?"

"Do we get the best in the house for rooms?" Malachi asked.

"Yep. The Queen has nothing but the best," Bear said.

"Well, how come the sign outside is hanging off its hinges?" Rose Ann asked.

"I'm working on that right now," Bear said.

"And why does the place look like it hasn't seen any paint in years?" Rose Ann asked.

"I can't find the right color," Bear said.

Rose Ann looked at Bear. "You can't find white?" she asked.

"You ask a lot of questions, girl. I can find white, but it's difficult to find someone to paint the place," Bear answered.

"Um-hmm," Rose Ann said. "A man like you owning a place like this and you can't find any one to paint?"

"This is your sister, huh?" Bear asked, as he gave Malachi a questionable stare.

Malachi shrugged. "What chores do we have to do?" Malachi asked, as he stared at Bear. "We ain't going to be no one slaves for a few dollars."

"Boy, this is ain't a damn plantation. Those days are gone...not all the way, but some. What's your name?" Bear asked.

"I'm Malachi and her name is Rose Ann."

"All right. Let me show you around. Cotton! Get your bum ass over here and watch the shop. I got to show my new workers their surroundings," Bear said.

A man with one leg shorter than the other appeared out of a side room. He was wiping his hand on a soiled rag. He came up to Malachi and Malachi could smell a wretched scent of alcohol emanating off him.

"Didn't I tell you about drinking that hooch and coming to work, man? Damn! I told you you can't smell like that around the customers," Bear said, as Cotton limped around the counter. "I told you to change that dirty shirt, too. Let's go kids."

Malachi and Rose Ann followed Bear up the stairs.

When they reached the top landing and began passing closed doors, Malachi could hear the sounds of moaning coming from some of the rooms and a few sounds of pleasurable shrieking. He glanced at Rose Ann, and her expression made him want to laugh. She was clutching the collar of her coat and her eyes were searching the floor. If she'd been a little lighter, he might've seen her knuckles begin to turn white.

"After I show you two youngins your rooms, I want to show you my other properties," Bear said, as he led them several more feet down the paint faded hallway.

He stopped in front of a door with two locks on it. "This is it."

Malachi and Rose Ann stood to the side as Bear reached into his pants pocket and pulled out a ring of keys. He fumbled with them for a few seconds until he found the right one.

"The room on your right is the adjoining room. I thought you might want to be close to your girl—"

"Sister," Rose Ann snapped.

"Uh-huh. However, whatever," Bear said quickly while rolling his eyes upward. "Welcome to the hotel Queen!" He pushed open the door.

Malachi and Rose Ann's mouths fell nearly to the floor from shock. They stared into a room that was empty.

"Beautiful, isn't it?" Bear asked. He walked into the room and spun around.

"Bear, ain't nothing in here," Malachi said. He walked into the middle of the room, and raised his arms as he turned around in a circle. "Nothing!"

"Right. Now you use your imagination to fill it with things. See, I got a plan," Bear began. He stopped. "Come on in and close the door, girl." He watched Rose Ann walk in and close the door. "Okay, this it. I plan to give this baby my attention. I want to name it Queen. That way it'd give it some class. I mean, right now I'm just starting out, but in three or four years I want to have this baby up and running like a well oiled engine." He slammed a big fist into the palm of his hand. "Yep, that's how I picture it. But to do this I need people I can trust. People who ain't involve with other people who are thinking of doing harm to my plans. Whatta think, huh? The way I see it, this town will one day be big, and I want to have my hand in its pocket when it does. You and your—"

"Sister," Rose Ann interrupted.

"Uh-huh. However, whatever. Can come in with me as well paid workers I can trust?" Bear asked.

"I thought it was already called the "Queen." You have a thing with trusting people, huh, Bear?" Malachi asked.

Bear pointed to his glass eye. "Wouldn't you?" he asked.

Malachi nodded.

"All right, then. Put your things in here, and I'll show you around some more," Bear said.

Rose Ann and Malachi dropped their things in the middle of the empty room.

"Good," Bear said. "Let's go." Bear turned to go back out the door when Malachi grabbed his big arm.

"The keys, Bear," Malachi said.

"Oh… Oh… Yeah," Bear said. He removed two keys from the ring, and handed them to Malachi. "I was going to give them to you."

"Uh-huh," Rose Ann said.

"You two are quick. How old are you, Malachi? Twenty? Twenty-three?"

"No. I'm seventeen. I'll be eighteen at the end of the year."

"No shit! You're a big bone young Negro. How old is your…sister?"

"She's young," Malachi replied with apprehension.

"Hmm. Don't wants to tell, huh? Don't worry about me. You better worry about them fools out there, though. You keep her close to you. They're animals out there. That's why I keep this next to me at all times," Bear said. He patted the .38 revolver in his waist for emphasize. "You never know where or how these fools might come at you. Come on. Let's go see my other future prospect."

Bear headed for the door with Rose Ann and Malachi behind him.

As Malachi followed the large, gruff looking Bear, he had to admit that he didn't feel the least slighted by the man. There was something interesting about Bear. Malachi thought the man was just trying to find someone he could trust without dropping his guard.

Bear led them down the stairs and out a back door. They went to a cellar door in the back of the hotel. Bear stomped down on the door twice, then waited a second or two, and then gave the door three more quick loud stomps. He quickly stepped away from the cellar doors.

It would only be a matter of seconds before the cellar doors opened, and two men carrying double-barrel shotguns emerged.

"How's business?" Bear asked.

"It's good, Bear. You know how Saturday night is. A

lot of moonshine and beautiful bitches with big tits keep the party jumping," the man to the left of Bear said.

"Watch your mouth, Cali. We have a young girl present," Bear said.

Cali, wearing his customary black business suit that was a size smaller than his actual size, glanced at Rose Ann.

"Sam, Cali, this is Malachi and Rose Ann. They're gonna be working for me," Bear said.

Malachi looked at Sam. The man's neck was as big as a tree trunk. His glistening baldhead gave him an even more intimidating appearance. But at least his suit fitted him.

"Any trouble, Sam?" Bear asked. He scratched his ragged beard as he glanced around.

"Nothing, Bear," Sam said.

"What about the Brown brothers? Anything I ought to know?" Bear asked.

"Ain't heard from them," Cali said.

Some things unheard are a good thing…Maybe. Let's go down, kids, and see my future unfolding," Bear said. He led the way down the stairs.

The lights and smoke was suffocating. The smell of unwashed bodies, and bodies with too much perfume assaulted Malachi and Rose Ann sense of smell. Malachi looked around and saw men wearing large lapel colorful suits standing next to men still wearing their overalls from the field. Women were dazzling in their sequined shimmering dresses and high heels. The place was very big for a cellar.

"This is my joint. On the right you see four poker tables. To the left you'd see my craps and roulette tables. On the stage up there is Sally. She sings here every Friday and Saturday night," Bear said as they slowly walked further into the gambling den. "I make my own moonshine. That's two dollars a jar. The stuff is so powerful that if a person gets too close to a fire while drinking it, they better get ready to roll their ass on the ground, because that baby is going to light their ass on fire. Literally."

"What do you want from us?" Malachi asked.

The noise was loud. Bear had to shout to be heard. He was walking between Malachi and Rose Ann. He put his arm around Malachi's shoulder. "I need you to be my eyes and ears around here. You'd sweep, mop, clean the tables, and keep the mason jars filled with moonshine," Bear began. "No one is going to think you're doing anything wrong. You keep you ears open for me and that's what I want from you."

"What about my sister? She ain't going to be working around no drunken men," Malachi said.

"Right. She'd straighten out the rooms when customers leave. You know. Change the sheets. Give them clean towels. Things like that," Bear answered.

"No funny stuff," Malachi said.

"No funny stuff," Bear repeated.

"Sally sings very nice," Rose Ann said.

"Yeah. She's a good girl. So, what do you say, Malachi?" Bear asked.

"I got to talk to my sister. Rose, come on."

"Take her over to the bathroom area. It smells a little, but it's quiet and you can hear yourself think," Bear said. "I'm going to make my rounds. Just look around. You'll find me or hear me when you finish."

Pulling Rose Ann along, Malachi found a spot by the

bathroom. He wrinkled his nose at the smell of urine, but he had to admit, it was quiet.

"What do you think, Rose Ann?" he asked.

"I don't know. We could use the money, but how long would we have to be here, Malachi? The place isn't all that great."

"This ain't jail. We can leave whenever we want," Malachi said.

"I know, but—"

"We'll be fine, Rose. I'm going to tell Bear we'll take his job."

Malachi and Rose Ann walked back to where they'll left Bear. He was nowhere to be found.

"There he is," Rose Ann said, as she pointed across the floor to Bear.

Malachi looked on stage, and saw Bear playing a drum set. His large arms and big head were bouncing with the music. Malachi was amazed at how Bear beat the drums with such force and inner ease. His rhythm was on time and consistent as he stayed with the band. Malachi took Rose Ann by the elbow and they got closer to the stage.

They were small tables arranged around the stage. Malachi tried not to block any ones view as he and Rose Ann tried to find an area in which to watch the show. Everyone was clapping and laughing as Sally sang a song about women not being appreciated until they went upside their man's head with a two-by-four, then they were loved. The song made Malachi smile. He noticed that Sally was wearing a cream- colored flapper short dress with beads at the ends. And whenever she turned her back to the audience to shake her voluptuous butt, the beads would shake uncontrollably, making the audience laugh. Her shiny black, bobbed hair fit her face perfectly.

"She really has them worked up," Rose Ann shouted so that Malachi could hear her.

"Yeah, she does," Malachi said.

Sally's voice was a sultry, baritone. Malachi found himself really staring at her. She was a full figured woman with large breasts. Her caramel, smooth enhanced her beauty.

"I ain't got me a man at home; I got me a little boy who can't work my neeeeeddddsssss. Heeeee wants to play in the sanddddddbox, and I need to have him play in my box," Sally sang. *"He says he loooovvvveeevesss me, but ain't been no loving going on laaaattteeeelllyyyly...I'm all woman...All woman...indeed whoooo has her neeeeeeeeeeeeeeeeds!"*

Sally held the note so long Malachi thought her breasts were swelling up to give her more oxygen to continue. He watched as Sally stomped her feet again and again as the note continued to hold.

"She better stop, she's going to kill herself," Rose Ann said with concern.

Malachi began shaking his head in disbelief. The woman finally ended her note and tossed the microphone onto the stage. Bear continuously beat the drums with a rhythmic fervor until the last note ended, and then he tossed the drumsticks in the air as he leaped out of his seat with his arms over his head, grinning.

The audience went wild with approval of their performance by clapping thunderously loud.

Sally took a lady gracious bow and walked to the edge of the stage. A man in a black tuxedo helped her off the stage. As she walked pass the audience, people were touching her and giving her accolades. The man in the tuxedo walked her toward the back. He opened a door, and they disappeared.

Malachi's back exploded with pain. When he turned around, he saw Bear laughing hysterically with an arm around Rose Ann's shoulder.

"That bitch can sing!" Bear shouted. "Ain't too many women I know in this life time can sing the blues the way Sally can. Whew! That woman keeps this joint packed. Come on. I'm going to introduce you kids."

Bear dragged, and pulled Malachi and Rose Ann through the thick crowd of people. When they reached the door, Malachi watched Bear take out a key and open it. He pushed them inside, and slammed the door closed.

Bear took the lead. "I pay that woman twenty dollars a week, and she triples my money every night," he began, as they walked down the short hallway with dull lighting. "I run a fun business. I like to make my customers happy when they're here. Not like the Brown brothers. Those lugs don't care about the people, only the money that's coming in. Here's Sally little hole in the wall."

Bear knocked on the heavy wooden door.

"Who the hell is it?" Sally asked through the door.

"Your goddamn boss!" Bear shouted.

"Well, come back later, I'm having a drink," Sally said.

"Open this damn door!" Bear snapped.

"Come back later, goddamn it!" Sally shouted.

"This bitch is crazy," Bear said. He reached into his pocket and pulled out the ring of keys. He fumbles for the one he wanted. A shiny brass one. He stuck it in the keyhole and turned it clockwise. "Ain't nobody gonna tell me to come back later in my joint."

When the door open, Malachi heard Rose Ann gasped. Rose Ann covered her eyes with both hands. Malachi, after the visual shock, let his eyes take in the sight. He gave his complete attention the naked Sally sitting at a small table with a jar of moonshine on it. She was wearing a pair of black underwear and black sheer stocking with black garters. Malachi's eyes immediately fell on her big, brown breasts. The nipples on her breasts were very large. He smiled.

"Boy, put your goddamn eyes back in that pretty face of yours. I know you done seen tits before. They might be big, but they're like any other two once you've seen them," Sally said. "You pay me to sing, you cheap bastard, so don't be barging into my motherfucking room in the future. Throw me my robe so that young girl can open her eyes before she bumps into something and hurt herself."

Bear ran over to a chair in the corner where Sally's robe lay. He grabbed it and walked quickly back to her.

Malachi watched Sally stand up. To him, she didn't seem embarrass at all about being naked. Sally looked Bear up and down from head to toe before slowly reaching for her robe. Malachi couldn't believe he was watching a naked woman so beautifully well rounded. When Sally turned her back to him, he could see how big, and sexy her butt stood out.

After tying her robe closed, Sally turned back around. "Okay, honey, old Sally is decent," she said.

Rose Ann slowly removed her hands from her face. She gave a sheepish smile.

Sally smiled back at her. "Who are your friends, Bear?" Sally asked. She reached for the glass of moonshine, and gulped down its remaining contents.

Bear stood there staring at Sally.

Bear, Malachi noticed, had also been transfixed on Sally's breasts. He didn't hear the question.

"Motherfucker, if you stop lusting at the sight of my tits, you would've heard my goddamn question!" Sally snapped.

Bear came out of his reverie with a shake of his head.

"Hi. I'm Malachi, and that's my sister Rose Ann," Malachi said.

"Oh, so you can speak. I thought I might have to go get my smelling salt for you... Malachi," Sally said. She slightly pushed Bear out of the way as she seductively walked toward Malachi with her chest purposely pushed out in front of her. "What else do you do?"

Malachi took a step back as she neared him.

"Don't worry, baby. Sally doesn't bite...Unless she wants to, and then there's nothing but pleasure after that," Sally said.

"Sally, come on now. He's young," Bear said, as he came up behind her. "I wanted you to meet them. They'll be working here."

Sally spun around on her three-inch heels to face Bear. "Working? Here? You cheap bastard! What are you going to pay them? You ain't been paying me a damn thing but promises and hollow ass dreams for the past month. Oh sure, you might give me ten dollars here and five dollars there from time to time, but I'm a woman who needs her money every damn day. The only reason I'm still with you is because your cook makes some mouth-watering pig feet, and collar greens. Other than that, I might've moved on a long time ago," Sally said.

Bear folded his arms across his chest and looked down on Sally. Who, at five feet, looked like a midget compared to Bear.

"Woman, is that all?" Bear asked.

Sally put a hand on her large hip and began tapping her foot. "Let me think about that question for a minute," she said.

"Yeah, you do that," Bear said.

Malachi watched Sally's expression turned from discontent and anger to a broad smile filled with warmth. She reached out to Bear and hugged him.

"You know the Bear is here for you," Bear said. He wrapped his arms around her.

Sally looked up at Bear. Bear leaned down and kissed her hard on her lips.

"You big cuddly bear," Sally said. She turned around and looked at Malachi and Rose Ann. "Sister and brother, huh? Where's the resemblance? You sure she's not your girlfriend. You're handsome enough, and she's…well, she's womanly enough."

Rose Ann pulled her coat over her breasts, and lifted her head. "No, he's my brother," she said.

"Cut the shit, Sally," Bear said. "They're good kids. Anyway, the way this town is growing, I need people I can trust near me."

Sally turned around to face Bear. She opened her robe. "You can't trust me? If you can't trust me, then you're a big fool, and no matter what, you'll never trust anyone," she said.

Bear picked Sally up by lifting her by her waist. Malachi was surprised at how easily he could do it.

"You know I trust you, woman. But the Brown brothers are really beginning to make me mad with their shenanigans, Sally. Three nights ago, Cotton goes up in the attic to do his spying, and he sees someone come running out of Jack Shin's barn. Ten minutes later, he says he sees the place catch fire. How many times have I told you that the Brown brothers have been trying to get to Jack out of the moonshine business so they can take it over? Too many times, that's how many. We all came to Blackenfield about the same time ten years ago. When I met them, they were jostling every pocket that looked like it had some money in it. They were rolling over drunken bums in the alley. They've never been any damn good. If they get their hands on Jack Shin's business, then I'm really going to be in competition with the bastards. Every new face that shows up in this hole of a town, they recruit them. If you ask me, I think they're getting an army together," Bear said. He put Sally back down. "Those three can never be trusted."

Sally gently patted Bear on the cheek. "All right, baby. But what about these two?" Sally asked, as she turned around to face Malachi and Rose Ann. "They seem awful young to be in your war with the Brown brothers."

"War? Malachi said.

Bear waved his hand as if to ward off Malachi's next question. "Not a war, Malachi, but a position of power for the money that is coming into this town. You see, boy, like everything in life, especially in a poor man's life, you got to grab what you can before someone else grabs it. You don't take chances with anything you can't control. You have to make sure you have your future in your pocket at all times. The Brown brothers are slowly building themselves an empire, and they're not going to wait for no one, or anything to make it happen. I know they're watching me and the Queen, but, hell, I'm watching them, too," he said.

Sally laughed and sat back down at her small-mirrored desk. She filled her glass with some more moonshine. She turned around in her chair to face Bear. "Look, big, and ugly. You put too much into thinking when it comes to the Brown brothers. They, like everyone else, are trying to survive in this shitty town, but they're just making sure they can swim when this baby fills up with a cesspool of dumb bastards and retarded cutthroats who think they might be smarter," she said. "Anyway, how is handsome, and his girl... I mean...his sister going to help you?"

Bear placed a cupped hand under his chin as he turned toward Malachi and Rose. "They are going to be my ace in a hole," he said. He laughed.

CHAPTER SIX

Putting a Puzzle Together

Malachi was sweeping the dusty, wooden floor of the Queen. The heat from outside was draining him. He had to admit, as sweat ran freely from his well-muscled, young body, that New Orleans was hot in the summer time. The shoulder cut-off black tee-shirt he was wearing was comfortable, he admitted, but he needed a cool bath to remove the sweat and grime he'd accumulated since working the entire day. As he swept by the tables of men gambling, he would linger beside the table to hear what they were talking about. If nothing sounded threatening concerning the Queen, he would move to the next table with his broom working the area and listening intently. He'd been doing the same routine for nearly three months.

Rose Ann was changing the sheets on a bed. She'd

already disinfected the room by wiping it down with water and ammonia. The washbasin that every room had in it was soaking in a bucket by the door. She knew before leaving the room, she would have to place it back on the dresser that was situated squarely in the middle of the room. As she slapped away the wrinkles on the sheet she'd unfolded and placed on the bed, she stood up.

"I like the view when you're bending over."

Rose Ann spun around to see a man standing by the bathroom door wearing only his pants and holding a towel.

"Well, sights are all you're going to see," Rose Ann said. She walked to the edge of the bed and gathered in her arms the soiled sheets she'd removed. She walked to the door.

The tall man grinned as he stepped in front of Rose Ann's path. He prevented her from opening the door. She stared the man down hard while displaying a courteous smile.

"I think we can have a good time together," the tall man said. He smiled.

Rose Ann's smile broadened. She looked at the man. His black skin was as dark as coal. His face, although round, had high cheek bones. And, she had to admit, he didn't look that bad. Dropping the sheets to the floor, she took a step back.

"Sir, I have work to do, and you're not helping me by standing in my way," Rose Ann said.

"Maybe we need to get a little more acquainted. My name is Stump. I know your boss, Bear, real good. We go a few years back together," Stump said. He took the towel and tossed it on the pile of sheets. "The last girl that used to work here, me and her used to have a nice time. "I'm a man who likes to pay for what he gets. You know what I mean."

Rose Ann rolled her eyes. "Really," she said. She reached for Stump's hand. Taking it, she led him to the bed. "Sit down. Maybe we can work something out."

Stump sat down on the bed. His eyes were hungrily taking in Rose Ann's simple beauty. "You're a real fine philly. I'll love to ride you all night long," he said. "I pay good money for a good time."

"I bet you do, and I gonna give you a good time," Rose Ann said. She lifted her right leg onto the bed while slowly pulling up her dress to reveal her sheer stockings. "A big man like you sure would take care of a little girl like me, won't you?" Rose Ann's voice had become high and girlish like. "I mean, you wouldn't hurt me, right?"

"Hurt you? Hell naw," Stump said, as he stared at Rose Ann's pretty leg. "I'll make you happy."

If Stumps' lust hadn't blinded his vision, his eyes would've caught Rose Ann other hand reaching under her dress.

"Stump's a man of his word. I'll give you a few extra pennies if it's really good," he said.

"And I'll give you the chance to pray before I cut your throat," Rose Ann snapped, as the edge of the pearl-handled razor she was tightly clutching suddenly appeared and dug into the skin of Stump's neck. Her words were rough. "Since you're new here, and the other guests haven't told you about me, I'll give you that one. My name is Rose Ann. I don't give anything away, and I don't sell my body. But I do cut bastards like you on a daily basis. So, I suggest--you don't mind if I suggest this to you--do you?" Rose Ann watched Stump shake his head. "Good." She pressed the edge of the razor a little harder into Stump's neck. "I didn't think you would. Anyway, if you ever approach me again in this way, I'll take your balls from you, and you'll be less of a man. Now, I'm going to take my razor away from your neck. You might feel a sense of shame by letting a woman do this to you. Don't worry, it's only us here, and I won't tell anyone if you don't."

Stump, his eyes hardening, nodded.

"Good," Rose Ann said. She put her foot on the floor. "I'm going to finish cleaning."

Stump watched Rose Ann walk over to where she'd dropped the soiled sheets. She bent over and picked them up. At that moment, he thought of rushing her, and putting her in a headlock, but for some reason, he had admiration for her. She was a strong, young, vibrant woman. He smiled.

Bear sat in his office going over some papers that were on his desk. He looked up when he heard his door open. It was Cotton.

"Hey, Cotton. How's it going?" Bear asked.

"Good. I finished cleaning the spittoons, and mopped and swept the floors upstairs. I brought three more cases of moonshine from the barn for tonight," Cotton said.

"You're a good man, Cotton. I'm glad you're with me. I have to take some papers over to the courthouse to have them on file. But you keep doing what you're doing. I appreciate it."

"What kind of papers? I hear the Brown brothers been talking about you," Cotton said. He sat down in the chair that was in front of the desk. "They say you making too much money for one man."

Bear looked up from the papers he was reading. He smiled. "Some legal papers. What else are they saying, Cotton?" he asked.

"You need to become partners with them," Cotton said.

"Partners? Fuck them! Those conniving bastards!" Bear snapped.

"It might not be all that bad, Bear," Cotton whispered. "I mean, I've been watching them for the past four months. They're growing. They're reaching into everything. I saw Red Boone the other day."

"Red Boone that owns the eat house on the east corner of town?" Bear asked.

"Yeah. He said the Brown brothers bought him out."

"How much did they pay him?" Bear asked. He began scratching his beard.

Cotton shrugged his shoulders.

"They didn't pay him. I'll tell you what they did. They told him to sign over his place to them, and in three months they'd give him his money, didn't they?" Bear asked.

Cotton nodded.

"Those goddamn bastards!" Bear snapped. He slammed his fist down. "They think they can keep scaring people with those bullshit ass tactics," Bear snapped.

"It worked," Cotton said.

"It only worked because Red Boone didn't have anyone behind him. They scare people with their threats, they don't ever do anything. Nope, Cotton, I can never become partners with those bastards. I'll rather buy them out, and then run them out of town."

"You ain't got enough money to buy them out. Anyway, you know how they think. To them, this town is theirs," Cotton said. With his hands in his lap, he began twirling his thumbs nervously.

"Maybe I don't and maybe I do," Bear said. He laughed. "I don't care about them. They'd never own the Queen."

Cotton looked at Bear. "God forbid, but what if you get killed walking down the street or something. You ain't got any family out here," he said. His voice cracked with emotion.

"It'd be all right," Bear said. "Nothing is going to happen to me."

"Good, because you've always done right by me," Cotton said. "I have to go clean the shot glasses." Cotton stood up.

"Go ahead. I'll see you later. And, Cotton. You're looking and smelling better now."

"Rose Ann helps me out now," Cotton said, as he headed to the door. "She treats Cotton kindly."

Bear watched Cotton go out the door. He looked down at the papers in front of him. He smiled. It wasn't much, he admitted, but it was enough to keep a person's head above water. Picking up a pen, Bear quickly signed his name to the papers.

When Malachi saw his sister coming toward him looking angry, he knew what had happened. He was standing behind the counter of the bar wiping it down with a wet towel as she hurried toward him.

"These bastards think every girl in this town is a hoe,"

Rose Ann said, as she stopped in front of her brother. "I had to use my razor on another fool's neck a few minutes ago. These old bastards need to cut those things off if they don't know how to keep them down between their legs."

Malachi laughed. His sister had changed since settling in at the Queen. To him, she seemed to be older. No, he corrected. More mature.

"What happened?" Malachi asked. He didn't look at Rose Ann. Instead, he surreptitiously kept his eyes on a man who was sitting at a table by himself drinking a glass of water. "Did someone grab your butt again?"

"No. That's not it…Well, yeah in a way. I mean how come men always think girls—"

"Women," Malachi said. "You're big, Rose Ann. Sure you're fifteen, but men don't see that in your body. How many times has Sally told you about every man that comes in this place are yearning for you?"

"Sally can kiss my black ass!" Rose Ann snapped.

"Rose Ann, that's not nice," Malachi said.

Rose Ann turned up the right corner of her mouth. "Sally doesn't care about anyone but herself. If she ain't always begging for money, then she's trying to always get out of her responsibilities."

"You don't like her be—"

"I don't like her because she has no self-respect. She's always flashing her breasts at men and that fat, flabby butt. Yeah, she can sing, I give her that, but she ain't no real woman in my court," Rose Ann said. She rubbed her tired face, and looked around. "It's kind of slow tonight."

"It'd pick up later on. Who did you have to pull your razor on this time?" Malachi asked.

"One of Bear's friends."

"One of Bear friends?" Malachi asked. His face became a mask of stone. "What was his name?"

"A man name Stump," Rose Ann said.

"Stump? I ain't ever heard of him before," Malachi said. Malachi stopped wiping down the counter. He looked at his sister. "You're sure he said he was a friend of Bear's?"

"Uh-huh. That's probably why I didn't make him bleed," Rose Ann said.

Malachi leaped from behind the counter, and stood in front of his sister. "Well, that's one that you didn't. Because the last time you clipped someone with your razor, Bear and I had to rush him over to the doctor. The man had lost so much blood, the doctor thought he was going to die," Malachi said.

"Good for the fool! He should've never grabbed my breasts, and then act like he could reach between my legs like he owned me!" Rose Ann snapped.

"I have to go see Bear. Do you think you can hold off on slicing anyone until I get back?" Malachi asked. Rose Ann smiled at him. "I guess that means yes."

"Yes," Rose Ann said. "I have to go finish a few more rooms, though."

"You do that. I'll see you in a few," Malachi said.

Malachi leaned into his sister and gave her a quick peck on her cheek, and then hurried off in the direction of Bear's office.

Ten minutes later, Malachi was standing in front to

Bear's office door. He knocked once, and then three quick times more. He heard Bear tell him to come inside.

Malachi walked in to see Bear sitting behind his desk counting money. On the desk was also his gun.

"Malachi. How's it going?"

Malachi walked into the room and closed the door behind him.

"Come sit down," Bear said.

Malachi took five long strides, and sat down in the chair. "There's some cat outside drinking water, and looking around. The thing about him is that he doesn't want anyone to know that he's casing the Queen," Malachi said.

"It's those damn Brown brothers. So now they're sending people over here to see what I'm doing." Bear scratched his beard. "I don't know about this bullshit."

"Rose Ann said she had a face-up with some new scab in room 323," Malachi said.

"I taught that girl what to do when those situations come up. Damn it! Did she cut him with her razor? We're still coming out of the mess from the last one she cut up. Do you know how much I had to pay that white, ignorant sheriff to keep him from locking her up?" Bear didn't wait. "Twenty-five goddamn dollars!"

"Thanks for that, Bear, but she didn't cut anyone this time," Malachi said.

Bear looked at Malachi. He leaned back in his wooden chair. "Oh, okay, so what's the problem?" Bear asked, as he calmed down knowing he didn't have to rush anyone over to the doctor.

"Rose said the man knows you, and that you're good friends."

"You know how that is, Malachi. These scabs are always throwing my name out there to get something free," Bear said. He opened the bottom draw and removed a strongbox. He opened it and began taking out wads of money wrapped with rubber bands. "I've been teaching you this for awhile now. Did she say what his name is?"

"Stump."

Bear froze. His hand hovered over the strongbox. He looked at Malachi.

"Stump?" Bear asked.

"Yeah," Malachi said.

Malachi was startled at Bear's next gesture. He watched as Bear moved quickly began placing the money back in the strongbox. Malachi squinted to get a better look at Bear. He noticed that Bear was talking but he couldn't hear what he was saying. Bear slammed the drawer closed and locked it. He stood up so fast that he knocked over the chair.

"Look behind that door and get that pickax handle," Bear said.

Malachi stared at him.

"Goddamn it, boy, move!" Bear shouted.

Malachi jumped out of his chair and ran to get the pickax handle. He turned around in time to see Bear sticking the .38 revolver in his waist. He watched as Bear came from around the desk like a madman. His strides were long and purposeful. Malachi opened the door, and Bear didn't break stride as he exited. Malachi followed him.

Malachi had to half run, and do a full trot to keep up with Bear. He glimpsed at the faces of those he passed. Everyone seemed to be watching them. He gripped the pickax handle as if his life depended on it. He and Bear ascended the stairs two and three at a time until they were standing in front of room 323.

Malachi watched as Bear removed the ring of keys from his belt buckle. He jiggled the keys quietly as he searched for the right on. When he found it, he stuck it in the keyhole.

"Listen, Malachi, when I open this door, we're going in there to bust some head," Bear said. He turned to Malachi. "Just follow my lead, ya hear, boy."

Malachi swallowed hard. His eyes widen, and he nodded. His right leg began to tremble with fear.

Bear turned back to the door. Malachi watched him as he slowly turned the doorknob. He swallowed hard again, and licked his dry lips. For some reason, he couldn't find any spit in his mouth.

Bear quickly opened the door and rushed in followed by Malachi.

Stump lay on the bed with his arms behind his head. His bed was facing the door. He smiled when he saw Bear and Malachi.

"Damn, Bear. You could've knocked, man," Stump said. He laughed at the expression on Bear's face. "Are you surprised to see me?"

Bear closed the door. He reached for his waist and removed the .38 revolver. "You're a sneaky bastard! I told myself if I ever see you again, I would put a bullet between your lying, no good eyes," Bear said. He walked toward the bed.

"Yeah, I thought you'd feel that way," Stump said. He sat up. "I never meant to hurt you, Bear. I just couldn't take it anymore."

Malachi watched Bear and Stump. Stump had an expression of solace, whereas Bear's expression was filled with anger. He gripped the pickax handle tighter as it lay against his leg, and hoped he didn't have to use it, but he knew, deep down, that if Bear called on him to weld it, he would split Stump's skull open without any hesitation. Bear had shown Rose Ann and him nothing but love since they'd agreed to be his friend, and friendship was hard to come by in Blackenfield. He knew that now.

"You couldn't take what, Stump?" Bear asked, as he took another step closer to the bed. "You couldn't take the Brown brothers putting pressure on you? You couldn't take the time to wait until we built something worthwhile? You couldn't wait for what, huh, Stump?"

Stump reached under the sheet.

Bear pointed the gun at Stump and cocked it.

Malachi gasped.

"Relax, Bear. I didn't come all the way from Canada to harm you," Stump said. "I came to bring you something."

Malachi watched as Stump rose up and tossed Bear a burlap bag. Bear caught it with his free hand. His good eye never left Stump.

"All debts are paid," Stump said. He lay back down with his arms under his head again.

Bear looked at the burlap bag. He offered the gun to Malachi. Malachi looked at it.

"Take the damn thing, and keep it on him," Bear said. "He's as slick as an eel."

Malachi continued to stare at the gun in Bear's hand. He'd never held a gun before, and was a little frightened.

"If you don't take this gun, boy, I will slap it up against your thick ass head!" Bear snapped. "Take it!"

Malachi reluctantly reached for the gun. Its handle felt hot in his hand. The weight of it felt heavy to him as well. He swallowed hard…again.

Bear reached into the burlap bag and pulled out a handful of money.

"One thousand dollars, Bear. I can't buy back what we had, but I can repay what I stole," Stump said.

Bear looked up from the bag at Stump. "It was only five hundred. What's the other five hundred for?" he asked.

"Guilt money," Stump said.

"Guilt money, huh?"

"Guilt money, Bear, that's all. Nothing more," Stump said.

"How long are you staying?" Bear asked. He stuffed the burlap bag into the front of his waist. "I mean, it don't make me no neither mind, but out of…curiosity."

"Not long. I just wanted to see Blackenfield. It's been a long—"

"Time! Yeah, I know," Bear said. "Even longer when my money was stolen." Bear said as he reached for the gun. He uncocked it, and placed it in the small of his back. "I hope you paid for your room in advance."

Stump laughed. "I gave your boy five days in advance when I took this room," he said.

"Good," Bear said. He gestured for Malachi to head to the door with a toss of his head. "Ain't nothing on the house, and don't be tossing my name around the Queen thinking you're going to get something free."

Stump said nothing as he watched Bear and Malachi walk to the door and open it.

"Bear?" Stump called out. "I've missed you and the Queen."

Bear didn't look behind him. "Go to hell, Stump," he said, as he slammed the door closed.

Stump laughed. His laughter could be heard down the hallway as Bear and Malachi walked.

"Who was that, Bear?" Malachi asked. He'd placed the pickax handle nonchalantly over his left shoulder as they walked down the hallway.

"He used to be my best friend."

Malachi glanced at Bear. "The one who took your eye?" he asked.

"Yeah. Best friends can one day become your worse enemy," Bear said.

CHAPTER SEVEN
Falling from Grace

Later that evening brought another headache to Bear as he paced Sally's dressing room shaking his fists in the air.

"What the hell do you mean you're not going on tonight, Sally?" Bear asked. He stopped in front of Sally. "The place is packed. They're out there begging for you."

Sally sat at her mirrored dresser sipping from a glass and swinging her crossed leg. She was wearing a thick beige robe with nothing underneath.

Bear slapped his hands on his big thighs. He spun around and began shaking his fists in the air again while pacing the floor.

Malachi was standing by the door watching.

"I don't give a raccoon's ass how pack it is. I want to know why you haven't proposed to me!" Sally shouted.

"You and I been doing the wife and husband thing for a minute now, and I want to know when we're getting married to make it real."

Malachi had been half listening to them argue. Considering they go through the same scenario twice or three times a week, but this was different. His ears perked up attentively at the mention of marriage.

Bear stopped. When he turned to face Sally, his mouth was hanging open.

"That's right, you bastard! I said it. Marry. When are we going to get M-A-R-R-Y?" Sally asked.

Malachi smiled. He didn't know Sally could spell without using a curse word in her sentence.

"Married? Sally, come on, baby, you don't want to marry me," Bear said. He walked toward Sally. He dropped to one knee, and placed his hands on her hands. "I'm not the marrying kind. You want someone who's going to be there for you. I'm not that person. Marriage is for people who will love and give love unconditionally, honey. Me, I'm that kind of person when the marriage gets rough, I got to get away."

"I understand," Sally said. She reached for the glass that contained the moonshine, and refilled it. "You want the milk, but when it's time to buy the cow, you don't want it anymore. Well, goddamn it! You will be buying this cow from this day forward! They'll be no more nibbling on your sausage for me. No more backdoor shots when my monthly cycle comes around and you're feeling horny. No more sucking on the man in the boat when you can't get your nature to rise. No marriage. No goddamn nothing! You're a cheap, no good, slimy, bastard!"

Malachi was smiling when Bear glanced over at him. Bear shook his head.

"I don't know why you're looking at Malachi. He ain't sleeping with you. I am!" Sally said.

A knock on the door made Malachi turn around and open it.

Rose Ann slipped through. "The crowd outside is getting mighty rowdy," she said, as Malachi closed the door behind her.

"Fuck them! They can all go to hell!" Sally screamed.

"What's wrong with the foul mouth woman?" Rose Ann whispered to Malachi.

"Bear won't marry her," Malachi said.

"If I were him, I wouldn't marry her either," Rose Ann said.

"Little bitch, I heard that," Sally said. Her words had become slurred. "The problem with you young bitches still smelling yourselves is that you ain't lived long enough to endure no real complications from men. Your titties are still high up and hard. Your ass is young and round, and you're still in the learning stage of a man teaching you what he likes. That being the case, you need to keep your little trap shut. And I mean both holes. The one on your face and the one between your legs."

"You know, when I first met you, I was a little scared of you, but that's because I'd never met anyone as disgusting as you before," Rose Ann said, as she walked closer to Sally. "It was only after I'd gotten to know your hot foul mouth, and all the things you say out of it, that I became less frightened of your ignorant ass. So what he won't marry you. Is it because you ain't marrying material? Maybe. And if that is the case, you need to change your ways if you want him to marry you. So, before you start putting me down as the girl who don't know shit, you ought to look at yourself first. You see, when this is all over with, you still gonna have to look in the mirror and see that ugly puss of yours. "

"Rose Ann!" Malachi snapped.

Rose Ann continued walking until she was standing in front of Sally.

"The problem is that you keep your legs open too wide and you don't know when to close them. Your mouth is as big as that thang between your legs. If you keep them both shut for awhile, you might get what you want," Rose Ann said. "Men don't want a woman who can cuss as well as them, or a woman who thinks she's God's gift to every man when she's lying on her back. I don't know much, but I know that…bitch!"

Rose Ann spun around on her heels and walked back toward Malachi.

Sally looked at Rose Ann. "So, the quiet, bashful, little girl has grown up," she said.

Rose Ann looked at Bear. "You don't need her to sing. Malachi can sing better than she can anyway, Bear," she said.

"Malachi?" Bear and Sally said in unison.

"Yep. Malachi can sing," Rose Ann said with pride.

Malachi wanted to will himself through the door and disappear as all eyes turned toward him.

"I didn't know you could sing, Malachi," Bear said.

"Hah! Malachi can sing my ass!" Sally snapped, as she brought the glass of moonshine to her lips. "Who the hell is going to pay to hear him sing?"

Rose Ann put an arm around Malachi's shoulder. "My brother can sing," she said.

"The Queen belongs to me when I'm on that stage," Sally said. She wiped her mouth with the back of her hand. She gave Rose Ann a threatening stare as she stood up. When she did, her robe fell opened to reveal her breasts. "No one can hold that stage floor like I can. It belongs to me."

"Malachi can hold it, and take it away from you," Rose Ann said, as she turned her head away from Sally's nakedness. "You only hold it because you never had any competition."

Bear walked over to Malachi. "You can sing the blues?" he asked.

"Huh? Uh...a little," Malachi said.

"He can sing more than a little, Bear. He can sing real good," Rose Ann said.

Bear stared at Malachi.

"I'm the marquee player on that stage, Bear. Without me, they'll be no Queen," Sally said.

"Go get what you need. Tonight, you gonna go on stage," Bear said.

"What? Bear, have you lost your damn mind?" Sally asked, as she turned to Bear. "What do you think you're doing?"

Bear ignored her.

Rose Ann opened the door. "Let's go to the stage," she said, as she bent in the waist while giving a sweeping hand downward toward the door. "Your audience is waiting for you, sir."

The three of them walked out of Sally's room.

When Bear closed the door behind him, they all heard the sound of glass shattering against it.

"I guess I won't be getting married this year," Bear said. "Unless you can't sing, Malachi. And, if that's true, then boy, you got an ass whipping coming, because that woman is not going to let me hear the last of this."

Ten minutes later, Malachi, wearing a bow-tie and white shirt with black pants, stood in front of thirty rowdy, drunk, and obnoxious men and women. He pulled a high stool that was several feet away toward him and sat down.

"What the hell are you doing on stage, boy?" a man wearing a dirty brown hat said. "You don't look like fat ass Sally to me."

"Yeah," shouted another man on the opposite side of the room. "I didn't spend all my money on this rot-gut moonshine to listen to you. Where's Sally? I come here to be entertained."

"Let his fine ass sing!" Screamed a woman dressed in all red who was sitting in the middle of the room between two burly looking men wearing suits. "I'll pay my money just to see him take off his shirt."

"Me too," said another woman standing several feet to the right of Malachi wearing a small cream colored blouse and matching skirt that fell to the top of her knees. "Go ahead, baby. Let Grace hear you sing, and when you finish I can take you to my room and let you hear me sing while I wrap these big, black legs around that pretty face of yours."

Her comment made the crowd erupt in laughter.

"Play with the guitar or play with yourself, boy, but

don't stand up there looking cute," the man in the dirty brown hat said. "I came here to hear some blues."

"If you don't want to play that guitar, I'll let you play with these," the woman in the red dress said, as she pulled down the front of her dress to expose her ample breasts. "They'll make a better sound than that guitar if you hit them with the right note."

Malachi watched the woman stuff her breasts back inside her dress as the crowd grew louder and rowdier.

"Malachi? Malachi?" Bear shouted over the noise from the side of the stage to the right of him. "Boy, I got faith in you. Take your time," he said. "You can do it."

Malachi sat down. He placed the guitar on his lap. He looked out into the crowd. He could see drunk faces, curious faces, and nonchalant faces all staring back at him. He knew if he'd been a shade lighter, he'd be sitting up there pale as a redneck backside. He licked his lips, and then he began to string the guitar with his pick.

"I'm a loneeeelllyyyly rider, riding on a donkey with no sense. An ornery thing that's kept my hide raw and sooooorrrreeeere. It pays me no miiimmnnndddd when I call its name. That's a painful shame… I ride this donkey strong. The donkey ignores me, and kicks me in my head when I'm wrroonnnonggg… I done rode that donkey until I can't ride no more, but if I get off, the damn donkey is going to go sleep on the floor."

Malachi played the guitar as if he'd been playing it for years. Every cord he strung appeared to come alive. His voice filled the room with a soothing blues comfort. He saw heads nodding along with the song, and feet tapping rhythmically with the cords of the song. A resounding hush fell on the room. When Malachi looked out into the crowd, he was amazed at the stares that greeted him.

"*I worked those fields… like a man… with no sense. My hands bleeding and the sweat running off my faaacceeeace. I scream at that donkey…Movvvvve, girl… cause a storms brewing. I got to get this job done… Run home to my woman and have me some fun… I ain't got no time to play… no time to stay. I got me a real woman home, donkey, and she needs her man on this hot and horny daaaayyyy.*"

Malachi hit three more cords on the guitar. Stringing them beautifully. When he finished, he smiled, for he'd made it through the song with a crowd that had never heard him sing before. To him, if they didn't like the song, he didn't care. In his heart, he gave it all he had.

No one in the crowd said a word.

The woman wearing the red dress walked up to the stage.

Malachi stared at her. He knew to expect the worse. He got off the stool and took a step back.

The woman wearing the red dress ripped off her top, and tried to climb onto the stage. "Take me, boy, I'm yours!" she shouted.

From that moment on, pandemonium erupted in the Queen. Men were slamming their glasses on the tables while striking the floor with their feet. The women began dancing around tables and grabbing any man or woman who would dance with them.

Bear rushed onto the stage, and grabbed Malachi in a strong bear hug while lifting him off the floor. "Goddamn it, boy! I've been in a lot of hole-in-the-wall joints during my days, but I have never heard anybody sing the blues the way you did," he said.

"Sing something else, boy!" shouted the man in the dirty brown hat. "Hell, you got these women in her creaming for you, son. When you got them wet, you got to keep throwing that juice on them. Sing another song!"

Bear put Malachi down. "Do you think you got another one in you, Malachi?" he asked. He stared hard into Malachi's eyes. "Do you, boy?"

"Malachi hesitated. "I think so," he said.

"No, Malachi. Do you have another real good one in you?" Bear asked. There was desperation in his voice. "Can you do it?"

"Yeah. I can do it."

Rose Ann, who was standing in the back, glanced over to see Sally still wearing her robe to the right of her.

"I told you he could sing," Rose Ann said.

Sally, a glass of moonshine in her hand, turned toward Rose Ann. "He ain't sang shit, as far as I'm concerned."

Sally walked pass Rose Ann and rolled her eyes. Rose Ann watched her. She looked at Sally's large ass. She waited until Sally had walked another few feet, and then she lifted her dress, and ran after her.

Sally smiled as men gave her room and compliments. She nodded her head in a friendly, but inviting way.

Rose Ann was nearly on top of Sally. Rose Ann stopped running as she quietly ease up behind Sally who was walking like a queen in her domain. Rose Ann was close enough behind her to raise her foot. Her foot found Sally's fat ass. Rose Ann kicked Sally so hard, that Sally's head snapped back as her body went forward. She hit the floor with her moonshine splashing all over her.

Stump was rolling over when he heard pounding on his door. He threw his feet out of bed and went to the door in his underwear. Before opening it, he glanced out the window. He saw the sun was rising. He groaned as he opened the door. Standing in the hallway was Sally wearing a revealing black lacey dress and a jug of moonshine. Her face was made up and her lips were covered succulently with red lipstick.

"Can I come in?" Sally asked.

Stump looked at her. He scratched his crotch area, and took a step aside. A crooked smile formed. Sally walked in. He closed the door, and watched Sally's hips swing from side to side as she headed for the bureau that was against the wall. She put down the jug of moonshine, and turned around.

"I heard you were back in Blackenfield, Stump," Sally said.

Stump walked to a chair in the corner and sat down. He leaned forward with his elbows on his knees. The crooked smile hadn't faded. "Sally Garber. You're still looking as fine as ever. What honor do I owe this visit?" Stump asked.

Sally smiled. She slipped free a shoulder from her strap on the dress, and stuck out a seductive hip. "Is this reason enough?" she asked. "Come on, let's have a drink."

"What would Bear think if he knew you were in my room, woman?" Stump asked. His crooked smile grew even more crooked.

"Bear can kiss my fat ass! Get some glasses and let's drink," Sally said.

"Look in that draw to the right of you. They're a little dirty, but we can work that out," Stump said. He leaned back in his chair and crossed his legs. "What do you want, Sally? I know game when I see it."

Sally reached into the draw and removed the glasses. She poured the moonshine into each glass, and then turned toward Stump.

Stump watched as Sally slipped her other shoulder strap off her shoulder. She let the top fall to her waist. Her full size 44-D breasts were exposed and inviting. Stump laughed.

"I want you, Stump," Sally said, as she stood in front of him.

"At what price?" Stump asked.

"There ain't never been a price between us, Stump, you know that."

"Get to the point, Sally," Stump said as he reached for the glass Sally offered.

"The Queen ain't been the same since you've been gone, Stump. I remember when you and Bear fought hard to get this place up and running. How many times did I patch you two up from the fights, and the stab wounds you two suffered? I lost count after the tenth time. How many nights did I watch over the both of you while you healed? Worried neither one of you would make it through the night. Countless times," Sally said.

Stump crooked smile broke into a wide grin. "You're gaming me again, Sally. Yeah, you, me, and Bear go back a long way. When this town was nothing more than a gaping hole with big boulders in the middle of the street, and tall trees everywhere. Between us and the Brown brothers, we built this town. When newcomers arrived, we staked them, then we doubled our money by charging them double interests to be paid back. Everything was one big partnership," he said.

"Then the Brown brothers wanted more," Sally said. Her face became a mask of hate, as her eyes narrowed, and she pulled her lips back to reveal her teeth as if she were some sort of animal caught in a cage. "All this was ours. We—"

"Ours, you mean, Bear's too, don't you, Sally?" Stump asked.

"Goddamn it, Stump! You act like you're still Bear's best friend or something. If Bear had seen you the next day after you'd stole the money, he would've put a bullet in your thin ass. I know because I watched him curse and damn you until the ends of earth for stealing from him for a month. So why are you sitting here acting like you care about Bear? Negro, you better think about yourself and how the Queen can be yours one day. It is yours in a sense," Sally said.

Stump shook his head. "The Queen belongs to Bear. I forfeited my half when I stole the money," Stump said.

"Negro, please. Look at those scars on your body," Sally said. She leaned forward and ran a finger down a scar on Stump's chest. "I remember the night you got that. I thought you were going to die. You had lost a lot of blood from that stab wound. Bear had carried you up the stairs to my room. When he put you in bed, he fell to the floor. He had two stab wounds in his back. Those were good days, Stump."

Stump looked down at his chest. There was a scar running from Stump's chest to the top of his navel. He looked at his stomach. The bullet wound scar gave him pain wherever it rained. He remembered the night he woke up screaming from the pain as Sally dug the bullet out. On his forearm was an indenture from the ax that nearly chopped a third of his arm off. By his abdomen there was a scar from another bullet that nearly took his life. As he reminisced, he had to admit, he had bled as much as Bear while building the Queen in their early years.

Sally stood in front of Stump looking down at him. "The past four years has been good to Bear since you left, but you can do better without him," she said, as she reached down, and pulled Stump up by the shoulders.

"How do you know all of this?" Stump asked as he looked down on her. "You become a fortune teller since I've been gone?"

Sally reached down and slipped her hands into Stump's underwear. Stump watched her.

"Bear's problem is he doesn't know when he's got a strong woman behind him. You, Stump, we always knew where our commitments lie," Sally said, as she let Stump's underwear fall to his ankles. "You know me, and I know you."

Stump's crooked smile returned as he watched Sally fall to her knees in front of him. He gasped as he felt the wetness of her mouth take in his engorged member. His crooked smile turned into a very large grin as he watched her head bob to and fro with a strong rhythm as her hands gripped his buttocks tightly.

CHAPTER EIGHT
Eyes open Wide

Two weeks later, Malachi became the Queens top billing. Bear took advantage of Malachi's good looks, and supplied him with fresh clothing every time he took the stage. He was singing four times a night, and Bear loved it as he began taking in new customers and money continued to flow from the drinks and his new occupation of running a new scheme called the numbers racket.

It was near nine o'clock in the evening when Bear looked up from his desk at hearing his door open to see Malachi walk in looking exhausted. Malachi was dressed in the same outfit he wore for his seven-thirty show an hour and a half ago. He sat down in the chair facing Bear, and unbuttoned the top of his crispy white shirt, then ran his hands through his black hair.

"You tired, boy?" Bear asked.

Malachi twisted his neck from side to side. He heard the crackling of the bones as he tried to work the kinks out. "A little," he said.

Bear put down the pencil. He leaned back in his chair, entwining his fingers over his stomach. "You should be. Boy, I ain't seen this much money since my days as a hot driver for some moonshine runners I used to work for as a kid. And it's my money, goddamn it! I knew when I first saw you that you'd bring me luck. Look at this place. Money is coming in from everywhere," Bear said.

"Yeah, and I'm tired," Malachi said.

"You said that already. What is it? You are gaming for some extra money?" Bear asked. He reached into the draw and pulled out a roll of twenty-dollar bills. Peeling a few from the roll, he put them on the desk and slid them over toward Malachi. "A little motivation to get rid of any rabbit fever you might have in the future."

Malachi smiled. He slid the money back to Bear. "It's all right. You do real good by me and my sister," he said. "We're okay. I've been watching Cotton, though. He's been running around here the past few days with a notepad and a pencil taking down people's numbers and taking money from them after he gives them a receipt. What's going on with that?"

Bear's eye grew bright. He picked up the twenty-dollar bills and placed them back in the pile. He put the money back in the draw. "Right. Stump came to me—"

"Stump?" Malachi said. "The same Stump who made you lose your eye?"

"Uh…Yeah. Well, let me clear something up about that eye business. Stump really didn't take my eye. We got into a fight one night in a town called…Hell; I don't even remember the name of that piss hole. Anyway, someone threw a bottle in the middle of the fight, and the shattered glass hit me in the eye. It became infected weeks later. During the passing of the weeks, I kept getting these headaches, and my good eye would become real blurry. My bad eye had become closed and swollen and had formed puss around it. It never stopped draining. Stump took me to a doctor who didn't know squat, but he did know that my eye had reached a point where it couldn't be saved. It had to be taken out or else I would go blind. The doctor gave Stump a medical book. For three days Stump read that book, and then one night we were out drinking. I mean, Malachi, I ain't never been that drunk before in my life. I was feeling no pain. The next morning I woke up with this patch on my eye, and no more headaches," Bear said.

"You trust him?" Malachi asked.

"Let me finish, boy. How old are you now?" Bear asked.

"Seventeen."

"Seventeen? When I was seventeen I was living on the streets in Alabama. Trying to find food wherever I could. In the wintertime I used to put plastic in my worn shoes to keep my feet warm because I didn't have any socks at the time. I lived at the homes of friend to friend until they got tired of me bumming from them and wouldn't let me in anymore. I ain't never had real family until Stump came along. We think alike. Yeah, he hurt me when he ran out on me four years ago with the money we'd been saving, but he stood back to back with me when I needed him during hard times. Can I forgive him? Yeah. Do I trust him? Hell no. Not one hundred percent and he know it. With this number racket he brought to me, it's a no risk and all gain situation. It's simple. Let's say a person plays their three digit number. That number can go straight, box, split, or combination. If a player puts a nickel on straight, a penny on box, a penny or dime on splitting or a nickel on combination for that number I win either way. Why? Because you can only win it one way. You see the money the person is playing for his number is also the money that he or she is going to be paid with if they win. Boy, I am a winner all around. It's Peter paying Paul, and I ain't paying anything at all."

"How does Stump get his share from this?" Malachi asked.

"That's the part I saved for last. Stump is the House," Bear said. He slammed his large hand down on the desk and started laughing.

"The House?" Malachi asked.

"Uh-huh. Being that I didn't trust the sonofabitch, he decided to put three hundred dollars up front to pay out if anyone hits. So, for the past two weeks, I've been raking in the dollars that didn't cost me one red cent," Bear said.

"I don't know, Bear. Money like that sounds too easy."

"Yeah, that's why I haven't returned Stump's three hundred dollars yet. The dirty bastard," Bear said. "I may have to hire me another worker to help out Cotton with taking numbers."

Malachi nodded. "How do you get the numbers?"

Bear's eyes became bright. He leaned forward over the desk and whispered. "The horses. You see, when the racehorses are on the track, there are certain times in which Cotton stops taking the people numbers. By the time the first race is over, that's the first number out. By the time the second race ends that's the second number. When the third race ends that's the third number. That's it. You now have all three numbers for that morning. The afternoon and the evening numbers run the same way," Bear said.

"Cotton's been looking clean and sober lately," Malachi said.

"Yeah, I've been on top of his nasty ass. I told him the next time I catch him unclean and walking around here smelling like garbage; I was going to fire his butt. You sure you don't need no money?" Bear asked.

"You are coming to the show tonight?" Malachi asked, as he stood up.

"Damn right. Hey, I took Rose Ann out of the rooms and made her my accountant."

"I know. She told me this morning," Malachi said. He walked to the door.

"I didn't know she knew numbers the way she does," Bear said.

"A very wise and good woman we know taught her," Malachi said.

"Hell, I didn't take her out of the rooms because she was doing badly; I took her out because she had another incident with a customer the other day. You two are like night and day," Bear said.

"I'll see you tonight," Malachi said. He was laughing as he closed the door behind him.

Malachi had finished the second song when he looked up and saw three nicely dressed men walk in. They were all wearing overcoats of mohair in different colors with impressive suits underneath. Malachi watched them as they headed to the back of the room and stood against the wall.

Malachi came off the stage and walked to his table in the far right corner of the room. He watched Sally take the stage in a white, beaded sequined dress with a fox fur slung around her shoulders. The band began playing her a beat as she walked around the microphone very slowly before grabbing it, and starting to sing.

"That wild woman knows how to bring in a show," Rose Ann said.

Malachi turned around to see his sister standing behind him. He pulled out a chair for her. "Where you been?" he asked.

Rose Ann sat down. "Counting Bear's money, and learning how to do the tally for the number racket he's got going," she said, as she sat down.

Malachi turned toward his sister. "How is that coming along? It sounds stupid to me."

Rose Ann placed her elbow on the table, and rubbed her right thumb and index finger together. "A lot of money is coming in from that, Malachi. A lot of money," she said. She winked her eye to emphasize her point. "Can't you tell by watching Bear? The man is smiling from ear to ear. I heard your last song. Nice. One girl came up to me and asked me if I could tell you she wanted to say hello."

"Another nightwalker?" Malachi asked.

Rose Ann shrugged. "She doesn't look like one. She's over there," Rose Ann said as she tossed her head to the left. "The one wearing that gray dress."

Malachi glanced over his sister's shoulder. "The one that looks like she's getting ready to run?" he asked.

"Uh-huh. If you asked me, I don't know why she wants to meet you," she said, sticking out her tongue. "You look like a bubble fish to me."

Malachi smiled. He watched Sally do her number, and then she hurried off the stage. The band played some music until it was his time to do his next show.

"That's because you're his sister," Bear said. He pulled out a chair and sat down at the table. "Good song, boy." He leaned forward and lowered his voice. "Do you see those three men back there in the matching overcoats?"

Malachi looked at Bear quizzically. "Why are you whispering? As loud as this joint is, no one hear us," he said. "Yeah, I saw them when they came in. Who are they?"

"The Brown brothers," Bear said. "The one in the middle is Chester. He's the oldest, and the one who has the brains out of that cutthroat outfit. The one to the left of him is Sylvester. He has the muscles when something important has to be done today, and the smallest of the three, as well as the most vicious one, is called Lester. You never take your eyes off Lester if you are in a room with him, Malachi. Never. That bastard will gut you as fast as he'd blink."

"Why are they here?" Rose Ann asked. "I've never seen them in here before."

Malachi looked at his sister. She looked a little frightened. "Its okay, Rose. They want to hear me sing the blues," he said.

Bear stared at Malachi. "Yeah, girl, your brother's right. Anyway, we have an open door policy. They can come to the Queen and I can come to their place, the Goldspot, whenever I like. I'm going to go over and see what they want." Bear winked at Malachi, as he stood up. "You better get ready for your next show."

"All right," Malachi said.

Bear leaned down and whispered in Malachi's ear. "In my room in the closet, underneath a pile of books, is a bunch of loose boards," he said. He placed a key in Malachi's hand. "Remember that."

Malachi stood up while pocketing the key. He watched as Bear made his way toward the Brown brothers. He was laughing and shaking customer's hands as he zigzagged through the crowd. Malachi headed to the stage to do his next number.

"You want me to stay?" Rose Ann asked.

"Naw. Go tell your friend I'll see her after the show," Malachi said.

"When did she become my friend?" Rose Ann asked.

"When you told her I was your brother," Malachi said.

By the time Malachi reached the stage, he saw that Bear and the Brown brothers were gone. He did see Stump hurrying to the back of the room where Bear's office was at and probably where Bear had taken the Brown brothers. Malachi gave his attention to the microphone and the audience.

"I see ya'll came here tonight to listen to me sing the blues," Malachi began. "Ain't nothing like a good song, do ya'll agree?"

The audience that wasn't drunk shouted out their agreement. The other half, Malachi noticed, were mumbling and nodding their heads to whatever their drunken ears picked up. Malachi smiled.

"I have this new song I want ya'll to hear. It's a tale about some tail," Malachi said.

The audience started laughing.

"I see ya'll like that," Malachi said. "If that's the case—"

Three gunshots rang out from the back of Bear's office.

Malachi watched as the Brown brothers, although, not actually running, weren't taking their time either seconds after the gunshots went off, as they headed for the front door. Malachi leaped from the stage and ran toward the back to Bear's office.

When Malachi exploded through Bear's door two minutes later, he found Stump standing a few feet from Bear's body that lay on the floor. He saw blood forming under his body. He stepped further into the room. Stump looked at Malachi. He was holding Bear's .38 revolver.

"It's not what you think, Malachi," Stump said, as he dropped the gun. "Let me explain, boy."

Malachi heard footsteps behind him. He knew it was some of the audience trying to get a look at what was going on. He looked again at Bear's unmoving body as blood continued to flow freely. Biting down hard on his teeth, he attacked Stump.

Stump, being a worldly man, stepped to the side as Malachi charged him. He was thin, but Stump knew how to fight. As Malachi approached, he threw his right fist into the side of Malachi's head. Surprising him and knocking him to the floor. As he was about to pick Malachi up, a crowd of onlookers rushed him and began pummeling him with fists and feet. Before he knew it, Stump was under a pile of fifteen bodies all trying to tear him apart.

Two hours later, Stump, his face swollen and dried blood on the corner of his lips, sat tied up in a chair under the intimidating eyes of the men and women who'd beaten him. Malachi stared at him as Sheriff Hays walked back and forth creating a scenario of what took place.

"Now you boys are telling me," Sheriff Hays began, looking at all the faces staring back at him. "That Stump shot Bear or that Stump along with the Brown brothers shot Bear, then the Brown brothers hurried on out of here like they'd seen the coming of the Lord. Now, don't get me wrong. I know Stump, Bear and the Brown brothers for a mighty long time. I can remember when they first came to this little old town called Blackenfield. Wasn't anything here. Anyways, ain't nobody actually witness Stump kill Bear, nor did anyone actually see the Brown brothers kill Bear. Right?"

Malachi stared at the dirty, blond hair sheriff. His fat belly hung over his gun belt and he continuously chewed on the tobacco that was in his rotten mouth with tarnished teeth. Malachi felt disgusted at what he was hearing.

"I do know there's been an assault on Stump. And all ya'll admitted to beating him up. What I don't know for sure is who killed Bear. No one saw Stump pull the trigger or the Brown brothers. What am I suppose to do? I'm the sheriff for both these towns, but I let you darkies do what you want as long as it's within the confines of the law, and ain't disturbing us other white folk," Sheriff Hays said.

"But Sheriff Hays," Malachi began. Rose Ann was sitting beside him, and he could hear her crying. "I saw Stump with Bear's gun in his hand. I don't mean to tell you how to—"

"That's right, boy. You don't ever want to tell me what or how to do my job. As a white peace officer that kind of disrespect would offend my sensitive side. I've been doing this before you were born. What's your name?" Sheriff Hays asked.

"Malachi—"

"So you're the mulatto who's been singing all sweetly to these here darkie girls. Hmm. You look like you got you some white in you. Is your father a white man?" Sheriff Hays asked.

Malachi stared at him. He gripped the arms of the chair he was sitting in so hard, that his knuckles had turned white. He felt Rose Ann gently touch his arm. He calmed down.

"You niggers got to realize you ain't got a sheriff. You make up your own laws in Blackenfield and when something happens, you call me. I can't do anything to Stump or the Brown brothers. Bear is dead. Ya'll gonna have to move on and forget about who killed him, because can't nobody point a finger at the killer. I suggest you let Stump go because if you don't I'm going to have to arrest somebody for unlawful imprisonment of his person as well as the fact that he was assaulted," Sheriff Hays said.

No one moved.

Sheriff Hays walked over to Malachi. "Did you hear what I said?" he asked. He tilted his beige Stetson hat back as he stared at him. "Do I have to repeat myself?"

Malachi looked at Cotton. He nodded at him.

Cotton walked over to Stump and began untying the ropes.

"I have a feeling, Malachi, you and I are going to have us a real misunderstanding one day," Sheriff Hays said. He leaned toward Malachi lowering his voice. "And if that day were to come anytime soon, nigger, I'm going to peel that half white, half Negro skin off you, and then I'm going to set your black ass on fire at the cross."

Malachi stared at him. His eyes narrowed to two angry slits. He felt Rose Ann squeeze his bicep. He leaned back in his chair. Exhaling very slowly.

"Your darkie girlfriend is pretty," Sheriff Hays said. "You take care of her now, ya hear."

"She's my sister," Malachi whispered through clenched teeth.

"What?"

"She's my sister," Malachi repeated, as he defiantly stared into Sheriff Hays' blue eyes.

"Your sister? Nigger, please don't take me for a fool," Sheriff Hays said as he stood back up. "Ya'll two don't look nothing alike at all. Anyway, bury Bear. If I remember, I'll send over some flowers for his funeral."

When Sheriff Hays turned around to address the crowd, Stump walked by and out of the door. Malachi followed his every step.

"Listen. Bear is dead. I'm sorry the boy is gone, but life goes on. Bury your dead, and think about the living," Sheriff Hays said. "Ya'll take care."

Sheriff Hays walked toward the door. He hitched up his gun belt and walked out.

Before the door had closed, Malachi was up and running toward Bear's office. There was a dark jacket on the back of a chair that he passed. He grabbed it without breaking his stride.

"Cotton, get this place jumping and give everyone a free drink," Malachi shouted as he continued to head toward the back.

When he entered Bear's room, Malachi quickly removed his white shirt. He dropped it to the floor and put on the black jacket he'd worn earlier to assist him in merging with the shadows. He moved toward the window. He opened it, and climbed out.

Sheriff Hays walked down the street spitting out chewing tobacco. He walked for twenty minutes enjoying the cool night. The men and women he passed on the street would walk to the other side when they saw him. He walked another ten minutes before he reached the barn he'd been told to come to. If he'd taken the time to look behind him, he might've seen the darting shadow that followed him in the darkness.

Closing the barn door behind him, Sheriff Hays looked around. "Where the hell are you?" he shouted.

A snickering sound came from the darkness.

"Get your ass out here," Sheriff Hays said, as he stared into the corners and other parts of the barn. "I can't be on this side of town all night."

"We know," Chester Brown said. He stepped out of the corner followed by his two brothers. He lit a lantern. "We appreciate you taking care of things with Stump."

"Hell, it doesn't make me any difference. One nigger killing another is one less nigger for me and my lodge brothers to lynch. Where's my money?" Sheriff Hays asked.

Lester Brown, still snickering, walked up to the sheriff and gave him a handful of money.

"Now what?" Sheriff Hays asked, as he counted the money.

"We take control of the Queen," Sylvester Brown said.

"Like hell you will. That nigger Malachi ain't going to let you boys get your hands on the Queen," Sheriff Hays said. He stuffed the money in his front pocket. "It's something about that nigger that makes a man want to think before he leaps when it comes to him. He has old man eyes."

"He's young. He can't handle the Queen," Chester said. He removed his wool hat to reveal a shining baldhead. "We can handle anything and anybody that comes into Blackenfield."

A sound of creaking boards from the barn's roof made everyone stop talking.

"What was that?" Sylvester asked.

Sheriff Hays shrugged. "The wind hitting old wood," he said.

No one took the time to look closely at the ceiling. If they had, they would've seen an eye looking through a small hole at them.

CHAPTER NINE

A new King for the Queen

The passing of the four months since Bear's death had been slow and difficult for Malachi. He'd decided to bury Bear in the back of the Queen with a large headstone. It was his way of keeping him near. At that moment he was sitting behind Bear's desk in his office reading the papers he'd found in Bear's closet the night he died. He'd read them so many times that he could now read them word by word without looking at them. It was Bear's will, and he'd made Malachi the beneficiary of the Queen and everything that went with it. At first, Malachi was dumbfounded as to what to do and who to rely on in running the Queen with the ongoing moonshine still, the gambling, and the number racket. But, to his surprise, Cotton had become reliable for him. He knew about it all, and had been teaching Malachi.

Malachi folded the will, and walked to the closet. He opened the closet. Bending down, he removed the floorboards, and pulled out the medium size locker with the large padlock. He reached inside his pocket and pulled out a set of keys. He opened the padlock. He smiled when he saw the contents. There were ten thousand dollars in the locker in hundred dollar bills. He nearly had a heart attack when he saw the money. He knew, though, he needed another place to hide the money and was working on something at the moment with Cotton.

After putting everything away, Malachi stood up. He stretched his body, and yawned. It was nearly twelve o'clock and he was exhausted. He walked back to the desk. As he pulled out the chair to sit down, the office door opened and Sheriff Hays walked in.

"How's it going, boy?" Sheriff Hays asked.

Malachi looked at the white sheriff with contempt. Sheriff Hays sat down in the chair in front of the desk...

"Slow, but okay," Malachi said. "You're here for your monthly pickup?"

"Goddamn right, boy," Sheriff Hays said, as he chewed on the tobacco. "I need to ask you something, boy. A couple of my lodge members were wondering if they—now these are their words, not mine—could invest in that number racket thing you got going with the niggers." Sheriff Hays leaned back in his chair and raised his hands outward as if he were about to ward off a blow. "Me, I told them that kind of thing ain't no good for us white folk, but they keep hounding me. What do you think?" He put his hands down.

Malachi looked at the sheriff. He had come to despise

the man. He examined the dingy white shirt with its soiled collar, and the sheriff's constant, annoying chewing of the tobacco. Why had he ever decided to deal with the bastard?

"You're right, Sheriff Hays. Your lodge brothers wouldn't want to get involve with a bunch of Negroes who can't do anything right. They'll just lose their money," Malachi said, as he opened the desk draw and removed a fifty-dollar bill. He pushed it toward him. "We appreciate you taking care of things for us, Sheriff."

Sheriff Hays looked at the money. He smiled as he reached for it. He placed it in his shirt pocket. "Well, I told them that you would say something like that. You know how you Negroes are. Ya'll like to keep things close to the breast. But since this is money, my lodge brothers are thinking of a bigger picture."

Malachi placed his elbows on the table while cupping his face in his hands. "Yeah, I can see where they're coming from. Since the money ain't black, they can take it and not feel...dirty," he said, and then smiled.

"Huh? Well, yeah," Sheriff Hays said.

Malachi nodded.

Sheriff Hays stood up. "For a young buck, you act mighty old," he said. He walked to the door. "I'll be seeing you next month."

Malachi watched as he walked out the door. When it was closed, he grabbed the paper holder, which was a red rock, and threw it at the door. He hated Sheriff Hays, but knew there was nothing he could do about him. Malachi knew Sheriff Hays was working with the Brown brothers and that infuriated him.

At that moment, he now knew why Bear thought

the way he did. He opened the desk draw and reached inside for a twenty-dollar bill. He needed to pay one of the girls. Beside the money, he saw the gun. Bear's .38 revolver lying menacingly in the back of the draw. He'd never fired a gun before, and he didn't know why he kept it. Maybe it was a reminder that it was Bear's, and gave him comfort if anything else, he thought. Malachi stood up. It was time to check out the place to see how things were running. He had no other person to emulate but Bear. Every action he did, he did it because that's the way Bear did it.

Ten minutes later Malachi was walking through the gambling den. Things were being setup for the night. He saw dice tables being cleaned as well as a roulette wheel being greased. He saw Monty. A fast talking medium size man who dressed well while creating his illusion of a three-card flip game standing in the far left corner. He'd allowed him to set up his table two weeks ago for a percentage of his winnings. He walked over to him.

"Hey, Monty," Malachi said.

Monty nodded. His concentration was on the three cards that were faced down on the table. He was dexterously flipping them with both hands one over the other. From time to time he would show Malachi the red queen, and the two black queens. Monty's fingertips were holding each card. Malachi was amazed at how Monty's fast hands moved.

"Find the card, boss, and win two dollars for one dollar," Monty said as he flipped the last card down. He spread his arms open to emphasize his point. "Find the red queen and I'll give you two dollars. But if you pick the black queen, you lose."

Malachi looked at the three cards faced down. The middle card seemed to be calling him. He tentatively reached for it, but then stopped as the sight of the card on the right of him caught his eye.

"If you wait too long, you wrong, boss," Monty said. He laughed at the perplex expression that filled Malachi's face. "The card ain't going to bite you. Pick one."

Malachi looked at him. "Naw, I'll pass on this one. You've won too much of my money lately," he said.

Monty laughter continued as he watched Malachi walk away.

Malachi headed toward Cotton who was standing behind the bar. Malachi had to admit, over the past few months, Cotton had changed. He was wearing fresh clothing everyday, and he smelled clean.

"That bastard, Three Card Monty. He won twelve dollars from me in an hour," Cotton said as Malachi approached. "I tell you, Malachi, those goddamn cards are bewitched. Can't any man do what he does with those three cards. And it ain't like I don't flip them all over after I pick the wrong one to make sure he ain't playing with them all black. But, dammit, that red queen is always there. Sally came and took the rest of her clothing."

"Good. Was Stump with her?" Malachi asked.

"He stayed outside," Cotton said.

"I'm going to the hotel to see Rose Ann. You'll be all right?"

"I've been doing this for a while, remember?" Cotton said, as he removed a glass, and cleaned it with the rag in his hand. "How are you coming along?"

"Okay," Malachi said.

"Your birthday is next week. What will that make you, eighteen?" Cotton asked.

"Uh-huh." Malachi looked at Cotton. "My sister told you that didn't she?"

"She told everybody," Cotton said, as he put down the clean glass and picked up a dirty one and began wiping it. "Your sister is…thoughtful."

Malachi shook his head. "I'll see you later," he said.

Stump lay in bed. He stared up at the ceiling. Sally walked back and forth taking clothing from the bed and putting them in the drawer across the room.

"Look, baby. How about if I wear this tonight when I come to bed," Sally said.

Stump didn't look. "That would be real nice," he said.

"Motherfucker, you didn't even look at the thing!" Sally snapped as she stood at the foot of the bed staring at Stump while holding the nightdress. "Your mind is wondering too damn much. Get over whatever you're going through. The Brown brothers have given you a job, and I'm singing here as the main event. So, what else could you want?"

Stump continued to stare at the ceiling.

Sally climbed on the bed, and slowly crawled up to him. She lay on his chest. "The Brown brothers have been good to us since Malachi kicked us out of the Queen," she said. She played in stump's kinky hair that was on his chest. "You're depress about Bear? Don't be. Bear wasn't shit anyway!" she snapped.

Stump eyes slowly shifted from the ceiling to Sally.

"Don't lose any sleep over that cheap bastard," Sally

said. "I never did like his little dick ass, anyway. Only reason I was giving him some of this nookie was because it made things easier for me. You've always been the man in my heart, Stump."

In one swift motion, Stump rolled to his left, throwing his entire body against Sally as he sat up. Sally, caught off guard by the move, rolled off Stump and landed hard on the floor.

Stump looked down at her as he planted his feet on the floor. "Bitch, any man that gives you what you want is your man," he said. "I'm your man now because that's what you're dealing with now. If you don't like whatever suites your fancy, you get rid of it. That's who you are. A conniving hoe who takes what she wants, and don't care about anyone else," Stump said.

Sally sat on her butt staring up at Stump. "That's not true. You mean the world to me, Stump. Ain't nothing I wouldn't do for you," she said.

"Yeah? We'll see," Stump said. He stood up. Stepped over Sally, and walked to the chair that had his shirt. He grabbed it and walked to the door.

"Where you going, baby?" Sally asked.

"I need some air. The room is getting stuffy, and it's starting to stink," Stump answered, as he opened the door and stepped out.

"How long you gonna be gone?" Sally asked.

Stump answered her by slamming the door.

By the time Stump reached outside, his mind had cleared. He stood by the pole and watched the people making there way to either the Queen or the Goldspot as the evening began to settle. He reached into his right pants pocket and removed his smoking tobacco pouch.

He reached inside and pulled out several rolling paper sheets. As he folded the paper vertically down the middle, he then poured smoking tobacco into the paper sheets. When he felt the tobacco was enough, he put the drawstring of the pouch in his mouth and pulled on it. Closing the top. He put it into his pocket. With both hands free, he began rolling his cigarette. When it was complete, he stuck it in his mouth, and then lit it.

Standing there smoking his cigarette, he thought about forgetting everything and heading back on the road. He'd never been a person to stay in one place for too long. Bear knew that about him, but still befriended him. He exhaled.

"My brothers want to talk to you."

Stump turned to the side of him. Standing below his shoulder was Lester Brown.

"Why?" Stump asked.

"Don't know," Lester said, as he started snickering. "I'm just the messenger."

Stump turned his attention back to the street. "And you're a good one," he said.

Lester stopped snickering. "What does mean?" he asked. He stepped closer to Stump. His face nearly touching Stump's shoulder as he looked up at him.

"Mean? It doesn't mean anything," Stump said. He flicked his half smoked cigarette out into the street. "Let's go see what your big brothers want."

Lester stepped aside as Stump walked pass him and back into the Goldspot.

"That boy has a mind like a door trap," Chester said. He was sitting at his large, red colored, mahogany desk as Sylvester stood beside him. "We need to get in on that number racket Malachi got going. He's bringing in more money than us. If this keeps up, in three or four years, the boy could eventually buy us out."

"Naw. That boy ain't got smarts like that. With Cotton giving him a hand and a few others, he's keeping the Queen floating, but that's about all," Sylvester said. "Don't give him more than he's worth, Chester."

"We can buy him out," Chester said.

Sylvester shook his head.

"We can ask him if he wants to become partners," Chester said.

Sylvester shook his head.

"Then what?" Chester asked.

Sylvester stared at him.

Chester nodded. "Yeah, those thoughts might be true. It might be our only option. But he's only a kid," he said.

"They grow up to become men, and then you're confronted with a manly situation," Sylvester said.

Chester put a hand to his mouth and closed his eyes.

The door opened and Stump and Lester walked into the office.

Chester opened his eyes. "How man times have I told you to knock, Lester?" he asked. He looked at his brother, and shook his head.

"All the time," Lester said. He continued to walk into the room followed by Stump.

"Do you listen?" Chester asked.

"All the time," Lester replied. He found a chair in the corner and sat down. Crossing his arms over his chest, he smiled at his brother.

Chester shook his head. He gave his attention to Stump. "Come on in and sit down, Stump. You want something to drink?" he asked.

Stump looked around the nicely furnished office. He was impressed by the arrangement of furniture and its coloring of beige, brown and black.

"No. I'm okay," Stump said. There was a couch against the wall facing Chester's desk. He sat down.

"You're working out nicely handling the management duties for the Goldspot," Chester said. "What we need to know is how does that number racket work that Malachi is running over there at the Queen?"

Stump leaned back into the comfort of the couch. He crossed one leg over the other. "I wished I knew. He looks like he's doing mighty swell over there," he said.

"I thought it was you who introduced that number game to Bear," Sylvester said.

"Me? Nope," Stump said. He turned his hand around and began examining his nails. "I don't know anything about that."

"That's not what Sally told us," Chester said.

Stump uncrossed his legs. He rubbed his chin and looked upward. "The only thing Sally knows how to do is give a man some good head. You should know about that one, Chester. Other than that, she's talking out of the side of her neck," Stump said. He put his hand on his thigh.

Chester gave Stump an ominous stare while rubbing his bald head.

Lester began snickering.

"Cut that bullshit out, Lester!" Chester snapped.

"Stump, that situation we got you out of with Sheriff Hays cost us a piece of money, but, hey, friends are—"

"Friends? When did we become friends, Chester?" Stump asked.

Sylvester stepped out from behind the desk. He walked to the front of it and sat down on its edge. "Motherfucker, we ain't here to play games with you. We brought you into our fold because we know you and Bear were tight." He began. "Now, if we really wanted to hang your skinny ass for killing Bear, we would've—"

"Killing Bear? I saw the three of you running out of his office between the gunshots. So, if anything, I figure one of the three of you killed Bear," Stump said.

Sylvester took two quick strides toward Stump. He grabbed him by the shirt collar and lifted him in the air.

"You want to play games?" Sylvester asked. "I'll break your thin ass in half, and then from those two halves, I'll break some more of you."

Stump felt Sylvester's hot breath in his face. He stared into his black eyes, and decided that maybe he'd went a little too far in provoking him.

"All right, Sylvester. Maybe my mouth got ahead of my brain. I apologize," Stump said. He heard Lester's snickering become louder. "We can talk about anything. Relax."

Sylvester looked at him. He lowered him back onto the couch. Stump watched as Sylvester walked back to the desk as he straightened out his collar.

"Now, let's start from the beginning. How does Malachi do that number racket thing?" Chester asked.

Stump stared at Chester. He pierced his lips together as if thinking. "I really don't know, Chester, but give me some time to run around, and I could find the answer for you," Stump said.

"How you gonna do that?" Sylvester asked. "Everybody in this town wants to see you either hung from a tree, or shot dead and left you in the street."

"I'll go ask Malachi," Stump said.

Silence filled the room.

Seconds went by and no one said anything.

"Goddamn, this Negro is a fool!" Sylvester shouted.

Lester erupted with laughter.

Chester stared at Stump. "Man, if they catch you in the Queen, your ass is dead," he said.

"Well, they won't catch me," Stump said.

"How are you gonna make Malachi tell you anything?" Sylvester asked.

"I'll ask him," Stump said. He smiled.

Malachi was standing behind the clerk counter waiting for his sister to return from the bathroom when he heard the front door open. He looked up to see a yellow man come shuffling in carrying a bundle of clothing. The bright red kimono made Malachi stare hard at him. The man's baldhead wasn't as surprising as the long, white braid that fell to the center of his back.

"How can I help you?" Malachi asked cautiously.

"I...bring...clothes,"

Malachi could tell by his words that he'd just learned how to speak English. "Who are you bringing clothes to?" he asked.

"Room 252."

"Room 252? Is that what you said?" Malachi asked.

"Yes."

Malachi stared at the man. He then looked down at the sign-in book to see who was in the room. "Oh, Mr. Grant is in that room. Leave the clothes and I'll make sure he gets them."

"No leave. Give myself."

Malachi stared at him. "Uh…What is your…race?" he asked. He looked around to make sure no one heard him ask the embarrassing question.

"I am Chinese."

"Chinese? Where is that?" Malachi asked.

"It is in China. Far away. Over many, many miles of water," the yellow man said.

"What is your name?" Malachi asked.

The man raised his chin. "I am called Kai-Chang."

"Kai-Chang? What kind of name is that?"

Kai-Chang looked at him. "What is your name?" he asked.

"My name is Malachi Moon."

Kai-Chang nodded. He raised his chin a little higher. "What kind of name is that?" he asked.

Malachi laughed. "Yeah, you're right." He looked at Kai-Chang hard. The man's silk kimono fell down to his feet. On his feet were a pair of black slippers with thick black soles. "How would you like to work for me, Kai-Chang?"

"I have job already. Why I leave from one job washing clothes to another job washing clothes?" Kai-Chang asked.

"No, you wouldn't be washing clothes for me," Malachi said.

"What I do for you?" Kai-Chang asked.

"You'd be like my…watcher," Malachi said.

"Watcher? What does a watcher do?" Kai-Chang asked. His slanted eyes became even more slanted as he gave Malachi a dubious stare.

"You keep your eyes open for me. Tell me when you hear things that might hurt me," Malachi said.

"Like a bodyguard?" Kai-Chang asked.

"Bodyguard? Uh…I guess."

"How much you pay?" Kai-Chang asked.

Malachi smiled. "How much do you get washing clothes?" he asked.

"I make two dollars and seventy-five cents a week," Kai-Chang said.

"I'll give you twenty-five dollars a week," Malachi said.

"Where do I sleep?"

"I'll give you a room in the hotel," Malachi said. "If you need time to think—"

Kai-Chang stopped Malachi by holding up his hand in front of Malachi's face. "I shall return with my things," he said.

Kai-Chang dropped the bundle of clothes he'd been carrying on the counter, and turned around and headed for the door. Both of his hands were stuck in the sleeves of his kimono.

"What about your delivery, Kai-Chang?" Malachi asked.

"Kai-Chang no longer works for the imbecile name Tong. He has shown Kai-Chang no respect since Kai-Chang come to this country two years ago. So, for his imprudence, Kai-Chang shall not complete his delivery. Kai-Chang now works for Mala."

Malachi watched Kai-Chang walk out the door. He

glanced at the bundle of clothing. He'd get someone to take the clothing up to room 252, he told himself.

"Who's Mala?" Malachi shouted after Kai-Chang.

The next morning, Malachi awoke to the sounds of a bird in his room. He sat up in bed to find Kai-Chang sitting in the middle of the floor on a rug with his legs crossed and his hands snuggly concealed inside the sleeves of his brown silk kimono.

Malachi wiped the sleepy crust from his eyes as he tried to adjust his vision. He looked at the window and saw that the sun was about to rise.

"Kai-Chang, how did you get into my room?" he asked.

Kai-Chang continued to hum.

Malachi watched him.

What appeared to be an hour of humming turned into thirty minutes of impatience as well. The fact that he was listening to Kai-Chang hum had put him to sleep again.

"Mala? Mala?" Kai-Chang said.

Malachi opened his eyes to see Kai-Chang standing above him. He sat up on his elbows.

"Mala, Kai-Chang has finished his morning prayer."

"That's what that was?" Malachi asked with a sleepy voice. "How did you get in here?"

Kai-Chang pointed to the door.

"I locked my door before I went to sleep," Malachi said.

"Kai-Chang has his ways," he said.

"Why are you here, Kai-Chang?" Malachi asked.

"I come to start work."

"Okay, but it's too early," Malachi said. He dropped

back down on the bed, and pulled the sheet over his head. "In a few hours we'll start working."

The sheet was yanked off his head.

"Kai-Chang wants to know if you pay him in American money?" Kai-Chang asked.

Malachi sat up on his elbows. He yawned. He looked at Kai-Chang. He reached for the sheet that was now at the end of the bed. He felt embarrassed with no clothes on except his underwear. "Of course. What else could I pay you with?" he asked. With the sheet in his hand, he lies back down. "You could've waited until later in the day to ask me that, Kai-Chang."

"Kai-Chang does not want to be paid with yen."

"With Yen? Who is Yen?" Malachi asked. "I don't even know Yen. I'm going to pay you alone. I don't need another person. So tell Yen to go somewhere else for a job."

Kai-Chang looked from left to the right. He arched his left eyebrow, and went and sat down on his rug.

Five hours later, Malachi awoke to find Kai-Chang sitting in the same spot.

"I thought I was dreaming," Malachi said as he sat up. He threw his feet out of bed. "You've been sitting in that same spot since I went to sleep?"

Kai-Chang's eyes were closed. He nodded. His hands were in the sleeves of his kimono.

"Don't your legs hurt?" Malachi asked.

"No."

Malachi stood up. "Today, I'll show you what you have to do around the Queen," he said. "First, where are your things?" Kai-Chang pointed to a bundle in the corner. "That's all? Well, don't worry. I'll buy you some clothes."

Malachi walked passed Kai-Chang. He stopped and looked down at him.

"How did you get in my room, Kai-Chang?"

"Kai-Chang has his ways."

Malachi was going to pursue the conversation but let it go when Kai-Chang began to hum again.

CHAPTER TEN
Enemies and Friends

The morning sun rose and fell on the Queen that was very busy. It was a Friday morning, and everyone was preparing for the night, because that's when people would come out to play. Malachi and Kai-Chang were walking down the street. They were headed to the general store when Malachi saw the young lady that Rose Ann had said wanted to talk to him a few. She was walking on the other side of the street. He was about to go say hello to her when he saw Chester and Sylvester walking toward him.

"The two men walking toward us are not really friendly, Kai-Chang, so be on your toes," Malachi said.

"Are they your enemies?" Kai-Chang asked.

"Neither enemy nor friend. They're in between," Malachi said.

Chester and Sylvester walked up to Malachi. Malachi stopped.

"How's the Queen, boy?" Chester asked. He held eye contact with him.

"Okay. How's the Goldspot?" Malachi asked. He really didn't want to say anything to the Brown brothers, but he knew if he didn't it would only create more friction, and, he admitted, he was a little frighten of them. Yet he knew if they suspected it, they would come at him hard. He had to hold face. "How's Stump?"

"Stump is coming along fine," Sylvester said. He walked slowly around Malachi. "He's making money for the Goldspot."

"Malachi," Chester said. He placed an arm around Malachi's shoulder and turned him around to start walking back the way he and Kai-Chang had just come from. "We need to have a talk about us joining up and becoming partners with that numbers racket thing you got going."

Malachi walked with Chester apprehensively. He was tensed as he tried to slip from under Chester's vise-like grip. He didn't know if the man was trying to pull him in an alley and stick a knife in his gut.

"Yeah, boy, we think your coming into partnership with us will make the Goldspot more attractive," Sylvester said, as he walked on the other side of Malachi. "As well as the Queen."

Malachi turned to see if Kai-Chang was beside him. To his dismay, Kai-Chang was still standing where he'd left him with his hands in the sleeves of his kimono. And, to Malachi's amazement, he could've sworn he saw Kai-Chang whistling as he watched them. Malachi felt a sense of dread engulf his body. His breathing became labored. His legs went weak and he felt his bladder become heavy.

"Stump said it was Bear who came up with that number racket, and, if that's true, of course Bear explained everything to you," Chester said. "How else could you be still running it so smoothly?"

Malachi looked at Chester. "Stump told you that?" he asked.

"Yeah, and it must have been so secretive to the point that Bear didn't tell Stump how the system work because he didn't want anyone else to know about it," Sylvester said. He squeezed Malachi's bicep very hard. "We'll like to know how it works."

Malachi sighed. "I don't know how it works," he said. He looked at Chester and then Sylvester.

"You don't know?" Sylvester repeated. "Then how do people know if their number didn't win? How do the people playing know that you're not cheating them? No, you slick bastard, you are a part of that system and you know how it works. Now, we're trying to be nice to you, but...."

Malachi felt his throat expand from fear. He swallowed. "I don't know," he said.

"How do you know what numbers is going to come out during the day and night?" Chester asked.

"The numbers do their own thing. Man, I don't know what you guys are talking about," Malachi said.

They stopped walking.

Chester removed his arm from Malachi's shoulder. He stared at him. "Listen, boy, I don't want to hear that bullshit about you not knowing how that game is played.

We're offering you a good partnership. At your age, you could be rich by the time you're twenty-five. The next time we talk, you better have something better than what you said here today, you hear?" he said.

Sylvester removed his hand, but not before squeezing it hard enough to make Malachi wince from the pain. "Listen to what my brother has said. We'll hate to send our little brother over to talk to you. He sometimes talks a person…to death," he said.

Malachi stood there and watched the Brown brothers walk ahead of him. His legs were shaking, and his mouth had gone dry. He turned and walked back to Kai-Chang.

"You had a good talk with them?" Kai-Chang asked when Malachi approached.

Malachi stopped in front of him. "Why didn't you come with me? Those two fools could've stuck a knife in me and left me lying in the street," he said.

"You said they were not your enemies, so why should I be concerned?" Kai-Chang said.

Malachi scratched his head. "So, you're telling me if I don't tell you someone is my enemy, you won't be concerned?" he asked.

"Yes, for Confucius said that a wise man sees his enemies before they can see him," Kai-Chang said.

"Who is Confucius?" Malachi asked

"A very wise Chinese philosopher of old who wrote many wise words during his time," Kia-Chang said.

"How old?" Malachi asked. He gave Kai-Chang a dubious stare.

Kai-Chang looked at him. He arched his right eyebrow. "He's dead. That's how old he was," he said.

"So why are you listening to a dead man?" Malachi asked.

"His wisdom is eternal. His words are like fire that motivates the unwise," Kai-Chang said.

"Eternal? What does that mean?" Malachi asked.

"It means that what transpires on this lowly plane has already been lived by Confucius on a higher plane. To listen to his reasoning is to prepare one-self for the unexpected that flows with life."

Malachi scratched his head as he stared at Kai-Chang.

"I see that your expression of confusion must be taken into consideration when trying to explain one as wise as Confucius," Kai-Chang said.

"Yeah, I guess. Come on," Malachi said.

"Why do these men want to harm you, Mala?" Kai-Chang asked.

Malachi was walking with his head lowered. He looked up. "I guess they feel that I'm doing more with what Bear left me than when he was alive. They feel threaten by me making more money than them," he said.

Kai-Chang nodded. His eyes were closed. When he opened them, he stopped and turned toward Malachi. "There are times when your enemy must think he is your friend, and then when he least suspects it, you must pounce on him like a tiger on an elephant. Giving him no quarter and releasing all your might to prevent the elephant from gaining any advantage with its size to crush you," he said.

Malachi turned toward Kai-Chang. He squinted, and twisted his lips upward. "What the hell did you say?" he asked.

Kai-Chang sighed. "To beat an enemy that is bigger than you, you must let that enemy think it can win. To be successful in winning your fight with him, you must first gain his confidence."

Malachi scratched his head. "Okay. So you're saying I should lead the horse to water and when he gets ready to drink it, I should poison it, right?" he asked.

Kai-Chang looked at Malachi. He shrugged. "Right," he said.

"Oh. Well, why didn't you say that?" Malachi asked. "Come on."

Malachi and Kai-Chang shopped in the general store for paint, brushes, and plywood. They had to get a cart to put the things in. By the time they reached the Queen, Malachi was exhausted.

They stood in the lobby of the Queen when Cotton walked up wearing new clothing and smelling like fresh mint cologne.

"Hey, boss," Cotton said. He stood beside Malachi. He looked at Kai-Chang and frowned. "You hired new help?" he asked.

Malachi shook his head. "Nope. Well, he is in a way. He'd be doing odds and ends jobs around here. Where's Rose Ann?"

"She's in the office doing the books. I was just back there. She wanted something to eat," he said. He inched a little closer to Malachi. He leaned forward and whispered into his ear. "Uh…he's a chink, boss."

Malachi turned toward him. "I remember when you were walking around here not smelling too good, and looking even worse, Cotton," he began. "I know what he is. So, being that he works for me, he's to be respected. At all times."

Cotton gave a weak smile. He nodded. "You're right, boss," he said.

"Find something for Kai-Chang to fix around here. I'll be in the office," Malachi said.

As he walked to the office, Malachi began to think. If the Brown brothers were thinking about getting rid of him, what would he do? How would they go about it? And whom would they use to get to him?

Opening his office door, he was shocked to see Stump sitting on the desk facing him. He wanted to slam the door close and run, but his pride got the best of him. With nervousness and apprehension running rampant through shaking body, he took in a deep breath and walked into the room as he closed the door. When he turned back around to face Stump, his body braced itself for the bullet he knew would be coming his way.

"You're really filling out, Malachi," Stump said. "How's your sister?"

So that's where the Brown brothers were going to take their intimidation. Malachi bit down on his bottom lip. His breathing became shallow. He stuffed his shaking hands deep into his pocket so Stump couldn't see them.

"Don't worry about my sister. She has nothing to do with how I run the Queen. She's not in anything that I do, so don't be trying to threaten me with her!" Malachi snapped.

"You scared, ain't you, boy?" Stump asked. He slid off the desk, and walked toward Malachi. "Ain't nothing wrong with being scared. Fear keeps you strong. I mentioned her because I want you to tell her that I was sorry about the first time we met. "

"I'll tell her, but you don't scare me, Stump. Whatever you want to bring to me, I ain't scared," Malachi said. He balled his hands into fists to stop them from shaking. "I know Bear wasn't scared when you shot him in the back either."

Stump was close enough to Malachi to breath on him. He stared down at Malachi. "That's what you think? It's only right. A lot of people are thinking that I killed my best friend because of our differences," he said.

"Think? Everybody in Blackenfield knows you killed Bear and sided with the Brown brothers!" Malachi hissed with hatred. He felt his hands stop shaking. He was becoming angry. "And now you're here to kill me for the Brown brothers so they can take over the Queen."

Stump spun around and walked quickly away from Malachi. He walked to the door. He stood there with his hand on the doorknob, and then just as quickly, he turned back around and headed toward Malachi. He walked around the desk. He opened the draw. Malachi's eyes popped out of his head when he saw Stump take out Bear's gun. He looked at Malachi with the gun in his right hand.

Malachi wanted to fall to the floor and beg for his life, but he didn't it. He pushed that thought out of his mind, and lifted his chin while defiantly staring at him.

"Killing ain't nothing, Malachi, do you know that?" Stump asked, as he stood in front of him. He lifted the gun inches from Malachi's nose. "Once you've killed, any other killings after that are meaningless. You become… less caring."

Malachi stared into Stump's eyes.

"But you have to be heartless to kill a friend. A real good friend at that," Stump said.

Malachi eyes harden. He bit harder on his bottom lip. He could taste blood in his mouth. And, the fear he thought would make he run out of the office was gone. Instead, it was replaced with an urge to grab the gun and shoot Stump between the eyes. Although he'd never fired a gun before, he would chance it if it meant avenging Bear. He took his hands out of his pocket.

Stump flipped the gun expertly over his index finger making the butt come into Malachi's face. The point of the gun was now directed at Stump. He offered the gun to Malachi.

Malachi looked at the butt of the gun, and then Stump.

"I gave this gun to Bear when we first came to this town. They were a set. I have the other one," Stump said. He lifted his shirt. In the waist of his pants was the other gun just like Bear's. "They're matches."

Malachi looked down and saw that the guns were matches.

"Take the gun, boy," Stump said.

Malachi hesitated.

"Go on, take it, Malachi. Everything that was Bear's is now yours," Stump said.

Slowly, and, with caution, Malachi reached for the gun. When his hand gripped the handle of the gun, Stump let it go and took three steps backward.

Malachi looked at the gun.

"All right. You have a gun now. Do you want to use it? Would you like to take a shot at me?" Stump asked.

He placed his hands on his hips and stood in wide-leg stance. "You were scared before, are you scared now?"

Malachi looked at the gun, and then Stump.

"You feel I killed Bear, and I'm going to tell you right now, I didn't," Stump said. He turned slightly to his right. He slammed the side of his fist against the wall, and a section of it popped out. "I would never kill my best friend."

Malachi lowered the gun to his side. He walked over toward Stump. The lines in his forehead were lines of confusion.

"Bear and I had a getaway made in this office. We had to get out of this office other than the front door. This getaway leads to a room one flight above this office. I thought only Bear and I knew about it, but someone else did, and they used it to get out of this office after shooting Bear," Stump said.

Malachi placed Bear's gun on the desk.

"When I saw the Brown brothers running toward me after the gunshots, I thought one of them had done it. When I ran into the office I was hoping to catch the killer. I was thinking it was Lester. When I pushed open the office door, I saw this," Stump pointed to the secret door. "It was closing. I could've run after the person who shot Bear, but instead, I tried to help him. He stared at me and smiled before he closed his eyes. I don't know why I picked up his gun. Maybe it had to do with reflex, I don't know, but when everyone busted through the door, it looked like what it looked like."

"I never knew about a secret passageway," Malachi said.

"And whoever did, had Bear's trust, because he

wouldn't have just told anyone," Stump said. He closed the small secret passage doorway by pulling a metal lever on the side of the wall by the window. "You never tell anyone about your escape route."

"So you didn't kill Bear?" Malachi asked.

"No, boy, I didn't."

Malachi nodded. "The Brown brothers cornered me earlier. They wanted to know how the number rackets worked. They said that you didn't know how it worked. That Bear had told you about it," he said.

Stump smiled and nodded.

"But you're the one who told Bear how it worked," Malachi said.

"Yeah. I wouldn't tell those bastards the correct time of day," Stump said.

"I heard them talking to Sheriff Hays about how they appreciate him getting you off for killing Bear," Malachi said. "I saw them give him money that night when Bear was killed."

"The Brown brothers must have set that up after they ran out of the Queen. I figure they knew I'd be the one to blame for the death of Bear, and contacted that white, crooked cracker, Hays. They probably figured no one in town would trust me and, that they could use my situation to get what information they could out of me and go after you," Stump said.

"Do you think they know who killed Bear?" Malachi asked.

"If they do, they're keeping it close to their breast, because I ain't heard anything," Stump said.

Malachi walked behind the desk and sat down in the chair. He placed his elbows on the table and his hands under his face. "The Brown brothers are coming after me," he said.

"They'd be coming after the Queen. You're young, Malachi. Those boys will throw everything at you to get this hotel and everything that comes with it, but you have an advantage now," Stump said.

Malachi looked up at Stump. "Really? What's that?" he asked.

"You'll have me working on them from their side of the fence."

Malachi moaned.

Saturday night brought out the best and worse dress people in Blackenfield. The Queen and the Goldspot were the most prestigious places to go to on a warm spring night. As everyone pampered themselves to start the night, Lester Brown was sweating profusely as he searched for his moment of pleasure.

"Come on, woman, give me what you got!" Lester shouted, as he wiped the sweat out of his eyes with his bare shoulder. "I know you want it hard!"

Sally, her legs spread wide open while lying on her back, stifled a yawn by placing a hand over her mouth. She looked up at the sweaty face of Lester while he pounded on her with his eyes closed. She turned to the right of her and cursed. Lying on the small table out of her reach were her cigarettes. She needed a smoke to calm her nerves, and to put some excitement into what she was currently enduring.

"Go ahead, baby, you riding that horse good," Sally said without much enthusiasm. "Hold those reins, big boy! Ride mama good!"

"I got you now! Shit! I got you now!" Lester screamed, as he continued to thrust himself into Sally.

Sally could feel the buildup inside of her. She was happy that it only took Lester two minutes to reach his climax. She watched his face contort in different stages. There was a face of agony as Lester pulled back his teeth in a snarl. And the image of his face becoming one of pleasure as he began shaking his head and smiling. His eyes rolled up into the back of his head. His body began to convulse as veins popped out of his neck. He went stiff, and then he collapsed on top of her.

"Goddamn, woman! You make a man want to cry," Lester said. He was out of breath as he lay on Sally's naked breast. "Give me an hour or two and I could go at it again."

Sally grunted, as she rolled Lester off her and reached for her cigarettes on the table. "I can't wait another hour, big boy, I have a show to do," she said, as she sat up with the pack of cigarettes in her hand.

Lester's face fell onto the pillow when she moved. He lay there breathing hard.

Sally sat on the edge of the bed with her legs open like a man. She lit her cigarette, as she felt Lester's seed run down the side of her leg.

"You know how long I've been trying to get into that bush of yours, Sally?" Lester mumbled while his face was in the pillow.

Sally turned toward him. She exhaled smoke in his direction. "How long, big boy?" she asked.

"Loooooonnngggg time!" Lester said. He rolled over. He looked at Sally. "So, was it good to you?"

Sally displayed a cold, harden smile. "It was the best I ever had," she said.

"Was I better than my brother Chester?" Lester asked.

"He's a little boy compared to your manliness," Sally said. She took a long pull on her cigarette, filling her lungs with smoke.

"What about my brother Sylvester?" Lester asked.

Sally lifted her head, and blew the smoke upward. "Negro, please. He's even less of a man when it comes to you. Sure, he's tall and whatnot, but you are the real man among men, Lester," she said.

Lester smiled. With blinding speed, he reached up and grabbed Sally by the mane of her thick, black hair, yanking her head back as he pulled her to him. "That's right, bitch! I'm the big nigger you gonna be giving that trim to from now on," he said.

Sally, her face close to Lester's stared into his brown, eyes. She'd slept with many men to get what she wanted in life, but as she stared into Lester's eyes, a sense of dread engulfed her.

"It'll always be you, baby," Sally said.

Lester yanked her hair harder. "It better be," he said.

"But things could be better if we had our own thing going," Sally said.

"What thing?" Lester asked, as he slowly stroked Sally's hair.

"Your brothers always think that they're smarter than you, but I know that you're the real one running things," Sally said.

"Damn right!" Lester said. He pulled harder on her hair.

"Well, baby, I know you can do things without them. You're the man to be respected and feared. They take your actions and use them to make themselves look good. What they do, you can do better," Sally said.

"You think so?" Lester asked.

"Yes. You need to really start thinking about if something happened to them—and I'm not wishing anything would—it might be you who would be running things in Blackenfield," Sally said. She pulled hard on the cigarette. "No one can live forever."

Lester reached between his legs. He felt himself coming to life. "If I became the man around here one day, I'd need a good woman behind me," he said.

Sally turned toward him. "Ain't I a good woman, Lester?" she asked.

Lester tightened his fingers in Sally's hair. He reached over and removed the cigarette from her fingers with his other hand. He crushed it out in the ashtray. Settling back down, he looked at Sally.

"Yeah, you're a real good woman," Lester said.

Lester pulled Sally's hair to the point of pulling out a few strands as he directed her head toward his crotch. "Let me see how really good you are with your mouth," he said.

Sally, a tinge of fear running through her body, grabbed Lester's hips as she moistened her mouth.

Lester looked down at her and started snickering while watching Sally's head bob up and down in his lap.

CHAPTER ELEVEN
Everything Changes

Malachi was walking into the gambling area of the Queen when he heard Cotton calling out to him. He stopped and turned around.

"That damn slant eyed fool, don't want to do nothing!" Cotton said, as he neared Malachi.

Malachi watched Cotton approach. He saw that his clothing had paint on them. "Where is Kai-Chang?" he asked.

Cotton tossed a thumb over his left shoulder.

Malachi moved his head slightly to the left of Cotton's frame. He saw Kai-Chang slowly walking toward them with his hands in the sleeves of his yellow silk kimono.

"I'll take care of it, Cotton," he said. "Go on and get cleaned up."

Cotton glanced back at Kai-Chang as he walked by him. Kai-Chang nodded slightly while passing Cotton.

Malachi walked to a chair and sat down. He watched Kai-Chang take his time. When Kai-Chang reached him, he stood there.

"Take a seat, Kai-Chang," Malachi said.

"Kai-Chang will stand."

Malachi nodded. "What happened?" he asked.

"I do not know what you speak of," Kai-Chang said.

"Cotton said that you don't want to help around here," Malachi said.

"I shall help when it is needed, Mala," Kai-Chang said.

"What does that mean?" Malachi asked.

"Kai-Chang is one who helps when there is no other help to be rendered," Kai-Chang said.

Malachi tilted his head while arching his eyebrows in confusion. "What does that mean, Kai-Chang?"

"One does not know that one needs help until one asks. That might be the simplest form to enlighten you, Mala. Help comes when one least expects it. That's when it is really needed," Kai-Chang said.

"What does painting, sweeping, or carrying supplies have to do with what you're talking about?" Malachi asked. "You wanted a job. I—"

Malachi stopped when he saw Kai-Chang raised an open palm.

"Kai-Chang took your job to assist you, Mala. Kai-Chang was fine with his other job, but your offer of more money persuaded Kai-Chang to vacant his old job and come work for you. Yet, Confucius has said that a man who leaves one labor for another labor is a man who is trying to catch his own tail," Kai-Chang commented.

Malachi sighed. "And that means...."

"To evolve in life, one must move forward not backward to achieve great things and higher enlightenment," Kai-Chang said. He bowed.

"So, you don't do anything?" Malachi asked.

"I do what is expected of me, Mala."

"And what is that?" Malachi asked.

"That is what may come to past," Kai-Chang said.

Malachi shook his head, and rolled his eyes. "What am I paying you for?" he asked. He placed his hands over his face as he sighed with exhaustion. "You said you wanted the job."

"Kai-Chang was pleased to accept your offer of a job, but you did not ask Kai-Chang what he did. Kai-Chang only delivered laundry to help, but that is not my job. Kai-Chang has many jobs."

"What is your job?" Malachi asked with exasperation.

"To assist those who may need my assistance," Kai-Chang said.

Malachi slapped himself on the forehead hard. "Okay, Kai-Chang. "I'll think of something for you to do...later," he said.

"Kai-Chang shall be patient in awaiting your decision, Mala."

Malachi looked at him. "I bet you will," he said. He stood up. "Come on, let me show you around."

Kai-Chang bowed as Malachi stood up.

"Gambling is making money," Malachi began, as Kai-Chang followed him. "When Bear taught me how to run the Queen, I didn't know if I could do it, but as time went on, I became comfortable, plus Cotton helped me a lot."

"I do not like him. The one you call Cotton. He expects too much from one such as I. And he is too headstrong," Kai-Chang said.

"In other words, you don't like him asking you to work," Malachi said.

Kai-Chang said nothing.

Sheriff Hays was standing in a large cornfield surrounded by thirty other men dressed the same way he was. Night had fallen. The evening was muggy and humid. The men were passing around several jugs of moonshine.

Sheriff Hays could feel sweat running down the back of his shirt. He snatched off the white hood that covered his head. He exhaled and inhaled quickly as if he were short on breath.

"It's hot as hell under that damn hood!" Sheriff Hays snapped. He spit out a mouthful of tobacco juice. "Why, for sweet Jesus, do we have to wear these things?"

"Goddamn it, Barney, why do you always start this crap when we're going through the ritual?" said a man whose stomach looked as if he was pregnant, and who was dressed the same way. "Why can't you wear the damn hood?"

Sheriff Barney Hays looked at John Hawkins as if the man were a fool. He was considered the Grand Dragon of their lodge. To Sheriff Barney Hays, John Hawkins reminded him of Santa Claus at that moment with his big, red shiny sheet.

"Look, Johnny Boy, I ain't wearing that sweaty hood until it's time for us to burn the logs," Sheriff Hays said. "Anyway, you ever try to spit out tobacco juice under one of these things?"

Johnny lifted his hood. "Hell, yeah," he said, as he spit out some tobacco juice. "That damn stuff gets all over my shirt." He pulled his red hood back down.

"I'm tired of these meetings in the woods. Why we can't meet in a house or some place more comfortable?" Sheriff Hays asked. He placed his hood back on his head but not before spiting out some more tobacco juice. "So what if the niggers know who we are. We get tighter ropes to put around their dark necks when it's time to hang the bastards."

"We've been best friends since our daddy's shined shoes together, Barney. The boys thought you weren't hungry enough to be in the Lodge, but I told them you can make this thing work. Now this is the first Lodge for our order on this side of the state, and we have to set an example for future ones," Johnny said. "Now bring your white, lily ass on. I have a meeting to conduct."

With lead feet, Sheriff Hays followed his best friend.

Johnny walked to a wooden pulpit. He stepped on the metal crate that was behind it, and looked down into the faces of white hooded sheets. Sheriff Hays stood beside him.

"Boys, we're gathered here tonight for our first official meeting as Ku Klux Klan members. We're the first chapter in New Orleans to acknowledge the purity of the white race. Our purpose is to put fear in these dark, jungle bunnies that some free-minded liberal set free from our chains of bondage. We have to get these niggers back in their place to continue the purity of the white race," Johnny said to the boisterous applause of the men in front of him. "We have to protect our white women from these niggers who are soiling our white land and our white women's virginity with their antics of bestiality and devilish ways."

"I ain't ever had me a white, virgin woman, Johnny Boy," someone from the crowd shouted.

The crowd erupted in laughter.

"That don't mean they ain't none out there, Hubert Wallins," Johnny shouted back. "And don't be cutting in when the Grand Dragon is talking. All right. We need to keep fear in these niggers everyday to let them know that the Ku Klux Klan is not to be toyed with. Every other Wednesday, we'll meet and stra...uh...strate...What's the word I'm looking for, Barney?"

"Strategize, Johnny," Sheriff Hays said as he rolled his eyes.

"Right. We'll strategize to bring about the destruction of these niggers. Because we can't let them demand what the white man has. We refuse to give them the rights that will make them act like they're equal to us. Niggers are not the same as us!" Johnny shouted.

"What about your uncle Henry from Tallahassee, Johnny Boy!" Another person shouted from the crowd.

"Uncle Henry ain't a nigger, Charlie! He's a little dark because my family has a little Injun in them from my great great grandma's side of the family!" Johnny shouted. "It's none of your damn business anyway! Now ya'll stop cutting me off so I can finish my speech. Now getting back to them niggers. The way I see it, we're gonna have to set an example. We got us a town full of niggers in

Blackenfield down yonder, and we better let them know that we're the boss. So, I, the Grand Dragon of this Lodge, suggest that we start lynching us some niggers! What do you boys say?"

The crowd of white sheets erupted with yells of joy.

"All right, Charlie, light up our Christmas tree," Johnny said. "And pass around more of those jugs of moonshine," Johnny said. He stepped down from the podium.

"We're gonna mess with them niggers in Blackenfield, Johnny Boy?" Sheriff Hays asked.

"Damn right, Barney. Now our policy has been a simple one. As long as they stayed on their side of town, we ignored them, but this is a new age. Niggers are acting too uppity with the entire world looking on. Once we lynch one, two, or twenty of them, they'll know their place," Johnny said.

"Some of them niggers we've known for years," Sheriff Hays said. He raised his face hood, and spitted out tobacco juice. He left it up. "And some of them pay good money to be left alone."

"Pull down your goddamn hood, Barney," Johnny whispered. He watched as Sheriff Hays pulled down the hood. "It doesn't make a difference as to how much money they're giving us. They're niggers, and like any nigger, they get lynched, burned, and killed if a true white man wanted to do it. That's our right as white folk. Ain't no laws in this county gonna convict a white man for killing a nigger. That being the case, we gonna set some examples with these niggers right next door."

Johnny stopped as the night around them became ablaze. He and Sheriff Hays turned around to look at the sudden illumination of a twelve-foot tree that had been crisscrossed in the form of a cross.

The gasoline Charlie had tossed on it was a little too much, because Charlie was running through the woods setting trees on fire with his burning body while screaming in pain.

"Somebody better put Charlie out," Sheriff Hays said calmly. He looked on as Charlie ran back and forth as his screams became louder and louder while the flames ate his clothing and skin.

"Goddamn it!" Johnny said, as he stomped his foot. Somebody throw Charlie to the ground and put him out before the boy is charcoal. Then we'll have us a white nigger in our midst".

Sheriff Hays looked on as three men, one with a blanket, began chasing Charlie. When they finally caught him, he was tossed to the ground and the men began smothering the fire with it as they rolled him around.

"Ku Klux Klan my ass. They're all a bunch of assholes," Sheriff Hays mumbled as he lifted his face hood, and spit.

Malachi was on the stage finishing up his last song. He looked out into the audience and saw the girl. He waved at her. He watched her look over her shoulders, then point to herself. Malachi nodded and waved again. She smiled and waved back. Malachi strung the last chord on his guitar, and stepped down from the stage. The audience gave him a standing ovation. He was dressed in his best double-breasted gray suit. He'd slicked down his natural curly black hair with some thick pomade. He felt confident as he approached the girl because he'd awoken two days previous to find that he had peach hairs growing on his top lip. He was becoming a man.

As he walked to the table where the girl was sitting, he glanced in the corner to the left of him and saw Kai-Chang sitting on a stool with his hands inside the sleeves of his dark blue kimono. He smiled. He saw Cotton and three other workers making their rounds taking numbers on their small writing pads.

"Hello," Malachi said as he neared the girl who was wearing a beige dress with matching purse and shoes. Her white hat was pulled down snugly on her head. "You like the show?"

The girl, obviously embarrassed, looked up at Malachi and nodded. When she did look at him, Malachi gasped. Her beauty was mesmerizing. He'd seen her only from distances up to that moment. Up close, he realized that she was gorgeous. Her almond shaped face with light brown eyes made a person's brain shut down. He'd never seen anyone as beautiful as her.

"Hi," the young woman said.

Malachi sat down on the seat across from her. "What is your name?" he asked. He could barely make his lips move. Maybe it had to do with his singing, but he knew that was not true. His mouth was dry because the girl's beauty was breathtaking.

"My name is Betty Mae Johnson."

"My name is Malachi Moon."

Betty Mae smiled at Malachi. Malachi mouth hung open. Her smile was so innocent.

"I know who you are. Most people in town know you're the young boy who owns the Queen," Betty Mae said. "I have two girlfriends who came with me tonight. They said you were more than handsome."

"You do? They did? I didn't see them," Malachi said, as he glanced around.

Betty Mae waved her hand. "They're around here somewhere. Where's your sister?" she asked.

"Rose Ann? I don't know, but she's around here working. I'm going to tell you something, but I know you hear it all the time," Malachi said. Betty Mae smiled at his awkwardness. "You are beautiful."

"No," Betty Mae said.

"No what?" Malachi asked.

"I'm not that beautiful," she said.

"Stop lying to yourself. You're more than beautiful," Malachi said. He leaned forward. "You can make a grown man fall to his knees with your beauty."

Betty Mae laughed. "That's sweet," she said.

"How old are you?" Malachi asked, as he leaned forward in his chair.

"Didn't your mama tell you never to ask a girl her age?" Betty Mae asked.

"Mama and I didn't have that discussion yet," Malachi said.

"Oh. Well, take my word for it. Girls don't like to talk about their age. We feel it makes us old. How old are you?" Betty Mae asked.

"Seventeen," Malachi said. He pushed out his chest.

"Seventeen? Dear me. I thought you were…Well, your sister told me you were twenty-two. You look much older than seventeen," Betty Mae said.

"I had good looking parents. So, if you thought I was

twenty-two that would make you about twenty or twenty-one. Right?" Malachi asked. He smiled.

"Twenty-one," Betty Mae said.

"Boss?"

Malachi turned around to see Cotton hurrying toward him. When Cotton reached him, he bent down to whisper in his ear.

"About six of the Brown brothers' men just came in acting rowdy and drinking heavily," Cotton said. He moved his head to the right. Malachi followed his direction.

Toward the left of him, Malachi could see six men dressed in weather worn, ragged clothing drinking and talking loudly.

"How do you know they're the Brown brothers' men, Cotton?" Malachi asked.

"One of the girls overheard some of them talking about the Brown brothers giving them some extra cash."

"Go get my Louisville Slugger behind the bar, and tell the other men to surround them but don't make it look too obvious," Malachi said.

Cotton nodded and quickly dashed off toward the bar.

"What's happening?" Betty Mae asked.

"Nothing for you to be worrying your little head about. I'll tell you what. I have some business to take care of, but I don't want you to leave. Do you see that doorway over there?" Malachi said, as he pointed to the far right corner. "Stay over there no matter what happens."

Betty Mae stood up. "What about my girlfriends?" she asked.

"Believe me, they will be all right. Now you go on like I told you."

Cotton returned. His arm was concealed behind his leg. He slipped Malachi the Louisville Slugger baseball bat as he stood up. He watched Betty Mae make it to the door where he'd told her.

"Did you tell Blackie, Dun, Moose, and Mack about the situation?" Malachi asked Cotton.

"Yeah. They spread out so the Brown brothers' boys are in the middle of us," Cotton said. "They did it without looking suspicious."

"I hate this. For a Saturday night like this one, I can lose money like it was water running out of a facet if a fight broke out. Did you tell them not to break too much of the furniture?" Malachi asked.

"I told them, boss."

"Let go take care of business," Malachi said, as he took the lead and the bat.

Malachi and Cotton made their way to the front of the club. A man wearing a brown derby hat who was part of the crew was sitting at the table. He turned toward them. Malachi watched as he said something to the other men. When he finished, they all turned toward Malachi and Cotton.

Malachi approached the table with a smile. The Louisville Slugger was concealed behind his left leg. "How you boys doing?" he asked.

The man with the brown derby hat grunted. "We were doing all right until you showed up," he said. "Look, boys, we got ourselves a little big man."

They all started laughing.

"Get your asses out of here!" Cotton snapped. "You're flunkies for the Brown brothers and don't belong in the Queen."

"Hey, Slim, we got us a loud mouth," said brown derby hat.

Everyone turned to Slim. A man as thin as a rail stood up. Malachi gulped at his height. The man was over six feet, three inches tall. In his hands he was holding a crowbar.

"Yeah, I heard him," Slim said. His voice was a full baritone. "What'd you think about that, Tomcat?"

Tomcat stood up. Wrapped around both his fists were two thick, heavy linked chains. "Shonuff! I think you gonna have to put my ass out with some help," he said. "Because you two ain't gonna be able to do it yourselves. But I might be wrong. Whatcha you think, Buster?" asked Tomcat.

Malachi looked at the men's faces who were still sitting to try to determine which one was Buster. No one stood up.

"This young punk doesn't know who he is messing with."

The voice came from behind Malachi and Cotton. They turned around to see a man dressed in all green whose size was as big as a house towering over them.

"So you want to play with the big boys," Buster said, as he took a step forward.

Malachi heart skipped a beat. When Buster moved toward him, he thought he felt the entire building shake.

"I thought you said there were only six of them," Malachi whispered to Cotton.

"They must have slipped him in separately," Cotton whispered back.

"Now you were telling us that we needed to move our asses out of here, right?" The brown derby hat man said.

Malachi and Cotton turned back around.

"Now, my boy, Sweet," the brown derby hat man began, he nodded his head in the direction of Sweet. When he did, an ugly looking dark skinned man stood up brandishing an eight-inch knife and a sinister grin. He tossed the knife down into the table. It stood menacingly. "Sweet is a good man, but Marcus is even better." Marcus stood up. He lifted his shirt to reveal four bricks tucked into his waist. "And of course there's Cully." Cully stood up. In his hand was a fat, long whip. "I'm Taz," the brown derby hat man said. He stood up as well. He raised his shirt to reveal a .44 revolver. "You boys come to a party carrying paper when you need some knives, or better yet, a gun."

"Damnit, Cotton," Malachi mumbled. "Uh...Look, we can talk about any misunderstanding outside," Malachi began. "You should think about what you're getting into before you start anything."

Taz laughed. Malachi saw that the top rows of his teeth were encased in silver. "Boy, all that is too late," he said. "You crossed over into a man's world, and in that world, you either eat your prey, son, or be eaten."

"Mala, maybe I can be of assistance to you," Kai-Chang said, as he walked up to them. "Confucius says that all men can be brought to peace if they will it to be."

Everyone turned toward Kai-Chang. He bowed.

"Who the hell is this chink?" Taz asked.

"He looks like a woman with that braid running down his back and that shiny dress," Sweet said.

"Mala, your friends are...insolent," Kai-Chang said.

"They're not my friends, Kai-Chang," Malachi said.

"No, Mala?" Kai-Chang asked. He turned to Malachi. He arched his right eyebrow. "Not your friends?"

"They are my enemies, Kai-Chang," Malachi said.

Kai-Chang closed his eyes and nodded.

"Buster, get rid of this chink," Taz said.

"My pleasure," Buster said.

Buster stepped through Cotton and Malachi while cracking his knuckles.

"The enemy of my friend is my enemy," Kai-Chang said.

From that moment on, Malachi witness pandemonium explode as he grabbed Cotton by the arm and pulled him out of the way. Malachi came to understand why Kai-Chang wanted to know his enemies as he watched him go to work with efficiency.

Buster reached out to grab Kai-Chang by the shoulder. When his hand touched Kai-Chang, Kai-Chang twisted his body to the right away from Buster's grip, and grabbed Buster's hand with his right hand. He maneuvered his fingers around Buster's wrist. A chilling crackling sound of bone was the end result.

The scream that exploded from Buster's mouth was ear-shattering even over the loud music being played. Buster fell to his knees while reaching out to try and pull his wrist away from Kai-Chang's grip. It was a fruitless effort, for he realized that Kai-Chang's grip was like steel.

Malachi watched as Kai-Chang threw a leg over Buster's outstretched arm, and brought his weight down on it. The bone in Buster's shoulder snapped. Kai-Chang drew his other hand back above his head. It was the heel of the hand extended outward. He slammed it into Buster's nose. Maneuvering it upward and in. The crackling sound of bone and cartilage could be heard.

The bone in Buster's nose shot straight upward into his

brain, and killed him. Kai-Chang let go of his wrist and Buster fell dead to the floor.

The music had stopped playing. There was a quiet that fell on the club as everyone stared at the dead fat man lying on the floor.

"Motherfucker!" Taz shouted as he reached for the gun in his waist.

Kai-Chang, his silk kimono flowing gracefully around him, moved toward Taz. Kai-Chang's speed was unbelievable as he appeared behind Taz at the exact moment he was trying to pull the gun from his waist. Kai-Chang gripped Taz's wrist tightly, keeping the gun in his waist while grabbing him in a headlock as he kneed Taz in the back of his thigh, forcing him to the ground. As Taz fell to the ground, Kai-Chang pulled the gun from his waist, and tossed it to Malachi all in one swift motion.

With Taz kneeling on the floor, Kai-Chang lifted his arm to apply pressure to Taz's outer throat. Kai-Chang didn't want to aphysiate him, so he kept his grip tight but not to the point of choking him to death. Taz struggled but to no prevail. Within seconds everyone watched as his eyes grew heavy, and began to slowly close. Seconds pass before Malachi watched Taz's body go limp. Kai-Chang let him go. Taz fell to the floor unconscious.

Cully swung his whip at Kai-Chang. Kai-Chang leaned opposite and away from the incoming edge of the whip. It went pass him. As Cully pulled the whip back, Kai-Chang grabbed it, and pulled hard. The strength of Kai-Chang surprised Cully. As Kai-Chang pulled on the whip, Cully flew across the table. Kai-Chang's hands hit Cully in several places on his upper body with blinding speed. Cully's body shook each time Kai-Chang hit him. The blows were fast and hard. Cully did not move after Kai-Chang's last blow to his chest. Kai-Chang pushed him off the table. Cully hit the floor with a loud thud. He didn't move.

Slim looked at Tomcat. Tomcat glanced at Sweet. Sweet licked his lips dry and looked at Marcus who, in return, looked at Slim.

"Uh… I guess we'll be heading out right about now," Sweet said, licking his chapped lips as he slowly edge his way pass Tomcat.

Tomcat dropped his chains and nodded at Malachi for his approval.

Marcus grunted a reply that was unintelligible, and covered up his four bricks by pulling down his shirt.

Slim cleared his throat, and then quietly lowered the crowbar to his leg and let it drop. He looked around and hurried to the door.

Malachi and Cotton watched as the four of them walked out of the club and didn't look back.

Everyone was silent.

"Hot damn!" Cotton screamed, startling Malachi. "That slant eyed, thin man can kick some ass! Whoooeeeee!"

The club came to life. Music blared, and laughter could be heard throughout the Queen.

Malachi walked over to Kai-Chang. Kai-Chang bowed as Malachi approached.

"So, that's what you meant when you said what you said about everyone being different," Malachi said.

"A person's skill is not always displayed on their sleeve, Mala," Kai-Chang said. "Confucius say that a man who lives by the—"

"Sword dies by the sword," Malachi said.

Kai-Chang shook his head.

"No? You weren't going to say that?" Malachi asked.

"A man who lives by the sword must be willing to cut the flesh in hopes of bringing together a peaceful solution. If one were to die by the sword he welds what would be the purpose of welding the sword if you were to be bested by someone who is more knowledgeable in its use of the sword than yourself?" Kai-Chang said. "Every action one takes must be conducted in the hopes of bringing an end to a confrontation without ultimate death as the answer."

"Uh-huh," Malachi said, as he gave Kai-Chang a dubious stare.

Kai-Chang nodded.

Everyone turned when the front door bursted open.

"What the hell is going on in here?" A slurred voice asked.

Malachi turned and looked at the haggard, wrinkled appearance of Dave the Drunk. The only thing impressionable on his clothing was the shiny sheriff's badge on his shirt.

"Dave, you're a little late. The ruckus is over now," Cotton said.

Dave the Drunk walked up to Malachi and Cotton, as his constantly shifting eyes always searching his surroundings. When he was near enough, Malachi blinked rapidly as the horrid stench of moonshine and not too many bathes emanated from Dave the Drunk's body.

"Ya'll making a lot of racket in here, Malachi," Dave the Drunk said. "Ya'll are in an ordinance violation that could lead to a fine. If I was ya'll, I'll keep the noise down."

"You need to take your drunk ass out of here, Dave!" Cotton snapped. "When the town council voted to make you sheriff, that meant that your black ass get in the middle of the commotion and try to break it up. It's not for you to arrive five minutes later talking about you gonna give somebody a shitty fine."

Dave the Drunk turned around and looked at Buster, Taz, and Cully lying on the floor. "What's wrong with them?" he asked. "Ya'll have a party in here and didn't invite your local sheriff?"

Malachi turned to Cotton. "Get the sheriff a drink," he said. "And get some boys together and throw out the garbage."

Dave the Drunk walked over to Buster. He bent down and touched his chest. "Good heaven, man. He's dead!" He snapped, as he stood up wiping the hand on the front of his pants. "You better make that a double on that drink." He turned to the crowd. "Everyone in here is a witness, and I'll be going around asking questions as to how the big fellow died. That's all right with you, right, Malachi?"

Malachi laughed.

CHAPTER TWELVE

My Brother's Keeper

Five days later, with the evening sun settling, Sheriff Hays was standing by the door of Chester Brown's office. He was wiping the sweat from his forehead as he lifted his large cowboy hat.

"You're telling me, Hays, that your friends feel it's time to come into Blackenfield and take Negroes for some lynchings?" Chester asked. He was standing behind his desk with his hands folded behind his back. "When did the Klan get here?"

"Johnny Hawkins—"

"That fat, redneck, bastard!" Sylvester shouted. "Years ago when he first came to this area I should've killed his white, coward ass. He's always running around acting like he's pure white bread with that fat, nasty wife of his."

Sheriff Hays put his hat back on. He looked hard at

Sylvester. "Look, boy, I won't have that kind of talk about any white man as long as I'm standing here," he said.

"Fuck you!" Sylvester snapped. "You're telling us this now because you think your money train is coming to an end. I ought to get some angry Negroes together and go whip his redneck ass. Put a noose around his fucking neck!"

Sheriff Hays hefted his gun belt, and pulled in his large stomach. "You could do that, Sylvester, but before the day is over, ya'll boys will have so many white men wearing sheets over their heads, and running through this town that it'd make your heads spin. Oh, and I'll be with them," he said. "You can bet your sweet, black ass on that."

"You'd bite the hand that feeds you?" Sylvester asked.

Sheriff Hays looked around for something to spit his tobacco juice in. Finding nowhere, he turned toward the corner and spit.

"Goddamn it, Hays! Show some fucking respect!" Chester shouted.

"Not only will I bite the hand. I'll bite the foot, the leg, the thigh, and even the ass if it meant going against my white brethren," Sheriff Hays said. He took three steps forward.

"You ain't shit, Hays!" Sylvester hissed. His anger made him kick at the desk.

"You know, boy, I've been putting up with your disrespect of a white man because the money is green, but don't take my weakness for kindness, ya hear?" Sheriff Hays said.

"Relax, men," Chester said. "There's no need for us

to be going at each other's throat. We just have to talk this out."

Sheriff Hays and Sylvester stared at each other.

"The Klan needs some Negroes to go into their nooses, huh? All Right, we'll give them as many as they want," Chester said.

Sheriff Hays and Sylvester looked at him.

"The Queen has a lot of Negroes," Chester remarked.

"Let me ponder that for a moment," Sheriff Hays said. He walked back to the corner, and spit more tobacco juice in it. He turned back around wearing a smile on his cherubim face. "I guess that will do. You know what they say about Negroes."

"What do they say? You fat, white, cracker," Sylvester said as he balled his fist.

"They all look alike," Sheriff Hays replied. He laughed so hard that his stomach shook. "Now ain't that funny?"

Sylvester looked at his brother, and shook his head.

Malachi was sitting in a chair staring out the window as the sun came up. He was wearing only his underwear. His hair was tied down with a silk handkerchief. He heard keys by his door, and knew it could only be Rose Ann.

"What are you doing?" Rose Ann asked, as she came into the room after locking the door.

"Sitting here thinking. That's all," Malachi said.

Rose Ann came over and sat down on the bed across from him. She was dressed in a dark green summer dress with matching shoes.

"Why are you looking so down?" Rose Ann asked. "Is it because of what happened a few nights ago? If it is, don't worry about it. The Brown brothers will get their poison one day when they least expect it."

"It's that and other things," Malachi said.

"Like what?" Rose Ann asked. She stood up and walked over to her brother. She lifted his shoulders, and placed her back against the headboard. Malachi's head rested on her stomach. She began massaging his shoulders. "You're filling out."

"Yeah. You know, Rose, sometimes I don't know what I'm doing. I'm seventeen and—"

"Eighteen in another three weeks," Rose Ann said.

Malachi smiled. "It's kind of hard to know who to trust, and who wants to put a knife in my back. Now I can understand how Bear felt. He gave me too much too soon," he said.

"Boy, too much is when you want to run away from everything. That's too much. You're still here and you're doing some good. The Queen is alive because you keep it going. No one perfect, Malachi. Your shoulders are big enough to handle anything. Now what's happening with you and the Chinese man?" Rose Ann asked.

"Kai-Chang? I thought I was hiring someone to do the chores around here. I didn't know I was hiring a man who does things with his hands and feet you wouldn't believe, but he can be trusted, and he makes sure nothing will happen to me, or anyone I tell him to protect," Malachi said.

"People are talking about how you have come into your own by hiring a killer to protect you," Rose Ann said, as she applied pressure to Malachi's shoulders. "Rumors are going around that you're smarter than your young years show. People are starting to really respect you."

"Gossip. I didn't know what Kai-Chang was until the night he took on the Brown brothers men. To me, he was just a laundry man. How are we coming along with the Queen and the numbers racket?" Malachi asked.

Rose Ann smiled. "You're making a real profit. Last month you made seven thousand dollars," she said.

Malachi spun around to look at his sister. "Seven thousand dollars? We made that much? Whew, I'm so glad Maybelle taught use how to do math," he said.

"Not we. You," Rose Ann said, as she pushed him back down and continued massaging his shoulders. "And then you taught me."

Malachi nodded. "I wonder how much money the Goldspot is raking in."

Rose Ann slapped Malachi on the head. He sat up, placing his feet on the floor. "Don't worry about them," she said. She stopped massaging his shoulders. She stood up, and came around in front of Malachi. She dropped to her knees as she folded her arms on Malachi's thigh. "I have something to tell you."

Malachi looked at his little sister. "What?" he asked.

"Well, I…I met this boy…No. He's older. Twenty years old. I met him a few weeks ago. He didn't know who I was or that you were my brother. Anyway, we started talking, and, well, I like him," Rose Ann said. It was all said fluidly and in one sentence.

"You'll be sixteen next year. What does this boy do? I mean. Is he a farmer? A grocery clerk? What?" Malachi asked.

"He's going to school to become a dentist," Rose Ann said. "He's not from around here. He's from up North, and he came down here to see his grandmother before going away to school. He reminds me of you a little. I mean…he's not as handsome as you, but he has some good points."

Malachi laughed. "How much do you like him?" he asked.

Rose Ann hugged her brother's thigh. "I like him a lot, Malachi," she said.

Malachi stroked his sister's back gingerly. "What's his name?" He asked.

"Roger Edmond Toussaint the Third," Rose Ann said.

"I want to meet him," Malachi asked.

"All right," Rose Ann said.

"I think I met someone, too," Malachi said.

Rose Ann lifted her head and looked at her brother affectionately. "Who?" she asked.

"You told me about her," Malachi said.

"I did? What does she look like?" Rose Ann asked.

"She looks like Heaven," Malachi said.

"In your eyes, you mean," Rose Ann said. "Because you've never seen Heaven." She laughed

"Uh-huh."

"What's her name? Heaven?" Rose Ann asked lightly.

"No. It's Betty Mae Johnson," Malachi replied. He smiled when he saw his sister smile grow bigger.

That afternoon, Stump was making his rounds for the Brown brothers. He would walk to the shops around Blackenfield and demand payment from the storeowners. It was part of the Brown brothers' tacit extortion ring. He'd been doing it for four days, and hated every moment of it, but he endured the pain to get closer to the Brown brothers. He was standing in front of old man Morton's hardware store. He dreaded going in, but he knew if he didn't, Lester would come and make things even worse for the old man and his wife. Stump inhaled deeply, and then opened the front door to the store.

"How's it going, Mr. Morton?" Stump asked, as he entered the store while closing the door behind him.

Bailey Morton looked up from the counter. He reached for his thick eyeglasses, and placed them on his wrinkled nose to see who he was talking to.

"Oh, it's you," Bailey Morton said when he recognized it was Stump. "You're still bumming around with those Brown brother bastards?"

Stump walked to the counter. "Yeah. How's Mrs. Morton doing?" he asked.

"None of your damn business, that's how she's doing!" Bailey snapped. He reached under the counter.

"I know things look bad, but they're getting better," Stump said.

"Boy, take this little bit of money I owe you and kiss my ass with the kind words you're trying to lie at my feet," Bailey said, as he slammed his hand down on the counter.

Stump saw the money when Bailey removed his hand. He reached for it.

"You tell those Brown boys they won't get another red cent from Bailey Morton," he said.

Stump began counting the money as he headed for the door. He stopped and turned around. "You're a few dollars short, Mr. Morton," he said.

"Well, that's all I got," Bailey said. He shrugged his shoulders.

Stump sighed. He walked back to the counter.

"Mr. Morton, you know how those boys feel about their money. They'll come in here and tear your shop down for a few dollars. You don't have anything else to go with this?" Stump asked.

"That's all I got. The rest they got to take out of my skin to get," Bailey said.

"You take care, Mr. Morton," Stump said. He turned around and walked out of the store.

As he headed to his next store to collect money from other owners, Stump reached into his pocket and added his own money to Bailey Morton's. The Brown brothers wouldn't know the difference.

Two hours later, Stump was sitting in a chair across from Chester who was going over the daily haul from the collection of storeowners. Sylvester was behind Chester's chair.

"Stump, how could you let them hit you with the crying game about not having any money?" Chester asked, as he counted some money.

"I don't know. I'm a sucker for sad stories," Stump said, as he leaned back in the chair. "Why do we take money from them anyway? All the money the Goldspot is raking in from the gambling and the prostitution combined with the moonshine you boys are making, I don't see why we have a problem with a few dollars missing. Hell, you boys ought to be pulling in a nice piece of change every month."

Sylvester smiled at Stump as he began to roll up his sleeves.

"We make money from the weak or the strong. It doesn't make a difference who they are, but if we don't get our money, then other people will think we're weak and come after us. Next thing you know, we're being extorted," Sylvester said. He walked around the desk, and stood in front of his brother with his back to Stump. "If we can't make old men pay, then what are we going to do when we go against cats that are as competitive as us?"

"Share?" Stump said.

"Naw, man. That's not an option. We got to correct the little mistakes in hopes that they won't turn into bigger ones down the road," Chester said.

"Maybe," Stump said.

Sylvester had placed both his hands on the desk as he leaned toward Chester.

"Or we just keep losing money," Chester said.

Sylvester kicked his left leg out at Stump. Stump, a man always attentive, pushed himself backward. He rolled out of the chair, and stood up in a boxer's stance.

"That's good, Stump. I didn't think you'd see it coming," Sylvester said, as he turned around to face Stump. "That trick usually works."

"When you started rolling up your sleeves, I took notice. Now you want to prove a point. Okay. This office is big enough for you to prove it," Stump said, as he tossed his head from side to side to get the kinks out of his neck. "You're a big man, Sylvester, so I'm going to have to beat you in the body because your head is too thick for my hands, and there's no sense in me breaking my hands on that thick, empty skull of yours."

Sylvester threw his arms out to loosen up his muscles. He twisted his upper torso to loosen up his back. He walked toward the right side of Stump. He flexed his large biceps as he stared hard at him.

"I hope your boxing skills is better than your intimidation game, Sly, because you ain't doing nothing yet," Stump said, as he backed up two feet. "You think you might need Chester to help you out on this one?"

"Negro, I'm going tear into you like a starving dog biting into a T-bone steak who ain't ate in a week," Sylvester said.

"That'd make you right about starving, huh?" Stump asked.

Sylvester put his fists up in front of him in a boxing stance. He relaxed his shoulders, concentrating on putting all his power into his fists as he slowly circled Stump from the left. To him, it was going to be an easy task to beat up Stump.

A smile broke out on Stump's face. Sylvester was big and brawny, but he knew he had the edge. He was smaller, and quicker. As fast as the smile had formed, it disappeared just as fast when Sylvester lunged at him.

Sylvester knew if he threw a punch at Stump he would easily avoid it, so, instead, he charged Stump. His large body moving with unbelievable speed.

The move was unexpected. Stump, though, not missing a beat, pivoted to his left, and let loose a powerful left hook that hit Sylvester in the stomach. Stump heard Sylvester let out a small groan, but that didn't stop Sylvester's torpedoing body as he continued forward. Sylvester went with the momentum as he threw a wide right hand at Stump's head. Stump casually sidestepped the telepathy blow and stepped into Sylvester's midsection by placing his head directly into the middle of Sylvester's chest while letting loose a volley of punches to Sylvester's stomach and kidneys.

Sylvester was surprised at how fast Stump moved. He was even more surprised when Stump stepped in close enough to suddenly begin raining blowing into his chest and mid-section. Sylvester felt each punch harder than the last. He tried to get away from Stump's wicked assault, but each time he backed up, Stump stepped in, not giving him a quarter to breath while continuously pummeling him with blows.

Stump knew he was winning the battle by the way Sylvester was trying to get away from him every time he landed a hard punch into his body. He pressed the attack by occasionally throwing an uppercut into Sylvester's exposed chin. The first time he did it, his fist landed square on Sylvester's chin, snapping his head back, and giving Stump an opening to come across with a powerful right hook to the side of Sylvester's head, staggering him and making him take a step further back. As Sylvester stumbled from the blow, Stump stepped in to deliver a vicious punch to Sylvester's chest just under his heart. He watched as Sylvester's eyes grew wide from the heavy-handed punch. Stump knew Sylvester's heart had jump erratically in his chest from the blow. Sylvester gasped from the blow, and fell to his knees. Stump took one step back, as he towered over Sylvester breathing hard with his fists balled. The knuckles on his hands were skinned from the contact to Sylvester's rough skin. They were bleeding. But he couldn't feel any pain. All that he was feeling was pride as he stared down at the bully.

"Okay, big man. You're used to beating on people who don't know how to use their fists, but when you run into someone who does, you find your big ass on your knees and bleeding," Stump said. "Get up. Let's go another round. I think you got another round in you. What do you think?"

Sylvester stared up at Stump with eyes that were filled with hatred. Blood ran freely down his shirt from his split lip. He was hurting. Every time he took in a deep breath, it hurt. He knew that pain. It was a few years ago when Lester had hit him in the ribs with a lead pipe. His ribs were broken on his right side. He growled as he slowly began to rise. He watched Stump take two steps back.

"I'm going to break your god...damn... back, Stump!" Sylvester hissed.

"You can try," Stump said coolly.

Sylvester, now on his feet, looked at Stump. His eyes opened in shock, and he shouted. "Nooo!"

Stump looked at him. What was he saying no to? Stump was about to angle himself to the right when his head exploded in pain. A shearing white light filled his vision. He felt his legs go out from under him. He fell to the floor unconscious.

"That boy was whipping you like a slave, Sly," Lester said, as he stepped over the motionless Stump. "I was going to let him go at you again, but you know what mama used to say. If your brother is losing the fight, reach out and smite his enemy."

Sylvester watched Lester put the gun he'd used to cold-cock Stump back in his waist. He exhaled from weariness, and sat on the edge of the desk gingerly cradling the right side of his ribs.

"What were ya'll fighting about anyway?" Lester asked.

"Mama used to use that saying for you, Lester. You were the one always getting your ass whipped as a kid,"

Chester said. He stood up and came from around his desk to look at Stump. "Don't you remember? How are you feeling, Sly?"

Sylvester waved off the question.

"What are we going to do with, Stump?" Lester asked. "Does it hurt when you breathe, Sly? If it does, we know what that means."

"That's a good question. What are we going to do with Stump?" Chester asked. He looked at Lester. "Where you been?"

"Around," Lester said. He went and sat down on the old leather couch in the far corner. He crossed his legs and snickered.

"Around, huh? You digging into Sally, ain't you?" Chester asked.

Lester looked at him.

"You be careful with that bitch. She's as deadly as a rattler snake," Chester said.

"How would you know?" Lester asked. His question was defiant as he stared at his brother.

Chester turned toward his little brother. "You ain't ever been the smartest one of all of us, Lester. I tell you this because I know women like Sally. She'd use you, and when she's finished with you, she'll throw your ass into the street with no clothes on just so she can get a laugh. If you sleeping with her, I don't care, just don't let the bitch know your business. Ya hear?" he snapped. "Let me correct that. Our business!"

Lester stared at his brother.

Chester returned the stare.

Lester broke out into a heartily laugh. "Okay, big brother, I'll be careful with her," he said.

Chester continued to stare at Lester.

"Okay, Chester, okay," Lester said.

"Now, what do we do with Stump?" Chester asked, as he turned around and looked at the unconscious Stump.

"First, lift him up and place his right hand on the desk," Sylvester said. "Lester, give me your gun."

Chester bent down and lifted Stump up. Lester gave Chester a hand after giving Sylvester his gun.

Sylvester took Stump's right hand and placed it palm down on the desk. He raised the butt of Lester's gun and brought it down fast and hard on Stump's hand. The first blow, Chester felt Stump jump in his unconsciousness from the pain. Sylvester did it three more times before handing Lester back his gun.

"Toss his ass in the alley out back," Sylvester said, as he went and sat down behind the desk. Perspiring heavily, he tried to control his breathing to adjust to the pain from his broken ribs.

Sylvester watched Lester and Chester struggle with the unconscious Stump through the door, he called out to them. "Hey, and bring back the doctor. That bastard broke my ribs," he said.

Malachi was eating dinner when Cotton casually strolled in and told him that Stump was in the alley a few doors down unconscious. Malachi had gotten some men together and they brought Stump into the Queen. The men he'd picked were reluctant to help because of the allegation of Stump killing Bear. Malachi had to threaten and then bribe them to help.

With Stump in one of the rooms upstairs, Malachi

had returned to finish his dinner when Betty walked in. He'd asked her to sit down with him.

"How do you run all of this?" Betty Mae asked, as she watched Malachi bite into the roast beef on his fork.

"I don't. Everyone else does, and I supervise it all," Malachi said. He smiled when he glanced at her. "It's hard."

"You're too young to own a hotel and the other things that come with it," Betty Mae said.

"It was kinda thrown at me. I had no choice but to take it and learn as I walked through it all. Why aren't you married with two children and a husband yet?" Malachi asked.

"That's a serious question to be asking a woman you've just met," Betty Mae said

Malachi shrugged.

"Just like a man," Betty Mae said.

"I'm still a young boy, remember?"

"Don't get cute with me. You're a young boy in an old man's body," she said.

"Sometimes I feel like that. What do you do?" Malachi asked.

Betty Mae lowered her head. She picked up her cup of tea that Malachi had ordered and sipped it. "I'm a seamstress," she said.

"You act like you're embarrassed," Malachi said. "I wish I knew how to make clothing. Did you make that dress you're wearing? It's nice."

Betty Mae looked up. Her brown eyes were bright. "Yes, I did," she said. "I was thinking about making it a different color, but I thought tan fitted me better."

Kai-Chang walked up to the table. He bowed. "The

one you call Stump is requesting your presence, Mala," he said.

Betty Mae stared at Kai-Chang. She looked at his eye-catching gold colored kimono. "That's a beautiful...."

"Kimono," Kai-Chang said.

"Uh-huh," Betty Mae said.

Malachi stood up. "Finish drinking your tea. If I'm not back in fifteen minutes, then I'm caught up. Come to the show tonight," he said.

"Oh, that's what I wanted to ask you, Malachi. Who taught you to sing so beautifully?" she asked.

Malachi shrugged. "I was born with a voice, I guess," he said.

"It's a beautiful voice, Malachi," Betty Mae said.

"I'll see you," Malachi said.

When Malachi and Kai-Chang open the door to Stump's room, he was sitting on the edge of the bed cradling his right hand that was in a cast from his wrist up to his elbow. He was wearing nothing but his underwear.

"Get me a gun, Malachi," Stump said.

Malachi closed the door. He walked to the corner and picked up a chair. He carried it over, and placed it in front of Stump. He sat down. He stared at Stump.

"Boy, don't give me no mess right now. All I need from you is a gun," Stump said.

"What happen to yours?" Malachi asked.

"Ain't it a damn shame? Just when I decide not to carry it, I needed it tonight," Stump said, as he cradled his cast.

"Confucius says that a wise man that uses his mind

is more powerful than any weapon conceived by man," Kai-Chang said from the door.

Stump looked at Kai-Chang. He nodded and then looked at Malachi.

"That's Kai-Chang," Malachi said. "Confucius is a dead man whose wise words are used everyday by the Chinese to teach patience and understanding." He shrugged.

"Confucius can't be dead if his wisdom is passed on to the living," Kai-Chang said.

"I don't give a damn about Confucius. I want a gun, Malachi!" Stump snapped.

"If I get you a gun and you go after the Brown brothers, you don't think they will be waiting for you? No one likes you because they think you killed Bear. You have no friends in Blackenfield except me. Rose Ann would stab you in the back if she knew you were in the Queen. The men who carried you in here wanted to drop you in the well down the road. It took a lot of threats and extra money to stop that from happening. The doctor who looked you over wanted to poison you. I had to pay him an extra fifty dollars not to do that and not let anyone know that he'd fixed you up. Now, you tell me. If you go over there, and they kill you—and they will kill you, Stump—who will care? Dave the Drunk would have one extra shot of whiskey at you being dead, and nothing else. Like you told me. We have to play this by ear," Malachi said.

Stump nodded. He leaned toward Malachi and whispered. "Where did he come from?" he asked. Tossing his head in the direction of Kai-Chang.

Malachi sighed. He'd grown weary of telling everyone

about Kai-Chang. "I hired him as an extra hand around the Queen, but that's not what he does," he said.

"So what does he do? Walk around wearing women dresses?" Stump asked.

"It's not a dress. It's a...."

"Kimono," Kai-Chang said.

Malachi and Stump looked at Kai-Chang. They were surprised that he could hear them from the doorway since they'd been whispering.

"Right," Malachi said. "Anyway, you stay in this room for a few days. I'm the only one with the key and only Kai-Chang and I know you're up here. This way the Queen will run smoothly."

"What about the men who brought me up here? How long are a couple of days, Malachi?" Stump asked, as he watched Malachi stand up.

"Those men won't say anything. I paid them good money to keep their mouths shut. It won't be long, Stump," Malachi said.

Malachi and Kai-Chang walked to the door.

"How long?" Stump asked again.

"A month or two," Malachi whispered.

"What?" Stump shouted as he ran to the door.

Malachi closed and locked the door just before Stump reached them.

"Your friend seems to be upset about staying out of sight," Kai-Chang said, as they walked down the hallway.

"A month is a long time to be somewhere by yourself, Kai-Chang," Malachi said.

Kai-Chang, his hands in the sleeves of his kimono stopped. He turned to Malachi. "Not necessary, Mala. I once spent three months in a cave to practice my isolation technique, and to become one with nature," he said.

"Three months, huh? That's a long time," Malachi said.

Kai-Chang began walking again followed by Malachi.

"Not really. One must let go of the things that he feels are important to him. Once you let go of your needs, then life takes on a natural understanding than when one feels the need to be more communicative," Kai-Chang said.

"Meaning what, Kai-Chang?"

"Less talk gives you more time to think. You talk less, you learn to plot more against your enemies. Giving you the advantage," Kai-Chang said.

"That's something to think about, Kai-Chang," Malachi said.

"Exactly, Mala."

"Exactly what, Kai-Chang?" Malachi asked.

"You're beginning to think," Kai-Chang said.

Malachi glanced at him.

Kai-Chang smiled.

Chapter Thirteen
Fire in the Night

Johnny Hawkins was sitting down to dinner when his wife of ten years walked into the dining room and announced that Sheriff Hays was at the door. He told her to let him in.

"You want something to eat, Barney?" Johnny asked as Sheriff Hays walked into the dining room.

"No. I just stopped by to tell you that we can go and get us a Negro whenever you want," Sheriff Hays said.

"Good. Because we have to set an example to the other small towns around here and let them know that we're doing our job when it comes to lynching. Who do you have in mind?" Johnny asked.

"Someone… special," Sheriff Hays said.

"As long as it's a nigger, I don't care," Johnny said. "You sure you don't want some of this fried chicken and mash potatoes? If not you can have some corn on the cob. My wife has a sweet potato pie in the oven for dessert."

Sheriff Hays looked at him. He raised his index finger and pointed to his mouth.

"There's a spit can in the corner, Barney," Johnny said. He watched as Sheriff Hays walked to the corner. "You chew that stuff too much. It's gonna rot your teeth."

"What the hell. As long as I'm happy in the end I don't care," Sheriff Hays said, as he walked back to the table and sat down.

"The boys were talking about you," Johnny said.

Sheriff Hays looked at him. "Yeah," he said.

"They think you've gone soft while messing with those niggers over in Blackenfield," Johnny said, as he stuffed his mouth with a spoonful of mash potatoes. "I told them they'd lost their minds if they think you were throwing in with some niggers. Am I right?"

"Yeah," Sheriff Hays said, as he chewed on his tobacco.

"Uh-huh. Don't let money come between your brethren, Barney."

Sheriff Hays watched as Johnny continuously stuffed his face with mash potatoes and fried chicken. "I won't, Johnny Boy," he said. "Maybe you ought to slow down on the fired chicken while still trying to swallow the potatoes."

"When do you want to go and get our nigger?" Johnny asked.

"A week from now will be perfect. It'd be Malachi's birthday, and all the niggers will be out wearing their Sunday's best," Sheriff Hays said. He chewed heartily on his chewing tobacco.

"Good. We need that kind of stimulation in Gatesville. You know the boys get bored being home listening to their wives nag them all day and night. This gives me a good standing among them, and you, too, Barney," Johnny said, as pointed a fork full of mash potatoes at Sheriff Hays. "It's things like these that will keep us all together."

"Uh-huh."

"You sure you don't want some fried chicken? Jean makes it like you want to lick your hands off instead of wiping them on a napkin," Johnny said.

"Nope. I got to be going, Johnny Boy," he said.

His fat cheeks protruding outward, Johnny Hawkins nodded. His lips were smeared with chicken grease as he raised a chicken bone at Sheriff Hays. Acknowledging his departure.

Sheriff Hays was standing on the porch of Johnny Hawkins house when a thought came to him. Life has always been about money, he told himself, as he walked down the short steps. Anything other than that was stupid. The Ku Klux Klan was stupid, but he knew to go against them would be like cutting his own feet off, because they voted him in office. Before he became sheriff, he worked on a dead farm that yielded nothing but pennies compared to what he was making now shaking down the Negroes. Well, he guessed. You got to give something up to make something else happen.

He spit out some chewing tobacco juice, as he headed down the road toward his car he'd named Sweet Dixie. He'd been thinking about running for mayor once Chuck Gray retired. The man didn't do anything but sit on his ass all day and tell boring jokes to anyone who'd listen.

Sheriff Hays meant to ask Johnny about that possibility coming to fruition in the near future. He spit out some more tobacco juice as he kicked a rock.

Malachi was standing in front of the mirror in Stump's room straightening out his collar as Stump paced back and forth. Kai-Chang was on his floor mat humming with his eyes closed.

"Why can't I come?" Stump demanded. "I've been coped up in this room for so long, I can't breathe, man. Look, I can put a hat on and blend in with the crowd in the party. It's been three weeks, Malachi. Look at me. I even grew a beard. I got to get out of this room!"

Malachi looked down at the full-length mirror at his new clothing. It was his birthday, and he'd become a man by turning eighteen. He watched Stump through the mirror.

"Everyone thinks you skipped town, Stump. If you show up now, the Brown brothers will kill you, and that will mess up my party," Malachi said. He smiled.

"Your party? I ain't had a woman in three weeks! Don't you think it's time for me to party? Malachi let me out of here for a few hours. No one will see me," Stump said.

Malachi turned toward Stump. Stump stopped pacing. "Stump, that cast on your wrist stands out too much. At the moment we have the Brown brothers running around trying to find you. Anyone who comes into the Queen tonight might be a spy for them. We have the advantage at the moment. Do you want to mess that up?" he asked.

Stump cradled his cast. He looked hard at Malachi.

"Give me a gun, and two hours, and the Brown brothers will be gone," he said.

Malachi could see the malice in Stump's penetrating eyes as he stared at him. Stump rarely blinked when he had someone's attention. His eyes appeared to narrow with coldness. He cleared his throat. "Stump," he began, "if you miss one of them, we'll have a war on our hands, and then we all lose. Let's do things slowly...for now."

"Malachi, I'm not used to doing things this way. There were times when Bear and I...." Stump stopped. He placed a hand over his face and sat down on the edge of the bed. "I'm tired of...waiting," he said.

Malachi walked over and sat down next to him. He put an arm around his thin, strong shoulder. "I know how you feel, Stump. You think I don't want to go at them for killing Bear? It takes a lot of restraint to hold back, not because of fear—although I am a little scared of them— but I have to, or everything Bear put into creating the Queen will be gone with one lighted torch through the front window," he said. "I don't want it like that. We have to go at it differently. Patiently."

Stump nodded. "You're right," he said. He looked at Malachi. "You're an old, Malachi. Sure that young, innocent face of yours shows youth, but that mind of yours is very old. Bear taught you right in handling business."

"To be patient is to manipulate your enemies' weakness of imprudence. An enemy who believes it to be invincible, is an enemy that will fall on its own sword when he sees an attack from a full force coming his way," Kai-Chang said. His eyes were still closed. "Only a fool reacts to his feelings. A master tactician reacts to what advantages can be gained by being observant as well as being patient. Knowing his enemies every move before initiating his attack is a man of thought and shrewdness. A commander who will be feared on the battlefield once he displays his ingenuity."

Malachi and Stump looked at Kai-Chang.

"There once was a great emperor in China name Tsui-Wang. He was very powerful in the Eighth Dynasty. A man who'd conquered nations with his brutality and cunning. One day he decided to send his army into a small village on the northern side of the country that had refused to pay their tribute to the state. It was a simple village of no more than two hundred men, women, and children. Tsui-Wang sent in one hundred of his lackluster guardsman. These soldiers were not of any high rank, but he believed they would do to conqueror a village with no military expertise. His greatest asset at the time was his arrogance," Kai-Chang said.

Kai-Chang stopped talking. His eyes were still closed.

Malachi glanced at Stump. He shrugged. They both returned their attention to Kai-Chang.

"Tsui-Wang's men," he began, "were set upon by the villagers with such furiousity, that those soldiers that who'd survived—which had only been ten—decided not to return to the kingdom because of their shame. This failure infuriated Tsui-Wang to the point that he sent out his second to best guardsmen to retaliate. This simple village of peasants destroyed them as well. Their number consisted of five hundred men. Professional soldiers had fallen to the wiles of the small village that showed no military prowess. These hardened warriors were considered to be second best only to Tsui-Wang's personal bodyguards. They were deemed the elite of men."

Kai-Chang opened his eyes, as he turned to Malachi and Stump.

Malachi and Stump waited for him to continue. Seconds ticked by which eventually turned into minutes. Finally Stump sighed.

"Shall I continue?" Kai-Chang asked.

"Yeah," Malachi and Stump said simultaneously.

Kai-Chang nodded, and then closed his eyes again.

"Tsui-Wang became so explosive with anger that he cut off the head of his second in command to set an example for those that had witness his failure," Kai-Chang said. "His anger set off a ripple effect that went out through the ranks of his military. He wanted to know what army was hiding in the village that was skilled enough to kill his second to best fighters."

"All right," Malachi said. "Who was in the village that could do such a thing to his warriors, Kai-Chang?" he asked.

"Wait! There are only women and children in the village," Stump said. "How could they defeat men like that?"

"Men, women, and children," Kai-Chang said, as he nodded while raising a manicured finger.

"Men, women, and children," Malachi repeated.

Kai-Chang looked at Malachi.

A smile slowly began to form on Malachi's face.

Kai-Chang smiled.

"I know the answer," Malachi said. "The men had to be warriors at one time. They taught their wives and sisters how to be warriors, and the women taught the children, making them all a dangerous army."

Kai-Chang nodded. "I am impressed, Mala," he said. "So what Tsui-Wang thought was a village of weak peasants turned out to be a village of warriors. In the end he released the village from its monthly tax, and learned a lesson."

"What was the lesson?" Stump asked.

Kai-Chang smiled. "To underestimate your enemy is to die a thousand deaths on a thousand shards of glass," he said.

"You could've just told us that in the short form," Stump said.

"But I rarely get a captive audience," Kai-Chang said.

Malachi erupted with laughter.

The past three weeks had been a weeks of sleepless nights for Rose Ann in her preparation for Malachi's eighteenth birthday. She had run from corner to corner in the Queen setting up the arrangements of food, balloons, drink, and entertainment. By the time Tuesday night rolled in for Malachi's birthday, the Queen was packed with well-wishers bringing gifts. Malachi had to get away from everyone wishing him happy birthday as the night wore on. He went back to Stump's room after a few hours.

Malachi used the key to enter Stump's room. As he closed the door behind him Kai-Chang appeared and eased his body through the door. With the door locked, he turned around and his nostrils were assaulted by the smell of moonshine. He looked and saw Stump sitting in a chair without his cast in the semi-dark room.

"Happy birthday, Malachi!" Stump shouted, as he raised his tin cup. "I can remember when I turned eighteen. I got a kick in my ass from my step-father and a red shiny apple from my mother."

"I see the doctor took your cast off," Malachi said. He walked over to a chair in the corner. He picked it up and walked to where Stump was sitting, placing it in front of him, he sat down. "How's your wrist?"

"Achy. Can I come down and help you celebrate your birthday?" Stump asked.

Malachi shook his head. "The Brown brothers are coming to my party," he said. "But here, I brought you some of my birthday cake."

"You invited them bastards!" Stump snapped. Moonshine flying out of his cup from agitation as he stood up. "I don't want any damn cake! I want to kill the Brown brothers, and get me a woman afterward."

"The cake is good. The Brown brothers invited themselves, and the woman thing is out of the question," Malachi said.

"I've been in this room too long, Malachi. I need some air, and I need a woman!" Stump snapped.

"I've been thinking about that. And I might have a solution to our problem," Malachi said. "You know Dave the Drunk's six month term for sheriff is over at the end of next month."

"Yeah. So?" Stump said.

"So…." Malachi repeated.

Stump looked at Malachi. Malachi smiled at Stump.

"What is it, boy?" Stump asked, as he brought the tin cup to his lips. "Don't smile at me without telling me what you thinking." He stopped. Stump's eyes narrowed.

He looked at Malachi. "I know you're not thinking what I think you thinking."

Malachi nodded.

"Oh, hell naw! I'm not going to do it, Malachi. I ain't never like those bastards!" Stump shouted.

"It can give us an edge to get to the Brown brothers," Malachi said.

Stump gulped down the contents in his tin cup. He shook his head. "I'm not running for sheriff of Blackenfield. I don't like it one bit," he said. "Anyway, I couldn't take the Brown brothers on by myself."

"You'd need some deputies," Malachi said.

"Right," Stump said. "Where am I going to get deputies?"

"My boys," Malachi said.

Stump looked at him.

"We'll get the deputies from the Queen. This way they're legitimate to go after the Brown brothers with the town backing them. Especially those people who are being extorted by them. Everyone would be on your side, Stump," he said.

Stump rubbed his tired eyes with one hand while extending his tin cup out to Malachi to have it refilled. Malachi reached for the moonshine jug that was on the floor near Stump's feet. He filled Stump's empty cup, and watched Stump sip from it.

Stump removed his hand. He stared at Malachi. "Boy that brain of yours is working! Hot damn, it might work! Either way it goes, I'll be out of this damn room. It sounds like you got yourself a plan, son," he said. "Wait. People will still dislike me thinking I killed Bear. No one will trust me."

Malachi filled his cup with some moonshine. He drank it fast. As the burning sensation of the moonshine went down his mouth, Malachi eyes opened wide. He began coughing. Stump stood up and began slapping him on the back to clear his air passage.

"You're a thinking boy, I give you that, but you ain't a drinker," Stump said, as he laughed.

Through short breaths, Malachi said, "I will take care of that, Stump."

"I know you will. You're shrewd, Malachi. Very shrewd," he said.

When Malachi and Kai-Chang left Stump's room, they'd both agreed as to what had to be done to achieve success. At the end of the month, Stump would begin preparing to run for office. As Malachi walked around the crowded Queen greeting everyone, he was smiling. He was glad it was his birthday. He saw Betty Mae standing alone and walked over to her.

"Hi, Betty Mae," Malachi said.

Betty Mae turned toward him. She was attractively dressed in a black shimmering dress with long tassels that fell to the top of her knees. She casually walked over to Malachi. When she was close enough, she threw her arms around his neck and pulled him to her. Her lips found Malachi's. Malachi gasped as he felt her tongue enter his mouth. He didn't know what to do since it was his first time he'd been kissed.

Betty Mae broke their kiss, and looked at him quizzically. "What's wrong?" she asked. Her arms were still locked around his neck.

"Huh? Oh…Well—"

"That's the first time you've been kissed, isn't?" Betty Mae asked.

"What? No!" Malachi said indignantly. He looked at Betty Mae, and then looked down at his new shoes.

"Yes, it was. I thought I'd wait until you turned eighteen so we can have some fun, but I may have to hold your hand along the way," Betty Mae said. She smiled at Malachi's uncomfortability. "I'd be gentle with you."

"Malachi! Malachi!"

Malachi spun around at the hysterical cry from his sister. Rose Ann ran up to him crying.

"What's wrong, Rose?" Malachi asked.

"They took him!" Rose Ann screamed.

"They took who, Rose?" Betty Mae asked, as she came around Malachi and began rubbing her back. "Calm down, girl. What happened?"

"We were walking in the woods about a quarter of a mile out of town. Just holding hands and…and enjoying the night. Next thing we know, they're all around us. Roger pushed me ahead of him and he tried to fight them, but they were everywhere. I ran. I just kept running," Rose Ann said. She was out of breath and was hugging Malachi with all of her strength.

"Rose, where is Roger?" Malachi asked.

"The…The Klan. The Ku Klux Klan took him away," Rose Ann said, as she collapsed into Malachi's chest, sobbing and screaming.

"The Klan, huh?" Stump said as he stared out the window. "I ain't never known them to be in this part of the county."

Malachi, with his hands behind his back, paced the room, as Kai-Chang sat on the floor near the door on his rug. "What am I going to do, Stump? My sister is…out of it," he said.

"Yeah, those crackers like to lynch us niggers to the highest tree," Stump said as he stared out of the window.

"How can we find them?" Malachi asked. He stopped pacing Stump's room and stared at him. "I got to get him back, Stump, before they…hurt him."

"Well, dealing with the Klan, they ain't the smartest of white folk that I know. All you got to do is climb the highest house or tree, and you'll see them," Stump said, as he turned toward Malachi.

"What?" Malachi asked.

Stump raised his arm and pointed out the window.

Malachi rushed over to the window. He couldn't believe what he was looking at. About five miles out of town, a blazing cross was burning.

"Those crackers are the dumbest sheet wearing fools I've ever met. You got to be a fool to be walking around with sheets over your head, and none on your bed," Stump said.

"We've got to get out there, Stump," Malachi said.

"Um-hmm," Stump said.

Malachi walked to the door. He looked down at Kai-Chang. "Kai-Chang, we have to go," he said.

Kai-Chang eyes were closed. "Why does, Mala, want to go into a storm? A storm that will surely sweep you into the tortuous sea and may cause death," Kai-Chang said.

"Huh?" Malachi said.

Stump turned to look at Malachi. "What he's saying

is that if we ain't prepared, the Klan will lynch us, too," he said.

"How do we get prepared?" Malachi asked, as he turned to face Stump.

"I need a gun," Stump said.

CHAPTER FOURTEEN
Sheets and Hoods

They rode about four and a half miles in Cotton's car. When they thought they'd ridden close enough to not be seen, they exited the car, and walked thorough dense foliage with Stump leading the way.

"What if they have a lookout, Stump?" Malachi asked, as he followed Stump.

"This is a Klan lynching, Malachi. What are they going to have lookouts for?" Stump asked. He walked with caution while looking around. "If the Klan needs to have lookouts, then they're doing something good. It's a damn lynching. They know ain't no one coming out here but other crackers."

"Sometimes the least suspecting is usually the one to be caught," Kai-Chang said.

Malachi and Stump stopped.

Kai-Chang, who was bringing up the rear, stopped as well. He was dressed in all black. The kimono he usually wore was now replaced with a black, tight fitting pantsuit. His long hair was tied and pinned up in a bun. He was wearing some kind of head gear that concealed his features. That was also black. If he stood in the darkness of the tress, he appeared to disappear entirely.

Stump turned around and looked at Kai-Chang. "Why are you here again?" he asked.

Malachi touched Stump on the arm. "We need, Kai-Chang," he said. "Take my word for it."

"Sure we do," Stump said sarcastically. "You got your gun?"

Malachi touched the gun in his waist. He shivered. "Yeah," he said.

"Let's keep it moving," Stump said. He turned around and began walking. Malachi and Kai-Chang followed

They walked for thirty minutes before they heard the voices ahead of them. If it weren't for the moonlight, the darkness would've had them all walking in a complete circle, Malachi thought, as he fingered the butt of the gun in his waist.

"All right, boys. Tonight we will initiate the new recruits by the spilling of this nigger's blood," Johnny Hawkins said.

Stump, Malachi and Kai-Chang were crouched down looking through several bushes at the crowd of over thirty Klansmen dressed in their white sheets and holding burning torches.

"Bring the rope and the nigger out," Johnny said.

The crowd of white sheets parted to reveal a shirtless,

frightened, Roger being escorted by two Klansmen who were holding his arms tightly.

"That's him?" Stump whispered to Malachi.

"Uh-huh," Malachi said.

"I don't know how we can get to him. We only got two guns…Well, one really. Boy, you ain't never shot a man before, have you?" Stump asked.

"No," Malachi said in a voice.

"All right. Listen, firing a gun is easy. You aim it at the person's biggest cavity. In this case, it's the man's chest. Pull the trigger, and the bullet will do the rest," Stump said.

"I…don't…know—"

"Damnit, boy, don't go…Forget it. Give the gun to the chink," Stump said, as he and Malachi turned around to locate Kai-Chang. He was gone. "Where the hell did he go?"

"Argggg!"

"Who is screaming like that?" Johnny asked, as he looked out in the crowd of white sheets. He was standing on a large rock.

"I think it was Tommy," a Klansman several feet away answered.

Sheriff Hays, who'd been standing around spitting out tobacco juice, looked on indifferently as he scanned the area

"Owwww!"

"Now who was that?" Johnny asked. He rose up on his tiptoes to look around. "This isn't a game, boys. We got serious business here tonight."

"Johnny, I swear to God, Buck was standing beside me, and then he was gone a moment later. If it wasn't for the scream, I wouldn't even have noticed he was gone," a man of small size said from the back.

"Ohhhh!"

"Cut it out!" Johnny shouted. "This is serious, boys. This nigger has to swing tonight, so other niggers will know the Ku Klux Klan holds sway over this county."

"Ahhhhh!"

"Goddamn it! What the hell is going on back there?" Johnny asked. He looked at Sheriff Hays. "This ain't anything to play with." He returned his attention to the crowd of white sheets. "When you come into the fold of the Klan, you've entered the cusp of our wonderful nation. And the next one of ya'll that holler out like that again, is going to be disavowed as a member."

"What is disavow, Johnny Boy?" Charlie asked.

"Huh? Uh...Well, it's a word that...Forget it, Charlie. How's that salve my grandmother gave you for your burns doing?" Johnny asked.

"It's great, Johnny," Charlie said. "I—"

"Nooooo!"

"Didn't I tell you fools that if—"

"Johnny Boy, a dark shadow came out of the darkness and grabbed Mo-Mo," Hubert said.

"A dark shadow? You've been drinking again, Hubert? I thought you said you gave it up after hearing voices coming from the corn fields every night when you went to bed," Sheriff Hays asked, as he hefted his gun belt over his big belly that he'd strapped on outside his white sheet. "We're in the woods ain't anything out here but dark shadows."

The crowd of white sheets slowly began to part in the middle.

"What are you boys doing?" Johnny asked, as he watched men step to the side, creating a passageway in front of him.

"You are in possession of a friend of my employer and I would like to claim him," Kai-Chang said.

The appearance of Kai-Chang made some of the men remove their hoods and gawk at the sight of him.

"Damn it. That's a China man!" Charlie shouted.

"What the hell? How did he get here from China?" Johnny asked, as he stepped forward.

"It ain't how he got here, it's what we gonna do with him now that he's here?" Sheriff Hays asked. He put his hand on the gun butt, and stared at Kai-Chang.

"All right. What we have here boys is a situation that is to our benefit," Johnny said. "Instead of one nigger hanging from the tree, we're gonna have a yellow nigger hanging with him. Get an extra rope!"

"Malachi, where did this chink come from? He's a damn fool!" Stump said. "He's standing in the middle of a bunch of crackers wearing sheets with rawhide ropes in their hand. What the hell is he thinking about? He done lost his mind!"

Malachi smiled.

"Instead of us saving Roger, now we got to go get him as well," Stump said.

"Maybe not," Malachi said. "Let's watch it a few more minutes and see what happens."

"Watch? Boy, them Klansmen is going to kill the both of them. Get your gun ready, we going in," Stump said.

Malachi grabbed Stump by the forearm. "Wait! Stump, give it five minutes, and then we'll go in to get them," he said.

"Five minutes! Boy, I know you scared, but fear can be your strength at times. Let's go get them now," he said.

"No, Stump!" Malachi said. He held onto Stump's forearm. Gripping it hard. "Take my word for it and give Kai-Chang a chance."

"Chance? Malachi, those crackers is going to hang that yellow man and your sister's boyfriend if we don't go in," he said.

"Five minutes, Stump," Malachi said.

Stump looked at Malachi.

"Some of you boys garb the China man, and bring him up here along side our nigger," Johnny said.

Two Klansmen stepped out of the crowd and approached Kai-Chang. The bigger of the two got to Kai-Chang first. He reached for Kai-Chang's shoulder. As his hand hovered in the air, Kai-Chang, with shocking speed, stepped in, and released a volley of punches beginning from the big Klansman midsection up toward his chest and into his face. The punches were accurate and hard. The big man fell to the ground. He twitched for a moment, and then went limp. The small Klansman saw what took place, and stepped back.

"Well, I'd be doggone," Hubert said. "That yellow chink knocked out Bubba! I mean, he's out cold!"

"Well, don't just stand there. Get him!" Johnny snapped.

As if on cue, the passageway that had been opened for Kai-Chang closed with the conversion of white sheets and hoods all attacking him at once.

"Did you see what that chink did?" Stump asked.

"I told you," Malachi said.

Kai-Chang, his feet, lifting off the ground, found a mark each time he placed his foot into a Klansman's chest, stomach, face, or throat. The crackling sounds of knees, arms, and wrists were heard being snapped along with horrible, painful screams.

Malachi was in awe as he watched Kai-Chang's brilliance of speed and powerful punches landing on men, and, the men, falling to the ground and rolling over in pain and spitting out blood from busted ribs and broken jaws. When the sound of a gun being fired entered the fray, everyone stopped moving and looked around to see who had fired it. Or, who had been shot.

"Get the hell out of the way!" Sheriff Hays shouted. He was pointing his gun into the crowd as he searched for Kai-Chang. He watched his brethren of Klansmen part ways for a better view. "Where is he?"

They all turned around to look at the spot Kai-Chang had been standing. He was gone.

"What the hell was that?" Johnny asked. He stepped closer into the crowd of Klansmen. "You idiots couldn't take down one yellow man wearing his goddamn pajamas!" He screamed.

He received his answer as men began rolling around on the ground and screaming out in pain.

"He's gone," Sheriff Hays said.

"Gone!" Johnny snapped. He walked into the middle of the crowd. He looked at his fallen Klansmen. He put his hands on his fat hips, and shook his head. "Ya'll all a bunch of women! You let one skinny chink whup ya'll. Then you let him get away. Okay, what the hell. We'll take it out on the nigger. Hurry up and lynch him. I got to get home and get me some apple pie."

"The nigger is gone!" Charlie screamed.

Everyone turned around. The two Klansmen who'd been holding Roger, lay on the ground unconscious.

"What the hell happened to our nigger?" Johnny asked.

Twenty minutes later, Stump, followed by Malachi, Kai-Chang, and Roger were getting into the car.

"Kai-Chang, you one fighting mother," Stump said, as he started the engine.

Kai-Chang nodded from the back seat.

"Roger, you just had your neck saved by a chink," Stump began. "Those Klansmen would've hung you like a rag doll from the tallest tree if they had ten more minutes to get it done."

Roger, his eyes nearly popping out of his head, stared at Stump and nodded. "Not only was them white men going to lynch me, they wanted to pour hot tar over my body, and then feather me before hanging me. That's not right what they were planning to do," he said. His voice was cracking with emotion as he nervously glanced back over his shoulder to look out the back window.

"Boy, ain't nothing right about the Klan. They do what they do because they are the white folk, and we are the Negroes," Stump said.

No one said a word as Stump threw the car into gear, and drove down the dark road.

Six months later, the streets were filled with people running around shouting and having fun as the warmth of the day contributed to the festival. It had been an easy win for Stump to beat Dave the Drunk. Considering that Stump had won by ninety-eight percent of the vote and Dave the Drunk had disappeared without conceding defeat had encouraged the voters to take to the street in jubilation. That jubilation, Malachi knew, could've been a riot if he hadn't begun planting the seed that it wasn't Stump who had killed Bear weeks ago, but the Brown brothers. The Brown brothers didn't dispute the rumor, which, Malachi knew they wouldn't due to their arrogance.

Malachi, dressed in a nice gray suit and new shoes, stood on the steps of the Queen and smiled as he saw the Brown brothers look his way as they walked by him. Their expressions were one of anger. Malachi didn't have anything to fear from them at that moment because Kai-Chang was standing beside him.

"You are happy, Mala?" Kai-Chang asked.

"Yep."

"Because your friend has won this thing?" Kai-Chang asked.

"Uh-huh," Malachi said.

"But would not this act bring more trouble to you, Mala?"

Malachi turned toward Kai-Chang. "The Brown brothers think they own this town. But by Stump becoming the new sheriff, it gives us an edge to counterattack their moves," he said.

Kai-Chang looked at Malachi. "No, Mala. It makes your adversary more desperate to seek your demise to achieve his own destiny. Confucius says that any man who denies another man his future is a man whose future is doomed for the present."

"What?" Malachi asked. He tilted his head to the side, as he tried to understand what Kai-Chang had said.

Kai-Chang, his hands deep inside his burgundy kimono, sighed. "If you stop another warrior from gathering his fruits and spoils among the masses, that warrior will only become more confrontational and belligerent. He will no longer hide in the shadows and conduct his war, he will create a battle that everyone will see, and one he must win to contain his dominance," Kai-Chang said.

Malachi stared at Kai-Chang. "So, you're telling me that this will only make the Brown brothers angrier?" he asked.

Kai-Chang nodded.

"Come on, let's go inside," Malachi said.

As Malachi and Kai-Chang walked through the doors of the Queen, a bottle came crashing at their feet. Malachi was startled. Kai-Chang didn't flinch. They both looked up. Dave the Drunk was sitting at a table with four jugs of moonshine in front of him. He had one bottle at his mouth, gulping down its contents. Most of it though, was spilling out onto his clothing.

"Goddamn it!" Dave the Drunk shouted as he slammed the jug down. "I was railroaded, Malachi. The people didn't give me a chance," he said.

Malachi and Kai-Chang walked toward him.

"Dave, what are you doing?" Malachi asked.

"Drinking! Hell, that's what I do," Dave snapped.

Malachi sat down at the table. The look of concern was sincere as he stared at Dave. "Look, man. What do you want? All the people in town know that…you're…Well, that you're a drunk, Dave. It was a fair vote. These are the same people who voted you in as sheriff, remember?"

"I was a good sheriff. When something happened, I

was there. Oh, yeah. I might've been a few minutes late after the incident, but I was there," Dave said.

His words were slurring, and Malachi had to lean forward to understand what he was saying.

"Dave, the town is going through a change, and people felt you weren't right for that change, that's all," Malachi said.

"Who?" Dave asked.

Malachi watched as Dave the Drunk brought the jug of moonshine to his lips, and let the liquid flow freely down his throat, onto his shirt, and his pants.

"Did you vote for me, Malachi?" Dave asked, as he brought the jug down to his chest, and gave Malachi a look of sadness.

Malachi smiled.

Dave slammed the jug down. "You didn't?" he asked.

"I voted for you and Stump. You're both good men," Malachi said.

Dave looked at him. He arched his right eyebrow. "Could you do that?" he asked.

"Yep," Malachi said.

"You voted for both of us?" Dave asked. He watched Malachi nod his head. "Okay, if that's the case, then I'll go shake Stump's hand and call it quits." He stood up. Knocking the chair over. "Wait! What am I going to do about a job?"

Malachi laughed. "What about working behind the bar at the Queen?" he said.

"Huh?"

"It's my way of keeping a good man working," Malachi said.

"I don't need any handouts, Malachi. You're a good boy and all, but I can do for myself," Dave said. He pushed out his small chest.

"I'm not asking you to be less of a man, Dave. I'm asking you to work for me because I need you," Malachi said.

"Yeah?"

Malachi nodded.

"All right, then I'll work for you. I got to be going now. I have to find Stump and congratulate him," Dave said. "You boys can finish drinking these other three jugs of moonshine."

Malachi and Kai-Chang watched as Dave staggered out the door a few minutes, and fall down the five steps of the Queen into the street.

"You are a good man, Mala. Instead of harping salt into a wounded man, you closed his wounds by showing kindness and compassion. That is wisdom beyond those your age," Kai-Chang said.

Malachi smiled. "What was I going to do? I couldn't let him drink himself to death. In his mind he felt he was a failure, but it was me who brought about his failure. I wouldn't have slept well tonight if I didn't try to give him something back, Kai-Chang."

"True words of benevolence," Kai-Chang said. He nodded as he bowed. "So, you have been listening to me."

"When I can understand what you're trying to say," Malachi said, as he turned toward Kai-Chang.

The right corner of Kai-Chang's lips lifted.

"Was that a smile, Kai-Chang?" Malachi asked.

Kai-Chang said nothing.

"It was a smile," Malachi said, as he smiled.

Two weeks later, Stump had deputized four men who were out of towners and who hadn't been corrupted by the Brown brother. They were four, big, brawlers who he coerced into joining him by offering them thirty-five dollars a month instead of the usual ten dollars. He told his deputies to watch for the Brown brothers men, and if the Brown brothers men went into any stores to follow them in and make them feel uncomfortable to the point of them walking out without collecting their extortion money from the storeowners.

By the end of the month, the tension in Blackenfield was so thick; a person could cut it with a butcher's knife. Everyone in the town seemed to be walking on needles. Stump sat in the sheriff's office with his feet on the table, and his head leaning back staring at the ceiling. The crashing sound of his door being opened didn't bulge him.

"You fucking bastard!" Chester shouted, as he stood in the doorway with Sylvester and Lester. "You think because you're the sheriff, we won't kill your black ass? You're thinking wrong, Negro, because we can and will if you keep pushing us."

"You got these field niggers all in our business, and messing with our money, Stump. You cross the line with that bullshit!" Sylvester snapped.

Lester said nothing as he quietly eased off to the side.

"We know you and that punk, Malachi, is trying to take over this town, but it ain't going to work," Chester began. "We been running this town since it sprung up."

With slow deliberation, Stump looked at them.

"You want to take us on, Stump, then bring your ass to the fire, because we're gonna burn you something good!" Chester shouted.

"First, this town was never yours. Don't you boys remember it was me and Bear who named this town, and brought it to where it is today," Stump said, as he slowly removed his feet from his desk. "You three have forgotten who the brains were behind this town back in those days. We split the town up. You remember what it was like back then? So now you three think because Bear is dead, and I was in hiding that you own this town. That will never happen as long as I live."

"Well, maybe it's time for you to stop living. Maybe it's a time for you to stop breathing, too," Lester said. He snickered.

"That sounds real good coming from a short man with an even shorter mind," Stump said. He smiled at Lester.

Lester quickly reached inside his jacket for the gun that was in his waist.

Stump pushed aside the basket that hid his hand, and pointed Bear's gun at Lester. "If it ain't your balls you're grabbing, and I know you ain't got any of those, then I suggest when you pull your hand out of your pants it better be empty. If it is a gun you're reaching for, well, you can pull it out now while I'm holding this gun, and I'll put a bullet through your chest before you can blink. It don't make me a difference how I shoot you, or where I shoot you, Lester. It's your choice," he said.

Lester watched Stump. A smile slowly began to emerge.

"Lester," Chester said. "Let it go."

"Yeah, Lester, let it go," Stump said, as he continued to smile.

Lester snickered. He slowly removed his hand from his jacket. It came out empty.

"You made a wise choice today, Lester," Stump said.

"Today is your day, Stump," Lester said.

"Everyday is my day, Lester. Hell, I'm the sheriff. What else you boys want to talk about?"

"That little beating I gave you wasn't enough, huh?" Sylvester asked.

"Turn that around, Sly. I was whipping your big ass until someone cold-cocked me. And, if my guess is right, it was probably you, Lester," he said.

Lester began snickering louder.

"What do we have here, Stump? A Mexican standoff or something?" Chester began. "We can't make any money if we're going after each other throats. You want to sit down and work this out?"

"Nothing is going to work out. I'm changing how this game is played. No more extorting the old store owners who are trying to keep a roof over their heads," Stump said. "Instead, why don't you boys donate something to the town that the people can appreciate?"

"Donate?" Sylvester said. "We ain't donating a goddamn thing!" He took a step closer to Stump.

Stump cocked the gun as he set its aim directly on Sylvester's forehead.

"Come on, big man. Bring your cornbread and fatback eating ass over here. Let me see if your big head can stop one of these slugs from entering your body," Stump said.

Sylvester froze.

"Uh-huh. Just the way I figured it. You Brown boys like intimidating people when the three of you can gang up on someone small, but when it's time to face someone your own size, it's a different story," Stump said.

"Now you listen—"

"No, Chester! You listen! Either you boys gonna do things my way or you three can pack your bags and money, and find a new town. That's your only option right now. Anyway, personally, I hope you choose the wrong one, so I can start putting my boot in the three of your butts just for the hell of it," Stump said. A wide grin appeared. "This little meeting is over. You got two days to tell me what you gonna do about the donation to the town, and if you gonna change your ways."

Chester stared at Stump.

Stump's grin grew wider as he began to wave the barrel of the gun back and forth.

Chester nodded. "Let's go boys," he said.

Stump watched the three of them turn around and walk out the door.

As the Brown brothers made a purposeful stride down the street in the direction of the Goldspot. Lester, who was following began to whistle. Chester stopped. He turned around to face his younger brother. Lester smiled at him. With uncanny speed, Chester's right hand came up and struck Lester in the face. The blow was so hard it made Lester stumble backward several feet before he collapsed to the ground. He looked up at Chester rubbing his jaw.

"What'd you do that for, Chester?" Lester asked.

Chester walked over to his fallen brother. He pointed his right index finger several inches from his nose. "From this moment on," he began, "you are to find a way to kill Stump and that young pup, Malachi," he said.

Lester smiled, and began to snicker. Chester reached down and helped him up.

"You know what you're doing, Chester?" Sylvester asked, as he walked up behind him.

With Lester on his feet, Chester spun around, and unleashed a volley of blows to Sylvester's stomach, chest, and face. His hands were blinding fast, as each blow knocked Sylvester back and off balanced. Sylvester, big, and burly didn't go to the ground. Instead, he cowered up from the blows until Chester had exhausted himself.

Breathing heavy and hard, Chester leaned forward with his hands on his knees, and looked up at his brother, Sylvester. "No…more games…are…we… gonna…play with these…bastards," Chester said between breathes.

Sylvester said nothing as he tried to stop the blood from running from is mouth and nose with the handkerchief he'd pulled from his back pocket.

"I'm tired of playing these goddamn games!" Chester shouted.

Lester and Sylvester watched as their brother strode off leaving them behind.

Lester began to snicker.

Sylvester turned toward him and raised his left arm.

Lester's hand went immediately toward his waist. "Go ahead and try it," he said. "I'll put two quick holes in your ass, and I don't care how mad Chester gets after I do it."

Sylvester slowly lowered his arm.

"I thought you'd change your mind," Lester said. "Come on, let's go."

Sylvester nodded his head for Lester to go first.

Lester placed one foot in front of him, and then stopped. "Nope, Sly, you go first," he said.

Sylvester smiled. He turned around and followed Chester. He heard Lester behind him snickering.

Chapter Fifteen
No place to Dream

Two hours later, Lester sat in a chair as Sally pampered him with cold compresses to his swollen jaw.

"You see, baby, if they really love you they wouldn't do these things to you," Sally said, as she applied the cold compress to Lester's jaw. "And why is it that you have to do all the dirty work while they get all the fame. I tell you, baby, you are the guts and brains of your brothers. You just have to step up and take what is yours."

Lester said nothing as he watched Sally lean over him. She was only wearing her bra and panties. After she applied the cold compress to the right of his face, he simply stared at Sally as she walked back and forth.

"If they were any real men—like you, baby—they would do themselves what they're asking you to do. Why is it they act like they're running things around here when it's really you? May I make a suggestion?" Sally asked.

Lester nodded as he stared hungrily at Sally's breasts.

"Don't do what they ask. Let Stump handle your brothers, then when he finishes, you take on Stump. But let me tell you, baby, Stump ain't no push over. Sure, Bear might've been big and threatening, but it was Stump who put fear into anyone. That man is mean. Mean as a shark eating dead fish that floats by. If he bites you, you're going to lose a lot of blood poison. You go up against Stump, you make sure you take two guns," Sally said. She went to the edge of the bed and sat down. She looked at Lester. "One time, Bear and Stump had some trouble with these two drifters. Bear, he wanted to talk to the men and tell them they were getting into something that would…you know, be harmful to them. Not Stump, though. Stump wanted to go to the men's room and kick their ass before the sun came up."

"Did he?" Lester asked.

"No. Bear held him back for about a week until finally, one of the men beat one of the girls who'd been cleaning the rooms. When that happened, Bear unleashed Stump," Sally said.

"Unleashed him? What does that mean?" Lester asked. He grimaced as she touched the compress to his jaw again. Hoping the swelling would go down by the next day.

"There seems to be something building up in Stump. He's always been quiet naturally, but finding out the man had beaten one of the girls to the point of almost killing her, Stump had no mercy for him. Stump snuck into the man's room one early morning before the sun was up. He had a bull's whip in his hand. The man was sleeping naked with another woman in the bed with him. He opened his eyes to see Stump standing over him. The man tried to grab a gun that was on the small night table beside the bed. Stump slammed the man's hand with the handle of the knife he had in his other hand, then he began to whip the man with the whip."

"What's mean about that? The bastard deserved it," Lester said.

Sally began to shake her head. "Stump had been standing over that man for thirty minutes just watching him sleep. I don't know what made the man wake up, but when he did, I bet he'd wished he'd died in his sleep, because, Stump beat the skin off him with that whip. And, because he was screaming so loud he'd awaken everyone on the floor he was staying on, didn't help his partner. When his partner ran into the room to stop Stump, Stump put the knife he was carrying into the man's stomach up to the hilt. He held the partner's shoulder while he pulled the knife upward toward his chest. While the second man, bleeding badly, lay on the floor dying, Stump returned his attention to the man he'd been beating with the whip. When he finished, the man was dead, and so was his partner. Stump, without the slightest remorse, stepped over the two dead bodies, went outside to the barn and washed the blood off his face and hands," Sally said.

Lester stared at her. He stood up and walked toward Sally. He bent down as if to give her a kiss. "Bitch, is that story suppose to scare me!" he screamed inches from her face. Sally jumped back. "Because it doesn't! I'll kill him and anyone else if I want to," he said.

Sally crawled onto the bed backward while staring at Lester as she tried to get away from him. "I didn't mean to say you were scared of him, sweetie. Maybe we ought to get away for awhile until this thing blows over, then we will come back and pick up the pieces that will benefit you, baby," she said. "I know you're not scared of anyone."

Lester stared at her. "Leave my brothers?" he asked.

"They don't care about you. I'm the only one who cares about you! They just want to use you, like they always used you when you were a child. You remember you telling me that it was you who finished the fights they started. It was you they asked to clean up problems they'd made. It's you who's the backbone of the both of them. You don't need them. They need you! Baby, I know you're better than the both of them," Sally said, as she reached out and caressed Lester's arm. "It's you who should be commanding them."

"I'm I better than Bear and Stump?" Lester asked, as he slowly walked toward her on the other side of the bed.

"Huh?"

"I'm I better than the both of them in bed?" Lester asked.

Sally, hunched in the middle of the bed, stared at Lester. She didn't know where the questioning was leading, but she knew when an opportunity presented itself, and when to grab it before it got away. If it was an opportunity? Lester was mercurial, she knew. She had to be careful with him.

"Come on, babbbyyyy," Lester purred. "You slept

with both of them. What were you doing? Sharing your ass because of friendship?"

"Huh? I…No, I liked…them," Sally said. "I loved… Bear."

"You like any man you think you can control. You loved Bear, huh? I didn't see you mourning too much when he was killed," Lester said, as he reached her.

Sally lowered her head.

"Sure, you loved him. You'd love anyone you open your legs to, bitch!" Lester snapped.

Sally looked up. Her eyes had become feral as her chest rose and fell. Her teeth pulled back into a snarl. "Motherfucker, you don't know shit! I gave Bear my heart. My damn soul and he didn't appreciate it or cared that I gave it to him! Only woman he ever loved was the Queen!"

Lester stopped. He stared at Sally and saw a woman he'd never seen before. He watched as Sally stood up on the bed. Her voice was beginning to rise with anger.

"All you fucking men ain't shit! A woman gives you her heart, and you bastards rip it from her instead of caressing it, and showing that you can be kind enough to hold it and love her back. No, not you limp, small dick fools! Ya'll all think a woman want you because of what you can do for her in bed. Well, it ain't that at all. We love you bastards because we just asking to give us what we give you every miserable day. Do you know how many times I told that to Bear? Too many damn times! And he always told me to move on. That he wasn't good enough for me. I should try and find me a man who'd make me happy all of the time of each day. Goddamn asshole! I was a good woman to him. Sure, I know I've been around, but hell, that doesn't stop a damn thing." Sally said, as she came off the bed and walked up to Lester. Lester took a step back. "Real men don't need to be told what a woman wants. They just know it. Bear didn't know shit, but the Queen! The Queen! The Queen! I was tired of listening to what plans he had for the Queen, and nothing for me. Me! The woman who was fucking him! Pleasing his fat ass! Letting my body be ravaged because of that love, and all I wanted was for him to say he loved me. He loved the damn Queen more than he loved me, I tell you!"

Lester stared into Sally's, pitiless eyes. He saw something he never thought he'd never see, especially in the eyes of a woman. He knew those eyes staring angrily at him. He saw those eyes every day. They were the eyes of a mad person. A person whose mind had been gone a long time ago. They were the same horrific eyes he possessed whenever he looked in the mirror.

"It hurt me a little but the pain went away after a couple of days, and being with you substituted for that love lost, but now you have to be a man and remove yourself from these bastard who are only trying to use you like Bear used me," Sally said.

Lester stared at her. "Bitch, you've lost your fucking mind," he said.

The blow snapped Lester's head back as Sally's open hand landed across his face. His eyes filled with confusion and became watery, as he stared at Sally dumbfound.

"That's the last time you're gonna call me that," Sally said. "It hurt me when I killed Bear, but that hurt is gone now. I have to live with myself knowing that, and love the man I'm with."

Lester's mouth fell open as he rubbed the other side of his face. "You killed Bear?" he asked.

"Motherfucking right, I did! Ain't no man gonna keep putting me down when I'm trying to love him with every ounce of my being. That bastard! I snuck in through the secret passageway in his office that Bear had told me about earlier that night. We talked. I told him I wanted to marry him. The bastard laughed at me, and told me to go lay down. When he heard ya'll coming, he walked to the door to greet ya'll. I went to his desk and took out his gun. When I called out to him and he turned around, I shot him. I killed him because he didn't love me like I loved him. And he ain't the first one I killed when it came to me being loved back," Sally said with pride. She raised her chin, and stared at Lester.

Lester stared back at her. He blinked once, and then again. He took another step back only to have Sally take a step forward toward him.

"I want you to know that I love you, Lester, and anything I say or do is for the best of us and how we can make our future better," Sally said.

"You...love...me?" Lester asked.

"Yeah," Sally said, as she took a step closer to Lester.

"You...love...me?" Lester said again.

"Yeah, motherfucker. I love you!" Sally snapped.

Lester slowly began to shake his head. He did not take his eyes off Sally's face. His fists began to open and close rapidly. His hands, with blinding came up fast around Sally's throat. Sally's eyes snapped open wide in surprise. She grabbed Lester's wrist to break free. Lester began to squeeze.

"You can't love me. No one loves me but my brothers,"

Lester hissed, as he continued to squeeze harder. "My brothers are all that I have and trust. You started a lot of shit by killing Bear, bitch. Too much shit and we're feeling it."

Sally reached for Lester's face. Her nails were sharp claws as she scratched Lester's face from the top of his eyebrow and raked her hand downward to the bottom of his chin to break free, but it was no use, for Lester only tightened his grip.

Moments before she lost consciousness. Her eyes nearly popping out of her head, Sally looked to the right of her and saw Bear standing in the corner smiling. Darkness engulfed her seconds later.

As darkness fell that night, the Queen became full. Malachi was standing at the bar listening to the man with his back to the stage playing his guitar. He was sitting down in a chair. He'd turned the chair around with his back to the audience, and had begun to play blues songs. Malachi was impressed by the man's guitar skill. He'd never heard anyone play that way. The man chords seemed to come to life as he sang.

"Hey, he can play," Stump said, as he walked up to Malachi.

"Yeah. I put him in the act," Malachi said, as he straightened his tie and smiles.

"The Brown brothers stopped by about two hours ago," Stump said. "I told them that they had to change their ways."

Malachi laughed.

"Yeah, I should've been laughing too, but those boys play a hard game," Stump said. "I thought I might have to shoot that crazy bastard Lester. Man, that cat can really sing. And listen to how he's plucking that guitar. Beautiful. "

"His name is R.J. That's what he said to call him. He's just passing through heading to Mississippi. Maybe I can get him to show me a few chords before he leaves, you know," Malachi said.

Malachi and Stump watched as Cotton hurried up to them.

"Boss," Cotton began, "I hear someone found Sally dead in bed over at the Goldspot today. Her dress was over her head, and she wasn't wearing any knickers. How a woman gonna be walking around with no draws on? That's a damn shame."

"Well, let me head on over there and see what's going on," Stump said.

"Uh-huh. That's what being sheriff is all about," Malachi said. "Who would want to kill Sally, though?"

"It's the Goldspot, so anything can happen in that den of sin," Stump said. "I'll see you later, Malachi."

Malachi nodded. He and Cotton watched Stump walk away.

"The few days Stump's been the sheriff, a lot of things have changed for the better around here," Cotton said, as he leaned up against the bar. "This boy really knows how to pick that guitar."

"Yeah, he does," Malachi said.

"But, Boss, why does he play with his back to the audience?" Cotton asked.

"I don't know. Maybe he doesn't want anyone to know which strings he's playing. If I played the way he did, I'll probably do the same thing. A person can't steal your style if they don't know how you playing it," Malachi said.

"What the hell did you do that for?" Chester screamed. He was standing over the calm looking Lester with his arms flailing to make his point. "You didn't have to kill her. For what, Lester? What was the purpose of killing her? And then you rape her. What sick shit is that all about?"

Lester looked up at his brother, and then leaned back in the chair as he crossed his legs. He glanced at Sylvester, who gave him a smirk full of malevolence.

"I killed that bitch because she killed Bear," Lester said. "I raped her after killing her to let the world see her humiliation."

"What?" Chester and Sylvester said in unison.

"Which what? Are you asking me what in why I raped her or why she killed Bear?" Lester asked. "Do you want to know why she killed Bear?"

"Why?" Chester asked. He'd changed his tone to a less threatening octave.

Lester snickered. "Bear didn't love her the way she wanted him to love her," he said. "He loved the Queen more than he loved her," he said.

Chester shook his head, and walked back to his desk. He sat down in his chair, and looked from Sylvester to Lester. He placed his elbows on his desk as he ran his hands over his bald head.

"Lester, you couldn't think of a better place to kill her beside the Goldspot?" Chester asked. He looked up to see his brother's response. Lester shrugged. "Now we got to deal with Stump and the questions. I don't care how you do it, but Stump has to die to prove a point to these mindless fools that we're not to be taken lightly."

"You told me that already!" Lester said, his voice going an octave high with a tinge of annoyance. "I'm working on it."

"Well, work faster!" Chester snapped. He slammed his hand down on the desk. "I don't need this right now. Our business is already sluggish, and now this. Hell, we might as well put a sign out front saying we going out of business."

They all fell quiet at the pounding on the door.

"Who the hell is it?" Sylvester shouted.

"It's your friendly sheriff," Stump replied.

Chester rolled his eyes.

Malachi waited until R.J. finished shaking hands with everyone before beckoning him to come over to the bar.

R.J. nodded and headed toward Malachi.

Malachi watched him approach. The man looked like he was in his early thirties. The hat on his head was broke down at the rim on the right side giving him a cool and suave look. He was average in weight and height, thought Malachi.

"That was a nice song," Malachi said, as R.J. came up to him. "I never heard anything like that before."

"Yeah, I wrote that piece myself a few years ago," R.J. said.

Malachi watched R.J. lean his guitar against the bar. "Do you mind if I see your guitar?" he asked.

R.J. looked at Malachi. "You're kind of young ain't you, Malachi?" he asked.

"Eighteen," Malachi said.

"How does an eighteen year old kid get to own a nice

hotel, an after-hour spot, and, a numbers racket?" R.J. asked.

"Someone gave it all to me," Malachi said.

"Someone gave it all to you, huh? This someone wouldn't be the same someone who gave me my...gift, would he?" R.J. asked.

Malachi turned to him. The confusion etched on his face made R.J. smile.

"Forget the question, Malachi. You answered it for me. Go ahead, you can see my guitar," he said.

Malachi reached for the guitar. It was your basic wooded guitar. As he gripped it, it felt like the guitar was warm not just on the neck where R.J. had been cradling it, but the entire guitar. He placed it on his stomach while clutching the neck. As his fingers hovered over the strings, he felt a sense of warmth emanate from it. From then on he had a compulsion to start playing. His fingers neared the strings as if they had a mind of their own without him consciously willing them to do so. His mind became light. He was jerked out of his thoughts when he felt the guitar being snatched out of his hands.

"You weren't listening to me, Malachi," R.J. said.

Malachi cleared his head as he watched R.J. lean the guitar against the bar again.

"That's a...good guitar," Malachi said.

"It's not a guitar that makes a good player, it's the fingers and the voice," R.J. said. "I heard you singing and playing before I did my gig. You're good...to a point."

Malachi smiled. "I'm not a professional," he said.

"I can tell. What you want to do when you're up there, Malachi, is bring the audience in with the song. Don't just sing the song, feel the song. When you play your guitar let the strings become an extension of your fingers. Everything must become one. One voice. One string," R.J. said.

Malachi was mesmerized by R.J.'s voice. It sounded sultry and mysterious to him.

"You're young, son. It gets better when you get older," R.J. said.

"How long you're gonna be in Blackenfield, R.J.?" Malachi asked.

"Just passing through. Sing a little to make me some money to keep my beak wet and keep it moving," R.J. said. "You got yourself a good thing here. You're young and staying here and growing old could fit you. You got a girl?"

"A girl? Not...really," Malachi said.

"So she kisses you and let's you play with her chest, but nothing else, huh?" R.J. asked. He smiled.

"Huh? Uh...."

"Don't worry about it. She will eventually. They all do," R.J. said. "Hey, I'm going to go call it a night. If I see you tomorrow night, then I'm still in town. If not...."

Malachi watched R.J. pick up his guitar and walk away. He watched R.J. shake a few more hands before he went out the door.

When the sun came up the next morning, Sheriff Hays was getting out of bed. His fat stomach protruded over his boxer underwear. He walked to the bathroom scratching his butt with his left hand while scratching his scrotum with the right hand.

As he stood over the toilet relieving himself, he was startled by the pounding on his front door, making him miss the toilet and peeing behind the toilet. He cursed as he headed for his bedroom to get his gun.

With gun in hand, and his hand on the doorknob of the front door, Sheriff Hays took in two quick breathes before yanking the door open, and pointing his gun.

Chester and Sylvester wasn't startled at seeing door quickly open in front of them. They did smile at seeing Sheriff Hayes standing there holding the gun in front of their faces with his gun belt over his underwear and nothing else.

"Put some clothes on, Hays," Chester said, as he and Sylvester barged into the house.

Sheriff Hays stepped aside to let them enter. Before closing the door, he looked out to make sure no one had seen the Brown brothers enter.

After closing and locking his door, Sheriff Hays spun around. "What the hell are you two Negroes doing coming into town? Better yet. How did you know where I lived?" He asked while holstering his gun. He ran to the window and looked out. "Damnit, I hope no one seen you nigg…Well, maybe no one did see you." He turned around and faced them.

"Look, Hays, we need you to take care of Malachi," Chester said.

"Malachi? The young pup that runs the Queen? I hear that boy is making a nice piece of money over there. He keeps my hand greased. It seems like he's trying to run you boys out of business. And he can sing. Ain't nothing like a Negro who can sing and look kind of fair skin to boot to keep those young dark chickens running to his coup to get some of his bird seed," Sheriff Hays said.

"With Malachi racking up the business and the sheriff—"

"Who? Dave the Drunk? Give him another jug of moonshine, Chester, and he'd leave you alone. That's the best damn sheriff that Negro town can have. One who ain't around when you need him," Sheriff Hays said. He started laughing.

"It's not Dave," Sylvester said.

"It's Stump," Chester added.

"Stump? Who the hell voted him in?" Sheriff Hays said. He walked to a chair and sat down with his legs wide open.

"Do you mind closing your damn legs, Hays, we don't want to see what your mama gave you for birth," Sylvester snapped.

Sheriff Hays looked down at his crotch, and then back up at the Brown brothers. "Fuck you. This is my house and I can sit anyway I damn well please," he said. To make his point, he opened his legs wider.

Chester shook his head. "Listen, Hays," he began. "Get rid of Malachi and it will be two thousand dollars in it for you."

"Two thousand dollars? Hmm," Sheriff Hays said, as he crossed his legs one over the other. "I don't know, Chester. I might need to bring in some people on this and it might be my loss instead of my gain."

"The bastard is trying to hustle us, Chester," Sylvester said.

"I ain't got to hustle you. I'm the sheriff of this town, so I can make my own rules," Sheriff Hays said. "And, the way I figure it, another thousand ought to cover everything."

"Three thousand dollars?" Sylvester snapped. "For a fat sheriff who can't run one block without falling down from being out of breath you want a whole lot."

"Let him keep talking and I can throw in an extra thousand dollars, Chester," Sheriff Hays said.

"All right we'll get you the three thousand dollars, Hays, but Malachi has got to go in the next few days," Chester said.

"All right. I'll take care of it. You can rely on me," Sheriff Hays said.

"We will be relying on you, Hays," Chester said.

Sheriff Hays winked at the both of them and smiled.

CHAPTER SIXTEEN
A day of Recognition

Malachi rolled over. When he did, he felt some heavy weight fall onto his chest. He opened his eyes. Smiling at him was Betty Mae. He smiled.

"So that was your first time being with a woman?" Betty Mae asked.

Malachi laughed. "How could you tell? When I couldn't find the hole, or when I started screaming out with joy when I did find it?" he asked.

Betty Mae laughed. "You're an old spirit, Malachi Moon," she said. "How was it?"

Malachi leaped out of bed and started dancing.

Betty's Mae's laughter grew harder and louder as she watched Malachi do a split and come back up still dancing.

Malachi jumped back in bed, and began to tickle

Betty Mae's ribs. She playfully fought him off. When the sound of someone knocking on the door made them stop.

"Who is it?" Malachi called out.

"Rose Ann. You decent? I have to talk to you," she said.

Malachi glanced at Betty Mae. "Uh...yeah. Let me put my pants on, Rose," he said. "Is Roger with you, sis?"

"No," Rose Ann said.

"Okay, I'll be right there," Malachi said. Getting out of bed, he went to the floor and picked up his pants. He leaned in close to Betty Mae and whispered. "Pull the covers over your head and be quiet."

Betty Mae stared at him. She shrugged as she slid down off the pillows and under the sheet and blanket. Malachi hurried to the door after putting on his pants and shirt. He looked behind him to make sure Betty Mae wasn't detected. He opened the door. He stepped aside as Rose Ann rushed into the room.

"I have to tell you something," Rose Ann said anxiously.

Malachi closed the door and turned around. "What is it, sis?" he asked.

"Roger wants to marry me!" Rose Ann exploded with happiness, as she began jumping up and down. "We're going to get married, Malachi!"

Malachi walked toward his sister. He smiled. He'd never seen her so happy before. Rose Ann leaped into his chest and gave him a big hug.

"I'm going to give you a big party, Rose," Malachi said.

"Yes, and I'll help decorate," Betty Mae said, as she sprung from under the blanket.

Rose Ann and Malachi turned around.

"Oh. Hello, Betty Mae," Rose Ann said. She let go of Malachi and gave her attention to Betty Mae. "Did you just arrived or are you recovering from the night before?"

Betty Mae displayed a shy smile. She sheepishly batted her eyelashes, and slid back down as she pulled the blanket over her head.

Rose Ann looked at Malachi.

"Just trying to get the feel of things," Malachi said.

Rose Ann tilted her head while piercing her lips together. "I bet," she said. She began tapping her left foot as she crossed her arms over her bountiful chest foot while she stared at her brother. A grin appeared, and she jumped into Malachi's arms again. "I'm getting married!"

Fall began to set in with cool brisk days rolling in with a blast. Betty Mae and Malachi began preparing things for the party. Betty Mae was decorating the lobby of the Queen that evening when she saw Stump walk through the front door.

"Hello, Sheriff," Betty Mae said.

Stump kept walking without answering.

"Sheriff?" Betty Mae said.

Stump stopped. He slowly turned around. When Betty Mae saw the front of his shirt, she let out a horrific scream as Stump fell to his knees, and then fell face first to the floor. She watched as blood began to form underneath him.

Malachi came running out of another room with Kai-Chang hot on his heels. He arrived to see Stump fall to the floor. Malachi ran to Stump. He bent down and turned him over. When he looked down at Stump's stomach, he saw three knife punctures. Blood was everywhere.

"Betty Mae, go get the doctor," Malachi said.

Betty Mae, her hand to her mouth, nodded and ran out the door.

"Press on the pressure point under his right armpit, Mala," Kai-Chang said.

Malachi didn't hear Kai-Chang. He moved toward Stump's head. He placed Stump's head on his lap.

"Mala, the pressure point," Kai-Chang repeated.

Malachi, instead, pressed on Stump's bleeding wounds to stop the flow of blood.

Kai-Chang patiently bent down and lifted Malachi up by the shoulders. Malachi looked at him with confusion. Kai-Chang quickly bent down and reached for Stump's right underarm pit. He applied pressure while at the same time pressing his left hand on Stump's chest above his heart. Massaging it very slowly.

"What are you doing, Kai-Chang?" Malachi asked as he watched.

"Saving your friends life," Kai-Chang said.

Malachi was amaze as he watched the blood that had been flowing from Stump's body so quickly, began to slow down.

"The pressure I am applying will give him more time to control his breathing, his heart rate, as well as slowing down the blood. This will give him time to consciously want to live," Kai-Chang said. "If I had waited another minute, he would've crossed over into limbo and would've never returned,"

Malachi dropped to one knee. He leaned into Stump. "Who did this, Stump?" Malachi asked.

Stump eyes fluttered. He opened them very slowly. He turned his head toward Malachi. His lips moved but Malachi couldn't hear anything. He leaned closer to Stump's lips.

"It...It...was...Lester," Stump said in a low voice.

Betty Mae came running in with the doctor behind her. The doctor pushed Kai-Chang aside, and began working on Stump wounds. Kai-Chang stood up. He looked at Malachi. Malachi stood up. He looked at Kai-Chang. He tossed his head to the stand. Indicating for Kai-Chang to follow him.

When Malachi passed Cotton, he stopped. "Get some men to help get Stump to the doctor's office," he said. Cotton nodded. "Cotton, get some men to watch over Stump while he gets well. No one gets to him without me knowing about it."

Cotton watched as Malachi and Kai-Chang headed to the back of room. He called out to several men to help carry Stump.

Malachi walked to the desk. He opened the bottom draw and removed Bear's .38 revolver. He stuck it in the front of his pants and closed his jacket. He looked at Kai-Chang. "You can stay if you want," he said.

"Why would I let you go into battle by yourself, Mala? You are a good man. You pay me to work for you, if I were not to come with you on this...quest, I would be in dereliction of my responsibilities," Kai-Chang said.

"I'm tired, Kai-Chang," Malachi said, as he rubbed a hand across his face. "I got to end this now or it won't end."

"What you seek may not go as you plan, Mala," Kai-Chang said.

"Maybe it won't go the way I want it, but I can't keep letting this happen," Malachi said.

"So, my friend, to battle we go," Kai-Chang said. He bowed.

Malachi nodded as he tucked the gun in his waist. He stepped from behind the desk, and headed to the door with Kai-Chang hot on his every step.

Chester slammed his fists on the desk. "How the hell did Lester let him get away without making sure he was dead? We set it up for Lester to get him when he passed the alley. What went wrong, Sly?" he asked.

Sylvester looked at his eldest brother and shrugged.

"That's your answer! Where the hell is Lester?" Chester asked.

"I told him to disappear for awhile," Sylvester said.

"Well, that's the smartest thing you said all week. Damn! If Stump ain't dead, then when he does get better, he's going to cause us hell on earth," Chester said. He placed an index finger on his lips. "All right. This is what we're going to do. Get a couple of the boys together. We're going to sneak into Doc Ben's place and finish Stump's ass off."

The office door slammed open. Chester and Sylvester turned around.

"Mr. Brown, Malachi and that China man are outside asking where you and your brothers are."

"Thanks, Fred," Chester said in a calm voice to the lanky man with the big pants standing in the doorway. "Go get some of the boys and tell them we got trouble."

"Yes, sir," Fred said, as he closed the door behind him.

"All right. We were going to pay that shiftless cracker, Hays, three thousand dollars to take care of Malachi. Now, at the moment, we're going to do our own work. That young boy walked in here like he owns our joint. That's a no-no," Chester said.

Malachi felt a little nervous entering the Goldspot. He'd never been in it before. He'd always had an invitation, but never took it up. He searched around the place looking for the Brown brothers. He didn't see any of them. His mouth felt dry, so he licked his cracked lips.

"To be in the enemies den is to be in the pit of a fire, Mala," Kai-Chang said, as he stood beside Malachi looking around.

Malachi glanced at him. He took in Kai-Chang's black, silk pajamas. The ones he'd worn the night they'd rescued Roger. His hair was tied into a ponytail.

"They probably know we're here already, Kai-Chang," Malachi said. He turned his attention back to the people walking back and forth. "And if that's true…."

Kai-Chang nodded. "It is better to bring the battle to the aggressor than for the aggressor to bring the battle to you, Mala," he said.

"Malachi!"

Malachi and Kai-Chang looked up at the steps above them. Standing there was Chester and Sylvester and three other men. Each man had a hand inside their jacket.

"Welcome to the Goldspot!" Chester said.

Malachi watched as the patrons who'd once been quietly mingling began to hurry out the front door.

Within minutes the Goldspot had become empty. The only men left were the Brown brothers and their men.

"I count ten of them," Malachi whispered to Kai-Chang.

"Is that all?" Kai-Chang said. His tone had a sense of arrogance to it.

Malachi had to blink on that question. He swallowed hard. From his peripheral vision, he saw Kai-Chang start to unbutton the jacket part of his black pajamas.

"What are you doing?" Malachi asked.

"I am preparing for battle, Mala," Kai-Chang said.

"Malachi, since you took it upon yourself to come in here alone, I'm going to give you an offer. You sign over the Queen to me, and I won't kill your sister," Chester said.

Malachi's head snapped up to look at Chester.

"That's right, boy. I'm going to kill you after you sign over you rights to the Queen, but I might let your sister live if you agree quickly to my offer," Chester said.

Malachi felt the heat in his toes begin to slowly ascend upward to his head. The heat he was feeling was anger. An anger that was intensified by the fact that Chester would threaten his sister who had nothing to do with what they were going through. Who was innocent? It infuriated him. He glanced at Kai-Chang. Malachi saw what was in his waist. There were several shiny palm-size, silver metal objects stuck into the black silk scarf.

"Mala, when I make my move, you find shelter and use your weapon," Kai-Chang whispered.

Malachi nodded.

"What's it going to be, Malachi?" Chester asked.

"Where's Lester?" Malachi asked.

"Why?" Sylvester asked.

"Stump made me a deputy. He said it was Lester who stabbed him. I came here to arrest Lester," Malachi said.

"Boy, you're a damn fool!" Chester said. "But you're a fool with a whole lot of guts. I'll give you that. Maybe Bear did right giving you the Queen. There's something about you that can make a man think before reacting when it comes to you."

"Look, Chester, I ain't got no quarrel with you and your brother. I just want Lester," Malachi said, as he licked his chapped lips for the fifth time since entering the Goldspot.

"I don't think my dead mama would appreciate me giving my young brother to the courts," Chester said. "Anyway, Lester ain't too good when it comes to being locked in a cage. He gets ornery."

Malachi watched as Chester's men began to split up. The other men of the Brown brothers had materialized while they'd been talking. The Brown brothers' men began taking up different positions throughout the room while nearly circling Kai-Chang and himself.

"Should I send down the paper and pencil?" Chester asked. He laughed.

"Yeah. Send it down," Malachi said.

Malachi watched Chester turn to the man to the right of him. Chester reached into his pants pocket.

"Now, Mala!" Kai-Chang shouted.

Malachi didn't flinch. He dived under a table to the side of him. As he rolled under it, he kicked it over while pulling free the .38 revolver. Behind the turned over table, he looked over to point his gun when he saw Kai-Chang moving with an ease that was unbelievable as he flung the palm-size silver metals he'd had in his waist at the Brown brothers' men. Whenever one of the silver, star shape metals struck a man, they'd let out a scream as the metal protruded either from their chests or their throats. Malachi had to admit Kai-Chang's accuracy was perfect as he watched him go to work.

Taking in a deep breath, Malachi fired the .38 revolver at one of Chester's men who was trying to shoot Kai-Chang as he hid behind the bar. When Malachi pulled the trigger, the recoil from the gun was so powerful that he nearly dropped it. He decided that holding it with two hands gave him more control. His aim for the man was slightly off, he admitted after seeing the results. He'd aimed for the man's head, but the bullet went into the man's chest. The bullet from the .38 revolver knocked the man off his feet. At that moment, Malachi didn't have time to feel sorry for anyone he was shooting. It was kill or be killed, he told himself.

The people standing outside the Goldspot, saw flashes of gun muzzles and the constant sounds of guns being fired as they tried to hide behind wooden barrels, and doorways. Rose Ann, who'd only been told what had happen to Stump by Cotton a half hour earlier, was, at that moment, in the lobby of the Queen being restrained by Roger who was preventing her from rushing out the door and going to the Goldspot to be with her brother.

Chester and Sylvester had decided to split up. The Goldspot had twin winding stairs on opposite sides. Chester headed to the right of the stairs and Sylvester took the left. Each one held a double-barrel shotgun tightly in their hand. The men who'd been with them were told by Chester to go down stairs before him. The first man who made it to the bottom of the stairs was greeted with one of Kai-Chang's silver metal stars in the side of his neck. The sharp metal cut through his artery. He died clutching his neck as he tried to stem the flow of blood. The dark blood sprayed through his fingers like a water fountain as he fell to his knees.

Malachi had ducked behind a table to reload. His fingers shook as he filled the cylinder of the .38 revolver with new shells. As he picked his head up to look over the table, the table exploded, sending wood splinters into his face. He was knocked back down behind the table.

Sylvester had waited patiently until Malachi had shown his face before firing both barrels of the shotgun. He admitted that if he'd waited three more seconds, he would've had a better shot at Malachi's head, but he was impatient and pulled the trigger too soon.

Malachi could feel his face on fire as the buckshot and the wood splinters burned. He felt the wetness of blood as it ran freely down his right cheek. He blinked rapidly to clear his vision. He tried to concentrate as to where the shot came from as he nervously looked around. He estimated it to be to the right of him. He changed his position and moved to the other end of the oblong table. He would aim more accurately, he told himself. Taking in a deep breath, he leaped upward.

Sylvester had taken shelter behind a wall that was at the bottom of the stairs. He was reloading the double-barrel shotgun when shots rang out. The first shot hit the shotgun, knocking it out of his hands. The second shot hit the wall he was partially being protected by, sending plaster into his face. He stepped out from the wall as he surreptitiously wanted to know where the shots were coming from.

Sylvester was too big to be hiding behind a partial wall. He admitted that when he heard the third shot. The bullet struck him in the chest, sending him backward. When he struck the wall, he slowly slid down leaving a trail of blood. His eyes rolled up into his head as his lungs expunged air.

Malachi's aim had been right as he watched Sylvester slide down the wall.

"Sylvester!" Chester shouted, as he sprang from behind a wall similar from the one Sylvester had been hiding behind. He ran toward his brother recklessly.

Malachi took aim at Chester. The sight of one of Kai-Chang's sharp, silver stars came into view as it flew through the air. He held off from shooting Chester. Chester, Malachi thought, must have felt the danger, because he turned toward the sharp object. The star kept twirling toward him until it found its mark directly in his chest. Chester screamed and stumbled backward. He dropped the double-barrel shotgun, as he leaned up against the wall.

Malachi watched Chester use the wall to pull himself up. He clutched his chest as he walked toward his dead brother. Blood dripped from his mouth. Each step he took, he moaned. Each step he made became slower and slower. When he was close enough to Sylvester, but not near him to reach out to him, he fell to his knees and crawled the rest of the way. Malachi saw Chester reached out and touched his brother's hand, and then he stopped moving.

Kai-Chang watched as the last remaining men of the

Brown brothers' ran out of the Goldspot. He walked over to Malachi.

Malachi stood up as Kai-Chang approached.

"No battle is a good battle, Mala," Kai-Chang said, as he stared at Malachi's bloody face. "Are you all right?"

Malachi looked around at the dead bodies. He nodded, as he touched his bleeding face. "Yeah, I'm okay. At least it's over with, Kai-Chang," he said.

"Is it? I only see two of the brothers who are dead. Is there not a third one?" Kai-Chang asked.

Malachi looked at him. He was right. Where was Lester Brown?

Three weeks later, as the wind blew its brutal cold, Malachi, Cotton, and Kai-Chang watched as Rose Ann and Roger drove off in the new car he'd given them for a wedding present. Malachi lifted his coat collar to ward off the wind. He smiled as Rose Ann waved to him.

"Hey, I'm going to miss that wild child," Cotton said. "There were days when I enjoyed her chasing the male customers around the hotel with her razor when they tried groping the girl. Boy, those were funny times. Where they off to, boss?"

"To live with two people who Rose Ann and I consider family," Malachi said, as he watched the car get smaller in the distance.

Cotton nodded. "You want me to head over to the Goldspot and see how things are working out, boss?" he asked.

"Yeah, and tell Monty not to beat too many people with his three cards, Cotton," Malachi said. "I'll be over shortly after I check on Stump."

"Okay, boss," Cotton said.

Malachi and Kai-Chang watched Cotton walk off.

"What does one as young as you, Mala, do with two hotels?" Kai-Chang asked.

"Enjoy it and make money," Malachi said. He turned to face Kai-Chang. "What else does a poor Negro do with money?"

Kai-Chang bowed.

Twenty minutes later, Malachi was knocking on Stump's room door at the Goldspot.

"Come in!" Stump shouted.

Malachi entered the room. He closed the door behind him. "How you feeling, Stump?" he asked.

Stump was propped up in bed with four pillows behind him. He smiled when he saw Malachi.

"I'm feeling good, son. How are you?" Stump asked.

Malachi walked further into the room. He went to the corner and picked up a chair. He brought it over to the bed, and sat it in front of Stump.

"Your face is healing okay," Stump said, as he leaned in closer to look at the right side of Malachi's face. "Hell, it gives you a sinister look if you ask me. It takes away that pretty boy face you used to have."

"What did the doctor say about your healing?" Malachi asked.

Stump leaned back into his pillows. He sighed. "Doc said that my lung had collapsed. If I don't smoke cigarettes in the next five years, my other lung ought to carry me until it's time for me to kick the bucket. Have you heard anything about where Lester Brown might be?"

"No."

"That's a sneaky bastard, Malachi. If you don't find

him, you'll be looking over your shoulder forever," Stump said.

"I'm not worried about Lester—"

"Well, you better be, boy!" Stump snapped. "Look what the mean bastard did to me, and I always figured myself to be on my toes. Don't ever underestimate anyone, Malachi, because there's always someone out there who's sneaky and more vicious than you. How's that girlfriend of yours?"

"She's okay. She took care of my face," Malachi said.

"Did Rose Ann like the gold bracelet I gave her for a wedding gift?" Stump asked.

"She loved it, Stump," Malachi said with a smile. "That's all she talked about for about a week. Are you going to run the Goldspot for me when you get better?"

"Damn right. I'm getting out of the law business. It's too damn dangerous," Stump said.

Stump and Malachi looked at each other and started laughing.

CHAPTER SEVENTEEN

Chickens comes home to Roost

Malachi watched the people around him being entertained in the Queen. It was a busy Saturday night and he'd seen a lot of new faces in Blackenfield over the last three years. He was twenty-one years old and had filled out considerably. He'd started to cut his curly, black hair close. His chest had barreled out, and his voice had become deeper. As he sat perched high on the stool in the corner of the room for a better view of the floor, an image of Bear came to mind. He smiled. He missed Bear, and knew if he were alive, he would be dancing in the middle of the floor from the fact that he was making a lot of money.

The sight of a Negro woman in a bright red dress

289

with matching shoes and a blonde wig caught Malachi's eye. He leaned forward a little. It wasn't her appearance that held his attention. It was something else he couldn't figure out at that moment. He continued to watch her as she let one man after another walked over to her to buy her a drink while whispering in their ears. For the ten minutes that Malachi watched her, he realized what she was doing. She was a whore trying to get someone to pay for her services.

After about the eighth man, she finally found someone. Malachi watched them drink, and whisper in each other's ear for ten minutes. The man slipped the blond wig Negro something in her hand. He went to the bar and got a jug of moonshine as the woman sat at the table waiting for his return. Malachi reached into his pocket and removed the white handkerchief. It was a signal for the manager to come to him. That night it was a new manager he'd hired a month ago by the name of Red.

Malachi climbed down from the highchair. "Red," he began, "I need you to do me a favor."

The blonde wig Negro woman didn't know why her customer had wanted her to go to the room by herself, but she'd agreed to go because he'd added an extra two dollars for her services. Other than that, she might've refused. She didn't like any kinky games from her tricks or any surprises.

After knocking on the door, the blonde wig Negro turned the doorknob, and felt it give to her touch. She opened the door and walked into a darken room. She hesitated a moment before going all the way in to let her eyes adjust to the darkness. The small light illuminating from the hallway let her see the lantern on the small table to the left of her by the bed.

"Where you at, big boy," the blonde wigged woman asked, as she closed the door behind her.

"Lock it," a male voice from somewhere in the room said.

The blonde wig woman turned around and locked the door. When she turned back around, she searched the darkness for her trick. She was wondering how he got into the room as she searched the room. With the door closed, she had to use her blindness to remember exactly where the lantern was at. She walked further into the room and bumped into the bed.

"I see you like to play games," the blonde wig woman said, as she reached behind her and began unzipping her dress from the back. "Well, whatever turns you on, baby. You're paying for this ride. I'm just here to make sure you have a good time."

"How long you've been whoring?" The male voice asked from the darkness.

"It seems like too long, but the money keeps me from going hungry. Anyway, I'll rather lie on my back and get money for it, then give it away free to some damn fool who ain't appreciating it. Some men you can tell they just want to talk when you walk into the room with them. They begin by saying they got a wife home but she don't do this and she won't do that. They pay me to listen to their stories. Their wives don't satisfy them and their girlfriends don't listen to them. My job is to make you happy, baby. If you want to talk. Talk. But if you want to some nookie, then I'm here to make sure you get it good."

Her dress was now around her ankles. The blonde wig woman stepped out of it, and kicked to the side. "Come to bed, baby, and let mama put you to sleep," she said.

When the lamplight came on, the blond wig woman covered her face from the light.

"Hello, mama," Malachi said, as he leaned forward with his elbows on his knees.

The blonde wig woman opened her eyes, but blinked them rapidly to clear the white spots in her vision.

When her vision was cleared, she stared at Malachi. "You're not the man who paid me. I don't do two men at once. You need to go find one of those young girls for that. My body can't take two of ya'll," she said.

"It's been a long time, mama," Malachi said.

"Long time? Oh, so we've been down this road before, huh?" The blond wig woman asked while blinking to clear her vision.

"Rose Ann got married a few years ago," Malachi said.

"Rose...Ann?" The blonde wig blonde face changed from confusion to one of recognition, and then a mask of horror as her mouth fell open. She let out a small scream and picked up her dress trying to quickly get into it.

Malachi stood up and walked toward her. "It's been a very long time, mama," he said.

Emma Jean Moon had been a woman of integrity all of her life. But as middle age set in, she began to realize that men could do nothing for her but abuse her psychologically, physically, and emotionally, she stopped living for what men wanted from her several years ago and began to live for herself. In her decision to let go, she also consciously let go of all things connected to her. It had been hard during the first two years after leaving the farm, but once she'd started to use her body to get the material things she sought, it became easier for her to accept who and what she wanted to be. She became a whore.

Malachi watched his mother turn her back to him and put on her dress. She removed the blonde wig and dropped it on the floor. He was surprised at how much her hair had grayed. To him, she still looked the same except for the gray hair and a few wrinkles around her eyes and mouth.

After putting back on her dress, Emma went to the bed and sat down. She placed her face in her hands and began to cry. She cried so hard that her entire body racked with deep sobs.

Malachi stood over his mother. He looked down at her and felt both sadness and anger toward the woman who'd disappeared from his and Rose Ann's life.

"Mama, did you know that Pa was...a strange man?" he asked.

Emma wiped her face with the palm of her hand. She looked up at her son. A son she realized at that moment had grown to become very handsome. "What do you mean?" she asked. "What happened to your face?"

Malachi waved the question away. "Did you ever see Pa do...things when he was with Rose Ann?" he asked. His words were cold as he stared at Emma.

"I don't understand what you're saying. What 'things' are you talking about?" Emma asked. She was fully dressed and looked at her son.

Malachi sighed. "Pa raped Rose Ann when she was

twelve years old, mama. And I want to know if he was doing those kind of things when she was younger or around you and you let it happen," Malachi asked.

Emma eyes, though red from crying, widened in shock as she stared at Malachi. "I…How do you…I'm a fool," she said.

"Pa—"

"Wait!" Emma said as she held up her hand. "Buford is not your father."

"What?" Malachi said. He took a step back as if he'd been punched in the stomach. His breathing had become short and labored as he stared at his mother.

"Let me tell you something about Buford," Emma began. "He was a damn farmer and wanted nothing else in life but that. Sure I married him, but I was already pregnant with you and he knew that going into the marriage. At the time I was young, pregnant, and ignorant and didn't have two nickels to rub together. He liked me and thought that marrying me would give him a sense of feeling like a man, but the fool didn't know what a man was. In his silly mind, he thought it meant farming, farming, and more farming. That wasn't what I wanted Malachi."

Malachi sat down on the bed. He felt weak. His hands began to tremble as he squeezed his knees to stop them.

Emma kneeled down in front of her son. She placed her hands on top of his. "Malachi," she began, "oh, my sweet baby. Forgive a young woman who didn't know what it was she wanted at a young age in life. I was an only child and felt a sense of freedom when I got away from my God fearing parents. I drank. I smoked. And I had sex as freely as I wanted to. I was young and stupid.

I can't change that like you can't change me from being the woman who gave birth to you. I can give you a dozen reasons as to what makes a person do what they do, but that wouldn't change your life, son."

Malachi nodded. Inside he felt a void of emptiness. An hour ago, he thought he had it all. But like Kai-Chang once told him. No one knows their future, and a person barely knows their past. At that moment, Kai-Chang words fitted his situation perfectly as he stared at the woman he knew as his mother.

"So, Buford is Rose Ann's father?" Malachi asked.

"No!" Emma said. She stood up and sat down beside Malachi.

Malachi placed his right hand onto the bridge of his nose and squeezed it to relieve the pressure that had materialized in his head. He took in a deep breath, and turned to the woman he thought he knew as a child.

"Rose Ann is not your sister," Emma said, as she placed her hands in her lap. "Do you remember the times when I would disappear for a few days—"

"A couple of weeks you mean," Malachi said.

"All right. Anyway, I didn't know it, but those getaways would be what would finally lead me to get away from that man altogether. The time before I actually left, I met a woman in town who didn't want to keep the baby she'd just given birth to. She was a young girl. Dark and lovely she was. Her baby—Rose Ann—was beautiful. I knew what it was like to have a baby out of wedlock and being young at that. The girl was going to leave the baby in front of a doorstep, and just disappear. We talked. She told me I seemed like I had a good heart and that Rose Ann would be happy with my family. I took her and brought her home. From that day, you'd known her only as your sister, and that's what she is, Malachi, your little sister. Buford can be a vindictive man. I guess he figured since I'd left him, Rose Ann would become his... plaything. The bastard!"

"Ma, who is my father?" Malachi asked. He refused to look at her.

Emma took Malachi's hand. She pressed it against her chest, as she turned and looked at him. "His name is—"

"No!" Malachi shouted as he snatched his hand away, and stood up. He walked a few feet away. "All my life I've known...Buford to be my father. He's always been a mean sonofabitch, but he was the man I knew to be my father. If you tell me who this man is, then I'd probably be looking for him just to get to know him, and for what? If he wanted to be in my life he would've stayed with you. No, my life is complicated enough now and I don't need anymore complications to go with it." He turned around. "Your sudden appearance back into my life is even more complicated. I'm never going to tell Rose Ann she's not my sister, but I will tell her Buford isn't her father. Maybe that fact will make life a little better for her."

"Whatever you think is best, son," Emma said. She stood up.

"What brings you to Blackenfield?" Malachi asked.

"I heard it was becoming prosperous," Emma said.

Malachi looked at her. He could see her eyes watering. Seconds later tears flowed freely down her face.

"Can an old fool of a mother get a hug from her son?"

Malachi smiled. He walked toward his mother with hesitancy.

Emma, feeling a sense of weight lifting from her very soul hurried to her son. As she laid her head into his chest, she cried. Malachi caressed her back as he lay his head on top of her head. It had been a long time since he'd hugged his mother. A tear fell from his eye.

By 1935, Blackenfield had become more populated as the town grew. In the course of its growth, so did Malachi and his business dealing with the Queen and the Goldspot. The spring late evening air had a fresh grass smell to it as Malachi placed his last piece of luggage in the back seat of the car. When he turned around, he was greeted with the sad faces of Stump, Cotton, Red, Emma, and Betty Mae.

"Don't look so depressed," Malachi said.

"I'm not looking depress. This is my happy face knowing you won't be around looking over my shoulder while I count the receipts," Stump said.

Malachi laughed.

"Don't worry about a thing, boss, everything will be everything by the time you get back," Cotton said.

"When are you coming back?" Red asked.

Malachi didn't answer. He watched as his mother walked down the stairs toward him. She'd changed over the years. She and Rose Ann had begun to write each other, and she was proud to find out that she was a grandmother. She would show pictures of the baby to everyone she talked to. She acted the part as well. She no longer wore wigs or applied make-up to her face. Emma had decided to let her hair grow its natural color. Sure they'd been stories around town how she'd been a whore who'd turned out to be the rich, young Negro's mother who own two hotels, but when the rumors started, Malachi had sent Red out into the street to squash it, or bust open any person who'd mentioned it. The rumors came to an end a week later.

Emma stood in front of Malachi. She gingerly touched the scar on his face. "You're like me, you know," she began. "The urge to go when you think you've done all you can do. Where you are going, son?"

"I need to do something with what I have, ma. I'll travel awhile, then sit for a spell in some town, and then move on again. I really don't know, but I do know I got to get to moving," Malachi said. "An unknown calling I guess might be a better way of explaining it."

Emma nodded. "Take this with you," she said. She handed Malachi a folded piece of paper with tape on the ends to keep it sealed.

"What is it?" he asked, as he reached for it.

"It's a name. You'll never have to open it if that's your decision. I just wanted you to have it. Put it in your wallet or in a box somewhere in the back of a closet. I don't care, but I couldn't let you go without having that name near you. I couldn't go to my grave comfortably knowing you didn't have that paper, son," Emma said.

Malachi looked at his mother. Her eyebrows were beginning to show streaks of gray in them. He removed his wallet from his back pocket and placed the small, folded, taped paper into it, and then returned his wallet to his back pocket. He kissed his mother on the cheek.

"You take care of yourself, Malachi," Emma said.

Malachi nodded as he watched his mother walk back up the stairs.

"If Kai-Chang was here, boss, he'd probably be making one of those philosophical remarks," Red said.

Malachi laughed again. Red was right, he admitted. If Kai-Chang had been there, he could hear him telling him about some journey of taking off to the unknown. How he'd disciplined himself to withstand the elements of nature. He missed Kai-Chang. It was over a year since he walked with Kai-Chang to the ship that had taken him back to China. He could still remember their conversation as they waited for the ship to dock.

"What are you going to do when you get back to China, Kai-Chang?"

"Enjoy my grandchildren, Mala. It's been a long time since I set foot on my native soil."

They were standing side by side as they watched the ship nearing the dock. Malachi had glanced at Kai-Chang. He could see that he was happy by the smile he rarely displayed.

"I've learned a lot from Westerners," Kai-Chang began. "Your bodies are like fat jelly that can never find its solidity with discipline, but your hearts are light and kind."

"I will miss you, Kai-Chang. Do you have enough money?"

Kai-Chang nodded. "You have been very generous to me, Mala. I thank you. Maybe I shall open me a restaurant when I return home or a small living abode for travelers."

"No, Kai-Chang, you have been good to me, and you taught me a lot, and I know whatever you decide to do, it will be something on a grand scale."

Kai-Chang bowed. "Friendship is like a rare jewel that

*is created once in a lifetime, Mala. And your friendship to
me is rare and sincere," he said.*

*"Your friendship has been good to me also, Kai-
Chang."*

*"Friendship should never part ways, Mala. Let us keep
our fond memories close to heart. I shall board the ship
without your presence."*

*Malachi knew what he was saying. He hated to see him
go as much as Kai-Chang hated to board.*

"Goodbye, Kai-Chang."

*Kai-Chang turned and looked at Malachi. "The word
goodbye seems so…forever. We have a saying in China. If
you say goodbye today, you won't be able to say goodbye for
the long journey across the sea of bliss. Instead of goodbye,
Malachi, I shall say, my thoughts for you will always be in
my heart, my friend."*

*Malachi smiled. Kai-Chang had never said his name
before.*

*"Then I will say the same to you…friend," Malachi
said.*

Kai-Chang bowed.

Malachi bowed.

Malachi returned his thoughts to the present as
he watched Betty Mae, who, he had to admitted, had
become even more beautiful to him over the years, walk
down the stairs toward him. She was wearing a gray skirt,
and a dark gray blouse with black flat-heel shoes. Malachi
enjoyed the way she was always color coordinated.

"So, you're just up and going," Betty Mae said. "No
reason. No direction. No place. Just hitting the dirt road
without a compass to guide you or anything like that,
huh?"

"Come on, let's take a walk," Malachi said, as he took Betty Mae's hand and guided her around the car.

They walked on the side of the street. Malachi glancing from time to time as Betty Mae wiped the tears from her eyes.

"I could tell you two or three stories why I'm leaving, Betty Mae, but you don't want to hear it. To you, I'm abandoning what we have, and, for me, staying will only let me live with half a sense of happiness in a world where you, as an individual, should feel happiness all of the time," Malachi said.

"What about me? Am I being selfish for asking what is going to happen to us? How do I survive not knowing where we're going in this relationship, Malachi?"

Malachi stopped. He gently turned Betty Mae around by her shoulders. He looked into her tear-filled eyes. "Betty Mae, I don't know what tomorrow will bring. I can't make any promises, and I won't keep you chained to me with false hopes and dreams. I have to go and find out who Malachi Moon is. If you were to find someone who would make you happy, then you grab that man and make yourself happy. Don't deny your happiness in hopes of looking for an unknown happiness by waiting for me," he said "If I told you anything other than that, then I would be selfish.

Betty Mae's lips began to quiver.

"Betty Mae, I have to do this to better understand me," Malachi said.

"What about me?" Betty Mae asked, as she stomped her foot. "Don't I count? Where am I in your search for yourself? Nowhere, that's where. I...I...love you, Malachi."

"You were my first girlfriend, and my first woman. I could say I love you, too, and would mean it, to the point of not knowing what love is. I say that because you've been the only woman I've ever been with. That doesn't make me love you any less or more. I can love you for what my heart feels and what my mind can understand," Malachi said.

Betty Mae wiped away a tear and stared at Malachi. "That is the most confusing thing I have ever heard," she said.

Malachi smiled. "Right," he said.

"I won't promise you I'll be here waiting for you when you get back—if you ever get back," Betty Mae said. "But I'll be here as long as I can.

"I'd be wrong if I asked you to wait for me any longer than that," Malachi said.

"Everything is a step at a time, Malachi."

"I wouldn't ask for anything more, Betty Mae," Malachi said.

They walked back to the car.

Stump came up to Malachi and gave him a hug. "You take care of yourself, boy," he said.

"I will," Malachi said. He leaned in closer so only Stump could hear him. "You watch out for my mother, Stump."

Stump nodded. "I will, son, he said.

Malachi opened the driver side of the car, before getting in he turned and looked at the smiling faces. He smiled back, and then entered the car. As he drove away, he felt a little dread as well as a sense of relief. Maybe the responsibility of running the Queen had taken a toll on him to the point of exhaustion and he was finally feeling the weight of it being removed from his shoulders. Maybe. He looked ahead and gripped the steering wheel with purpose and determination. Where he was going, he didn't know. Did he care? He didn't. The ride in itself was exhilarating to him. A ride into the unknown was stimulating.

The silhouette figure standing in the alley several doors down from the Queen watched what was transpiring. When Malachi drove away, the silhouette figure smiled as it blended into the darkness and slipped away.

Malachi didn't know where he was driving. To him, at the moment, it didn't make a difference in which direction to go. He had no destination. He didn't even care as he drove from town to town. Days eventually turned into weeks, and weeks into months. Every other town he would stop in, he would wire Stump asking him to wire him money. Stump never let him down. The money from Stump would be there before he left the town. The money he had in the bank in Blackenfield, didn't help him much considering he was traveling. There were towns he stopped in to play and sang to kill time and to see how receptive the unknown audience would react to him. There weren't too many standing ovations, but he did get feedback as to what some people were looking for during his performance. Six months later, Malachi glanced to his right at the sign that said he was entering Memphis, Tennessee.

By the time Malachi pulled up to a boarding house that had a sign for rooms to rent on the edge of a town called Larquos, he was exhausted. The sun was going down and he was hungry. He parked his car on the street, grabbed his bags and guitar, and walked up the stairs to the boarding house. He knocked on the door.

As he stood there waiting for a response, he looked around the area. There was another house down the dirt road. It looked like it hadn't been painted in years. The boarding house looked homely, he thought. It was painted beige and white. It was a colonial house with two large pillars. The front door opened to reveal a woman with a thin cigar in her mouth, and wearing a pair of men's tweed black trousers and large white long sleeve shirt with frills around the collar.

"What can I do for you?"

Malachi looked at the woman. Her left hand held a thin cigar and was missing her pinky finger. She possessed a dour look as she cocked her head to the side and stared at him.

"Uh…I saw your sign on the house for empty rooms," Malachi said.

"Umm. Well, can you pay the weekly rent? I don't want any bums coming in my place with no sob stories. I want my rent at the end of the week and no excuses."

Malachi was shocked at how direct the woman was. "How much is the rent?" he asked.

The woman put the cigar in her mouth and inhaled. She looked Malachi from foot to head with a slow examination. She exhaled. "Five dollars a week. I want two weeks in advance. I serve breakfast and lunch. Dinner you can find on your own. I don't want no cats, dogs, hoes, or drinking in my place. Friday and Saturday you can have guests from six in the evening until one o'clock in the morning. No one stays in my place overnight."

"Okay," Malachi said. "My name is Malachi Moon. What is your name? If you don't mind me asking?"

"Lady Marmalade," she said, as she swung the door open for Malachi to enter. "Welcome to my home."

The next morning when Malachi awoke, it was the smell of biscuits, eggs, bacon, and grits that made him open his eyes. He dressed quickly, and hurried down stairs.

When Malachi entered the kitchen he was greeted with a sight that made him stop. Sitting at the table was a large, black man whose size was unbelievable with white hair. Next to him sat a woman with bright red lipstick stuffing her mouth with eggs. She looked up at Malachi, and winked at him. Malachi looked away. His sight fell on a midget sitting on three encyclopedia books at the table. Lady Marmalade was standing by the small black cooking stove. She turned around at Malachi's entrance.

"Breakfast?" Lady Marmalade asked.

Malachi went to the end of the large, wooden table and sat down.

"Everybody, this is Malachi Moon," Lady Marmalade said. She headed to the table with a large plate of bacon and eggs. She sat it in the middle of the table for everyone to reach.

"Malachi Moon? Is that your real name?" The midget asked.

"Yeah," Malachi said. "What's yours?"

"Tom Thum," he said.

"Tom Thum?" Malachi repeated.

"Uh-huh. You got a probably with that?" Tom asked as he stood up on his chair and reached for some eggs.

Lady Marmalade looked at Tom, and smiled. She

shook her head. "And the lady wearing the 'I want to be kissed' lipstick sitting beside you is—"

"Jane Deville," she said. Offering her hand.

Malachi took it. He noticed when Jane offered her hand that her breasts were extremely large. He didn't want to get caught staring at them, so he quickly looked away. Although, his mouth was open from the sight of them.

"Close your mouth, boy. Staring is not nice."

Malachi glanced at the large Negro who'd made the comment. He was filling his mouth with eggs and bacon at the same time.

"That big, strong looking man feeding his face is Aaron Blaze. He likes to be called AB," Lady Marmalade said.

"Where are you from?" AB asked. He gave Malachi an intimidating stare while drinking a cup of coffee.

"The South," Malachi said, as he reached for a plate and began filling it with eggs and bacon.

"Hell, we're all from the South," AB said. "Where are you from in the South?"

"No place in particular," Malachi said.

"What kind of work do you do?" Jane asked. She batted her eyelashes invitingly.

"I own two hotels," Malachi said with hesitation. He wished he could take it back before it had come out of his mouth. He put a fork full of eggs in his mouth, as he averted his eyes, regretting he'd offered information that could be detrimental to him.

"Nigger, you don't own two hotels," AB said. "What do you really do? Burglar? Beggar? Thief or hustler?"

"You're too young to own two hotels," Lady

Marmalade said, as she brought over another plate of eggs, and sat the plate down. "If you ask me, I think by you carrying that guitar it would make you a musician."

"Yeah, I'm that too," Malachi said. "It's not like I bought the hotels. They were given to me. Sort of...."

AB looked at Malachi. AB's big face took on a scowl as his fat jaws chewed the food. "I've never liked a liar. Especially a liar who tries to act like he's better than me," he said.

Tom Thum looked from AB to Malachi. He smiled.

Malachi placed his fork on his plate and looked at AB. He pushed back his chair, and placed his elbows on the table. "Do we have a problem, Aaron?" he asked.

AB pushed back his chair, and turned his entire body to face Malachi. He placed his hands on his large, tree trunk thighs, and stared at Malachi.

"AB, you ought to stop trying to scare people with that mean look," Jane said. She batted her eyelashes and smiled at Malachi.

"I just want to know why the young boy is lying." AB asked.

"You don't know me that well to be calling me a liar," Malachi said.

"I don't, huh?" AB said.

"No," Malachi replied, as he stood up. He was scared, he admitted that, but he refused to be cornered by a man who had more muscle than brains. "If I called you a big, stupid tree, how would you feel?"

AB stared at Malachi. He stood up, Malachi watched him grow bigger and bigger as he slowly rose from his chair. He could tell by his size that AB stood over six feet, four inches in height. At that moment, Malachi realized he might've bitten off more than he could chew.

"Are you calling me that?" AB asked, as he towered over Malachi with an aura of intimidation.

Malachi swallowed hard. "What I'm saying is that I don't appreciate someone calling me something I'm not," he said.

"Well, I am what you called me, and I can whip your little butt and think nothing of it because I'm just a big, stupid tree," AB said.

"AB, leave the boy alone," Lady Marmalade said. "He didn't mean any harm."

"Yeah, he did. He hurt my feelings," AB said. "No one hurts my feelings unless I'm hurting their body for it."

"Ain't going to be no fighting in my house!" Lady Marmalade shouted, as she hurried to the stove. She removed a cast iron frying pan, and turned around. "If it's going to be any fighting in here, I'm going to be the one splitting heads. Now if ya'll want to fight, take out back!"

Malachi could tell that AB was a bully. If he let him get away with trying to goad him, he knew it wouldn't be the last time.

"I don't want any trouble, AB," Malachi said.

"You got trouble when you came in here lying, boy," AB said, as he took a step closer to Malachi.

Lady Marmalade walked up to the both of them. "Take it outside, or I'm going upstairs to get my single-shot shotgun and let some buckshot's fly in somebody's ass!" she snapped.

"I don't think he wants to go outside," Malachi said. He smiled as AB's mouth fell open in shock.

"You…You don't think I want to go outside?" AB asked.

Malachi exhaled slowly to stop his heart from racing in his chest. "Nope. I don't think you want to go outside," he said.

AB stared at Malachi. AB started taking off his jacket, and then his shirt. He laid them both on his chair. With his tee shirt on, he flexed his arms and chest muscles.

"I'm ready to go whenever you are," AB said.

When he smiled at Malachi, Malachi felt a shiver go down his spine. He thought he could outthink the man, but his psychological reversal role backfired on him, and, at that moment, he wished he had Kai-Chang with him.

"Let's go," Malachi said. He turned around and walked out the kitchen.

"I hate to see that fine looking boy get his head bashed in," Jane said. "Well, if it's going to happen, I might as well be there to help the boy off the ground and stop the blood that's going to be flowing from his busted, handsome face." She pushed back her chair and followed them.

"Sometimes you can bite off more than you can chew, and the next thing you know, you're choking on it," Tom said. He jumped down from his chair, and ran after Jane.

"Wait for me," Lady Marmalade said. She dropped the frying pan on the table, and hurried out of the kitchen. "First, though, let me get my shotgun, because they ain't gonna be no killing on my property."

CHAPTER EIGHTEEN

A Journey

Malachi watched as AB warmed up by throwing punches in the air and feinting while bobbing and weaving. He shook he head, asking himself why did he have to provoke the man, but he knew the answer. Someone like AB thrived on others fear. He glanced to the right of him and saw Jane and Tom sitting on the stairs watching them. Jane smiled at him and waved. Tom just started shaking his head. Malachi sat on the grass and began removing his shoes.

"Come on, boy, I ain't gonna kill you," AB said. He started laughing. "Although, I'm a heavyweight in the boxing division. Don't worry, I'm gonna take it easy on you. That scar on your face will barely be noticeable when I finish with you."

Malachi removed his socks.

"Take it all off, baby!" Jane screamed, as she clapped her hands while laughing like a banshee.

The screen door slammed closed making everyone turn in the direction of the house. Standing there holding a single-shot shotgun, was Lady Marmalade. She had one of her thin cigars in her mouth as she nodded.

"AB, if I see you hurting that boy too much, I'm gonna fire a warning shot in the air," Lady Marmalade began. "If you still hurting him, I'm gonna put one of these slugs in your big ass."

"This ain't gonna take long, Lady Marmalade. I'm gonna hit him with a one-two combination, and he's going to hit the ground and that's going to be it," AB said with a smile.

With his socks and shoes off, Malachi stood up. He stretched, and then threw several punches into the air to warm up. He snapped his head from left to right to get the kinks out of it. He looked up at AB. He smiled.

"You ready, boy?" AB asked.

"Ready," Malachi said.

"AB, remember what I told you," Lady Marmalade said, as she cradled the single-shot shotgun.

AB grunted as he slowly approached Malachi in his boxer's stance. He was right-handed and possessed a powerful left hook that rendered his opponents senseless when he laid it on their kidneys.

Malachi, using his right foot for balance and his left foot to guide him, began to inch forward on the balls of his feet toward AB.

It was funny, he thought, as he drew nearer to AB. The many times he would laugh whenever Kai-Chang would encourage him to learn how to fight. He couldn't grasp the concept of the kicks and punches, or how to center himself when it came to building his power within, but after two years of Kai-Chang's nagging and tedious practices, Malachi had finally giving into him. He learned how to fight what Kai-Chang called Tai Kwon Do. The art of fighting, Kai-Chang would tell him it came from knowing how to find your opponents weak points and manipulate them to your advantage.

"That's how you guard yourself, boy?" AB asked, as he came within striking distance of Malachi. "This is going to be easier than I thought."

They slowly began to circle one another.

Malachi could tell that AB was a professional at boxing by how he guarded all his flanks by keeping his elbows in and his fists covering his face. When AB feinted with a jab at his face, Malachi knew it was nothing more than an opening shot to get him to divulge his strategy. Malachi simply bobbed his head to the opposite direction of the jab, never taking his eyes off AB's eyes, his fists, and the movement of his shoulders.

"Oh. So you know a little about this game, huh?" AB said. He gave a short laugh.

Malachi was near enough to AB to block the second jab AB threw at him. He could tell by the light power of the blow that AB was trying to feel him out once again.

With the quick feint of his left jab, AB knew that it was thrown only to setup Malachi with an overhand right to his temple. When he saw the opening, he let go of his right hand with as much power as he could muster.

Malachi waited.

AB knew he had Malachi the moment he let go of his punch. It was a sweet setup so beautifully that he congratulated himself even before the blow fell on Malachi.

When Malachi saw the blow coming from the corner of his eye, he leaned back and away from it while pivoting to the left of AB as AB's punch went by him. When Malachi stopped his pivot, he found himself directly in front of AB. Inches from AB's chest.

Malachi's first blow found AB's heart as his second and third punches found AB's left and right top shoulders to render his arms useless. His blows were hard and to the point. He used his fourth blow to leap back and kick AB in the side of his head with his right foot. When he came down on his feet, he saw AB staggered back. Malachi made three quick strides, and, with an open hand side chop, he struck at AB's throat.

AB had never seen anyone throw punches as fast as Malachi's or as hard. He felt each blow with stunning revelation rack his body. The blows shocked his body into submission. He let out a small scream when Malachi struck him in the throat. A scream that could be heard a block away. He fell to the ground and grabbed his throat as he rolled around on the ground, grasping for air.

"Kiss my ass!" Tom shouted as he jumped off the stairs and ran to the fallen AB. "Did you see that? He whipped your ass, AB!"

"I ain't ever seen that before," Jane said. She looked at Lady Marmalade.

Malachi ran over to AB as he lay on his back fighting to get air into his lungs. He flipped him over onto his stomach, and began massaging his back while pressing on AB's thighs. Seconds later, Malachi could feel AB relaxing as he began to get control of his breathing.

"You okay?" Malachi asked as he turned AB over, and helped him sit up. "I tried not to hit you too hard."

"Goddamn, AB, that boy beat the hell out of you," Tom said, as he stood beside the both of them.

Lady Marmalade and Jane came over to stand beside.

"I hope you learned your lesson, AB," Lady Marmalade said. You can't go around trying to scare everybody because you're big and all."

"The boy can fight and he's cute," Jane said. She touched Malachi on the arm and giggled.

"You want me to help you up?" Malachi asked.

AB looked at him. His eyebrows furrowed as he gave Malachi a hard stare. Seconds pass before he softened his look, and nodded. Malachi reached out and took him under his arms as he assisted him from the ground.

"Good fight," AB said in a hoarse voice, as he clutched his throat.

"I didn't want to fight you," Malachi said.

"Well, it's a fight his big ass got," Lady Marmalade said. She looked at AB as she smoked her thin cigar. "I hope this taught you a lesson?"

AB glanced at her and growled.

Lady Marmalade flicked the ashes off her cigar, and gave AB an intimidating stare, as she affectionately caressed the shotgun.

"I guess the fight is over. Ya'll want to finish breakfast," Tom said.

"No." Everyone said at once.

Tom shrugged.

The evening came with a cool breeze as Malachi and AB sat on the porch swing of the house.

"Man, if I were you, I wouldn't tell too many people

that story. Everyone you run into will think you're lying," AB said.

They were sitting side by side. Malachi glanced at him. "Like you did?" he asked, as he passed the jug of moonshine to him.

AB nodded. "Yeah. It's difficult to believe something like that at this time in age in a Negroes life. We got whitey telling us we ain't nothing while trying to sleep with our women or trying to get us in debt by selling us worthless farming tools and charging us our soul to pay them back," he said.

"We are on the bottom of the totem pole, man, we'll always be looked down on," Malachi said.

AB nodded. "I got a fight next week. You think you can make it?" he asked.

Malachi watched AB take the large jug of moonshine and raise it to his mouth. He watched AB gulp it down in three large swallows. Never once taking the time to breathe as he swallowed.

"Yeah, I can make it," Malachi said.

"Good," AB said. He handed Malachi back the jug.

Their attention was drawn to the front door opening, and the strong smell of perfume hitting them hard in the nose. Lady Marmalade stepped out wearing an outlandish lime green dress with matching heels. On her head was a hat that covered most of her face. She saw them and smiled.

"You two need to stop drinking that nasty, gut killer moonshine, and come over to the Club and listen to me play the piano," Lady Marmalade said.

"You can play the piano?" Malachi asked.

"I can sing, too," she said.

"Why the hell not?" AB said, as he stood up. He grabbed his belt and hiked up his big pants. "I ain't had a good laugh in a long time."

"Neither had I until I saw Malachi put your big, lug ass on the ground gasping for air," Lady Marmalade snapped, as she cautiously walked down the stairs.

AB gave her an angry stare. His anger only lasted a minute, for Malachi touched him on the shoulder. "Well, he's a good fighter. And you know what they say—"

"Yeah, if you get your butt whipped, then you're second to the best. Cut the bullshit, AB. You two meet me at the Club. I'll buy ya'll a drink," Lady Marmalade said.

They stood there watching Lady Marmalade walk down the dirt road with her head held high, and her bright green purse swinging.

AB looked at Malachi.

"Where's the Club?" Malachi asked.

"I'll show you," AB said. "Wait for us, Lady!"

Malachi followed AB down the stairs.

They ran after Lady Marmalade.

The Club was a simple one. It had been a barn that was converted into area that could hold over one and fifty people. It had been sectioned off with plywood and sheet rock to create separate rooms as well as create a bar that began a few feet from the entrance and ended near the back of wall of the Club. The placed was enormous. Malachi entered it to the sounds of loud music and boisterous voices. There was so much smoke that he hand to squint his eyes to prevent them from burning.

"It's big, ain't it?" AB asked as they made their way further into the Club. AB began to straighten out his shirt by pulling it down at the ends. "This place can make you want to find a bed and never leave."

"Yeah," Malachi said, as he followed AB.

"Bigger than your two places?" AB asked.

"Much bigger," Malachi said.

Malachi looked around. In the center of the room he saw a large wooden, raised floor. He tapped AB on the shoulder. "What's that?" he asked, as he pointed to the area in front of them.

"That's the stage, Malachi. When you see the musicians on there, believe me, they come to entertain the people," AB said. "Come on, let's get a table."

AB led Malachi to the far right side of the room. They found a table. After knocking off the empty bottles onto the straw covered floor, they sat down.

A young girl no older than eighteen came over and stood in front of them.

"Hi. My name is Gail. Can I take your order," she said.

"Girl, you know what I want," AB said. He slapped Gail on her butt lightly.

"Oh, hi, AB," Gail said, as she removed the small writing pad from her face that she'd been holding up in front of her. "I didn't recognize you."

"This is Malachi," AB said. "Bring us some whiskey, and none of that watered down garbage. Let Egghead know I'm here, child."

"Mr. Sneech, you mean," Gail said.

"Egghead," AB said.

Gail stared at him for a moment, and then she turned and walked away.

"Egghead?" Malachi asked.

"Yeah. I've known him for years. When I first came here, he was working out of this barn shoveling horseshit. One day he comes to me and tells me he has an idea but he needs the money to make it work. At the time, I was doing well with my boxing game. Malachi, I was laying punches to heads and knocking them off their feet. The fight game was good back in those days. Well, of course I told Egghead his plan wouldn't work and I wasn't giving him any money to invest in a fool idea like this," AB said, as he raised his arms. "As you can see, I was more fool than he was because the man has been making money ever since. When things were going bad for me, and I began to lose my fights, Egghead gave me a shot. He built that stage up there and let me hold fights. I won one or two, but didn't realize how smart Egghead was until I noticed that he was getting a third of the purse and a third of the cut from the front door. The man is smart."

"You called, Aaron?"

A voice asked from behind Malachi. Malachi turned around in his chair.

Malachi was shocked to see a blond hair, blue eyed white man standing there wearing a dirty apron and smoking a cigarette.

"Why do you still call me that, Aaron? The workers know me as Mr. Sneech," Egghead said.

"Old habits are hard to die...Egghead," AB said. "Anyway, I want you to meet Malachi. He's a business man, too."

"Really?" Egghead said, as he came around and sat down at the table. "What kind of business are you in?"

"Something like this, but not as big," Malachi said.

"This is big. Did Aaron tell—"

"I told him already, man. You ain't got to rub it in!" AB snapped.

Egghead smiled. He reached in his pocket and removed a pack of cigarettes. He shook one loose. He lit the fresh cigarette with the one he was still smoking.

Gail walked over with a bottle of whiskey and two shot glasses. She placed everything on the table and waited for payment.

"Don't worry, Gail, Egghead will take care of this," AB said.

Egghead laughed. "I got it, Gail. Go on and get to another table," Egghead said. He put out the first cigarette in the ashtray on the table.

Gail tossed her head, and walked away.

"That's a big piano on that stage," Malachi said, as AB pushed a glass of whiskey in front of him.

"Only a few people I know can play that baby," Egghead said. "But that is only part of the Club style. When we have our jam session, you be here. It's something that you'd always remember."

"There goes Lady Marmalade," AB said.

Egghead exploded out of his chair. "Damnit, I forgot she thinks she's going on tonight. She got pass me," he said. "I got to go. Aaron, don't leave before I talk to you. I want to talk about the fight next week."

Malachi and AB watched as Egghead hurried away knocking people to the side as he tried to make it to the stage.

"What's wrong?" Malachi asked.

"You never want Lady Marmalade to get on that stage without giving her instructions," AB said.

"Why not?" Malachi asked.

AB raised his glass to his lips. He smiled. "Watch," he said, as he drank.

Malachi turned his chair around to get a better view. He watched as Lady Marmalade sat down on the piano chair. She placed her hands on the keys at the same moment Egghead was running up to the stage. Egghead stopped when Lady Marmalade hit the C Major Chord. He turned back around and walked down the short stairs shaking his head.

"Ya'll drunk ass bastards are here to hear some great music, or ya'll here to get pissy drunk. Either way, it doesn't make Lady Marmalade any difference. I'm here to play these damn ebony and ivory keys. So ya'll listen real good, the Lady is here!" Lady Marmalade shouted.

Malachi watched Egghead walk off the stage with a look of dejection as he continuously puffed on his cigarette.

"What's the problem?" Malachi asked AB, as he turned toward him.

AB answered by pointing at the stage as he reached for the whiskey bottle. Malachi turned his attention back to the stage.

"I wrote this song a couple of months ago," Lady Marmalade began. "To all you heartless men out there, this song could be you that I'm talking about, or it could be your brother or your daddy. It don't care who you compare it to, you shiftless bastards. I just want ya'll to listen!"

Malachi noticed that everyone seem to turn to the stage. He realized that the sound in the barn was reverberating leaving an echo that lingered.

The piano began to play. Lady Marmalade opened her mouth and began to sing.

"I started loving me a man named Bluuuueeeee…I gave

that man my heart…but he didn't know what to dooooooo. A woman can love a man and try…I say trrryyyy to make it work, but—and this is a sweeeeetttt but—if he ain't giving baccckkkk what I'm giving, then I'm gonna kick…kick… kick, his narrow ass to the street curb. Because the worthless bastard can't return it worth a fart."

The audience roared with laughter and cheered as Lady Marmalade continued to sing. Malachi had to smile at the song as well. He noticed that Lady Marmalade's voice was off-key and raspy, and she couldn't hold a note too long, but what she lacked in musical scale, she gave back in entertainment.

"Can't trust no man…Can't love no man…Don't want to live with you…Bluuuueeee…Cause if I dooooooo…I have to get my knife…And gut you throuuuugggghhhhh."

Malachi watched as the crowd went crazy while Lady Marmalade played the piano like some kind of possessed demon. She made the keys come to life as she pounded on them.

"I'll need you today…but if you hurt me…I'll bleed you dry tomorrow…my…sweet…sweet…Bluuueeeue. Love can be goooooodddd…Love can be baaaaddddd…If I love you now…Don't make me cut you later…When I'm maaaadddd."

Malachi smiled. The woman could hold her own. She made the crowd shout out her name while they clapped their hands in jubilation.

"Boy, I know her man is in some trouble at home," Malachi said.

"He sure was. When Lady Marmalade caught him sleeping with a young girl, she ran him out of town," AB said.

"What do you mean? He moved on with the other woman?" Malachi asked.

AB shook his head. "Lady Marmalade chased him out of town," he said.

"You said that."

"Malachi, Lady Marmalade strapped on a pair of boots and some pants. She grabbed her shotgun and chased the man out of town by firing at him. She chased the man from one end of the town to the other, and, the man was in his long underwear and nothing else," AB said.

Malachi stared at AB expecting him to start laughing. When he didn't, Malachi returned his attention to the stage. He realized that AB was telling him the truth.

"It ain't what you knooowwwow...It ain't whhhhhooooo you know...its how you make it worrrrrkkkk in bed..." Lady Marmalade sang. She hit several more keys on the piano. She stood up knocking over the small stool she'd been was sitting on. *"It can't be trrruuuuueeerue...When your Buuuueeeelue acts up and messes with yoooouuuuu."*

Hitting the last chord on the piano, Lady Marmalade walked to the edge of the stage and bowed. The crowd gave her a powerful, cheerful resounding ovation.

"That's why Egghead doesn't like for her to go up there without talking to her," AB said.

"Why?" Malachi asked.

"Look," AB said.

Malachi turned to the stage. He watched as Lady Marmalade picked up the piano stool and sat back down in front of the piano.

"Here we go again," AB said.

"I don't give a damn about no man," Lady Marmalade began, as her fingers struck a chord.

Four o'clock in the morning found Lady Marmalade, AB, and Malachi walking back to the boarding house. AB was staggering to the point of nearly falling to the ground. Malachi and Lady Marmalade had secured each arm to keep him upright.

"I didn't know you could sing...like...that," Malachi said.

"Boy, I've been singing the Blues for twenty years. But how would you know, you've only been in this world for a minute? I sing it like I mean it, and I mean it because I've lived it. Any fool can get on stage and act like they singing the Blues, but it takes a special person to sing it from their soul," Lady Marmalade said. "I hope this big bastard don't fall because I'm not helping him up. I'll go to the house and get him a pillow to sleep on right out here on the ground."

Malachi laughed.

"You're laughing. I'm about as serious as a frog leaping to get to dry land. A horny stallion that is about to get some ass from a small mare," Lady Marmalade said.

Malachi laughed harder as he struggled to keep AB upright.

Two weeks later, the stage had been rearranged and setup into a boxing ring. The tables that were there during the singing were now placed circular around the ring. The cool evening had brought in people from all the neighboring towns to see AB fight. Egghead gave the first twenty people that entered a free drink and a meal.

AB was in the back room warming up by throwing jabs and punches at his shadow. Perspiration ran down his large body like a waterfall, as he pivot, weaved, and kept his feet moving. Malachi, sitting in a corner, watched AB do his preparation.

"I can beat him," AB said. "It's all about who has the greater courage."

Malachi nodded.

"You see, Malachi, a man is his worse enemy when he starts to lose faith in his skills. I ain't as young as I use to be, but my skills can still hold me up," AB said. "All I got to do is pace myself, and keep my hands up. Keep my head moving, and don't get flat-footed."

Malachi nodded.

AB stopped. He looked at Malachi. "You got something you want to say?" he asked.

Malachi slowly walked toward AB with his hands deep in his plaid pants pockets. When he stopped in front of him, he was smiling.

"What the hell is that suppose to me?" AB demanded.

"If you want to win this fight, you got to let your opponent think he can beat you," Malachi said. "He's young, but he didn't get this far fighting like he doesn't know what he's doing."

"Huh?" AB said, as he stopped shadow boxing and looked at Malachi.

"AB, this boy is young, strong, and... maybe...stupid, but we don't know that," Malachi said.

"Huh?"

"When you're young and strong, you think you can beat the world. Use that to beat him," Malachi said.

AB looked at Malachi. He tilted his head a little to the right. "I don't understand what you're saying, boy. Damn right he's strong, but not too many young boys I know can get this far in the boxing game without having some kind of skills," he said.

Malachi rolled his eyes. He placed a hand on AB's shoulder. "Come closer," he said.

The crowd was eager to see some blood as Egghead kept the drinks coming to the paying customers. Those that didn't drink, he gave them drinks free from time to time to keep the place jumping. He was standing beside the bar when he saw AB come out of the back with his robe draped around his massive shoulders and throwing short punches in the air. Malachi followed him carrying some towels and a bucket.

"Gail," Egghead began, "AB is going to get the hell beat out of him tonight."

Gail, standing beside him glanced at him. She was dressed in the customary red, short, frilled dress that all the waitresses wore during fights. "Why do you say that? AB can hold his own when it comes to fighting," she said.

A crowd that had be rowdy and rude came to silence when AB's opponent entered the ring followed by two beautiful Negro women in black and white dresses that did less to a man's imagination than his eyes. They were followed by the manager of the champion who was dressed in a suit that was candy apple red with slick down pomenade hair that fell to his thin shoulders.

"That's why," Egghead said, as he pointed to the young fighter stepping into the ring.

Gail turned and gasped.

"You ever saw a young boy that big before?" Egghead asked.

Gail, holding a tray with drinks, shook her head as

she reached for a drink, and swallowed its contents in two quick gulps.

"That's why I said what I said," Egghead said.

Gail reached for another drink and gulped it down as she continued to stare at the young, massive, muscled boxer who was going to fight AB. She groaned.

"That young boy is going to bash AB's head in," Egghead said.

Gail's eyes held the vision of the young champion as she raised her third drink to her lips. Egghead stopped her by placing his hand over the drink.

"You've drank one too damn many of my alcohol, Gail, and you're not paying for it. I am. Get those drinks to the customers," Egghead said.

Gail nodded as she slowly walked away. Her eyes still transfixed on the ring.

"Goddamn!" AB exclaimed as he sat on his wooden stool in the corner. "You ever see anybody that big before, Malachi? Look at that boy's thighs. I swear to you they are as big as tree trunks. They're bigger than mine."

Malachi was in shock as he stared at the young Negro who stood as tall as AB, but whose body looked to be chiseled out of granite. He had muscles everywhere on his body. The thickness of his neck was beyond belief. It looked like he didn't have a neck from the thickness around it. The young boy's stomach had rows of muscles in it. His glistening body of sweat only enhanced his muscles.

"Uh…AB," Malachi began. "That boy is going to kill you."

AB looked up at Malachi. "Thanks for the show of confidence," he said. He returned his attention to the young boy he was about to fight. "I can take him." His words were barely discernible.

Malachi began rubbing down AB's shoulders. Trying to get him to relax. "All right. This is nothing, AB. Sure he's big, he's strong, and he's probably going to hurt you the first couple of rounds, but you remember what I told you," he said.

"What you told me don't mean squat at this point, Malachi. That boy is going to come at me with his gloves hot and heavy," AB said.

"Stick to the plan, AB. Stick to the plan," Malachi said.

An old man wearing a worn gray hat with too many holes in it, stepped into the ring and walked to the middle of it. Everyone watched him. He motioned for AB and his opponent to come to the center of the ring.

With AB and Malachi standing on one side, and his opponent and his people across from them, the old man with the gray hat looked out into the crowd.

"My name is Bluefoot. Ya'll know how I referee these fights. I don't want no kicking. No elbows. No crotch punching and no spitting in a person's eye. Ya'll follow those rules and we gonna be all right. You break them, and I'm gonna break some heads in this here ring tonight," he said. "In the right corner is the challenger. Ya'll know him. It's AB. A washed up, worn out fighter who don't know when to hang his damn gloves up after being whipped on more than I can count."

Everyone in the crowd started laughing. Lady Marmalade, sitting in the front row laughed while stomping her feet and slapping the man next to her on the back.

"In the left corner is the champion. Iron Man

Michaels'. Has won twenty-one of his champion fights from here to…Well, the boy has won in a lot of places and he's here to win tonight. This is going to be a good fight, and a fair fight. May the best damn man win," Bluefoot said.

Malachi and AB walked back to their corner.

"Not too many people out in that crowd have much faith in me winning this one, huh?" AB asked.

Malachi smiled. "I don't think so, and if that big boy lands one of those hard hitting fists square on your chin, you'd be thinking the same thing," he said.

Egghead ran up to their corner. He was holding a small writing pad with a pencil in his hand. "AB, you want to drop some money on your loss. The odds are twelve to one against you," he said.

AB growled.

"Twelve to one?" Malachi said.

"Yeah, Malachi, the people's confidence ain't what it used to be," Egghead said, as he stepped away from their corner. I'll be praying for you to win, AB, but my money will be on Iron Man Michaels'. No hard feelings. It is just business."

AB looked up at Malachi. "You think I can beat him?" he asked.

Malachi, in his heart, wanted to tell AB the truth. To let him know that Iron Man Michaels' was a young man whose thirst for winning would overshadow AB's heart for bravery.

"Man, I think you're going to give him a run for his money, and surprise everybody," Malachi said.

AB nodded.

CHAPTER NINETEEN
Battle of Wits

They each cautiously inched closer together toward the middle of the ring. Iron Man Michaels' was a southpaw. When he was near enough to AB, he threw a right hand jab to feel AB out. AB was a cautious fighter. He knew that the jab was nothing more than an exploring expedition to see how he'd handle it. AB handled it by taking two quick side steps to the right to get out of the way. His dexterous feet moved with caution and speed to the opposite side of Iron Man Michaels' powerful left hand which followed immediately afterward.

As AB worked his way out of a harmful situation Iron Man Michaels' might throw at him, he was surprise at how fast the young man moved on his feet. Iron Man Michaels' began throwing a flurry of right hand jabs at AB to the point of backing him up on the ropes. It was there, as AB tried to protect himself that he knew why they call the young man Iron Man Michaels'. The young man's punches were hard and painful as they landed on AB's forearms and shoulders.

While on the ropes, AB used his elbows to protect his ribs. His gloves were tucked tight under his chin as he kept his head folded into them. He watched Iron Man Michaels' come toward him with continuous jabs. AB was waiting for the right moment to unleash a barrage of punches of his own as he looked up from the hole he'd made with his gloves to protect his face. When Iron Man Michaels' was close enough, AB dropped his right hand low to get in a right-hand cross to Iron Man Michaels' jaw. As he saw the precision of his right-hand cross fly toward Iron Man Michaels' jaw, he was surprise when he saw Iron Man Michaels' leaned back, and AB's blow passed by him harmlessly. When Iron Man Michaels' came back into position, his overhand right hand came barreling down toward AB's head. It connected.

The power of the punch from Iron Man Michaels' made AB bones rattle. Iron Man Michaels' next punch of a left-handed uppercut to AB's chin, snapped his head back. AB bounced off the ropes from the blow and into a straight right-hand to his chest, and then a left hook that made him stagger several feet before falling face down to the canvass. The crowd went wild.

Bluefoot ran toward the fallen AB. He fell to one knee and began counting. Each time he said a number, he threw out an extended arm across AB's prone body.

Malachi rubbed his sweat drenched face as he watched AB slowly; very slowly rise from the canvass.

"Get up, AB!" Malachi shouted at the top of his lungs. "Come on! Get up!"

AB used one knee as he placed his gloves on the canvass and used them for support to push upward. He staggered to the ropes. As he bounced off them, he clutched them as if his life depended on them.

Iron Man Michaels' was in his corner with his massive arms raised victoriously as he jumped around. An early knockout he was hoping.

Bluefoot ran over to AB. He stared into his eyes. "Can you go on?" he asked.

AB looked at Bluefoot. He shook his head to clear away the blurriness, and then he nodded.

"You sure?" Bluefoot asked.

"Yeah. I'm okay," AB said.

The bell rang. Ending round one.

AB staggered back to his corner. He sat down on the stool Malachi had placed inside the ring. His arms hung listlessly at his sides as Malachi rubbed him down with a cold wet sponge, and let him sip water from the plastic cup he had. Malachi raised the tin bucket for AB to spit out the water. When AB did, Malachi saw two of AB's teeth come out as well. Malachi looked at him.

"It's all right, Malachi," AB said with swollen lips. "They came out from the back."

Malachi nodded. He wiped AB down with a towel.

"Try to keep off the ropes, AB. That kid will kill you if you get on the ropes again," Malachi said.

Egghead came up to their corner again. He climbed up on the ropes. "All right, boys. This is it. AB, the odds just went up twenty to one against you," he said.

Malachi wiped the sweat from AB's shoulders with

the towel as he glanced at AB. He began massaging AB's arms to keep the circulation going.

"Malachi, can I borrow fifty dollars from you?" AB asked.

Malachi stopped. He stood up and looked down at AB. "Why? To bet against you losing?" he asked. He raised his voice angrily.

"No. I want to bet it on me winning," AB said.

Malachi looked at him. For some reason he believed in AB at that moment. Sure, he had to admit to himself he didn't think AB stood a chance of winning when he'd seen him fall to the canvass, but now it was different. AB had a glow about him that shined with confidence. Malachi reached into his pants pocket.

"Here's a hundred, Egghead. Place fifty dollars from me and AB on him winning this fight," Malachi said, as he gave the money to Egghead.

Egghead looked from Malachi to AB. He took the money. "Who am I to deny fools from parting with their money?" he said, as he jumped down from the ring and hurried away laughing.

Malachi and AB watched Egghead run back to the bar.

"Malachi? AB said.

"Yeah?"

"Keep that smelling salt close. I'm going to need it more than once before this is over," AB said.

"I will, but you won't need it," Malachi said. "Start doing the things I told you."

The bell rang. Round two began.

AB had a second wind. It wasn't much, he knew, but

it was enough to give him the push he needed. Surprise, he knew had to be on his side to win.

Iron Man Michaels' watched AB approach. He could see the same fear and hesitation in his eyes. It was fear from his opponents that drove him to win all of his previous fights. His blood thirst desire in crushing anyone who he fought. This fight will be easy. AB was too weak for him to think he could win, he thought.

AB, breathing through his nose, contained his apprehension by remembering what Malachi had told him. To beat a bull, you had to make it angry, because once it became angry, it didn't think. It reacted.

AB moved fast toward Iron Man Michaels'. When he was close enough to land a punch, AB pivoted to the right while letting loose a left-handed hook to Iron Man Michaels' ribs. The blow wasn't as powerful as he'd wanted it to be, but enough to get Iron Man Michaels' attention. For as Iron Man pivoted to prevent AB from getting away by trying to cut off the ring, AB quickly shuffled back the opposite way, throwing Iron Man Michael' off balance. It was that awkward imbalance that made AB rush at Iron Man Michaels' with a powerful straight right-hand that struck him on the chin, knocking him back several feet.

The blow surprised Iron Man Michaels'. He didn't think AB had it in him. As he regained his footing, he watched AB do some feet shuffling. He smiled.

Confidence, AB knew, was the building of a man. He saw he could hurt the big, young man, and with that, he had to use his boxing prowess to stay on top of his game.

Iron Man Michaels' began to stalk AB. Slowly approaching him with his hands up and caution is thrown out the window. Whenever AB shifted to one side of the ring; Iron Man Michaels' slowly began to cut the ring off. He didn't want to give AB any maneuvering space to avoid his hardest punches.

It had become a stalking game, AB thought, as he watched Iron Man Michaels get closer to him with each step. He repeatedly jabbed at Iron Man Michaels' to keep him away, but Iron Man Michaels' would bob and weave his way closer and closer.

The bell rang.

Sitting down in his corner, AB was breathing hard as he watched Malachi work over him.

"How you think I'm doing?" AB asked.

Malachi massaged AB's thighs to loosen them. He glanced up at him. "You can't keep running. Now is the time to do what I told you," he said.

"That boy is good," AB said. "I was like that when I was his age. Strong and ready to throw down on anyone."

Malachi threw water in AB's face with the wet sponge. "The old must teach the young," he said.

"What is that suppose to mean?" AB asked.

"Something Confucius said," Malachi answered.

"Confucius? Who is that? Is he a boxer?" AB asked.

"No. AB, surprise is what is going to let you win this fight," Malachi said.

The bell rang. Round three.

AB stood up. He kicked out his legs to get rid of the kinks. He tossed his neck from side to side, as he watched Iron Man Michaels' come to the middle of the ring. He took in a deep breath, and then he attacked.

Iron Man Michaels' didn't think the old goat AB had

it in him as he exploded from his corner toward him. The way he was moving, he didn't think the old fool would go around him, but forcibly at him.

AB knew that Iron Man Michaels' wouldn't bulge from the center of the ring. It was that assurance, he knew, that made him come at him with full force as he neared.

In the middle of the ring, Malachi witnessed the old lion and the young lion go at it toe- to- toe as they fought. The crowd went bombastic as the two giants fought with a frenzy of punch for punch. The crowd was on their feet and everyone was screaming for blood.

AB placed his head in the center of Iron Man Michaels' chest to ward off some of his punishing blows to his head and body while delivering some of his own powerful punches. AB worked several feverish punches to Iron Mans' ribs and stomach, whereas Iron Man Michaels' tried, without much connection, to hit AB with several head butts.

AB smiled, for he knew what he had to do. He stepped on Iron Man Michaels' right foot. Pressing hard on it to keep it from moving. When there was no resisting to get his foot away from AB's, AB tossed his head up and into Iron Man's Michaels' chin with so much force that AB nearly blackout, but the sound of Iron Man Michaels' groan brought him back to consciousness.

AB, while still stepping on Iron Man Michaels' foot, stepped back far enough to let loose a devastating right-hand upper cut to his chin. AB released his foot as Iron Man staggered back two steps from the blow. AB moved in with a left, right, left-hand hook to the head, and then a right-hand overhand that struck Iron Man Michaels' on the right temple. The blow was so powerful that AB felt it reverberate through his entire arm and up to his neck.

When AB's head had struck Iron Man Michaels' chin, the power of it had made him bite his tongue very hard. It nearly severed it. His eyes had watered but only for a moment, because the blows AB inflicted on him had him hurting. He'd never been hurt that way before. AB was laying the swift, powerful combinations on him. Iron Man Michaels' cringed and winced from the sudden assault of pain being inflicted to his disciplined body.

AB watched Iron Man Michaels' stagger back against the ropes. He saw his gloves fall to his waist. AB knew if the bell rang, he wouldn't have another chance. He charged at Iron Man Michaels' and let loose a volley of wild, yet controlled punches that found their mark through his protective gloves. AB pushed Iron Man Michaels' gloves aside from time to time in hopes of finding Iron Man Michaels' ribs, head, kidneys, and stomach. Each time he knew he'd hit a mark because he'd hear Iron Man Michael's grunt, or moan in pain.

AB could feel his heart racing wildly. The knockout was close. He could taste it. He had to wait for Iron Man Michaels' to remove his covered hands away from his face, as he continued throwing combinations at him, but it was difficult to get him to drop his hands completely.

Iron Man Michaels' hedged on the point of being thoroughly worked over. He had to clutch AB to prevent him from doing any more damage to his beaten body. He opened his gloves slightly to see if he could grab AB. A desperate move he knew, but one that couldn't be avoided. He had to clutch AB to get to another round.

AB knew he wouldn't be able to finish the round. He

was too tired. He was breathing hard. His heart was about to explode. He wanted to drop his hands and give up. Let the young pup win. He didn't care at that moment. Then, unexpectedly, he saw his opening.

Iron Man Michaels' opened his arms to clutch AB as he threw himself at him.

AB stepped back and pivoted to his left at the moment Iron Man Michaels' opened his arms to grab him. AB let fly a vicious left hook to his head. The punch landed solid, and sent Iron Man Michaels' staggering across the ring.

AB wanted to end it. He wanted to walk to his corner and tell Malachi to throw in the towel. Yet, the sight of seeing Iron Man Michaels' wobble to gain his balance sent AB running toward him. When he reached him, he let loose a far reaching, straight left hand that found its mark on Iron Man Michaels' nose. The power of the punch lifted Iron Man Michaels' off his feet and into the air. When he landed on the sweat, and blood covered canvass, the ring shook.

Malachi watched Iron Man Michaels' bounced once, twice, and then a third time. He lay on the canvas unmoving. He glanced at AB bending over at the waist with his gloves on his knees and breathing like a tired old bull.

Bluefoot ran to the fallen Iron Man Michaels' unmoving body. He began to count.

The Club was in complete silence.

Bluefoot was on a count of four.

You could hear a pin drop. No one moved.

Iron Man Michaels' stirred.

Bluefoot was on a count of six.

Iron Man Michaels' coughed.

Bluefoot was on a count of eight following the count of nine. And, finally, the count of ten was shouted out by the crowd.

Malachi looked from Bluefoot to Iron Man Michaels, and then he looked at the beaten, worn, AB. He leaped into the air and shouted. "You won! You won, AB!" he screamed.

AB walked over to his corner on weak legs. Each step was excruciating.

Malachi jumped into the ring and gave AB a hug.

"Ain't this a bitch!" Lady Marmalade snapped, as she leaped out of her seat. "I've lost all my goddamn money on this bum ass Negro! Somebody get my shotgun! There's gonna be some shooting tonight. I'm not gonna sit still for this shit!"

All eyes were on Lady Marmalade. When she'd finished screaming, the Club came back to life with shouts, moans and jeers as the reality of the situation dawn on them. AB was the new champion.

Egghead came into the ring and gave AB a hug while laughing hysterically.

"What are you laughing about?" AB asked, as Malachi helped him through the ropes and out of the ring. "My entire body is aching. I lost some of my teeth. My hands hurt, and you're the one laughing. I don't see anything funny about this night."

"You wouldn't until you know the story. I bet on you, AB," Egghead said. "I just won me a small fortune. Damn it! I won me a fortune!" he said.

Malachi looked at Egghead. He smiled. The man was shrewd.

The next day at mid-afternoon, Malachi, AB, Tom Thum, and Lady Marmalade were in the kitchen at the boarding house eating lunch. It was a late lunch. Lady Marmalade walked over to the table and dropped a plate of fried pork chops on it. She looked at Malachi and AB. She rolled her eyes and walked back to the hot stove.

"What's wrong with her?" Malachi asked, as he reached for a pork chop, and placed it on his plate.

AB looked at Malachi. His right eye was swollen shut. His lips were as big as watermelons and his left hand had swelled to the size of Tom Thum's head.

"I think she's mad because we won the fight last night," AB said. He could barely move his lips. In his hand he had a raw steak that he pressed against his swollen eye. "You thought she was playing when she said she was going to get her shotgun after the fight? That woman is serious. Too damn serious if you ask me."

"Damn right, I'm serious!" Lady Marmalade snapped as she spun around holding a knife. "The both of ya'll rent has gone up to five dollars more a week. And I want it in advance right goddamn now!"

"That's...sudden," Malachi said, as he filled his mouth with a piece of pork chop. He smiled. He reached for a bowl of rice. He began filling his plate with it while glancing at Lady Marmalade.

"Sudden my ass! You two made me lose a whole lot of fucking money last night. You couldn't be a regular bum, AB, and lose the fight. Oh, no. You had to go in there and show your ass," she said. She kicked the bottom of the stove to make her point. "Do you know people lost a bunch of money with your win, AB? Too damn much. I want my advance rent money today before you two leave this house!"

AB shrugged. He reached into his pocket and removed a wad of money. He peeled off a ten dollar bill. "How much money did you lose, Lady?" he asked. He placed the ten dollar bill on the table. "Hell, you could've won too if you had more confidence in me."

Lady Marmalade placed a hand on her hip while dangerously twirling the knife. She watched AB play with his money. "Confidence ain't had anything to do with it. You were a washed up bum who was suppose to lose," she said. "Anyway, I figure I lost about sixty or seventy dollars last night."

Malachi laughed.

"Washed up bums still have one more fight in them, Lady Marmalade," AB said.

Lady Marmalade grunted and gave Malachi the evil eye by forming her hand into a claw, and scratching the air. Malachi stopped laughing. She turned her attention back to AB. "Well, I believe it was seventy-five dollars," she said, as she quickly glanced over at Malachi.

Malachi was eating his food with his head down to avoid looking at Lady Marmalade.

"Okay, here's one hundred dollars," AB said. He placed more money on top of the ten dollars. Scooping it all up, he offered the money to Lady Marmalade.

Lady Marmalade took three purposeful strides and snatched the money out of AB's hand. "Thank you," she said while counting the money and walking back to the cooking stove. "Uh...ya'll can forget about that rent increase."

Malachi looked up. "I bet we can," he said.

Lady Marmalade ignored him.

"I've been thinking, Malachi. We ought to go into business together," AB said. He placed his money back in his pocket.

"AB, I lost a few dollars on you, too," Tom Thum said.

"That's a loss you gonna have to accept, Tom," AB said. "What do you say, Malachi?"

"I don't know, AB. First, I really don't know you that well to be putting my money up for a business with you, and second, I already have two businesses. I'm just traveling now. Getting my head together. I'm not settling down at the moment," Malachi said.

"I'm a good man. Sure I have a thick skull, but anyone can vouch for me that I'm a stand up guy. Anyway, I'm not asking you to settle down. I'm asking you to help me with a business, Malachi."

"I don't know, AB," Malachi said.

"Can you play that guitar, Malachi?" Lady Marmalade asked, as she walked over to the table carrying a tray of hot biscuits. She placed them in front of Tom, who grabbed three and placed them on his plate. "Because if you can, you can sit in on our jam session tonight."

Malachi looked at her. What's a jam session?" he asked.

"Something that will keep your mind filled with... thoughts," Lady Marmalade said. "And while you're there tonight, you can think about what AB is asking you."

"All right," Malachi said. "That might be nice, but I'm not agreeing to anything."

When the darkness fell on the town, Malachi, AB, and Lady Marmalade headed to the Club. Malachi had his guitar as he followed them to the Club. The night was humid and he'd worn a white short sleeve shirt to ward off the heat. His pants were cut at the knee and he'd grab a pair of sandals to keep his feet comfortable. When they reached the door, Egghead was there to greet them. He ushered them in, and locked it quickly.

"You three are the last ones. Everybody is waiting," Egghead said, as he led them into the stage area.

When Malachi saw the stage, he was amazed at the oddly looking people walking around strumming guitars or tuning up their instruments. He saw one lady standing in front of the microphone singing very low. He looked at the man dressed in a blue sharkskin evening tuxedo playing the keys on the piano. He was laughing as his hands fingered the keys expertly.

"Jack!" Lady Marmalade shouted. "Get you lousy fingers off my keys."

Malachi and AB watched Lady Marmalade hurry up onto the stage.

Malachi saw a portly man with caramel skin blowing hard on a trumpet. He nudged AB in the side. "Who's that?" he asked.

"Where?" AB asked, as he looked around. "You know I only got one good eye until the swelling goes down, Malachi."

"The one with the trumpet," Malachi said.

"Oh. That's Buddy," AB said.

"I've never seen anyone play one of those before," Malachi said.

"Then tonight you are in for a treat," Egghead said. He'd gone to the bar and brought back a pitcher of cold water, and a bottle of rye whiskey. "These musicians will have your head spinning when this session is over."

"Stop playing around and let's get this music flowing," shouted another man tuning up his guitar.

Malachi looked up at the man who'd said it. He was sitting on a stool with his mouth touching the microphone. He cradled an ivory tip guitar. He was dressed in a brown suit and he wore dark glasses. Clutched between his fingers was something like a cigarette.

"That's Blind Willie," AB said. "He has been blind since he was a youngster. He started playing guitar to get the music out of his head. And, uh…If you get too close to Bilnd Man Willie and smell what he's smoking. Don't inhale to deep. The other cat on the banjo is Charlie P."

"Why can't I inhale when I'm beside Blind Willie? Who's that singing?" Malachi asked.

"Because Blind Willie is into that wacky weed. He smokes that stuff thinking its' going to bring back some of his sight. Well, everyone has been telling him that his sight ain't coming back, but that haven't stopped him from smoking that wacky weed. He likes smoking it. As for the lady singing, that's Lilith Greene," AB said. "Whew! That woman can sing. She might be small, but those pipes of hers can make a person feel every word and letter of the song she's singing. And she ain't too bad on the eyes either. Look at her shake those hips. Damn, she can make a grown man beg for her attention."

Malachi had to agree with AB. Lilith wasn't bad looking at all. And her hips moved like they had a mind of their own. Every note she went into whether it was a simple note, or a long note that required her to hold it for a long duration. She made it look easy.

"Get off that stool, Jack," Lady Marmalade said.

Jack ignored Lady Marmalade as she stood above him hovering like a hawk. He ran his fingers through his pomade black hair, as he turned around and looked at Lady Marmalade.

Lady Marmalade stood so close to Jack that her breasts were nearly on top of his large shoulders. "Get up, Jack," she said.

"Hey, Lady. It's good to see your fine, beautiful self. I don't get to see much beauty in my day, but when I see you, my whole day is fulfilled," Jack said.

"Negro, save that sweet syrupy bullshit for those young girls. I don't need any compliments at this stage of my life. Now get your yeller ass off the stool!"

"Whoa, baby. Let me pound on these keys for a few more rounds, and then I can get my small ass off this stool and give it to you," Jack said.

"Damn! I wished I'd brought my shotgun!" Lady Marmalade snapped, as she kicked the leg on the stool Jack was sitting on. "You're gonna make me go home and get it, because you are trying my short nerves at the moment, Jack."

"Whoa, my sweet sugarcane. There's no need for that. Violence is not the way," Jack said. "Come on. Sit down beside me and we can hit these keys together, baby."

"Man, you're a boxer, Jack. And violence is your way, nigger. Now get off the stool!" Lady Marmalade snapped.

"Baby, yeah I'm a boxer, but that's when I'm in the ring trying to protect my pretty face. My life is about loving and not struggling with that woman who wants to love me back," Jack said.

"Well, love another stool and get off the one you're sitting on," Lady Marmalade said. She drew closer to Jack. "If I tell you one more goddamn time to get off that stool, Jack, I'm gonna knock your ass off it."

"Lady! Sit your loud mouth ass down and let us do our thing for a few hours," Blind Willie shouted.

Lady Marmalade turned around with anger etched tight on her face. Her black eyes were points of meanness as she stared hard at Blind Willie.

"I see you looking at me, girl. Don't let my blindness stop you from coming over here and doing what you want to do," Blind Man Willie said, as he sucked hard on the rolled up cigarette-like object between his fingers. He frowned as he inhaled hard. His large lips sucking greedily on the smoke. He looked around as if he could see the smoke. "Hell, if I can smell you, I can hit you. And make no mistake I can smell you with that perfume on. Go sit down, and let us do our thing. I heard how you pounded on those keys a few nights ago. Let Jack do his thing, woman."

Lady Marmalade continued to glare at Blind Willie.

"Don't look at me too hard, child, you might go blind," Blind Willie said. "Now go ahead and get that big buxom of yours off the stage and let us do this gig."

Lady Marmalade turned toward Jack. She gave him a heart-stopping stare for a second. Walking pass Jack, she kicked him in his leg before heading off the stage.

"I thought Lady Marmalade was going to jump on that blind cat and beat him up," Malachi said.

"Nope, that ain't Lady Marmalade style. She's gonna wait, and when the time is right, she's gonna take her revenge on Jack," AB said. "Come on, let's go sit down."

Malachi, AB, and Lady Marmalade all sat at one table as they watched the musicians continue to tune up their instruments. Egghead came over and sat down with them.

"All right, we're gonna do this on one," Charlie P said. All the other musicians nodded. "Ya'll know how we do this. Four...Three...Two...One."

As on cue, A G-chord on the piano filled the place with a harmonious sound only to be followed by an A-chord from Blind Willie's guitar. Lilith smooth soprano voice took hold as she began to sing the blues.

"What you gonna do when your old man steps out on you...What you gonna say when he ain't home by eight... It's hard to let him go when ya in love...Cause love is that painful thing ya keep in your heart...No matter how many times he sees ya crying...That man and his mean spirit is gonna keep on lying...He gonna keep on lying. And lying... and lying."

Malachi listen to the next chords, as Charlie P entered with a whining, strong E-minor chord from his guitar to back up Lilith. He walked to where Lilith stood and began plucking the strings with dexterous fingers as he stood beside her. He placed the guitar between his legs and began plucking it as he stayed in tune with everyone else. Removing the guitar from between his legs, he fell to his knees with the guitar on his chest and leaned back as he continued playing it.

"I know he's showing off again, ain't he?" Blind Willie said. "I hate doing gigs with Charlie P. Get off your damn knees and let Lilith sing. You bum!"

Malachi, AB, Egghead and Lady Marmalade laughed.

"*My man's heart is gone down a different road,*" Lilith continued, as she began to shake her hips to the music. "*It's a road I ain't about to take with him and no other woman...If he can't be mine...He won't be yours.* "*I'm a woman...a woman...with pride,*" Shrieked Lilith as she stamped her foot to the beat. "*Ain't no man...no man... gonna knock me to my knees with love while sticking a thorn in my side...For love is a rock that can sink your heart... And make you drown in sorrow...It's a painful thing, this thing they call love and it will be there tomorrow... This thing they call love can break your back...It's through strength and patience that's keeping me from snapping my man's neck...Love can make you mean...Love can make you evil...But ain't nothing like a cold plate of revenge to make things sweet when everything has gone sour...My man is gone now...I'm feeling a little warm...I'm feeling another man's heat in my bed at night...It's okay with me...Cause I got his arms around me tight when I fall to sleep.*"

Malachi couldn't believe how strong Lilith voice was. He had to admit, the song and the instruments were beautiful as they all seemed to blend together. He started clapping his hands when he heard the trumpet come into play.

Lilith danced around letting the music take hold of her.

AB leaned into Malachi. "Ain't this grand?" he asked.

"Uh-huh. I never seen anything like this before," Malachi said.

"Are you going to go into business with me?" AB asked.

"I don't know, AB," Malachi said. His eyes transfixed on the stage.

"It's a good business venture. We can buy Patrice's store and add a few things more to it. We could make a killing in profit," AB said.

"I don't know, AB," Malachi said.

"Go ahead. Finish listening to the music. We'll talk later," AB said.

Malachi turned toward him. He opened his mouth and closed it. Several chairs behind him, he saw a skinny white boy with pale skin wearing a pair of worn out blue jeans and a cream colored shirt that had seen one wash too many sitting at a table three rows behind him. He was smoking a cigarette and had an expression of enchantment as he listened to the music. At first Malachi thought he was a girl because of his effeminate features, but his mannerisms said something different. Malachi turned to Egghead.

"Who's that back there?" Malachi asked. Tossing a thumb over his shoulder in the direction of the young, white boy.

"White boy with black, greasy-like hair?" Egghead asked. Not taking his eyes off the stage.

"Yeah," Malachi said.

"He's okay. I let him in when we have these jams. He likes listening to the Blues," Egghead said. "A white boy with a Blues soul. Isn't that ironic?"

The music ended. Everyone began clapping.

Malachi stood up and clapped hard.

"Come on up. You carrying that guitar for a reason, ain't you?" Lilith asked.

Malachi stopped clapping. He looked at Lilith with apprehension.

"Go ahead, Malachi," Egghead said. "That group doesn't let many people mix with them. If they're asking you to join, then go ahead."

Malachi nodded and reached for his guitar. Taking in a deep breath, he headed for the stage.

"Give it your best, Malachi," Lady Marmalade said.

When Malachi hurried pass her, Lady Marmalade slapped him on the butt. "Go get them, big boy," she said, as she exploded with laughter.

Standing on the stage, everyone watched Malachi as he placed the strap around his neck. Malachi tuned up his guitar. As he was about to strike a chord, everyone stopped playing.

"That's dangerous thing you have there, son. You know what to do with it?" Charlie P asked.

"If he doesn't, he better learn how to play that thing between his legs, because this is no time for us to be teaching him," Blind Willie said. "Anybody got a match. My stuff went out."

Lilith walked up to Malachi. "You know how to read music?" she asked. Malachi shook his head. "Can you play by ear? Malachi nodded. "Cat got your tongue, huh? Take our lead and come in when you're ready. When I point to you, that's your cue."

Malachi didn't say anything as he watched Lilith walked back to the microphone. He was fascinated by her simple beauty. He thought she had the prettiest lips he'd ever seen. They were small and full. She couldn't have been older than nineteen. He sighed when she walked away, as he took in the smell of rose perfume. He moistened her lips, and tried to concentrate.

"We're going instrumental on this one, boys," Lilith began. "When I point to you, you got the floor. If you can't keep up, you lose your spot. "Ya'll ready?"

No one said anything.

"Four…Three…Two…One," Lilith said. She pointed to Jack.

Jack saw her. He smiled as he began to play the piano as if his life depended on it. He hit one chord after another with fluid motion. He smiled. He knew how to showboat when it came to making the piano come to life. He would start at a high-pitch and casually bring the chords into a blending mixture that made the audience clap.

Lilith quickly cut Jack off by running a finger under her neck and pointing to Buddy. Buddy didn't miss his turn. He was standing in the back and didn't say much, because he let his music speak for him. He came on with a powerful blow from his trumpet. He continued to blow the trumpet with unbelievable speed and heart-stopping rhythm. Malachi listened as Buddy made the trumpet sound as if it were a different instrument by changing the notes emanating from it with fluidity. It was beautiful.

Lilith continued by pointing to Charlie P. Charlie P, the flamboyant professional, ran toward the edge of the stage while continuing to play his guitar. When his feet looked as if they were going to fall off the edge, he leaped back, did a split and struck an ear-splitting B-minor chord followed by an A-chord, which he strung along so wonderfully, that it made Lilith smile. Charlie P began to inch his way back up on his heels while playing. When he was completely up, he placed the guitar behind his back, and began playing it. That act got him a rousing ovation from Lady Marmalade, Egghead, AB, and the effeminate young white boy sitting in the back.

Lilith ended Charlie P's play with a hand slice through the air. She turned to Blind Willie. "Your turn, Willie," she said.

"Well, come on. I ain't got all night," Blind Willie said.

"Two...One," Lilith said.

Blind Willie struck a chord that seemed to send a shiver through everyone's spine. From there on, his guitar appeared to pulsate with rhythm as he followed that chord with a B-flat chord, and immediately continued with an A-minor chord and a C-minor chord that blended magnificently.

"That's enough, Willie," Lilith said.

"What? Hell, I still had a few more chords in me, girl," Blind Willie said.

Lilith smiled. "I know you do. All right, young one. Let's hear what you got," she said.

Malachi could feel his hands sweating. He was a little nervous. He looked at Lilith.

"Three," Lilith began. "Two...One."

Malachi hit the string on his guitar hard, making it reverberate. He followed that up with an impressive combination of chords that had everyone looking at him and nodding their heads at the sound he was creating. The music was something new. Something fresh.

"All right. Everyone join in," Lilith said as she walked to the microphone.

With everyone taking Malachi's lead, all the

instruments became a symphony of beauty to the ear. Lilith began to sing.

For two hours they played music, and for those two hours, Malachi had to admit, he'd never felt so at home in his life.

CHAPTER TWENTY
The Wind is Blowing

Malachi and AB stood in the middle of the street watching the sign being placed on the building in front of them. It had started to rain very lightly. AB passed Malachi an umbrella.

"What do you think?" AB asked.

"It looks... Um...good," Malachi said.

"Good, huh? But?" AB asked, as he took a step closer to get a better look at the sign.

"I thought we'd agreed on a different...name," Malachi said.

"Huh? Well, we did, but after I sat down and put it on paper, I realized—and I know you would've thought the same way—that it didn't look right. The name now shows more promise," AB said.

"So the name M.A.L.A.B.A. sounds good?" Malachi asked. He scratched his head.

"Sure. I took your four first letters and added it with my two, and created the name," AB said.

"MALABA?" Malachi said. He looked at AB. "That's the best you could've come up with?"

"It will grow on you. MALABA supplies are a decent name," AB said.

"Let's go in and see what the place looks like," Malachi said.

They both walked into the store. When the door closed behind Malachi, he stopped and slowly looked around.

"Looks…Okay, huh?" AB asked.

Malachi rubbed his face. He, being a businessman, cursed himself for not going with AB to finalize the deal of buying the store last week. He had got caught up in the news from the telegram Stump had sent him regarding his mother being sick. The next day he had begun to pack his clothing to go back home while at the same time listening to AB with an half ear as he reminded him that they'd agreed he didn't have to be there at the closing of the deal. Malachi simply gave AB his half of the money and didn't think anything of it. The next day, he'd received another telegram from Betty Mae saying his mother would be all right after seeing the doctor, and he shouldn't worry. Now, as he stood in the store, he'd wished he'd gone with AB.

"Sure we got to do a few things to it," AB began, as he walked further into the store, but it was worth it."

As Malachi looked around, he nearly choked from the thick dust that was everywhere. He took a step forward, and the floor gave in. AB grabbed his elbow to prevent him from falling further. Malachi removed his foot from the hole as he glared at AB.

"All right, so it has a few rotten boards in the floor. Termites. We can fix that," AB said. "Look, I know you don't think it's much, but we got this place for a steal, Malachi."

Malachi shook his head as he fans away the dust.

"We can make it work," AB said.

Malachi continued to walk. He headed for the back of the store to see what the storage room looked like. He jiggled the keys in the lock. He had to play with the lock to get the door open. Using muscle to the point of straining, he opened the door.

Malachi looked around the room. There were stacks of old newspapers in the far left corner. Beside the newspapers there were empty wooden crates. Malachi stepped further into the room. His stomach was assaulted by the sudden stench of a foul, dead smell of rotten meat penetrating his nostrils.

AB had come up behind him and was looking over his shoulder. He placed a hand over his nose. "What the hell is that?" he asked.

"What happened to Patrice's husband?" Malachi asked, as he placed a hand over his mouth, and slowly backed out of the room, closing the door.

"Who Sam?" AB asked. "You know, you might have something there. Patrice said that Sam had to go back east a few months ago to handle some family business. Rumor started circulating that she was having a little thing with the barber, Rome, during that time. He owned the shop down the street. No one put anything together. You think that's Sam lying in there between those sheets?"

"If it is, then we know that it was done out of freedom rather than love," Malachi said. "We'd better get the sheriff."

Eight months later with a new paint job inside and outside the store had Malachi smiling like a child who'd been given everything he wanted for Christmas. As he stood behind the counter beaming with joy at the sight of fresh goods and other items that now filled the store. He greeted his first customer with a wave.

"How can I help you?" Malachi asked. He watched the man walking around touching cans and other items. "We have good prices here."

Malachi watched the man. He realized that the man was white. He wasn't too surprise considering the town was Willisburg where whites and blacks mingled without much fanfare. As he continued to stare at the white man, Malachi lowered his head and concentrated on the book that he'd been writing in before he entered.

"How are you? Do you have any peanut butter and bananas?"

Malachi looked up. He saw the effeminate young white boy staring at him.

"I'm fine. Yeah, we got what you need," Malachi said.

Malachi walked from behind the counter, and headed toward an aisle in front of him. When he returned he was carrying four bananas and a small jar of peanut butter. He placed the items on the counter, and walked back around it.

"That's it?" Malachi asked.

"You don't like white men much, huh?" The effeminate white boy asked.

Malachi stared at him.

"I saw you play that night at the Club several months ago," the white boy said.

"I saw you there," Malachi said. "Let me ask you something. It's not that I don't like white folk; it's just that I don't trust them much. Why does a skinny white boy who looks like a girl enjoy listening to the Blues?"

"Yeah, ain't that funny? Anyway, I like it because it gives me a peace of mind."

"What's your name?" Malachi asked.

"El."

"El? What kind of name is that?" Malachi asked.

"I have a full name to it. I just like for people to call me El."

"You are one strange white boy, El. You need anything else?" Malachi asked.

"You're coming to the Club tonight?" El asked, as he took the bag that Malachi had placed his things in.

"I might. You gonna be sitting in the back as usual?" Malachi asked.

"Egghead said that my white face might mess with the flow of things in the Club. He let's me in because I pay him two dollars every time," El said.

"Egghead is white!" Malachi snapped. He shook his head and smiled. "What instrument do you play?"

El looked at Malachi. "How do you know I play an instrument?" he asked.

Malachi rubbed his right index finger against the right thumb of his hand.

El raised his hand. On it, he saw the callous from playing his guitar everyday.

"One musician always can tell another musician," Malachi said.

El nodded, as he grinned. "Yeah, I play the guitar," he said.

"Why don't you get on the stage?" Malachi asked.

"Egghead said I'll mess with the color of things."

"I don't know how Egghead thinks. He's as pale as chalk and he's telling you that. Well, listen, I'll see you tonight," Malachi said.

Later that evening after closing up the store, Malachi headed to the boarding house. Since the evening had become a little colder, Malachi lifted the collar on his jacket. As he walked through the near empty street with lanterns on the tall poles to give the street more light at night, he saw a fleeting shadow to the left of him against the wall. He spun around. He searched the area as he strained his eyes looking out into the darkness. He didn't see anything. Shrugging, he turned back around and began walking.

By the time Malachi reached the boarding house, he felt a little apprehensive and nervous. He didn't know why, but the feeling he was having made him very cautious. Walking up the stairs, he was startled when the front door flew open, and AB came running out followed by Tom who was waving a knife. Malachi quickly stepped to the side to avoid being stabbed.

"You goddamn bastard!" Tom screamed, as he circled AB with the knife out in front of him. "You knew what you were doing!"

AB, jutted from right to left to avoid the swing of the

knife whenever Tom lurched at his knees and thighs. He was wearing only his boxer underwear.

"She—"

"I don't want to hear it!" Tom shouted as he leaped up while swinging the knife at AB's stomach. Making AB jump back. "That's my future wife."

Malachi walked to the swing on the porch and sat down. He smiled.

Lady Marmalade came out smoking one of her thin cigars. She leaned on the doorframe shaking her head.

"I was just trying to get her to bed. We were drinking and she damn near passed out, Tom. I wasn't trying any funny stuff," AB said, as he dodged to the right of him when he saw Tom lunge at him. "I swear to you!"

Malachi saw Tom's chest rise and fall rapidly as he began to get tired. He put his hands on his hips while breathing very hard.

"I don't see why you're getting all riled up, Tom. That girl would sleep with a corpse if it smiled at her," Lady Marmalade said, as smoke exhaled from her nose. "If AB said he was putting her drunken ass to bed, what's the problem?"

"The problem, woman, is that when I came in the room, his draws were down to his ankles, and he was between Jane's legs with her legs up in the air. What the hell does that look like to you?" Tom asked.

AB glanced at Lady Marmalade. Hoping she had an answer because he didn't.

"Well," Lady Marmalade began, as she brought the small, thin cigar to her lips and pulled on it. She slowly blew the smoke out, as she looked from AB to Tom. "It might seem to me AB's draws fell to his knees while he was laying her on bed. You know AB always talking about his draws being too big, Tom. It probably looked like something was going on, but...."

Tom looked at Lady Marmalade. He stared at her uncomprehendingly, and shook his head. "What the hell do you take me for, Lady? Tom snapped. "He was trying to take advantage of my fiancé without her knowledge."

Tom leaped forward. His sudden attack surprised AB. The knife found AB's leg. Opening a small wound that made AB scream as he jumped back, pulling the knife free.

"Hah! I got your ass!" Tom shouted.

AB grunted and moved to the left to avoid Tom's next assault. He was dragging his wounded.

"Tom! Put that knife down."

Everyone stopped and turned toward the house. Jane stood in the doorway with a sheet wrapped tightly around her body.

Malachi noticed that the sheet did very little to prevent a person's imagination from wandering. Considering he could see the outline of Jane's breasts, thighs, and nipples.

"Put the knife down, Tommy. AB didn't mean any harm," Jane said.

To Malachi, it didn't look like Jane was drunk.

"It's okay, baby," Jane said. "Come on in the house. We can talk about it."

"No! I'm gonna kill this bastard!" Tom snapped angrily. He feinted to the right while swinging the knife. "Come on, boxer man. You ain't scared of a little man like me, are you?"

AB answered by taking three fast steps backward when he saw the knife come at him.

"Tom, if you don't drop that knife and let AB go, you won't be having any more of this," Jane said, as she opened the sheet to reveal her nakedness to everyone.

Tom saw her. He dropped the knife and ran up the stairs. He covered Jane up with the sheet and ushered her back into the house.

"Ain't that a sight?" Lady Marmalade began. "The drunken harlot and the midget."

Malachi laughed.

"How are you feeling, AB? Did he nick you good?" Lady Marmalade asked, as she smiled. "Next time you'd be more careful trying to stick your stick in a matchbox."

AB hobbled over to the porch. He sat down and looked at his bleeding leg. "That fool is as crazy as a bed bug," he said. "Lucky it didn't go in too deep."

"No. The crazy thing is you were trying to sleep with his woman," Lady Marmalade said, as she inhaled after dragging hard on her thin cigar. She let out the smoke, and looked at AB. "You don't mess with someone's woman in the same house her man is living…dummy."

Lady Marmalade turned around and walked back into the house. The door slammed closed behind her.

Malachi looked at AB and shook his head.

"It's not what you think, Malachi. Jane and I have been…you know. Doing our thing for years," AB said.

Malachi smiled. "I don't know, AB. If you two keep on doing what you're doing, I don't think Tom is going to appreciate it," he said. "And next time he might get you when you're sleeping. You sleep hard, you know."

AB gave a weak smile as he reached down and

touched his wounded leg. "That little bastard. I hope he goes to bed praying that the Lord never makes him taller, because if he does get taller one day, I'm going to whip his little ass," he said.

"Uh-huh. Not if he's carrying a knife. We're going to the stage tonight?" Malachi asked.

AB looked at Malachi. "Yeah. You think I need a doctor for this?"

"I don't know. It doesn't look like much. If the knife was old, though, we may have to get you some shots to prevent you from getting gangrene," Malachi said. "I want to see if the white boy can play."

"White boy? What white boy?" AB asked. He didn't look at Malachi as he tried to stop the bleeding by pressing on the wound. "I think it is stopping."

"Yeah," Malachi said. He leaned forward to look at AB's leg. "You'll be okay. The white boy who comes to the jam sessions."

"I don't know about that, Malachi. Egghead doesn't like any new comers dropping it. Especially those with blue eyes."

"Egghead is white! Is it because he's always around Negroes that he's forgotten that? Don't worry. It'd be all right," Malachi said.

"Where would they shoot me? In the butt?" AB asked.

"Nope," Malachi said, as he stood up, and headed to the door.

"The arm?" AB asked.

Malachi opened the door. "They will shoot you in the stomach. In your navel," he said, as he walked into the house. "So you don't get lockjaw."

AB looked down at his wound, and felt a churning in his stomach. "Damn!" he said as he stood up and walked to the door. "Are you sure?"

It was nearing midnight. The group played one song after another for hours. Everyone felt good while listening to the music they were creating.

Malachi walked to the edge of the stage. "I want to see if this...guitar player can play," he said.

"Bring him up, and he better not be as handsome as I am," Jack said. He hit several keys on the piano to emphasize his point. "Because Jack doesn't like to look back."

"Well, bring him up. I want to see what the boy looks like and if he can play. Hell, everyone with an instrument thinks they can play the damn thing," Blind Willie said.

Buddy blew a note on his trumpet. It was long and beautiful. "Let him up," he said, as he licked his small red lips.

Lilith walked to the microphone. "Come on up. Let's hear what you got," she said.

"I can tell if he's a real player or someone trying to act like he knows what he's doing," Blind Willie said.

Everyone turned toward Blind Willie. He was sitting on his stool holding his guitar with one hand as his dark glasses hung on the bridge of his nose. His white orbs for eyes moved back and forth. He was puffing hard on the wacky weed between his fingers. As he exhaled, he blew out smoke rings.

AB laughed. It was a brief laugh that was cut short when Blind Willie pointed at him.

AB placed a hand over his mouth as Blind Willie stamp his feet along with the music.

Egghead, who'd been attending to the bar, looked around at who they might be talking about. When he saw El stand up, he leaped over the counter and hurried to the stage.

As El neared the stage with his guitar, Egghead blocked him from taking the stairs to the stage.

"Hold it, you ain't going up there," Egghead said with his hand in the middle of El's chest.

"Why not, Egghead?" Malachi asked.

"Yeah. Why not, Egghead? You know how we work," Jack said. He ran a manicured hand through his process hair. "Let the kid up and let us decide if he ain't shit."

"First of all. This is a Negro joint that caters to—"

"Aw, man, don't give us that bull about a Negro establishment. Goddamn it. I'm still waiting for my forty acres and two mules, but ain't nobody been knocking on my door," Blind Willie said. "I'm too old to play games with these white folks, and being blind makes things even worse. Wait a minute. Ain't you white, Egghead?"

"Sometimes he is, and sometimes he ain't," Lilith said. "When it ain't to his convenience, he's part white, and part Negro. When it is to his convenience, he's all white. Let him come up."

Egghead removed his hand. "It ain't about that. It's about...you know. About mixing the colors. What'd you think the customers are going to say when they come in here to hear ya'll and see a pale skin, girl like boy on stage with a guitar? I tell you what they're going to say. They're going to get the hell out of here," he said.

"Ain't this a bitch! A white man telling us Negroes what it's like to be dark skin in a world where we're spit on, shot, and hanged. Egghead, if you don't go sit your ass down somewhere, I will get off this stool, and, with Buddy guiding me as to where to punch you, I will whip you something good," Blind Willie said.

"Come on, Egghead, let the man play," Malachi pleaded.

Egghead looked at the faces staring at him. He shrugged and stepped aside.

El displayed a boyish grin as he climb on stage.

"Now what are you gonna sing now that you're up here?" Lilith asked, as she stepped away from the microphone. "All right, boys let's see what the kid got."

El walked to the microphone. "I want to sing a song called Love Me Sweet," he said.

"It better not be one of those mushy songs that make a person want to cry," Buddy said. "I hate those songs."

El smiled. He placed his guitar strap around his neck. "It's not my song. I did a few changes to it. If ya'll can pick up my lead, I'd appreciate it," he said.

"It better not be one of those Confederate songs, son, because if it is, I'm gonna…Well, you know where I'm coming from," Blind Willie said.

AB pointed a finger at El. "He ain't lying," he said.

El walked to the microphone. Lilith gave him room but stayed beside him.

Egghead and AB went and sat down at a table.

El opened his mouth as his fingers played on the guitar. No one did a thing as he took the lead.

El began to sing.

Two minutes into the song, they all began to add their instruments to El's voice. Malachi concentrated on the beat as the song was drawn out by El. He was surprise at how smooth and soulful El sounded. When Malachi looked out at Egghead and AB, he saw them nodding their heads to the music.

Lilith merged her soprano voice to El's voice and the song really took on a powerful effect as El began to shake his right leg and roll his hips in a circular, sexual motion. Lilith increased her singing as El lowered his voice to let her become the more dominant one.

Malachi had never heard a white boy sing a song as soulful as El. He had to admit; the boy held a note and could blend his voice wonderfully with the beat. He sang with urgency and power that made Malachi smiled.

"Damn! That white boy can sing," Blind Willie said. "Somebody get that boy a jug of moonshine. He deserves a drink."

AB leaned over. "I think you ought to let that boy come in on a regular basis Egghead," he said.

Egghead nodded.

An hour later the doors of the Club opened. AB turned around to see who entered. He saw a man of small height walk in wearing a big hat that covered his face, and a large black overcoat that hid his actual size.

"One of the late night listeners?" AB asked Egghead.

Egghead turned in his seat to see the man walking toward the stage. He stood up to prevent the man from walking further. He stopped when he saw the dark figure reached inside his overcoat and removed a gun and run toward him.

Malachi saw Egghead stand up and look behind him. Malachi eyes looked outward. He saw a man hurrying toward Egghead. At first he didn't think anything of it. That changed, though, when he saw Egghead dive to the right and roll under a table.

AB's peripheral vision caught Egghead leaping out of the way. He didn't think. He stood up and turned around. When he saw the man with the gun, his eyes opened wide. His boxing instincts took over. AB placed his head between his shoulders and grunted as he rushed forward to stop the man.

The man smiled as he watched AB rushed toward him. He didn't miss a stride as he raised the gun in his right hand. He found the mark where he wanted to put the bullet. He fired the gun.

Malachi and the other's stopped playing and watched AB heading toward the man with the gun. Malachi lowered his guitar and made a quick dash to the edge of the stage when he felt himself being lifted off his feet, and seconds later hearing the sound of the gun going off. When he landed on his back, a sharp pain filled his chest and he had difficulty breathing.

AB stopped at the sound of the gun being fired. He looked down and searched himself. Seeing no blood, he looked back up at the man who'd fired the gun. He watched the man in the black overcoat run out the door.

"AB!" Lilith screamed. "Malachi's been shot! Run and get the doctor."

AB turned around and saw everyone hovering over Malachi. He took a deep breath, and then took off running to find the doctor.

Egghead had found a pillow and brought it over to Lilith who'd placed it under Malachi's head.

Malachi looked at the faces looking down at him. The pain in his chest had become unbearable as well as the stickiness from the blood on his hand. Coldness had begun to fill his body. He heard Lilith telling him to hold on. The pain was excruciating. He squeezed his fist to try and ward off some of the pain.

"What's going on?" Blind Willie asked. "Who shot the boy? Did they catch the bastard?"

"Maybe we can get some towels or something and stop the bleeding," El said. The strain in his voice could be detected as fear.

"Maybe we ought to carry him over to the doctor," Jack said. He was leaning down beside Malachi. "He's yeller and his color is starting to change."

"Egghead get over here and help the men pick up Malachi!" Lilith snapped. "If we don't do something now, this boy is going to die."

For some reason, Malachi felt euphoric. He closed his eyes. Seconds later he felt his body become light as it went limp.

CHAPTER TWENTY-ONE
Making History

"What do you think it was about?" AB asked.
"I don't know. Why would someone shoot at you?" Lady Marmalade asked, as she walked around the bed tucking in the sheets. "You did make a lot of people lose a whole lot of money, AB."

"But for someone to try and kill me, that ain't right," AB said. He stood up and walked to the window. "To make things worse, Malachi gets shot instead of me."

"Well, as big as you are, I don't know how the idiot missed you and hit Malachi. Fool can't shoot worth a damn," Lady Marmalade said.

AB turned around and looked at Lady Marmalade. "It ain't right, I tell you," he said.

"Hush!" Lady Marmalade said, as she lowered her

voice, and straightened out her dress. "It's been a week since he was shot and he still ain't open his eyes."

"They're open now," Malachi said from the bed. His voice cracked. His mouth was so dry he could barely say a word. "Do you have any water?"

Lady Marmalade reached for the glass pitcher on the small nightstand beside the bed. She poured water into the glass as AB rushed over to the bed. While she'd been pouring the water, AB had been fixing Malachi's pillows to arch him up a little.

"It's good to see you talking," Lady Marmalade said, as she sat on the edge of the bed and guided the glass of water to Malachi's mouth. "We've been worried about you."

"Yeah," AB added. "Everybody has."

After a few sips of water, Malachi nodded, and Lady Marmalade removed the glass. She watched Malachi close his eyes, and then open them.

"How long I've been in bed?" Malachi asked.

"About a week," AB began. "This is the first time you've opened your eyes. A lot of people thought you weren't going to make it. The doctor told us you're too strong."

"The doctor said the bullet collapsed your lung," Lady Marmalade said. "He said it's all right now but when you get older you're going to have shortness of breath or some other breathing problem."

Malachi nodded. "Well, I'm glad I took the bullet instead of AB because he couldn't be in a situation like that while boxing," he said, and smiled. "Did they catch him?"

"No. After questioning a few people, some of them

say that the man was laughing as he jumped in a car and drove away," Lady Marmalade said. "Are you hungry?"

"A little," Malachi said. "You said he was laughing?"

"Uh-huh. Some say it sounded like he was snickering or something like that. I'll go get you some soup," Lady Marmalade said.

Malachi and AB watched her leave the room.

"She doesn't show it, Malachi, but she's been worried sick about you. There were nights I'd come in to check on you and she'd be sitting in that rocking chair in the corner asleep while watching you. When she heard you'd been shot, she ran around like a chicken with its head cut off to make sure you got everything you needed," AB said.

AB glanced at Malachi. He'd grown a light full beard. In comparison with the scar on his face, AB thought he looked like some kind of pirate.

"What are you looking at?" Malachi asked.

AB smiled. He walked to the bureau and brought back a hand-held mirror and gave it to Malachi.

Malachi took the mirror. He looked into it and didn't recognize the face.

"You have a…different…look," AB said.

Malachi turned his face from left to right. He brought the mirror in and then out as he tried to come to terms with the face looking back at him. After a few seconds, he placed the mirror on the bed.

"I do look different," Malachi said, as he looked up at AB.

"You do. How are you feeling?" AB asked.

"A little tired," Malachi said. "How are things over at the store? What about the Club?"

"Well, since your shooting, things slowed down for Egghead, but three days later everything picked up again. The store is okay. I've been running things very well," AB said.

Malachi leaned further into the pillow. "Are we making a profit yet?" he asked.

AB arched his eyebrows. "Well—"

"AB, don't tell me we're not making any money after all the shucking and shining you gave me to become a partner," Malachi said.

"It's not that we're really losing any money, Malachi. It's just that we're not getting enough to show a profit."

Lady Marmalade entered the room carrying a tray with a bowl on it. She sat the tray on the end table by the bed. She sat down on the edge of the bed with the bowl. Removing a large spoon from the apron pocket she was wearing, she began to feed Malachi.

Malachi took the soup in as if he hadn't eaten in months.

"All right," Malachi said between swallows. "We're gonna do something a little different."

"Oh, damn," AB and Lady Marmalade said.

1950 had come in with a blaze of raw heat as the summer blossomed. Malachi knew the moment he opened the store what he would do with it. It was an idea that didn't go over well with AB when he first mentioned it to him eight years previously while lying in bed recovering. He knew AB would go along with the idea the moment he had the walls in the store knocked down and had workers plaster and add sheetrock to create a larger room. The counter and shelves in the store were removed completely. From there he had a glass partition of forty-six by seventy-two inches placed directly in front of the large room he'd converted. From there he added some electronic equipment with two small turntables. The glass partition was directly in front of the large room. In that room, Malachi added a microphone. It had taken him more than a year to complete everything to his satisfaction.

Malachi walked in behind AB. AB stood partially inside the room with the electronic equipment. His expression was one of confusion as he looked around.

"You don't understand what you're looking at do you?" Malachi asked, as he came and stood beside AB. AB shook his head. "About a year ago I heard about a machine that made wax rec—"

"Wax? Like on candlesticks?" AB asked.

"No, AB. This wax you can play on the phonograph. I had to—"

"On a phonograph? Boy, you done gone and lost what little bit of mind you had left since getting shot all those years ago," AB said. "I didn't notice it much, but as the years went on and you kept coming up with all these ideas, I realized you had lost your mind, and like any friend, I encourage your ramblings."

"That big room can hold five men with their instruments. What Egghead has is only a steppingstone to what we can do in here, AB. Egghead didn't improve on what he had, but I saw it for what it was, and can be. You know those jamming sessions at his place? Well, we can do that too, but record the music on wax. Then we can sell the records for fifteen cents a copy. I hear this type of thing is going on up north. Think about it. What if we made…one hundred of these records at fifteen cents a pop? How much do we make? Never mind, don't answer it, AB. It's a lot of money."

AB looked at Malachi. "It's called a record?" he asked.

"Uh-huh. And if we do this right, we stand to make a whole lot of money, AB," Malachi said.

AB placed a hand under his chin. He rubbed his index finger and thumb over his lips as he thought about what Malachi had said.

"It's something new, AB, but it can work. What person doesn't want to hear music whenever they want? Malachi asked. "With those machines we can make it happen. We can make a musician as popular around here as your regular group gigs, and we'll control the master recordings."

"Where do I come in? I don't play an instrument," AB said.

"We'll both learn how to work these machines for the recordings. Don't worry about anything else. You'll be a manager," Malachi said.

AB nodded.

Within three weeks, Malachi had dispersed flyers around town letting musicians know that they could record their songs for a small price at their recording studio. When musicians began appearing in front of the studio to record, Malachi found his niche as a music arranger.

"Jack, don't stand beside Henry," Malachi said from the booth into the speaker-box that could be heard in the recording area. "If you two stand that close together, it will be too much guitar. Henry, go to the left of Dell by the drums."

Dell looked up at the mention of his name. "What the hell is he coming over here for? You know I need my space, Malachi. I got to keep my elbows free when I'm pounding on these skins, man. Put his fat ass next to Sonny Boy," he said. To emphasize his point, he did a quick pounding on his drums as he ended it by hitting his cymbals.

Malachi heard what Dell said. He shook his head. "Listen men, if you want to make this happen, I have to lead it the way I know how," he said.

"Goddamn it, then lead it, man!"

Everyone quieted.

Everyone in the microphone area took a step back when Smiley said something. He'd been standing to the right by the door adjusting the strap on his saxophone. His barrel chest and baritone voice made many men do a double-take when they saw him. He was someone not to be questioned.

"If we're gonna do this, then let's go," Smiley said. He walked to the microphone. "Any of you slugs who ain't with this, then I suggest you get your non-musical ass out of the booth. Me, I want to do this to see where it goes. If it works, cool. If it doesn't work and we're wasting our time, then we can all sit down with Malachi and find a solution."

Jack hit a chord on his small piano. "I'm with you, Smiley," he said.

Smiley growled.

Malachi glanced at AB sitting at the control panel. AB smiled.

"If Smiley says it ain't gonna be no bullshit in here, then it ain't gonna be none," AB said.

"Dell, you and Henry will be the introduction. You see your music sheet in front of you," Malachi said. "You two will come—""

"Come on, man, I don't know how to read sheet music," Henry said. "I don't even know how to read!"

AB nearly fell out of the chair as he erupted with laughter. Holding his stomach, he looked at Malachi. "So, this was going to be a good idea, huh?" he asked. Tears rolling down his cheeks.

"This idea is no different than the store idea you had years ago. Except this one didn't have any dead body in the storage room," Malachi said. "Henry you can play by ear, right?"

"Yeah. What're you taking me for? A deaf musician?" Henry said.

"Okay, you come in on the second chord, Henry. Start with a snare drum, then two cymbals, and continue with that for three sessions and after that double the snares and hold that follow-up. Who else can't read the sheet music?" Malachi asked.

"Look, nigger," Smiley said. "You ain't here to make these grown ass men feel good about their sorry ass. You're here to make this thing happen. Most of us in here can't read sheet music. So, now what do you do?"

"Uh, I beg to differ," Jack said.

"Jack, don't make me break a mud foot off in your slinky ass," Smiley said. "Malachi, you direct us, and we'd play it. That's it!"

Malachi nodded. "We're gonna do it like this. Dell, you come in after Smiley who will follow Jack. Sonny Boy, you will bring up a strong E-flat after Jack. Henry, we already worked out when you come in so this is easy. Follow my lead and everyone keep up with the beat and the rhythm," he said. He looked at all of them. "On my count of three. Three…Two…One."

Everyone followed directions to the letter. Thirty minutes later they were all in sequence with one another. AB started tapping his foot and clapping his hands as the music flooded into the room sweetly.

Nine hours later, they were all exhausted. The fans in the rooms were going full blast but they couldn't suppress the humidity and the stifling heat. They were all sweating like they'd all came out of a shower.

"Enough!" Malachi said. "Man, we done recorded so much music, I think we can call it quits for tonight," he said, as he fell down into a chair and leaned his head back.

"It's been a long session," AB said, as he watched everyone packing up their instruments. "Personally, I didn't think something like this would work. But…."

As everyone piled out of the room, they all acknowledged Malachi by raising a hand or knocking on the glass before going out the door. Smiley was the only one who actually came into the recording room.

"Hey, man. I ain't ever done anything like this before," Smiley began, as he walked up to Malachi. He offered his hand. "But it's been real."

Malachi looked at the large hand in front of him. It was big enough to cover his entire face. He took Smiley's hand and shook it firmly.

"You keep this thing going, Malachi," Smiley said. "It might turn into something one day."

Malachi watched Smiley exit the door. He glanced at AB. "I don't ever want to feel those mitts on my body," he said. "Did you see the size of his big hands?"

"See them? Hell, when he raised them, I thought I felt a breeze," AB said.

By 1951, Malachi and AB had created their own recording studio sound with the assistance of unknown Blues musicians who'd come from all over the South to lay their songs on wax. It had become so busy that Malachi hired Lady Marmalade to help with the arrangement in the booth.

One evening, Malachi was leaving the boarding house when a man caring a guitar case walked up to him.

"How are you doing?"

Malachi stopped. He stared at the man not knowing what he wanted. "I'm okay," he said. "How can I help you?"

"My name is Riley and I hear you got yourself a nice recording studio around here. I like to get in on a session or two."

Malachi looked at the man with suspicion. "You can play that thing in the guitar case?" he asked.

"This? Boy, I can pluck her like plucking feathers off a chicken," Riley said, as he held the guitar case up.

Malachi smiled. "All right, follow me. I'm heading over there now," he said.

By the time Malachi and Riley reached the recording studio, there were several other people outside waiting. Malachi told them all to come in to ward off the cool evening breeze.

Lady Marmalade, who'd been sitting in the booth eating, stood up when she saw Malachi bring everyone in.

"Malachi, I told those musicians to wait and I'll have them come in two at a time," Lady Marmalade said.

"It's all right, Lady. I want to try something different tonight," Malachi said. "Where's AB?"

"Taking a nap," Lady Marmalade said, as she sat

back down and began eating. She looked at Malachi as she placed a fork into the collar greens on her plate while pushing aside the two chicken breasts that were also on the plate. "He need to get his big ass up and come over here and help me with all these buttons."

Lady Marmalade was about to say something when a woman wearing a brown fox coat that fell down to her ankles walked in. The fox hat she wore hid her features, but the way she walked exuded sexuality. She walked right up to the microphone.

"Would ya'll like to hear me sing?" The woman asked.

A few catcalls could be heard, and a person howling like a wolf was the answer she received.

The woman reached for the microphone.

"Who the hell does she think she is?" Lady Marmalade said. "Damnit. I knew I should've brought my shotgun."

IIII'mmmmm about to tell you the pains my heart… Oooohhhhhh, it's enough to make mmmeeee shout out his name…He's a goooodddd fine man who does love me like sweetttt wine. A strong man…."

"I know that…voice," Malachi began. "It's stronger… But it sounds like—"

"IIIIII don't know any man like you. You bring me flowers when I'm sick…Candy to keep me sweeeeet…And words of love to—"

"Lilith Green!" Malachi shouted.

The woman stopped singing and removed her fox hat. When she looked up, her face was radiant with womanly beauty. "Hello, Malachi," she said.

"Little ole skinny Lilith Green?" Lady Marmalade said. "I thought she went up North."

Malachi hurried out of the booth and ran into the jamming room to greet Lilith.

Lilith turned toward Malachi with open arms.

Malachi stepped into her waiting arms. The moment he did, his lips found her lips.

"Take that to a bedroom!" Lady Marmalade shouted.

Malachi pulled away from Lilith's warm, sweet lips. He towered over her as he glazed into her eyes.

"I've missed you, Malachi," Lilith said.

"What are you doing here?" Malachi asked.

"I was passing through to go do a concert, and decided to drop in. How's AB?" Lilith asked.

"He's the same," Malachi said.

"Come on! If you ain't singing get out of there and let someone use the microphone," Lady Marmalade said.

"Let's go outside," Lilith said.

Malachi nodded. He followed Lilith out.

"That's my car over there," Lilith said. She tossed her head in the direction of the parked car in front of them.

Malachi looked and whistled at the Oldsmobile Super 88 convertible in candy apple red.

"Pretty, huh?" Lilith said, as she headed to the car while holding Malachi's hand.

Malachi opened the car door for her, and then he went and sat behind the steering wheel.

"Let's drive Malachi," Lilith said.

"Where?" Malachi asked.

"Anywhere," Lilith said. She inched closer to Malachi and laid her head on his broad shoulder. "I miss this."

"What?" Malachi asked as he started the engine, and pulled out.

"Lying in your arms at night and waking up with

you in the morning," Lilith said. "It's been a long time, Malachi."

"About ten years," Malachi said. "I hear you're really making things happen in New York City and Chicago. Some people say you sound like a young Etta James."

"That's a good comparison, right?" Lilith asked, as she snuggled on Malachi's shoulder.

"Uh-huh.

"Malachi...I love you," Lilith said. "I didn't tell you that before I left because I didn't want to...crowd you. Sure, I was passing through but the real reason is that I want you to go on the road with me. To be with me."

Malachi said nothing.

"You're the only man I can love and know you'll love me back for me and not because of what I've become. I know what I'm saying. I've had my share of men, and none of them came close to you, Malachi. "I know this might sound stupid—"

"No, it won't, Lilith. You can never sound stupid to me. You're always thinking it through."

Lilith smiled. She reached up and kissed Malachi on the cheek. "You've always made me feel like I was special. That's why I always felt so secure in your arms. The truth is this, Malachi. I drove one hundred miles out of my way to tell you what I'd already said, and I want to ask you something that ain't the normal thing to do," she said.

"If I can do it, you know I'd do anything for you, Lilith," Malachi said.

"I don't know about this one, Malachi," Lilith said.

"Ask me."

"I want to marry you, Malachi."

Malachi, his eyes on the road, didn't say anything. His mind was jumbled with thoughts.

"That one caught you off guard, didn't it?" Lilith asked. She smiled.

"Yeah," Malachi said.

"I could give you the world, Malachi, and all I'm asking is two words from you," Lilith said.

"The two words needed when standing in front of a preacher," Malachi said.

Lilith and Malachi laughed.

"You don't need me to make you happy, Lilith. You already are. If the love I've given you and the love you've returned to me ain't enough at this stage in our lives, then what is? I couldn't marry you. You don't need me to marry you. You want a…I don't know. A comforting partner to get you through those cold nights of traveling, but that's not an act to get married over. I do love you. It's knifed in my heart and I will always love you," Malachi said.

"Yet not enough to marry me," Lilith said.

Malachi nodded.

Lilith kissed him again on his cheek. She laid her head back on his shoulder. "I had to ask, Malachi. Let's head back to town," she said.

Malachi stopped on the road, and u-turned.

Twenty minutes later Malachi was standing in front of the studio watching Lilith drive away. He saw her raise her arm and wave. He waved back as he watched the dirt kick up and headed out of town. He watched until the car disappeared, and then he turned around and went into the studio.

"You boys head into the microphone booth and start

setting your things up," Malachi said, as he walked into the recording booth.

The men all headed into the microphone area and began taking out there instruments and tuning them up.

"What happened to Lilith?" Lady Marmalade asked. And what are you going to do with all those men?" Lady Marmalade asked.

"She had to get to a show. As for the men, we're gonna make music," Malachi said.

An hour later, everyone had their instruments out and was making all kinds of noise.

"Boys, since no one knows the other. I want ya'll to introduce each other by playing your instrument for a full minute, and then say who you are," Malachi said.

"Start to the right of me."

"Why did she come all this way?" Lady Marmalade said.

"She wanted to talk, Lady," Malachi said.

"Talk? Ya'll haven't see each other in years," Lady Marmalade said, as she flipped a switch on the board in front of her.

"Can we concentrate on this, Lady," Malachi said.

A rotund man in a plain white shirt nodded when Malachi pointed at him. He picked up his washboard and, to the surprise of everyone, began to play it with unbelievable expertise for a full minute. His fingers were moving so fast and with such fluidity that it was amazing. When he'd stopped playing, he turned to everyone. He received a thunderous round of applause.

"My name is Washboard Slim Brand. I've been playing this washboard since I could walk," he said. He smiled to reveal a gap in his top teeth. "If you give me another minute, I can really make this baby come to life."

The next instrument was a harmonica. Its reverberating sensation sent chills down everyone's back for the minute it was being played. When the player stopped, he bowed.

"My name is Howling Hank Parks. I've been pumping life into this here harmonica since I was eleven years old."

The musical string plucking on a guitar made everyone look at Riley who was sitting on a stool playing his guitar as if it were trying to get away from him. Malachi was impressed by the man's skill.

"I like that, Raley," Malachi said.

"Yeah, Lucille has a way of making you take notice when she's talking," Raley said.

"That's her name, Lucille? " Lady Marmalade asked, as she placed a piece of cornbread in her mouth while giving Raley a look of scrutiny. "You name her after your first… or second wife?"

Raley laughed. His stomach rolling with the sound emanating from his throat. "No, ma'am. I named her Lucille because that's the name she gave herself the first time I played her."

"She named herself, huh?" Lady Marmalade asked. She arched her right eyebrow. "Can it cook and wash your dirty draws, too?"

"Lady!" Malachi said. "Eat your food. I like the way you play, Raley. All right, let's hear the skins."

The man sitting at the drums looked up. When he did everyone saw the streak of white hair that was in the middle of his black, kinky hair. The leopard suit he was wearing did little to a person's eye. He smiled displaying three silver teeth. Two on the top and one on the bottom.

He looked back down at his drums, and with breathtaking speed, he began to play a rendition of *One Night.*

Malachi watched as the drummer made the pigskin come to life by beating the drums into musical submission with the quick movements of his wrist. The drumsticks appeared glued to his fingers as he pounded gingerly on a cymbal followed by a thrashing of the snare drum, then a hollow pounding on his foot peddle to the bass drum. It was all done so smoothly that Malachi smiled as he nodded his head, and clapped his hands.

"Beautiful! Beautiful!" Malachi snapped with joy. "Damn, you can play those skins!"

"Yes, he can," AB said, as he entered the recording booth.

Malachi turned around. "Did Tom come?" he asked.

"I'm right behind him," Tom Thum said.

Malachi looked down. He saw Tom standing behind AB's big leg.

"You're ready to do your thing?" Malachi asked Tom.

"Show me to a microphone, and a tall chair to stand up on and I'd show you," Tom said.

"Take him to the session booth, AB," Malachi said.

Malachi and Lady Marmalade watched as AB led Tom into the microphone area with the musicians.

"What the hell is his little ass going to do, Malachi?" Lady Marmalade asked.

"Watch and see," Malachi said.

"I hope he don't start dancing in there. He's so little someone might accidentally step on his little ass," Lady Marmalade said. She laughed. "And if he got that knife with him, somebody is going to get themselves a few wounds when the little man gets mad."

Malachi and Lady Marmalade watched AB help Tom onto a stool. AB pulled the microphone that was hanging from the ceiling down closer to Tom's face. When he saw that Tom was comfortable, AB walked back into the recording booth with Malachi and Lady Marmalade.

"All right, men," Malachi began. "We're going to follow Tom's lead. Your sheet music is easy to read. Tom, we're going to take it at two, okay?"

Tom smiled.

"What is he going to do?" Lady Marmalade asked, as she filled her mouth with a fork full of macaroni and cheese.

"Here we go," Malachi said. "One…Two."

As on cue, Tom opened his mouth and out came the sweet softness of a controlled voice Malachi had ever heard. Tom sounded something like him but more controlled. More determined and forceful in a light way. His words seemed to come from the bottom of his stomach and traveled with precision out of his mouth lovingly. He sung solo for two minutes until the instruments came into play.

Malachi turned around. He saw Lady Marmalade sitting there with her mouth opened, and macaroni and cheese falling out of it. He laughed.

For hours they made music. Malachi and AB recorded everything. It would be early morning on the next day that Malachi decided to call it a night. He sent everyone home, and then fell on the small sofa that Lady Marmalade was sleeping on. AB took the chair across from him and sat down. He leaned his head back.

"What are we doing with all of this again, Malachi?" AB asked.

"Making money, and recording history, AB. Man, you can take something special and turn it into something worth thousands of dollars if you know what and how to do it. There are some real special people out there with gifts the world needs to hear. Musical talent that could one day change the world the way we know it. Maybe these recordings won't be anything at all," Malachi said, as he shrugged. "Or maybe one day they might be their weight in gold, but the reality of it all is that we are doing something different than any other Negroes."

"Yeah, you're right. It is something different. Especially when Tom started to sing. Man, I didn't know that little bastard had a voice like that," AB said.

"I didn't either," Lady Marmalade said, as she sat up and wiped sleep from her crust covered eyes. "That little man can sing. How did you know he could sing, Malachi?"

"I heard him singing Jane to sleep one night," Malachi said.

"Whew. That little man can sing," Lady Marmalade said, throwing her feet off the sofa. "Well, I got to be getting back and making breakfast."

"We're going back with you," AB said.

Malachi locked the door to the studio as Lady Marmalade and AB walked ahead of him.

CHAPTER TWENTY-TWO
Life is a full Circle

Ten months later, Malachi and AB saw their fruits come to full bloom. Malachi had pressed the wax with different singers on it, and began to sell them out of the studio. He had singers who'd went by names that were more funny pronouncing than listening to some of their music, but in the end, Malachi knew everything would work out. He was making money selling the records, and had begun to charge one dollar every two hours for jam sessions. No one complained because they were getting their voices on wax.

By 1953, Malachi had seen and heard enough. He was becoming homesick. Sitting in the studio one summer night, he turned to AB. "How would you like to buy me out, AB?" Malachi asked.

"Buy you out? Whatta mean?" AB asked, as he stared at Malachi.

"How much money do you think we made in the past three years?" Malachi asked.

"You know how much. We looked at the books together last week," AB said.

"Yeah. We got a little over twenty five thousand dollars in the bank," Malachi said. "You give me fifteen thousand and half the master recordings, and everything else is yours, AB."

AB leaned back in his chair. He stared at Malachi, as he crossed his fingers over his now protruding belly.

"It's not hard to do, AB. It's a good deal for you," Malachi said, as he walked to the sofa and sat down.

"Why do you want to get out of this sweet thing, Malachi?" AB asked. "Everything is going good for us. We got people from all over coming to the studio."

Malachi touched the side of his scarred face. "I know, AB. It's just that I want to go home and…rest."

"Rest? That's all? Hell, you can do that here. Go grab one of Stella girls and disappear for a week or two. You know how Stella girls treat you when you come into her spot," AB said. He emphasizes the comment by twirling his index finger, and looking up at the ceiling.

"It's more than that, AB. I miss my sister."

"Oh. I see. Let me think about it for a minute, Malachi."

"Uh-uh. You'll think too long for me. You're an ex-boxer. You can think on your feet, and you sure as hell can think when you're sitting down. Give me an answer now, AB."

AB glanced at Malachi. He nodded. "I don't want you to go. Who's going to help me run all of this?" he asked.

"Lady Marmalade," Malachi said.

"Damn! I knew you were going to say that witch," AB said.

He and Malachi laughed.

"There's no way I can change your mind, Malachi?" AB asked. He watched Malachi shake his head. "Do we have to write a contract or something?"

"We didn't write one when we first started out as partners, did we?" Malachi asked.

"No, we didn't," AB said.

AB stood up. He walked to Malachi and opened his arms. "You're always going to have a friend, Malachi. And this place will always be here for you if you want to do something…different," he said.

Malachi stood up. He hugged AB. "I know, AB. I know," he said.

Four months later, fall was beginning to set in. Lady Marmalade, Tom, AB, and Jane led Malachi into the Club. When he entered the Club a band greeted him on the stage and a crowd of partygoers called out his name. Egghead came up to him and gave him a bottle of champagne.

"So, you're leaving tomorrow," Egghead began. "There have been some stories told about you, Malachi. Good stories and you're going to be missed. Tonight is your night. We're here to send you off in a blaze of glory."

"Thanks, Egghead. It's been a pleasure knowing all of you. I don't know if I'd ever get back this way again, but….," Malachi said.

"Forget the sad tidings, my friends," AB said, as he wrapped a big arm around Malachi's shoulder. "Let's go drink, get drunk, and listens to the music."

Malachi felt his eyes become moist, as he nodded his head. AB led him to a table that was decorated with an assortment of plastic bells, garter belts, and musical instruments. They all sat at the table situated in front of the stage. There was an eight-piece band playing great songs of Blues, Jazz and other grassroots tunes. There were men he'd recorded with on the stage and others sitting around at tables enjoying the festive. Malachi reached for the glass of champagne that AB had poured for him. He brought it to his lips.

The next five hours was filled with a party ambience. Malachi watched the changing of bands and drank champagne continuously. He had to admit, he was happy, and that happiness was watching some of the singers and musicians before him create history. A history he knew would one day become an anthem for other Blues artist who like singing those songs of deep, thoughtful messages of women gone bad while loving the man who sent them on their journey; men paying for their pain of sorrow and glory through alcohol and jealousy, as well as relationships spiraling out of control from terrible decisions. It was beautiful.

When Malachi awoke in the wee hours of the morning following his going away party, he opened his bloodshot eyes to the darkness in his room. He glanced out the window. It was still dark. He sat up. He blinked a few times to clear his vision. He licked his lips and tasted a chalk-like substance from his mouth being dry and too many glasses of bathtub champagne. He threw his legs out of bed. He cradled his throbbing head in his hands as he tried to stop the room from spinning. Malachi stood up very slowly on wobbly legs, and headed for the bathroom that was down the hall.

When he opened his door and walked out of his room,

he felt a chill. He didn't care, though; he was trying to relieve himself before he had an accident running down his legs. As he hurried down the dimly lit hallway, he heard a door opened behind him but he paid it no attention. His only concern was making it to the bathroom.

As Malachi stood over the toilet urinating, he looked down into the toilet. His eyes caught what he hadn't noticed earlier when he'd hurried out of his room. He was butt naked.

Malachi was started by the sound of someone pounding on the door.

"Hurry up! Get out of there!" Jane shouted.

Malachi cursed under his breath.

Jane pounded on the door again. "Come on! Get out!" she shouted impatiently.

Malachi, shaking his head, reached for the doorknob.

Jane took a step back at hearing the bathroom door unlock.

"Well, it's about damn time," Jane began, as she reached for the edge of the door and yanked it open further. "What—"

Malachi saw Jane's expression turn from anger to shock. He heard her purr. Her eyes seductively began a descent from his face, chest, crotch, thighs, and then his feet as she took a step back while biting her bottom lip. Her eyes rose and stopped at his crotch. She licked her lips seductively.

"Malachi?" Jane said. Feigning shock, as a smile formed. "You're naked, baby."

Malachi hurried pass her while his hands covered his crotch.

Jane stood there and watched Malachi half run and half jog down the hallway.

"I like your tight ass, Malachi," Jane said. She began to laugh as she continued to look at Malachi. "Keep it right and tight, you handsome devil."

Malachi ran into his room, and slammed the door closed. He leaned on the door as he continued to protect his crotch. It took a few seconds before he finally let his hands fall from his crotch. He shook his head and began to laugh. He walked to his bed, and climbed in.

Seven hours later Malachi was up again. It was mid-afternoon. With his bag packed and his guitar case slung over his shoulder, he made his way quietly down the stairs. As he reached the front down, the sound of someone clearing their throat made him turn around.

"You didn't want to say goodbye?" Lady Marmalade asked from the kitchen doorway. One of her thin cigars was clutched loosely between her fingers. There were big yellow rollers were in her hair, and she was wearing a multicolored cotton nightdress. "I would've been upset if I'd missed you."

Malachi put down his bag, and walked toward her.

As he and Lady Marmalade hugged, Malachi knew he would miss her rough, but loving ways.

"It's been a pleasure knowing you, Lady," Malachi said. He pulled away, and stared into her eyes. "Through all that meanest lies a good heart."

Lady Marmalade smiled. "Yeah, you've been a jagged edge around here also. But don't let anyone know that," she said. "Does AB know you're leaving?"

"He knows I'm leaving," Malachi said.

Lady Marmalade nodded. "Wait, I got something for you," she said, as she spun around and disappeared into the kitchen.

Malachi walked to the door and grabbed his things.

Seconds later, Lady Marmalade returned carrying a food basket. She walked over and handed it to Malachi. "Something to get you through your long journey," she said.

Malachi took the basket. He lifted it to his nose. "It's fresh biscuits? I also smell some beef stew and some fried chicken in there. How long have you been up?" he asked.

"Please, boy, you know I got to run this house. If breakfast ain't ready when they get up, I got to hear a lot of noise about people being hungry," Lady Marmalade said. "Can you get everything out to the car?"

Malachi nodded.

"You're going to be missed," Lady Marmalade said.

"So will you, Lady."

Lady Marmalade smiled. She turned around and went back into the kitchen.

Malachi opened the door. He walked down the stairs to his car.

Malachi sat behind the steering wheel of his new Buick Roadmaster for a few seconds. He let some things run through his mind as he savored good memories of wonderful people. He smiled, as he reached for the key in the ignition and started the car. As he shifted it into gear, an image of Rose Ann appeared of her learning how to drive, and he laughed. At that moment, he really missed her.

Malachi had been driving for three weeks. Some nights he would pull over and spend the night in his car on the road if he became too tired, and other nights he would locate a motel to stay the night and take a shower. To pass the hours, he'd listen to a new radio that played all blues songs. As he listened to some of the songs, he knew the names of the singers and musicians before the disc jockey announced it because he'd worked with the artist.

On this particular night as he drove, Malachi listened to a man who played his guitar with devilish dexterity. Malachi cocked his head to one side to listen more closely to the voice singing, and to get a better pickup of the chords being played. He knew that sound, he said out loud. Who was he?

It had begun to rain, so whenever Malachi found himself about to put a face to the music, he had to concentrate on the slippery road ahead of him. The song continued to play. Malachi glanced in his rearview mirror. There was a car behind him. He paid it no attention, as he tightly clutched the steering wheel to concentrate. The rain began to fall heavily. He glanced in his rearview mirror again and saw that the car behind him had picked up speed.

When the song on the radio had ended, Malachi listened to the disc jockey announce who it was. Malachi heard the man say that the singer had been rumored to have sold his soul to the devil one night on a crossroad leading to nowhere to learn how to play a guitar like no one else had ever done before. The disc jockey said the man's name was *Robert Johnson.*

Robert Johnson? Malachi let the name run off his tongue. He repeated it again. The name didn't fit the person playing the guitar the way he remembered the person. He glanced in his rearview mirror again. The driver was about twenty feet behind him and gaining. He must be in a hurry to get home, Malachi surmised, as he returned his attention to the road.

Malachi slammed his hand against the steering wheel.

He did know the person named Robert Johnson, but when he'd met him, he was calling himself R.J. The musician who'd played with his back to the audience. Malachi laughed.

Malachi's laugh was short because he felt his head snapped back when the impact of the car behind him rammed into the rear of his car. He was about to hit his brakes when he looked into the rearview mirror and saw the black Sedan swerved out to the left of him on the two-lane road. Malachi took a quick glance at the car as it pulled up beside him. He saw that the window was down. He couldn't see who was driving, but his instincts took over when he saw the brightness of teeth glaring at him. His foot slammed down hard on the accelerator. The car leaped forward. Pulling away from the black Sedan.

At that exact moment, a gunshot was heard. The back window exploded on Malachi's car sending glass shards everywhere. Malachi hunched his shoulders and leaned forward to see the road better, and to avoid being shot. He increased his speed by pressing down further on the accelerator.

The black Sedan also increased its speed as it followed along side Malachi's car.

It was the Ku Klux Klan. Malachi mumbled under his breath, as he concentrated on the road. Who else could it be? They see a Negro out on the road by himself and think that a lynching is due. Why not kill him? He was on a dark road by himself with no witnesses. Malachi cursed for the umpteenth time, as he took a corner on the road going at sixty-three miles an hour.

The black Sedan was inches from Malachi's car. The driver of the black Sedan drew up behind the back tire of Malachi's car, and rammed the side of it.

The back passenger side window of Malachi's car came crashing in as another shot was fired. Malachi ducked down further.

The black Sedan was now side by side with Malachi's car. The driver of the black Sedan twisted the steering wheel as hard as it would go to the right, slamming the full weight of the car into Malachi's car.

Metal grinding against metal was painful to the ear. The full impact of the black Sedan smashed into his car, Malachi felt his body shift away from the steering wheel as the car was ran off the paved road and into the dirt shoulder to the right of him. The car went into a spin. Malachi had lost control of it. There was nothing he could do as the weight of the car went with gravity.

Instead of forcing the steering wheel in hopes of controlling the car, Malachi let it go as he reached for the glove compartment while the car tossed him around like a rag doll. He knew at any moment he could suddenly be flipping over and there was nothing he could do about it. He was in the hand of fate.

The black Sedan came to a stop. The driver watched Malachi's car spin out of control as it continued to twist and turn down the embankment, spewing up dust everywhere as the rain continued to fall heavily. When Malachi's car had come to a complete stop, the driver of the black Sedan drove slowly down toward it.

Malachi could feel the blood running down the left side of his face as it lay on the seat. His head had hit the metal doorknob on the passenger side. He was bleeding profusely. He blinked rapidly to clear his vision. Blood ran into his eye. He felt lightheaded. His shoulder was throbbing with pain. He closed his eyes.

When the black Sedan came to a complete stop several feet from Malachi's car. The driver opened his door. The hinges needed oil as it creaked He stepped out. A brown hat covered the driver's face and the black trench coat hid any other distinguishing marks. In the driver's right black-gloved hand, he menacingly cradled a .45 automatic pistol.

The sound of footsteps approaching was barely heard in Malachi's semi-unconscious state of mind. The loud thunder and pounding rain made it difficult to hear. He had to strain his ears to hear anything. He sighed in despair. His right hand hung limply downward and out of sight as he forced his mind to concentrate on his surroundings while listening intensely.

The driver of the black Sedan was now standing inches from Malachi. Malachi's unknown assailant smashed in the driver's side window. The driver reached in and pulled Malachi up. He leaned Malachi's head against the steering wheel. The driver of the Sedan grunted, and pulled Malachi's head away from the steering wheel, and leaned it against the headrest of the back seat.

"Malachi Moon. It's been a long time," the driver of the black Sedan said, as he let the .45 automatic caress the side of Malachi's bloody face. "You've changed." The driver began to snicker.

It was then that Malachi became fully alert. If not for the snickering, he probably would've let death take him. But the snickering brought back memories for him. They were memories he'd forgotten over the years.

"I've come to take my pound of flesh, Malachi." The man with the .45 said.

Malachi felt the barrel of the gun being pressed into

his left temple, as his head lay against the headrest. A surge of adrenaline pumped through his body rapidly as his breathing increased and his nose began to flare. He slowly raised his right arm. Bringing it across his chest in one swift motion, he fell away from the .45 automatic while bringing up Bear's .38 revolver. Malachi squeezed the trigger two quick times. The .38 revolver roared to life as the two bullets found their mark.

The impact of the bullets hitting the chest and throat of the driver of the black Sedan was forceful. The man was lifted off the ground and knocked backward.

Malachi opened the car door, and staggered out. He was weak, and his vision was bleary. The rain picked up, and began to fall harder. The rain mingling with the blood on his face gave him a horrendous appearance when the lightening illuminated the sky. Malachi wiped his face with his jacket sleeve. With clearer vision, he looked down on the ground several feet away, and saw his would-be assassin. Malachi, with hesitation, walked toward the person who lay motionless on the ground.

Malachi could see that the hat the assassin had been wearing had fallen off. As he drew nearer, he saw the .45 automatic had come out of his hand. Malachi kicked it further away, as he looked down into the person's face.

Malachi shook his head. If it hadn't been the snickering, he thought, he would be laying there dead instead of Lester Brown.

"Today wasn't my day to die, Lester," Malachi said. "So it was you who shot me that night in the Club. You were gunning for me instead of AB that night. I had forgotten about you. Sometimes revenge ain't as good as one might make it out to be."

Lester, his eyelids flickering, gave Malachi a distant stare as they fell on him. His lips moved as he tried to form some words, but no sound came out. Blood ran freely down the right corner of his mouth. He coughed.

Malachi raised the gun toward Lester's head.

Lester stared at him. "Go...to...hell!" He shouted as blood spewed from his mouth.

"You first, and I'd catch up to you," Malachi said.

Lester arched his back as if to get up. His eyes open wide with anger. He tried to muster his strength by trying to use his elbows to sit up.

Malachi took a step back with the gun still pointing at Lester's head.

Lester expelled his lungs and fell back to the ground. His eyes closed, as his fingers dug into the dirt. A grin appeared. Seconds later, his entire body convulsed, and then it stopped. He was dead.

Malachi turned and walked back to his car. Hopefully it might be still able to get him to a hospital.

It would be three weeks when Malachi arrived at Blackenfield. He parked his car around the corner in an alley. With his suitcase and guitar in hand, he stepped out into the street. He stood there and searched. He had to admit. The town had changed since the last time he was there. There were taller buildings and more stores. He saw the Queen and headed for it.

"Goddamn it, man! We didn't order pigfeet. We ordered pigskin," Cotton said to the small man in front of him. "If you'd written it down the order, we wouldn't be having this misunderstanding."

The small Negro with big ears had a clipboard in his hand and a pencil. The bloody apron around his waist let anyone know who might be curious that he was the butcher.

"Look, Blass, the boss doesn't want any trouble with you and the delivery," Cotton began. "You take this order back and bring us what we ordered."

"This is what you ordered, Cotton," Blass said.

Cotton scratched his rugged cheek as he stared at Blass. He heard the front door of the Queen open and glanced in its direction. He was about to look away when something familiar about the man walking through the door made him slightly push Blass to the side.

"Uh…Excuse me," Cotton said, as he walked pass Blass.

Malachi looked up to see Cotton hurrying toward him. He put down his guitar case and suitcase as he approached.

"Damn, Malachi, it's good to see you," Cotton said, as he snatched Malachi's wrist and began shaking his hand. He stopped shaking his hand, and took on a sober look. "I'm sorry, boss,"

"You're sorry?" Malachi began. "Sorry about what?"

"Stump is in your office. I have to finish with Blass about messing up our order," Cotton said, as he rushed back to confront Blass.

Malachi watched him run away. He picked up his guitar case and suitcase, and headed for the back room that was to the right of him.

Stump sat behind the desk going over invoice papers when the knock on the door agitated him. He hated when Cotton bothered him when he was trying to do his business.

"Come in, and it better be serious, Cotton," Stump shouted.

Malachi opened the door.

"Malachi!" Stump said, as he stood up and came around the desk. "God, it's good to see you! Come in. Come in!"

Stump helped Malachi with his suitcase as he ushered him into the office. He closed the door.

"Sit down, Malachi," Stump said.

Malachi smiled. He went to the chair in front of the desk to sit down. Stump stopped him.

"No, Malachi, sit behind your desk," Stump offered.

Malachi laughed and shook his head. "No, Stump, it's your desk," he said. "I'll sit here."

"No, Malachi. Go ahead and sit behind the desk," Stump said.

Reluctantly, Malachi went and sat behind the desk. He smiled.

"I didn't think you'd be here this fast after receiving the telegraph," Stump said, as he sat down in the chair in front of the desk. "It was a shock to us all."

Malachi tilted his head. "What telegraph?" he asked.

Stump looked at him.

"I was on the road, Stump. I didn't come because of a telegraph. I was just coming back because I was heading home to see my sister. What was in the telegraph?"

Stump stared at Malachi.

"What's wrong, Stump?" Malachi asked. He could see that Stump had grown a few more gray hairs in his goatee. "Why are you looking like someone threw back the biggest fish you'd finally caught. The place looks good."

"I...your... mother—"

Malachi sighed as he rolled his eyes. "What? She ran away with someone's money?" he asked. "Don't worry. Tell the person I'd pay back what was taken."

"Malachi...Your mother died of pneumonia a week ago," Stump said quietly.

Malachi felt his heart skip a beat. His breath became short, and he felt a little lightheaded. He put his elbows on the big desk, and covered his face with his hands.

"My...my mother...is dead?" Malachi asked.

"I'm sorry, Malachi. I'm real sorry," Stump said.

Malachi nodded.

"No one knew what she had. It came on quick. When I found out she was sick, I did my best to get her help," Stump said.

"I know you did your best, Stump. Where did you bury her?" Malachi asked. His words were barely audible as he looked up and stared at Stump.

"In a plot behind the Queen," Stump answered.

Malachi stood up.

"You want me to go with you?" Stump asked, as he stood up.

Malachi shook his head. He walked to the door.

Stump watched him exit. His heart felt heavy.

It didn't take Malachi long to locate the grave. It was behind the Queen and under a large oak tree that had risen above the hotel. Malachi couldn't remember the tree being as tall as it was the last time he saw it. He looked down at the tombstone. It read:

Ella May Barres
Born: Unknown   Died: May 23, 1953
Rest in Peace

Malachi smiled. Even in death his mother had left an impression for anyone thinking they knew her. It was short and sweet. He touched the tombstone. He hadn't known much about the woman who'd given birth to him. She was a wanderer who did what she wanted whenever she wanted. A strong woman with her own way of thinking as to what she perceived life to be.

To the right, and ten feet away, Malachi saw Bear's tombstone. He walked over to it smiling.

Wayne Thomas Grant
(Bear)
Born: To have fun   Died: Living life to the fullest

Malachi gave a hearty laugh and walked away. At least he had the opportunity to meet his mother, and, befriend a good man like Bear. For those things, he was grateful.

The next day Malachi lay in his bed in his old room in the Queen staring at the ceiling. He heard his stomach rumble with hunger. He sat up and placed his feet on the floor. He was naked except for his underwear. He heard a knock on the door.

"Come in," Malachi said. It was probably Stump checking on him.

The door opened. A tall, statuesque woman wearing a burgundy dress suit with a black hat pulled down covering her face.

"You're in the wrong room," Malachi said, as he reached for the sheet to cover his body.

The woman removed her hat.

"Betty Mae!" Malachi said, as he leaped up.

Betty Mae placed a hand on her hip, and smiled. "I wanted to see you," she said. "It's been a long time. How are you, Malachi?"

Malachi walked toward her letting the sheet fall to the floor. As he stood in front of her, he had to admit, her beauty had matured over the years giving her polished, but eye-catching warmth.

"I was planning on coming to find you in a couple of days after I'd finished doing some business with Stump," Malachi said. "I've been well."

"Good."

"Come in and sit down," Malachi said.

Betty Mae shook her head. "No, I just wanted to say hello, Malachi," she said.

"Come on. I'm not going to bite you," Malachi said, taking her hand.

Betty Mae laughed. "No, that's not it. I don't think it'd look appropriate for a married woman to be in a man's room she'd once had relations with while he's in his underwear," Betty Mae said.

Malachi looked at her. "You're married?" he asked.

"For five years now," Betty Mae said.

"You're married?" Malachi repeated.

Betty Mae laughed. "You said that already. Malachi, I waited for you as long as I could. You use to write me, but that stopped after a year. I had to move on with my life. You can understand that?" she asked.

And he did. Who was he to have a woman like Betty Mae to be waiting for him? If he really cared for her, he would've made his way back to her.

"I missed out, didn't I?" Malachi asked.

"I don't think you missed out, Malachi. I think you are a person who enjoys adventure. The unknown is what attracts you the most. I couldn't have satisfied you for long. It's not the person you might love that will keep a man like you grounded. It's looking for that something you don't know what you want...yet. You're still searching for something, and life keeps throwing obstacles in front of you, and you keep climbing over them to get to the next obstacle. That's your life Malachi Moon," Betty Mae said.

"I—"

"It's okay, Malachi," Betty Mae said, as she place a hand over Malachi's mouth. "No need to explain." She removed her hand. She leaned forward and kissed him lightly on his cheek. "You take care of yourself."

Malachi watched Betty Mae put on her hat. She turned and walked out the door. He watched the door close.

Malachi stood there staring at the door. He scratched his head, and walked back to his bed. He sat on the edge of the bed. For some reason he understood everything Betty Mae had said. He smiled. He was more like his mother than he would admit.

A few hours later, Malachi and Stump were on the floor of the Queen. It was late afternoon.

"The place has changed," Malachi said as he looked around at the new paint, curtains, and a polished floor.

"Money does that. Do you know we make so much money from the numbers game that it doesn't seem real sometimes," Stump said. "Besides that money and the money coming in from the Goldspot you're a rich man," Stump said.

"No, we're rich, Stump. If Bear could see this now, he'd be dancing all night with a jug of moonshine in his hand and cursing," Malachi said.

"Yeah," Stump said quietly. "I miss that stubborn fool. There have been times when Bear would come to my mind while I'm walking down the street or sitting down and I get…I don't know…sad."

"How are Cotton and Monty?" Malachi asked. He wanted to change to conversation. He knew what Stump was saying because he'd done the same thing at times.

"Cotton is managing the Goldspot like it was some kind of fortress, but he keeps the money coming in. As for Monty, I still let him do his thing with his three cards," Stump said.

"Two black Queens and a red one?" Malachi asked.

"That's right," Stump said. He laughed.

"We need to talk, Stump," Malachi said.

"Sure. Is it about the money I been sending Rose Ann every month? I had increased it to four hundred dollars a month a few years back, Malachi," he said.

"No. No. It's not that, Stump. I want you to buy me out."

Stump turned toward Malachi. He stopped. "What? Are you crazy? No. that's not going to work. All of this is yours. You made me a partner. If anything, you ought to be offering me a buyout," he said.

"No, Stump. I won't be coming back this way again. How much money do we have in the back?"

"I don't know. About forty thousand," Stump said. "We have another fifty thousand in the bank."

"Go to the bank and have a separate account opened for me, and put forty thousand in it for me. I'm going to take fifteen thousand from the floor box in the office." Malachi said. "Everything else is yours."

Stump shook his head. "I'm not going to do it," he said angrily. "Bear left you the Queen and everything that followed after that belongs to you."

"The same way Bear left the Queen to me, I'm leaving it to you, as well as the Goldspot," Malachi said.

"No, damnit! Look, Malachi, you're not thinking. This business is growing. You don't give it up and walk away," Stump said. "It ain't good business sense. In another year or two you'd have double that amount of money in your pocket."

"I just want to find me a corner in a warm house and relax, Stump. I don't want to do the hard thinking for anything anymore," Malachi said. "I'm tired."

Stump took Malachi by the shoulders. "I'll tell you what," he began. "I'll give you everything you asked, and every month I'll send you one thousand dollars," he said. "If one month the money stops coming in, then you know we're even." Malachi was about to protest but Stump put up a hand. "It's not negotiable."

"All right, Stump. We'll do it your way...for now," Malachi said.

"Good, let's go see the Goldspot," Stump said.

"Betty Mae came to my room this morning," Malachi said. He started walking again.

"She's something, huh?" Stump said, as he began walking beside him. He led the way to the door. "She married a smart, businessman from back east who'd been traveling out this way to open a cigar store. He hadn't planned on staying in Blackenfield, but he met Betty Mae. You can fill in the rest of the story."

"Cigar store? Why one of those?" Malachi asked.

"You'd be surprised at how many people smoke those stinking things. He's doing all right I hear. He bought them a house about two years ago."

"That's good money. Is Sheriff Hays still coming around with his hand out?" Malachi asked.

Stump laughed. "That fat, redneck cracker lost his reelection about five years ago, and now he's sweeping the streets for a living. That's what happens when you do wrong. As for his Klan's men, most of them threw away their sheets and hoods and moved to different towns when they found out that John Hawkins was sleeping with a Negro girl," he said.

Malachi nodded. He smiled.

A week later, Malachi was sitting in his car looking at the town as he slowly drove through it. He glanced at his rearview mirror and saw Stump and Cotton wave to him. He stuck his arm out of the window and waved back.

It would be several days before Malachi finally saw the barn fifty yards away, he smiled. That barn had been the forming of a friendship between George Lewis and Maybelle that had turned into a motherly and fatherly connection. He also saw that there were two other houses on the property that wasn't there when he left. Malachi drove straight up to the newly painted house of George Lewis and Maybelle.

George Lewis saw the new car pull into his driveway, but made no move to greet whoever it might've been. He sat on the porch swing rocking back and forth as he watched the driver of the car.

Malachi opened the car door and stepped out.

"Are you looking for someone?" George Lewis asked.

Malachi hadn't turned to face him yet.

George Lewis stood up. "Hey, I asked you if you were looking for someone?" he asked again.

Malachi turned toward him.

George Lewis stared at Malachi.

Malachi smiled.

"Is that you, boy?" George Lewis asked. "Maybelle! Get out here woman. Our boy done come home!"

Maybelle rushed out to the porch wiping her hands on her apron. She stopped when she saw Malachi. Their eyes locked, and then Maybelle screamed and ran down to Malachi.

Malachi opened his arms as Maybelle ran into him. He felt her muscles squeezing his neck hard as he wrapped his arms around her and squeezed lovingly.

Maybelle pulled away, and stared at Malachi. "God, it's so good to see you," she said. "Come into the house. Did you eat? Do you need to take a bath? Why didn't you tell us you were coming?" She started dragging Malachi behind her as she led him toward the house.

"Darn, Maybelle, let the boy be for a minute. You're asking him a thousand questions without taking breath. Breathe woman," George Lewis said, as he neared the stairs.

Malachi and Maybelle climbed the four short stairs. George Lewis greeted Malachi with a firm handshake. For a moment they stared at each other, and then Malachi wrapped his arms around George Lewis.

"Come on now, you're too big for that," George Lewis said, but he made no attempt to break free.

"I've missed the both of you," Malachi said. He placed his arms around both of their shoulders and gave them a hug.

"We missed you, too, son," George Lewis said.

Malachi released him. He let Maybelle drag him into the house followed by George Lewis.

"Call Rose Ann, Maybelle. She'd come a running

down here like a bat out of hell when you tell her Malachi is here," George Lewis said.

Maybelle led Malachi to the kitchen. She sat him down and went to the phone hanging on the wall on the other side. She started dialing.

George Lewis sat at the table. "You want something strong to drink to wet your whistle?" he asked.

"No, George Lewis. I'm okay," Malachi said. He smiled. "I'm okay."

Maybelle hurried back to the table. She sat down beside Malachi. "Rose Ann is on her way," she said. "I have some ham from last night. You want me to fix you a sandwich?"

"I'm fine, Maybelle," Malachi said. He took Maybelle's hand into his own. "I'm okay."

"You look...older," George Lewis said, as he scrutinized Malachi's face. "You're sure everything is all right?"

"I'm fine, George Lewis. I look older because I am. I was a young boy when I left here. I'm just weary from the drive. That's all."

"How's your mother, Malachi?" Maybelle asked. She lightly rubbed Malachi's arm.

"She's dead. She had pneumonia. I got there too late to see her buried. They tell me she received the best of everything before she died," Malachi said.

"I'm sorry to hear that, son," George Lewis said.

"So am I, baby. Some years back, Rose Ann made it up there to see her," Maybelle began. "She cried for a week when she returned home. She had asked your mother to come live with her and Roger, but your mother told her she didn't want to be a burden. That they were grown folks who needed their own space and not to be bothered with an old woman crowding them."

"Yeah, that was mama. I'll tell Rose Ann later when I think the time is right," Malachi said.

"Whatever you say, Malachi," Maybelle said.

The front door could be heard opening. Everyone at the kitchen table turned to see Rose Ann. She entered with her large, pregnant stomach first.

"Malachi!" Rose Ann screamed, as she hurriedly wobbled over to her brother.

Malachi stood up to greet his sister, kissing her on the cheek while hugging her tightly. He gave her his chair as he eased her into it.

"Hold onto her arm tight, Malachi," Roger said, as he entered.

Malachi looked up as he guided his sister to a chair. He saw that Roger had grown a beard and put on some weight. "You're looking like a married man, Roger," he said. "This is the first one, huh?"

Rose Ann affectionately rubbed Malachi's arm. She laughed making everyone else laugh. "No," she began. "This is our second child."

"Second?" Malachi asked. "Where's the first one?"

Everyone turned at the sound of the door screen being pushed open, and then closed. A small boy wearing blue jeans with a matching blue shirt and nothing on his feet, walked in wearing an expression of curiosity. He looked the splitting image of Rose Ann. He stood in the doorway looking at the faces that returned his stare.

"Hi, grandma and grandpa. Grandma did you make any strawberry jam?" The little boy asked.

"Hey, son. Say hello to the man standing beside your mother," Roger said.

The little boy walked over to Malachi. He stared up at him with beautiful brown eyes.

"Hello," the little boy began, as he scratched his arm. "My name is Malachi," he said.

Malachi took a step back. He glanced at his sister. She smiled. Malachi looked down at his nephew. He bent down and picked him up. He ran his fingers through his kinky hair.

"What's your name?" Little Malachi asked, as he looked up his uncle. He leaned in close to Malachi's ear. "I hope it's not a funny name like mine."

Malachi laughed. "Why is Malachi a funny name?" he asked.

"Why? Well, you ever hear of anyone with a name like that? I don't know why my parents didn't give me a normal name," Little Malachi said.

"I don't know. I like my name," Malachi said, as he straighten Little Malachi's shirt.

"You do? What's your name?" Little Malachi asked.

"Malachi Moon," Malachi said. A smile filled his face.

"Malachi Moon?" Little Malachi repeated. He looked around at the faces that were staring at him. He looked up at Malachi. "Your name is Malachi? Are you funning me?" he asked.

Rose Ann took her son's little, pudgy hand, and stoked it. "Malachi, this is your uncle. My brother. I named you after him," she said.

Little Malachi's head snapped back around toward his mother. "My uncle? The one you're always talking about?" he asked.

"Uh-huh," Rose Ann said.

Little Malachi pressed his face into Malachi's chest.

"Okay, maybe I can come to like my name now that I know there's someone else with it," he said.

Everyone began laughing.

Later that evening, Rose Ann and Malachi were walking toward Rose Ann's house that Malachi had seen when he drove up.

"Your house isn't too far from George Lewis and Maybelle's," Malachi said. "I don't remember any other houses besides their house when we were here."

"I know. With the money Stump was sending me each month, I convinced George Lewis to let me build those houses," Rose Ann said. "I missed you, Malachi."

Malachi placed an arm around his sister's shoulder. "I've missed you, too. "I see Roger did right by you."

"Roger's a good man, Malachi. He treats me good," Rose Ann said.

"I'm happy for you, Rose," Malachi said. "He pointed to the other gray and white house to the right of him. "Why did you build that second house? For little Malachi when he gets older and married. Girl, you're planning too far ahead." He laughed.

"I had that one built for you if you ever came back. I wanted us to be across from one another but not too far," Rose Ann said.

Malachi stopped. He looked down at his sister. "You had a house built for me?" Rose Ann nodded. "Oh, Rose, you're always thinking in advance. Thank you," he said.

They started walking again.

"I have something to tell you, Rose, and it's going to be painful, but you have to know," Malachi said. He squeezed her shoulder.

Rose Ann stopped. "What?" she asked.

Malachi turned toward her. Letting her shoulder go and taking her hands.

As Rose Ann stared into his eyes, she could see there was pain.

"Mama is dead," Malachi said. His voice cracked.

"Mama...is dead?" Rose Ann asked. "But that's not true. I mean. I just found her, Malachi. She's only been in my life for a short time!"

Malachi took his sister into his arms. He wanted to shelter the girl he knew as his flesh and blood from any pain or suffering. He'd protected Rose Ann all of his life, and would never say or do anything that would harm her, but he had to tell her their mother was dead. And that's all he would tell her.

"Malachi, I was planning on taking the kids to see her in the summer," Rose Ann said as her head rested on Malachi's chest. "When I went up to Blackenfield to see her, we talked all night about everything."

Malachi heard Rose Ann begin to cry. He gave her a strong hug, as he laid his head on her head and listened to her cry.

It was 1957 and the heat could be seen rising from the ground. Malachi and George Lewis were sitting on the porch listening to the radio.

"It's going to be a scorcher this summer, Malachi," George Lewis said.

Malachi nodded, as he sat with is head leaned back and his eyes close. He felt comfortable to the point of going to sleep. He'd worn a pair of cut-off shorts and a tank-top shirt to keep cool.

The radio was blaring with Rock and Roll music.

"I don' know how you can listen to that racket on the

radio, Malachi," George Lewis said. "It's a bunch of noise that doesn't make any sense."

At the end of one song another one came on. Malachi's subconscious picked up on the chords from the guitar. He opened his eyes as the song continued to play.

"Now, I don't know much about music, but this is a good damn song," George Lewis said. "I can hear the Blues in every chord that boy is playing."

Malachi leaned forward and turned his head slightly to concentrate on the music emanating from the radio.

"I was down at the local store last week, and some of the boys were talking about the music and where it's going. My friend, Weasel, said he'd seen a white boy on television singing and dancing. He said if he hadn't seen him, he would've sworn up and down a stack of bibles that he was listening to a Negro," George Lewis said.

"Did he say that the white boy shook his hips a lot, and held his wrist down while shaking his legs as if he were going through one of those shaking fits?" Malachi asked, as he continued to listen to the music.

"Well, come to think, he did say something about the boy shaking his hips with rhythm. And you know that ain't right. white folks ain't got any rhythm, but he said this white boy did," George Lewis said as he wiped sweat from his forehead with the back of his hand.

"I bet he said the white boy could pass as a girl if you didn't know better," Malachi said.

"Hell, you've been talking to Weasel? That's what he said," George Lewis said. "I hear that white boy is making thousands of dollars sounding like a Negro. And they want to know why we act the way we do when it comes to our Blues. White folks always trying to take our thing and call it their own creation."

Malachi stood up and stretched. "I'm heading over to my place," he said.

"You're coming over for dinner, right?" George Lewis asked.

"Wouldn't miss it if the world ended, George Lewis. Are you taking your medication?" Malachi asked.

"Yeah. If I don't Maybelle gets to screaming and acting all crazy."

As Malachi walked toward his house. He pulled out his brown, worn wallet. He removed an old looking piece of paper that was folded over several times. He stopped. He turned the paper around in his hands a few times contemplating on whether to open it. He placed his wallet under his arm. He gripped the ends of the paper, and began ripping them apart. He tossed the shredded paper into the air and let the wind take them away.

"Uncle Malachi!"

Malachi turned around. His nephew was running toward him very fast.

"Where are you going?" Little Malachi asked.

Malachi looked down at his nephew. He was getting taller. He was ten years old and was sprouting out. "I'm going to my house," he said.

"Grandpa was going to teach me how to play the guitar today, but he said he's a little tired," Little Malachi said.

"Was he? Would you like for me to teach you?" Malachi asked.

Little Malachi laughed. "You don't know how to play a guitar, Uncle Malachi," he said.

"All right, if that's what you think," Malachi said.

"Could you, please. I could take it slow. Grandpa said

I should try one chord at a time. Then, maybe, I might be good enough to play," Little Malachi said.

"Hmm. Grandpa is right…to a point," Malachi said. "But listen. What if I taught you how to play it but I'd teach you two chords at a time."

Little Malachi looked at his uncle. His small doe-like eyes took on an image of confusion. "If learning one chord at a time is hard to do, then two chords will be really hard," he said.

"It might, but you'd learn it faster, and instead of waiting, my way gives you the chance to be more advance in your chords," Malachi said.

"I don't know, Uncle Malachi. It means I have to work harder at learning the chords," Little Malachi said.

"Yep."

"All right. If I did that, then I have to remember to do my chores at home, and the other little things grandma and grandpa want me to do at their house. Whew, that's a lot, Uncle Malachi."

"If you had ten times the chores placed on you, and you wanted to do something that would make you happy, it wouldn't make a difference what responsibilities lie ahead of you, you're do it was because in the end, you'll be happy learning something you wanted to learn," Malachi said.

"Well, now that you put it like that. I guess I can do it," Little Malachi said.

Malachi dropped a gentle hand on his nephew's shoulder. "My young nephew, there will be times when you think you can't do something, and times when you feel you don't have the strength to see something through. It's times like those that will call on your character to get stronger or lose the desire of what you want to do. Only you can make the choice of which road to choose in life. Do you understand?" Malachi asked.

"Yes, Uncle Malachi."

"Good. We'll start your guitar lessons today," Malachi said.

"Now! Oh, Uncle Malachi. I have too many things to do today. Grandpa wants me to help him chop some wood. Why? I don't know. It's hot today. Grandma wants me to help her peel some apples for an apple pie. Why? She has three of them still sitting in the window from last week. After that, Pa wants me to clean my room, which I think ain't right because it's my room, and if I can sleep in a messy room who should tell me when to clean it. When all that is—"

"Little Malachi. You're telling me stories that have nothing to do with you learning the guitar," Malachi said. "All those things are part of life. You can't get around them."

Little Malachi began kicking the dirt while looking at his feet. He dug his hands deep into his pockets.

"So, what do you want to do?" Malachi asked.

Little Malachi looked up. "Learn the guitar," he said.

Malachi smiled. He took his nephew's hand, and they began walking to his house.

"I hope you don't have any chores for me to do at your house, Uncle Malachi. I mean, everyone is working me like a mule, and I'm only ten years old," Little Malachi said.

Malachi felt a feeling of warmth course through his body, as he glanced down at the little boy who was given his name. To him, it felt good to have a place where a man could call home.

"To help you get through some of those chores, I'll tell you some stories," Malachi said.

"What kind of stories?" Little Malachi asked.

"Stories you can tell your kids one day," Malachi said.

"I hope it's not about chores, because I don't need to tell my kids anything like that," Little Malachi said. "Only thing I need now is a yoke, a harness, and a bit in my mouth, and I'll be a mule tending to the fields. Did you ever have to work like everyone is making me work when you were younger?"

Malachi looked at his nephew. He shook his head and began to laugh.

"It's not funny, Uncle Malachi. That's all I do around here is chores. I wish I had some help," Little Malachi said.

Malachi laughed harder realizing that life had come into a full circle.

"I really do need some help," Little Malachi said, as he looked up at his uncle. He frowned. "I hope you tell me the joke because I don't see anything funny about doing chores."

I dedicate this book to my children,
nieces, nephews, and god-children:

Jamel, Enjoli, Terrence, Tawana, Malikkqua,
Shayeeda, Latoya, Little Bob, Tyrone, Don-Don,
Dontay, Shanice, Muffin, Jeffery, Je'me, Marvin,
Ashawn, Danielle, Imanee, and Romello.
And, of course, my grandson, Tahmir.

Every day you will meet a challenge; it becomes easier
once you're able to confront it with your head held high.
Great men and women are not born, they are molded
from strife, pain, and suffering. Through despair you will
find your strength, and in that strength you will grow to
become men and women of respect.

About the Author

R obert Crudup has been writing stories since he was seven years old. He has a certificate in Radiology Technology and currently lives in New York City.